THE ODYSSEY OF WALKER GARRETT

MICHAEL GLENN

ISBN 979-8-9893595-0-9

❀ Created with Vellum

CONTENTS

A NOTE TO THE READER

This is a work of historical fiction. Fictional characters and events are products of the author's imagination, and any resemblance to any actual persons, living or dead, is entirely coincidental.

Real historical people frequently appear as characters, and real historical events are described.

An appendix of historical notes is provided at the end of the book, in which fact is separated from fiction. Notes are provided for each chapter, and the reader is encouraged to consult them as each chapter is read. Some of the most remarkable events described in the story actually happened.

1

—————

THE ODYSSEY BEGINS

A long shriek of the *Southern Belle*'s steam whistle pierced the stagnant afternoon heat, followed by three short blasts to announce its arrival at the Courtland, Alabama, depot. In the adjacent fields, workers welcomed an excuse to stop for a moment and straighten up, leaning on their hoes to watch the aged, huffing locomotive tow its few cars slowly around the bend and hiss to a wheezing stop, as if it just couldn't go any further.

The depot was a single story in height, made of weathered wooden planks wearing an ancient coat of whitewash, windows opaque with dust. The station platform was deserted except for a sleepy, speckled hound who, after twitching his ear at a buzzing fly, lowered his head back to the floor and with a groan, rolled onto one side to resume his nap.

An elderly black man in a faded gray uniform ambled out from the station doorway to exchange mailbags and retrieve a small package, then slowly made his way back into the slightly cooler shade of the interior. Momentarily he reappeared, this time with a wooden trunk bound with two wide leather straps, which he loaded into the freight car.

Inside the depot, standing stiffly beside the wooden bench where they had been awaiting the arrival of the train for the past hour, were three people dressed in the uncomfortable clothes that country folk wear on Sundays.

"Well, I reckon it's 'bout that time," the graying older man said gruffly, clearing his throat for the third time, holding his sweat-stained straw hat with both hands. Immediately the short, plump woman at his side began sniffling and dabbing at her eyes with a handkerchief. Her once-dark hair was twisted into a bun on the back of her head, and there were faint flour stains on her navy-blue dress.

"Yes sir, Pa," responded the tall youth quietly. He placed a round-brimmed, floppy brown hat over his slicked-back sandy hair. The anticipated moment having finally come, it was suddenly weighing on him more heavily than he had expected.

"Walker," the woman entreated earnestly through her tears, "we're so proud of you, son! You be careful now, you hear? Write us whenever you can. We're going to miss you so much." Her voice choked on the last words, and she turned and pressed her head into the shoulder of her husband, her breath coming in short, quick sobs.

"Yes, Mama," the young man said as he picked up the bulky leather satchel—his only piece of luggage—and took a hesitant step toward the door. "I better get on board. The train won't be here long."

Walker Garrett and his father clasped calloused hands firmly, eyes meeting for a long second.

"You still got that letter from the General?"

"Yes sir. Right here in my pocket."

He then turned to his mother and bent over for her to kiss his cheek and hug his neck. She clung to him so tightly that for a moment he thought she was going to hold him there until the train left. An ear-piercing scream from the train whistle was his cue to gently pry her arms loose and step back. Taking a deep breath, he walked out to the platform and climbed the steps into the single passenger car. Finding himself the only passenger in the car, he slid into a seat by an open right-hand window. He tried to smile down at them, his lips a thin, tight line, and extended his arm in what was more of a salute than a wave.

The cars lurched and the locomotive began to slowly chug forward, steam hissing and the engine puffing loudly. He opened his mouth to call out a good-bye, but another long, shrieking blast of the whistle drowned out his words. The plain couple on the platform stood waving for as long as he could see them, finally disappearing as the track curved and a stand of spindly pine trees blocked his view. Walker blew his nose into the handkerchief his mother had insisted he take in his pocket. Sighing, he settled back in the tattered leather seat and tried to find a comfortable position. It was going to be a long ride.

Sitting by the open window in the hot summer breeze, he told himself that the moisture in his eyes was caused by smoke blowing back from the engine. Walker, surprised at the tightness in his chest, forced himself to take several deep breaths. He had never been more than fifteen miles from home, and now he was going to see distant, new places, and experience exciting adventures. It was what he had always dreamed of doing—to actually be doing it was exciting, but also a bit frightening.

He reached into his jacket pocket and took out the letter which had arrived just days before, postmarked from Washington, D.C., and signed by none other than General Joseph "Fightin' Joe" Wheeler. As he read the letter for the hundredth time, his pulse quickened again. He was to join the General in Florida and accompany him to Cuba!

The United States had declared war on Spain in late April of 1898, and Wheeler had been appointed to serve as an officer in the U.S. Army in the impending campaign in Cuba. A Confederate Civil War hero, he had been a member of Congress representing the Eighth Congressional District in northern Alabama for almost twenty years. Everyone in the tiny town of Courtland—no, everyone in the entire South—had been thrilled that the legend would ride again! Young men had dashed to enlist in the army, eager to serve with the living symbol of The War. General Wheeler, who had ridden with Lee and fought the Yankees, and who had been there with President Jefferson Davis at the bitter end! To many Southerners, no one embodied the "Lost Cause" more perfectly than the small, white-bearded, spry General Joseph Wheeler.

Lemuel Garrett, Walker's father, had been at the side of the General throughout the war. Though not an officer himself, he had been indispensable to Wheeler and his staff by scavenging for munitions and victuals, tending the horses, and showing courage under fire. Garrett had made such an impression on Wheeler that, after the war, the General had hired him to be the overseer of Pond Spring, his Alabama plantation about four miles from the Courtland depot, as the crow flies.

For more than thirty years Lemuel Garrett had managed the fields, cattle, stables, and all of the daily operations of Pond Spring. Wheeler had remarked more than once that without Lemuel Garrett, he "wouldn't know his right hand from his left" on the plantation. The General was touched that Lemuel and his wife Hannah, after a series of miscarriages, had proudly named their only child after him —Wheeler Walker Garrett, always called "Walker."

Walker had grown up on the plantation, practically a member of Wheeler's family. His father and the General had taught him to ride and shoot, and he had always dreamed of what it would have been like to have ridden with them in The War. Walker loved his father, but he idolized the General and was determined to follow in his footsteps.

The General was a believer in the importance of an education. When Walker had progressed as far as possible at the small local school in Courtland, it was Wheeler's influence that had gotten Walker admitted to the Academy in Decatur, the county seat, fifteen miles away. It was the finest school in northern Alabama, and the students were from the leading families of the district. Wheeler had even arranged for him to board with a prominent family of the town, the Dancys, who were political supporters of his.

Walker had spent two years at the Academy, sleeping in a small attic room at the imposing Dancy house during the week and returning home on weekends to help his father on the plantation. Eighteen years old, he had just received his diploma, his good marks earning the praise of his parents, his teachers, and—most importantly—the General.

When the newspaper headlines had shouted, almost a month earlier, that war was declared upon Spain and that General Wheeler was to take up arms once again, Walker had known immediately what he had to do. He had written to the General, asking him to allow him to serve as his father had served during the Civil War. He had begged—promised not to disappoint, and vowed to do whatever he was told. Wheeler had answered with orders to join him in Tampa! He was traveling directly there from Washington, and he instructed Walker to bring a trunk of the General's personal items from Pond Spring with him.

Refolding the letter, Walker could hardly contain his excitement. He almost forgot to cross over to the other side of the passenger car to view Pond Spring from the window as the train passed the plantation. The sight of the big white main house and the outlying farm buildings seemed both familiar and yet strangely foreign to his eyes, and he realized that he already felt like a stranger to his own home. When the plantation was lost to view in the distance, he settled back into the seat and closed his eyes. The rhythmic click-clacking of the rails soothed his nerves, and he began to relax for the first time in many days.

The little country train meandered slowly eastward through the lush farmland of the Tennessee River Valley. The *Southern Belle* had been in service since before The War, and her tall smokestack and elongated cowcatcher gave her a distinctive profile compared to the sleeker, faster locomotives that ran on the main lines. She stopped briefly in tiny Hillsboro and Trinity, leaving their scattered houses, stores, and churches behind in a short moment or two. No one was on the streets—it was too hot to be out and about, even though it was not yet June. Even the cattle sought the shaded areas of their pastures. Only the bowed backs of field hands proved that the area was indeed inhabited.

In less than an hour, the train rolled into the Decatur station. The station, with its distinctive red-tiled roof, was on the north side of town, nearly on the banks of the broad Tennessee River. Decatur was the most important railroad hub in the region, and here Walker had to transfer to a southbound express train for the rest of the journey. He stepped out onto the platform, a place he knew well from his time as a student at the Academy. The interior of the station was not busy at the moment, with possibly as many as a dozen people walking or standing casually about, and a few others sitting on the benches looking rather bored.

He looked about anxiously, hoping to see a familiar face—one in particular. The Dancy family had a daughter just a year younger than Walker. Every boy in the school had idolized the lovely, dark-haired Abigail, but she had not acknowledged any of her admirers. Walker had despaired of her ever noticing him—a boy from the country.

The Dancys had been a leading family of Decatur for four generations, and lived in one of the finest houses in the city. However, lodging at their home for two years did not mean living as part of the family. The attic room where he had slept was reached by a back stairwell which was used, not by the family, but by the household staff, and he had eaten his meals with the help in the kitchen, not in the dining room. Frank Dancy had given him lodging as a favor to the General, but had not made any attempt to welcome him into the family.

He hoped that he would gain Abigail's approval now that he was departing to win glory on a foreign battlefield. He had written to tell her of his departure to join General Wheeler in Florida and, in a moment of reckless bravery—or was it foolish indiscretion?—had asked if she would meet him at the station to say farewell. Now he was wondering what had possessed him to do such a thing. *She's probably laughing at me*, he scowled, looking down at his scuffed boots.

Just then he felt a tug at his sleeve.

"Mista Walka?" It was Daisy, the ten-year-old daughter of the Dancys' black cook, Beulah, smiling shyly with lowered eyes.

"Howdy, Daisy!" greeted Walker, with genuine warmth. "How are you and your mama doing?"

"We's jis fine," Daisy beamed, still not looking up.

"What brings you down to the railroad station?"

"Miss Abigail done sent me to bring you dis letter. She say she sorry she cain't come herself." She held out a small pastel yellow envelope bearing Walker's name written in a graceful, cursive hand.

Walker felt a surge of excitement at the sight of Abigail's handwriting on the envelope, but also a pang of disappointment that she had not brought it herself. Still, a letter was better than nothing. Walker almost snatched the envelope from Daisy's hand.

"Thank you, Daisy! Tell Miss Abigail 'thank you' for sending the letter. And tell your mama that I sure do miss her good cooking. She's the best cook in Dixie."

Daisy grinned from ear to ear, almost squirming in delight.

"I sho will, Mista Walka. And Mama she said to give you dis." And from behind her back, with the other hand she held out a small parcel wrapped in newspaper. Walker took it and felt its warmth. Raising it to his nose, he sniffed.

"My goodness, Daisy! Is this some of your mama's biscuits?" Daisy grinned even wider and almost doubled over with delight.

"Yessuh, Mista Walka! Wid ham!"

"Lord a-mercy child!" he exclaimed. "You give your mama a big hug for me! This was mighty nice of her!"

"Yessuh, Mista Walka. I sho will."

She continued to stand in front of him, something clearly on her mind.

"What is it, Daisy?" Walker said, with a friendly smile to put her at ease.

"Mista Walka?" she asked, still smiling shyly with downcast eyes, swaying back and forth with nervous energy. "Is you gon fight the Yankees?"

Walker laughed before he could stop himself, and then quickly patted Daisy on the shoulder.

"No, Daisy, I'm not going to fight the Yankees. This time the Yankees are on *our* side. We're going to fight the Spanish together, down in Cuba."

"Oh," she said softly, looking down at the floor. "That's good."

"The Spanish blew up one of our battleships down there in Cuba, and we have to do something about it," he explained. "I'm going to join up with General Wheeler and the rest of the United States Army, and we're going to teach them a lesson.

"And we're going to help the Cubans gain their independence from Spain," he added quickly, almost as an afterthought. "They're fighting for their freedom. It's sort of like the American Revolution."

Daisy nodded vigorously, as though she understood perfectly.

"We be prayin' for you, Mista Walka," she said seriously. "Bye now." And she began to back away.

"Thank you, Daisy. Bye to you, too." She turned and walked quickly to the side door of the depot—the one for colored people— and reaching the street, broke into a run, her bare feet kicking up the ankle-length blue cotton dress behind her.

Walker was touched by her concern, and even more pleased that her knowledge of his mission, though imperfect, meant that he had been the topic of conversation at the Dancy house. How else would she have known he was going off to war? He smiled with pleasure at the thought that the household was discussing him and praying for his safety.

Since it was more than an hour before his southbound train was due, Walker found a bench and, putting the satchel between his feet, unwrapped the newspaper parcel. The aroma of the hot biscuits and ham sent tingles up his spine. He hadn't realized how hungry he was! It had been a long time since breakfast at daybreak. The Dancy mansion was only a couple hundred yards from the station, almost halfway to the river ferry, so it was no wonder that the four biscuits were still warm—they were practically straight from the oven. He wolfed down three of them and reluctantly rewrapped the last one to eat later.

Wiping his hands on his pants, Walker pulled the yellow envelope from his coat pocket with a sense of anticipation. He spent a long moment just gazing at the feminine script on the front, trying to imagine Abigail at her desk writing it by flickering candlelight. Inside was a folded sheet of unlined paper with a printed border of pastel blue flowers. Within the folded page was a delicate white, crocheted square with a red heart design in the center and a blue ribbon tied in a neat bow. Walker held it up and stared at it for several seconds, realizing that this had been crocheted by Abigail herself! He held it between his fingers, thinking of it being between her delicate, pale fingers. It was as if he held a holy relic of priceless value. His heart skipped a beat. Taking a deep, ragged breath, he read the short note, penned with the same graceful flourish:

May 24, 1898
Dear Walker,

We are all thrilled that you are to join the General and defend our country's honor against those horrid Spaniards. We hope and pray that God will keep you and all the boys safe until your return home. Please write and let us know how you are faring. When you return, you will have to tell us all about it. Forgive me for not coming to the station myself, but I am not well today. I know that Daisy will see this safely to your hands. Let this memento be a reminder to you of home. Forgive my limited crocheting skills!
With kindest regards,
Abigail Dancy

Walker read the note several times, trying to divine the meaning of every phrase. "We are all thrilled"—didn't that mean that she was also thrilled? "We hope and pray"—so it was true, as Daisy said, that they were all praying for him! That meant that Abigail was praying for him, herself! And didn't she ask for a personal account of his adventure when he was home again? And didn't she hint that, had she been feeling well, she would have come to the station personally to deliver the note? What did "kindest regards" mean? He was not familiar with this phrase, but it certainly sounded affectionate. He heaved a deep sigh and smiled. He hadn't realized until now that Abigail thought so favorably of him! She had concealed it so well! And the little crocheted square with the red heart and the blue ribbon—clearly intended as a token of her concern, something to remind him of her while he was away—was better than he had dared to hope!

By the time Walker had finished poring over the note for the tenth time and slipped it back into his inside breast pocket, it was almost time for his train to arrive. Stepping outside to the water pump for a long drink, he gazed down the street toward the imposing Dancy house. The two red brick chimneys were visible above the treetops. So close! He longed to walk down Railroad Street, up the steps to the front door, and offer his "kindest regards" for Abigail's quick recovery. However, hearing an approaching train whistle, he decided that he did not have time and returned inside the station to collect General Wheeler's trunk and prepare to board the train.

It was late afternoon when the *Dixie Queen* bade farewell to the river town of Decatur. This was a vastly different locomotive engine than the old *Southern Belle*, and its five-foot-tall driving wheels soon had the train flying along at more than fifty miles per hour. Buildings, trees, wagons, mules, and people were all a blur outside Walker's window as the train dashed through towns too small to merit the attention of such a proud train. Less than two hours were needed to reach Birmingham, seventy-five miles to the south.

2

———————

ON THE ROAD

Birmingham's Terminal Station was the most amazing sight Walker had ever seen. There were ten parallel tracks beside the platform, and he followed a hurrying crowd down a flight of stairs to a passageway beneath the tracks to reach the main building. He had caught a glimpse of its twin towers and dome from his window, and he was eager to get a closer look while the train took on freight and passengers.

Stepping out into the middle of the cavernous central waiting room, Walker was stunned. The skylight dome was well over a hundred feet above him, with colorful ornamental glass and tiles. The floor and walls were marble, and the numerous benches were of an elegant dark wood. The waiting room was ringed with restaurants, barber shops, newsstands, telegraph offices, a ticket office—he couldn't absorb everything at once, but simply stood there, mouth agape.

He was jostled back to his senses by the rush of hurried travelers bumping into him. They scurried off without speaking, giving Walker irritated glares over their shoulders.

Realizing that he had limited time before he needed to be back on the train, Walker made his way to one of the lunch counters and purchased a plate of eggs, grits, and sausage and a mug of coffee for twenty-five cents—he'd have to be careful if his money was to last the trip. The steaming plate was on the counter in front of him almost before he could get comfortable on the padded stool.

Eating quickly, he downed the last of the black coffee and reached for his satchel on the floor. The well-dressed man on the next stool was also leaving, and as he strode away, bowler hat and silver-headed cane in hand, Walker noticed that he had left his folded newspaper on the counter beside his plate.

"Sir!" he called out. "Your newspaper!"

The man ignored him and continued walking quickly out into the large, busy waiting room. Walker picked up his bag and the newspaper and hurried after him. By the time he got through the doorway into the vast waiting room, however, the man had disappeared into the crowd.

As he stood looking to see what direction the man had taken, his eyes locked on a company of soldiers across the room. They wore the blue uniforms of the United States Army and stood next to a pile of knapsacks, their hats pushed back on their heads, perspiring in the heat. They were apparently waiting for their commanding officer to give them instructions.

Civilians passing by were shaking their hands, patting their shoulders, and even from across the large room Walker could tell that they were voicing their support and encouragement to the troops, who were smiling and nodding in reply.

Walker did not feel a patriotic surge of admiration as he contemplated them, but instead felt a tinge of jealousy. He had not even been formally enlisted yet, and had no uniform—only a letter in his pocket from General Wheeler, promising that he would be properly inducted and equipped upon his arrival in Tampa. None of these people rushing past knew that he was on his way to join the staff of General "Fightin' Joe" Wheeler! *If they did, they'd be shaking my hand, too,* thought Walker, feeling a bit resentful.

He reminded himself that he was on a special mission and that it didn't matter if these ordinary people in the terminal did not recognize his importance. *Perhaps it is actually better if they do not know,* he thought. *I don't need anything distracting me from carrying out my orders.* Even though his orders were only to escort Wheeler's trunk to Tampa, the fact that he had a purpose unknown to anyone else made him feel reassured of his own significance.

He turned away, frowning, and his attention was caught by the opening of the door to the colored waiting room. Through the door he briefly saw several Negro recruits, looking very smart in their blue uniforms.

Well, if that don't beat all, he fumed, clenching his jaw. *Even the darkies have blue uniforms!* He had heard that there were Negroes in the U.S. Army during The War and that some were even fighting Indians out West, but he had not really believed it until now. He stared for a long minute before moving on.

Carrying the newspaper in one hand and his satchel in the other, Walker wandered across the broad floor toward the platform exits. Still gawking at the exotic Byzantine interior with its colorful marble, tiles, and arches, he also saw shoeshine stands, fruit vendors, a revolving door, and a doorway with the single word "Ladies" above it. Adjacent to it was another doorway, labeled "Gentlemen." He knew he needed to hurry to the train, but he could not resist exploring this new mystery.

Men were coming and going through this door, so Walker followed them and found himself in a large room with tiled walls and floor. There were sinks with faucets, and stall-like structures along one side of the room, with some doors open and others closed. He strolled casually past them, glancing into one of the open stalls. His eyebrows rose and he gave a low whistle. He had seen an indoor toilet at the Decatur Academy, but a whole room full of them was something! Along the opposite wall a horizontal pipe extended about three feet above the floor, with water running down from it into a gutter that led to a drain in the corner. Men were standing in front of it, facing the wall. Walker quickly surmised the purpose of this arrangement. This room was the most amazing thing he had seen all day. *Just wait until I write home about this!* he chuckled to himself.

After buying a shiny red apple for three cents from a vendor in the main room, Walker made his way out the exit to the platform. The platform roof was constructed in several separate sections so that natural light reached the ground. The dimming light of the early evening was soft and had a calming effect on him. After the noise and crush of the crowded terminal, the platform now seemed comparatively quiet and tranquil. The continuous sound of steam hissing and occasional clanging noises were soothing to Walker, who found it somehow restful.

As he made his way through the tunnel to reach his train, he suddenly thought about what was happening at this moment back at Pond Spring. This was the time of day when Mama would be putting a hot meal on the table, and Papa would inhale the aroma of the fried okra, black eyed peas, corn, and cornbread. He would always smile and say, "Mmmm! Sure do smell good!" He would have a tall, cool glass of buttermilk, fresh from a big jar in the bucket which was kept lowered in the well. Sometimes there would be baked sweet potatoes with butter or baked apples for dessert. These thoughts made Walker feel rather homesick, so he forced himself to focus on his immediate surroundings.

Once again settled into his seat in the dimly lit passenger car, Walker unfolded the newspaper, angling it toward the window to catch the fading light. Reading after dark would be almost impossible. There was a weak ceiling light in the center aisle near his seat, which helped.

The newspaper was Birmingham's *Age-Herald*, Tuesday, May 24, 1898—twelve pages of news and advertisements. The bold front page headline filled him with excitement: "A Naval Battle in Cuban Waters Momentarily Expected." *It's about to really get started,* he exulted. One naval battle had already been fought in the Philippines. About three weeks ago Dewey had destroyed the Spanish Pacific fleet with no American casualties, and now it seemed that Admiral Sampson was about to repeat that great victory in Cuba.

Other articles caught his eye: "No Fear of Yellow Fever" and "New Spanish Cabinet Determined to Fight to the Finish." The Spanish governor of Santiago declared, "We hear America proposes to assail us with 100,000 men. Some reports say 150,000 men. We invite four times that number to entrench our fields with their carcasses. The greater the number, the greater the glory."

We'll see who gets the greater glory, Walker thought grimly.

He skimmed over the next pages quickly. Alabama had mustered two battalions of colored troops. The USS *Oregon* had completed its fifteen-thousand-mile, ten-week voyage from Bremerton, Washington to Florida, traversing the tempestuous Straits of Magellan without incident. Prominent American women were retaliating against the French opposition to the U.S. going to war with Spain by refusing to buy French-made gowns. Germany was criticizing America's initial reluctance to go to war. The war was bringing profits to Birmingham's new steel plants. Reports of train accidents, weather forecasts, and advertisements for Lydia Pinkham's Pills and Sloan's Liniment filled other pages.

He could hardly believe his eyes when he read the column by Carola Leigh: "Women in War: A Feminine View as to the Part the Gentler Sex Might Play if Given the Opportunity." The author declared that "the old idea that 'men must work and women must weep' has gone out. . . . Just as certain seems the extinction of the soldier's traditional 'girl I left behind me.' Very few girls want to be left behind. . . . She wishes to be in the thick of the fight, to share his dangers as well as his joys and sorrows . . . ."

Shaking his head in disbelief, Walker emitted a short, contemptuous laugh. The very idea! Women in the army! *Abigail Dancy wasn't lining up to join the army! No sir, she understands that her place is at home, supporting and encouraging the boys in the fight.* He reached to touch his breast pocket, over his heart, where the crocheted square was tucked. *That was what women should do-- not carry rifles and knapsacks! What on earth are some women thinking? Why, some even want the right to vote. The next thing you know,* he reflected, *a woman would even be running for President of the United States! Ridiculous!*

Then his eyes spotted an article entitled "Picturesque Joe Wheeler." Walker bent over the paper intently, holding it closely and devouring every word.

> Joseph Wheeler, of Alabama, who has been nominated as one of the four major-generals chosen from civil life, is one of the picturesque characters of the house of representatives. He is a very small man physically, perhaps five feet and an inch or two in height and weighs 110 pounds, but he is a marvel of activity. He is always on the go, and at a very rapid rate.

Yup, thought Walker. *That's the General, all right. He's a human tornado.*

The article concluded with:

> There is a romantic touch in having such a man as General Wheeler, simple, honest, conscientious, end his military career and perhaps his public service in a war undertaken by the United States, after he had worked so hard a generation ago in the cause of secession. No doubt he is glad of this opportunity to make the closing chapter of his military history one of service under the stars and stripes; and no one doubts that that service will be brave and effective.

Walker folded the newspaper carefully and slipped it down into the satchel. He would read it many times over the coming days and weeks. He felt fortunate indeed to be going to war in the service of such a man as General Wheeler. He would follow the General to hell and back, if need be. They would show the Spanish—and the whole world!

The last passengers finally having boarded, the train jerked into motion. With a loud hiss, it lurched out of the station and chugged slowly past factories, steel mills, warehouses, and loading docks, gradually gathering speed. Walker could hear the repeated blasts of the steam whistle as the train rumbled through dozens of road crossings. Through the dusty window he studied every detail of the city.

There was a dream-like aspect to everything. In the fading light, nothing seemed real.

At first the roads were brick-paved, with heavy freight wagons drawn by teams of six or more mules waiting to cross the tracks. The bearded wagon-drivers slouched on their wooden seats, coldly returning Walker's gaze as the train rolled past. As the train reached the outskirts of the city, the roads were dirt and gravel, with smaller wagons and one-horse carriages. Finally leaving Birmingham behind, the train picked up speed until the clickety-clack of the rails was a continuous rhythm.

When the conductor opened the forward door and came into the car, there was a brief rush of wind and noise before the door slammed shut again. Walker produced his ticket, and after a quick inspection, the conductor pressed his stamp upon it.

"I'm on my way to Tampa to join the army and go to Cuba!" said Walker brightly, as he put his ticket back into his coat pocket.

"You don't say," returned the conductor a bit sourly and, without a smile or another word, moved on down the aisle. Walker could feel his face redden in the dimly lit car, and biting his lower lip, he turned back to the window, suddenly thankful for the growing darkness.

Then, from just a couple of rows behind him, Walker heard the conductor's indignant voice, "You can't be in this car! This is for whites only. The colored car is down at the end."

"I paid for my ticket just like these other folks, and I have the right to sit anywhere I want," a man replied.

Turning to see who was speaking, Walker saw a dark man dressed in a fashionable gray suit, with a white shirt, a black neck tie, and bowler hat.

"You can sit anywhere you like, as long as it's in the colored car," snapped the conductor. "Get moving before I put you off this train."

"I paid for my ticket—" began the man again.

"Don't you get uppity with me!" interrupted the conductor, raising his voice and poking his finger into the man's chest. "You'll be going straight to jail if you don't get out of here right now."

The pair went down the aisle toward the rear door of the car, with the conductor roughly shoving the man ahead of him.

"I have rights!" Walker heard the man object. "I protest this unfair treatment!"

"Take it to the Supreme Court!" jeered the conductor. "See what that gets you! You uppity n----rs better learn to stay in your place, if you know what's good for you."

The rear door opened to the noise of rushing wind and clacking rails, and then all was quiet again.

A large, bald man in the center of the car snorted indignantly. "Give 'em an inch and they want a mile!" he exclaimed. "Don't that beat all!"

The other passengers shook their heads and laughed. Walker joined in, feeling better now.

He turned back to look out the window, but in the darkness he could see only his own face, dimly reflected in the glass. For the first time in his life, he appreciated the significance of the color of his skin.

This is the way it is supposed to be, he thought. *Whites and coloreds ought not to mix. It just isn't right.*

With darkness concealing the landscape and stars shining in the nighttime sky, the *Dixie Queen* steamed into Montgomery, the state capital. Walker's heavy eyelids opened, and then he quickly sat up straight as he realized where he was. To one side of the track he saw the broad Alabama River with a white steamboat paddle-wheeling its slow way upstream. Under the light of a full moon, it looked like a scene from the Old South in the days before The War.

The train was suddenly in the city itself, already slowing to a stop. To his left he saw the downtown district rising on a hill in the distance, with a few lights flickering. Shining above them all, its white cupola almost glowing in the moonlight, was the state capitol building—a copy of the national capital in Washington, D.C.

He had heard many times the story of how Jefferson Davis had taken the oath of office as the president of the Confederacy while standing on the front steps of this building. Though the Confederate government had moved to Richmond, Virginia, within a few months, Alabamians had always been proud that the first capital of the Confederacy had been in their state.

Walker wished that the train would pause long enough for him to walk up the hill from the Union Station to the capital and see the bronze star that marked the spot on the portico where Davis had stood, but he knew this was impossible. At least he would be able to write home that he had seen the famous building from a distance. *Mama and Papa will be thrilled,* he smiled to himself.

The train did not tarry long in Montgomery but was soon on its way further south. It was too dark to see anything outside the train window now, so he shifted about in his seat, trying to find a comfortable position for sleeping. At least there was no one sitting next to him, so he had room to twist and turn until he finally gave up and resigned himself to leaning his head and shoulder against the side wall. As the train rocked rhythmically along the iron rails, the steady motion eventually lulled Walker to sleep.

3

TAMPA

The rising sun awakened Walker early the next morning. Standing up, he stretched painfully and tried to work his legs. He pushed open the door at the end of the car and went into the breezeway, where fresh air could be had. There he ate a cold breakfast of the remaining ham biscuit, washed down with gulps of water in cupped hands from the spigot in the lavatory.

The train was soon entering the outskirts of Tampa. He noted with surprise that only one set of tracks led into the city. Nearer to the terminal this line branched out into several more tracks, where rows of boxcars were shuttled off to the side. Trains appeared to be standing on almost all of the tracks, and Walker realized that the mobilization of the army was moving at full speed. Tampa was a beehive of activity.

Upon exiting the passenger car Walker hurried to the freight room, where he claimed General Wheeler's trunk. A black porter rolled it on his cart through the terminal to the street side of the station, set it down at the curb, and then stood looking at Walker expectantly, one hand extended. Walker reached out and shook the man's hand, saying, "Much obliged." The porter frowned and cleared his throat. Just then Walker observed another porter loading a heavy bag into a carriage for a lady, who then appeared to place a coin into the man's hand. It dawned on him that the porter expected to be paid for his service.

Rummaging in his pants pocket, Walker found some coins. Sorting through them, he picked out a nickel and offered it to the porter, who merely stared. Picking out a dime instead, he offered it, and the porter, with a raised eyebrow suggesting that he had never seen such a bumpkin before, took it and walked away without a word, shaking his head.

As he turned back toward the busy street, Walker beheld a scene of noise and confusion. Hundreds of men in military uniforms were standing or marching in lines. Men shouting, train whistles screeching, horses' hooves clattering on the pavement, and bells ringing as horse-drawn trolleys clanged on their way, warning pedestrians to beware—it was bewildering and invigorating at the same time. Newsboys seemed to be everywhere, shouting out the news and waving their papers.

He suddenly realized that he had no idea where to find the General. Tampa was a good-sized city of fifteen thousand, but its size was swollen by the sudden influx of more than thirty thousand soldiers, twenty thousand horses and mules, and hundreds of trainloads of military equipment. The single-pier harbor was full of ships of the U.S. Navy, waiting to transport all of this to Cuba. It didn't look like one more soldier, sailor, horse, wagon, or freight car could possibly be crammed into the town, which was bursting at the seams.

Looking about desperately for someone to ask for information, Walker spied an army officer on horseback picking his way down the crowded street. Dashing into the street, he was almost run over by a trolley, which rang its bell and sounded a warning horn. Jumping off the trolley track toward the middle of the street, he was nearly stepped on by a horse pulling a carriage, and the driver cracked the whip near his head and cursed.

Scanning in both directions for any other oncoming threats, Walker waved to the officer and shouted, "Sir! Sir! Can you tell me where the army has its headquarters? I have a trunk to deliver to General Wheeler!"

The officer had been about to pass him by without replying—until he heard the part about General Wheeler. Reining in his horse momentarily, he scowled down at Walker and pointed with his riding crop back toward the direction from which he'd come: "Tampa Bay Hotel!" was all he said before he continued on down the street at a quick trot.

Hurrying back to the safety of the curb, he looked this way and that, not really knowing what he was looking for. He approached one of the wagons being loaded with boxes and sacks by soldiers and tried to inquire as to who was in charge. The soldiers ignored him at first—and then cursed at him and told him to get away.

"Can't you see we're busy working? Get out of here and mind your own business!" one shouted at him.

"I have a trunk to deliver to General Wheeler at the Tampa Bay Hotel," Walker answered. "I need a wagon to carry it."

"Well, that ain't my problem, is it?" sneered the unshaven soldier, sweating, with his shirttail hanging from underneath the back of his blue jacket. "Figure it out for yourself, boy!"

Walker realized he would receive no assistance from any of the men in uniform, and for a moment felt frustrated and helpless. It suddenly occurred to him that his father had been forced to improvise throughout The War to provide Wheeler's men with needed supplies. "Necessity is the mother of invention," he'd often said to Walker. "When you don't have what you need," he would say, "you make do with what you've got."

Walker was filled with determination that he was going to get that trunk to the hotel somehow. This was no time to let the General down—he had to prove himself capable of carrying out his orders.

Spotting a one-horse open-top cab, he dashed up to the colored driver. Pulling General Wheeler's letter from his coat pocket and holding it aloft, he shouted in what he hoped was a commanding tone of voice: "Bring that cab over here to the curb! The United States Army requires your services to carry this trunk to the headquarters at the Tampa Bay Hotel!" And then he added, for good measure: "Immediately!"

To his satisfaction and a bit of surprise, it worked. The cab driver helped him lift the trunk onto the luggage rack on the back of the small carriage and strap it into place, and Walker climbed into the passenger seat behind the driver. However, just as the driver had gathered the reins in his hands, a man in an army uniform with the gold leaf insignia of a major on his shoulders grabbed the horse's bridle.

"I'm requisitioning this cab for the United States Army!" he snapped. Pointing to Walker, he ordered, "You! Get out!" and then to the driver again, "Take me to the Tampa Bay Hotel! Now!"

The driver looked at Walker, confused and uncertain what to do. Walker, knowing that this might be his only chance to get the trunk delivered, held his ground. Holding up the official-looking envelope, he spoke to the officer in a respectful but firm voice, "These are orders from General Joseph Wheeler to bring his personal trunk to him at the hotel immediately. I'll be happy to share the ride with you, but I cannot disobey the General's orders!"

The major hesitated, surprised and irritated at not being obeyed promptly. He looked at the letter for a brief second and then made his decision. "All right," he said brusquely, "Move over."

Relieved, Walker slid over to the right side of the cab seat, and the major squeezed in beside him. The driver touched his whip lightly to the horse, which began to trot briskly through the crowded street, taking a zig-zag course and bouncing through a multitude of potholes.

Walker took the opportunity to glance furtively at the officer's uniform. It was the first time he'd seen a U. S. Army officer's uniform up close. The blue fabric reminded him unpleasantly of the enemy invaders his father and the General had fought during The War. *That was more than thirty years ago*, he reasoned to himself, *and if General Wheeler can wear the Yankee blue coat, then I guess I can, too.*

Hoping to make some casual conversation, he remarked, "Isn't that wool uniform hot in this warm weather? The soldiers won't be wearing that in Cuba, will they?" The words had just left his lips when he realized that he had said 'they.' The United States Army was not 'we' yet.

The major sat stiffly, his face turned to the left, and did not offer the slightest indication of having heard the question. Walker could see that attempting to talk to this man would be fruitless, so he spent the rest of the ride observing the traffic on the street, determined not to speak again.

It was only about a mile from the depot to the hotel, but it took the cab more than an hour to get there. The streets were packed with freight wagons, carriages, mounted riders, and columns of marching soldiers, mingling with civilians. Everyone seemed to think that they deserved the right of way, and the resulting impasse was paralyzing. Besides that, a slow-moving train blocked their path at a crossing, and they had to wait half an hour at the Lafayette Street Bridge, which crossed the Hillsborough River.

The Hillsborough River was a picturesque stream about a hundred yards wide—not nearly as impressive as the Tennessee River, Walker thought. It ran practically through the middle of Tampa, and its four bridges were strained to accommodate the huge volume of traffic that demanded to cross back and forth daily.

Just as their cab finally reached the bridge and was beginning to advance across it, a loud, long warning horn sounded, and all traffic came to an abrupt halt. The cab driver cursed under his breath as he reined the horse to a stop. Not understanding what was happening, Walker stood up in the carriage for a better view.

To his utter amazement, the center portion of the iron truss bridge was actually rotating and turning on a pivot under its middle! Another even louder horn sounded to his left, and Walker saw the reason for the bridge's movement—a barge was ascending the river, pushed by two tug boats. The bridge continued rotating until it was completely perpendicular to the roadway at each end, opening the river for navigation. The barge crept past at a snail's pace, and before it was clear of the bridge, a steamboat appeared upriver, descending toward the harbor. The bridge remained open for the steamboat to pass, and finally began rotating back to its closed position, allowing bridge traffic to resume.

Walker, standing and watching the entire process, was mesmerized. He had never even heard of such a thing! He would have to write home about this, but would anyone believe him? He doubted it.

Forgetting himself, he turned to the major and exclaimed excitedly, "Have you ever seen such a thing! Why that is—incredible!"

The major turned slowly to face him with an icy stare.

"Boy," he said coldly, "where are you from?"

Walker cleared his throat, suddenly apprehensive.

"Courtland, Alabama, sir," he replied meekly, gingerly sitting back down on the seat.

"I thought as much. You should have stayed there." The major almost spat the words, and then contemptuously turned away.

Walker was speechless, his face reddening. The cab driver looked furtively back over his shoulder at him, and their eyes met. The driver looked quickly away, as if embarrassed for Walker's humiliation. Walker kept his eyes straight ahead after that, and kept his mouth shut.

His resolve not to speak again was severely taxed, however, by the next sight that met his wondering eyes. Just across the river he saw several tall spires reaching skyward. They looked foreign—like pictures he'd seen of mosques and palaces in the Middle East. He counted a dozen of them rising high over the treetops. As his eyes grew wider, the cab turned a corner and proceeded up to the most incredible building Walker had ever seen—the Tampa Bay Hotel.

The major leaped to the ground, flipped a coin to the driver and bounded up the stairs to the veranda and through the imposing doors, disappearing into the interior. Walker stepped hesitantly out of the cab and stood staring up at the hotel. The building was magnificent. He turned to the driver and asked,

"Is this the Tampa Bay Hotel?"

"Yessuh," the driver responded, walking to the rear of the small carriage. "Where you want dis trunk, suh?"

"Oh—ah, well, let's set it up there on the porch." Walker and the driver took the trunk between them and carried it up the steps, setting it down to the side of the entrance. The driver stood up, resting his hands on his hips, cap pushed back on his head. Knowing what was expected this time, Walker dug into his pocket and pulled out all the remaining coins—an assortment of pennies, nickels, and dimes.

"Dollah," said the driver shortly, looking at the small coins with distaste.

"A dollar!" exclaimed Walker. The driver bobbed his head sharply once. He returned the coins to his pocket, and reached into the other pants pocket, finding his only remaining dollar piece. Reluctantly he held it out to the driver, who took it with alacrity and was instantly down the steps, into the cab, and clattering back up the street toward the bridge.

"May I help you, suh?" a polite voice asked from behind Walker.

He turned to see a black hotel porter dressed in a fancy red jacket and tie, looking at him. Spotless white pants and shiny black shoes completed his outfit.

"Me?"

"Yes suh. Are you here for a room, suh?" The look in the porter's eyes as he surveyed Walker's wrinkled and dusty clothes and rough boots suggested that he had his doubts.

"Ah, yes. I mean, no. I've—I have brought a trunk—this one here —for General Wheeler—Joseph Wheeler—he's, ah—" Walker struggled to find words.

"Yes suh. I'll see that the General receives the trunk. Thank you, suh." The porter turned to leave.

"Wait! I have to see the General myself. He asked me to—" Walker fumbled in his coat pocket, pulling out the letter— "He asked me to meet him here and bring him the trunk myself."

Coughing to clear his throat, and standing up more erectly and squaring his shoulders, Walker tried to appear more confident.

"Show me to the General's room, please."

"Wait here, please suh." The porter gave Walker a questioning look, as if he were unsure whether to believe him or not, and quickly disappeared into the hotel.

Walker took advantage of the opportunity to look around while the porter was gone. He descended the steps to get a better view of the façade. The building was enormous—six stories high and hundreds of feet long, and there were more turrets, towers, and spires than he could count. He didn't even know what to call some of the architectural features. Balconies, arched windows, fancy gingerbread woodwork—he couldn't take it all in.

The grounds around the hotel were full of exotic tropical flowers and palm trees. It was an elaborate garden and appeared to go on for acres, with gravel paths, gazebos, pools, and park benches everywhere. Some flowers, like roses, he recognized. Others he had never seen before. It was an explosion of color.

Only a few yards away was a narrow set of railroad tracks for bringing hotel guests right up to the steps. A steady stream of carriages and cabs were bringing mostly military officers, but also a good many well-dressed civilians. Others were exiting the hotel and taking the now-empty cabs and disappearing in various directions. The constant hustle and bustle made Walker feel like a leaf caught in a whirlwind.

The porter reappeared and gestured to Walker to follow. Another porter wrestled the trunk onto a handcart and brought up the rear as the trio headed into the hotel.

Upon entering the lobby Walker involuntarily let out a loud gasp of amazement and stopped so abruptly that the porter wheeling the trunk on the handcart ran into him from behind. If the exterior of the fabulous palace was breathtaking, the interior was even more so. Gilded round tables on a wall-to-wall red Turkish carpet, plush armchairs, large mirrors, tall urns and porcelain vases, pillars and arches, winding staircases—Walker stumbled over his own feet as he tried to see everything at once.

The room was crowded with army officers, some sitting at the tables and some standing in groups talking. There were dozens of journalists asking questions and taking notes. Red-coated porters circulated through the large room carrying trays of drinks and other refreshments.

Suddenly the lead porter appeared in front of Walker, clearing his throat meaningfully. Walker was so immersed in surveying the lobby that he was startled by this interruption and blinked with comical exaggeration as he focused on the porter, who was directing him politely with an extended arm toward the side of the room. Gathering his wits about him as best he could, he dutifully followed his guide down a broad corridor, still trying to look back over his shoulder at the fantastic room. They stopped in front of a gated grill set in the wall, above which a sign said "Freight." Walker looked at the porter with a question in his eyes. There seemed to be no reason to stop here.

The porter pulled back the fence-like grill revealing a small room behind it, about eight feet square. He walked into the room, motioning Walker to follow. The porter with the trunk entered also. When all three were inside the room, the porter closed the gate and pulled up on a lever attached to the wall near the floor. Suddenly the room itself began to climb upward and Walker, startled, grabbed the porter with one hand while bracing against the wall with the other.

"What's this!" he exclaimed in a panic. The two porters gave each other a look of disbelief and began to laugh out loud, one of them bending over and slapping his knee.

"Man, ain't you never seen a *elevator* before?" laughed one.

The color came back into Walker's face, turning red with embarrassment. He had heard of elevators but had not expected to actually be in one of them.

"Of course I have," he answered coolly, adjusting his jacket. "It just caught me by surprise, that's all."

The two porters could not contain their mirth at that, and their shoulders shook with laughter until the elevator stopped on the fifth floor. Pushing back the gate, the porter again led the way, turning down the wide hallway and walking past a dozen numbered mahogany doors until he came to the one he was seeking. Knocking twice at the door, he then tried the knob, which turned easily.

Opening the door, he stepped into the room and turned and held the door as Walker and the trunk followed.

"Is this General Wheeler's room?"

"Yes suh, it is," replied the porter with a nod of his head. "He must be somewhere else in the hotel."

"Thank you," said Walker. Then noticing that the two were not leaving, remembered again that everyone expected something. He dug the coins out of his pocket again and looked sadly at them. He extended his hand toward the porter.

"That's all the money I have left," he said. "Take it."

The porter raised his eyebrows skeptically and took the coins. Poking through them with his index finger, he shook his head and gave the other porter a glum look. They exited together, still shaking their heads.

When the door closed behind them, Walker breathed a deep sigh of relief. He had completed his mission— he had delivered the General's trunk! He felt a sense of pride and satisfaction that he had succeeded in his first assignment, and he hoped that General Wheeler would be pleased.

He tossed his dusty, sweat-stained brown hat onto a silk-upholstered chair and looked around the room. It was, of course, far fancier than anything Walker had ever seen before, but after having seen the lobby downstairs, his mind was becoming numb. His eyes roamed over the rich carpet, the expensive drapes at the window, a fine sofa and armchair, the lamps, the wallpaper and the paintings. In the corner sat a roll top desk with a swivel chair. In an alcove just off the main room, he saw a fancy bed with several pillows piled on it. The carved wooden headboard stood at least eight feet tall. There were several silver candlesticks, and a gold tinted glass ball hanging by a gold chain from the fourteen-foot ceiling in the middle of the room— apparently for lighting, he assumed. So many new things to see!

He opened a small door near the sleeping alcove and peered inside. His eyes widened at the sight of a toilet, sink, and a bathtub. An indoor privy in a hotel room! Walker was beginning to feel as if he had been taken from nowhere and plunged into a completely different world.

Slowly crossing the room to one of the windows, he looked down to the ground. He felt suddenly queasy being up so high and stepped back from the window, holding his stomach. He had never been on the fifth floor of any building before. In fact, he'd never been higher than the second floor of a building. This was even higher than the big oak at Pond Spring which he had climbed all the way to the top as a boy. Edging back toward the window, he bent forward and peered toward the ground again. Seeing the milling crowd of officers and civilians far below, surrounded by statues, baroque lamp posts, and other decorations, he realized that the cab had brought him to the rear entrance of the hotel. The front was even more elaborate. He shook his head in disbelief—it was all really too much.

Just then he heard voices in the hallway outside the door, which abruptly opened and in came General Joseph Wheeler—walking briskly and talking even faster, as usual. The General was wearing a fine blue military coat with braided gold shoulder boards, two rows of shiny brass buttons, and a yellow sash across the chest. With his white beard and polished black cavalry boots, he was a sight to behold.

He was followed by two men in blue army uniforms. The diminutive Wheeler was dwarfed by the two officers, who each stood almost a head taller. However, they did not equal the General in dignity or in the sense of authority and confidence that he exuded.

He was halfway into the room when he suddenly saw Walker and stopped in his tracks.

"Walker, my boy!" he exclaimed warmly, advancing to greet him with both hands extended, taking Walker's in a firm grasp. "I see you've arrived safe and sound, and brought the trunk, too! Excellent! How was your trip?"

"Very good, sir," was all Walker could manage to say.

"Excellent! Excellent!" enthused the General. "Have you eaten yet?"

"No sir." He was about to add that he'd had a ham biscuit at sunup, but Wheeler was talking again.

"Well, we'll take care of that! And we need to get you officially inducted and equipped for duty! There's no time to waste!" With his typically quick, darting movements, he whirled about to face one of the officers standing behind him.

"Major Payne! Take this young man and get him something to eat —and then get him over to the quartermaster's office and enroll him and get him a uniform!"

Walker's eyebrows both raised as he realized that Major Payne was the same officer who had shared the cab with him just a little while earlier. Their eyes met, and Major Payne's expression was again cold and hostile. Walker swallowed hard and tried to look nonchalant.

"Yes sir, General Wheeler," said Major Payne solemnly. "And what unit do you want him enrolled into, sir?"

"That's a good question, Payne. He's to be attached to me, in some fashion—haven't decided how, yet. He'll have to be in the cavalry, of course. Put him in the First Volunteers."

"Sir, the First Volunteers aren't in Tampa yet. They're not due to be here for several more days. I could put him in the Ninth or Tenth."

The other officer spoke up. Walker thought he looked remarkably familiar but couldn't say for sure who he was.

"Father, the Ninth and Tenth are colored units. We can't put young Walker into either of those. He'll have to go into a volunteer outfit, and the First is the only one available in your Fifth Corps, but they've been training in San Antonio for a month already. I think we should just enlist him in the Fifth Corps for now and find a unit for him later."

Walker's mouth fell open as he recognized Joseph Wheeler, Jr.— the eldest son of the General. Joe had attended West Point and was assigned as an aide to his father.

"Howdy, Joe!" exclaimed Walker, breaking into the discussion. "Why, I haven't seen you since you went off to West Point!" The two had never socialized or been close friends, since Joe, at twenty-six, was eight years older than Walker and had spent a good deal of his youth in Washington while his father attended sessions of Congress, but they certainly had known each other in earlier times at Pond Spring. Walker had been much closer to Thomas, the youngest son of the General, who was a year younger than Walker.

"Hello, Walker," returned Joe, more politely than warmly. He looked very grown up and official, with captain's bars on his lapels. "It's good to see you again."

"Yes, Joseph, that sounds like the best idea. Very good." The General's words cut in like bullets, ignoring the pleasantries between Walker and the captain.

"In fact," he continued, as if a new idea had suddenly flashed into his busy mind, "Joseph—you take Walker with *you*, instead of the major. You two can get reacquainted, and I need to go over some things with the major. Bring him back here when you're done with him. He can sleep on the sofa in your room until we decide where to put him."

"Yes sir," responded Joe, saluting stiffly. Motioning to Walker to follow, he turned toward the door briskly, and Walker, snatching his hat from the chair as he passed by, almost had to trot to catch up. Striding swiftly along, a step behind, Walker got the impression that the captain was not exactly pleased at being given the task of tending to him.

"I guess it's a dream come true for you to get to serve on your father's staff in a war, isn't it?" He made a cheerful attempt at conversation.

"Yes," was all Captain Wheeler said, keeping his eyes straight ahead. Walker decided that his impression had been correct, so he followed silently after that, his eyes examining everything he passed.

Descending to the ground floor in a much fancier elevator car, one designed for guests, not freight, Walker could hardly keep from exclaiming about the furnishings again, but thought better of it. A soft chime sounded and the red-coated porter stopped the elevator at the third floor to take on two more passengers.

One of the two men wore a U.S. Army general's uniform and the other wore a suit and tie. The general was extremely corpulent, weighing at least three hundred pounds. He had sandy blond hair mingled with silver gray, a bushy mustache, and limped rather painfully and awkwardly. The suited man was clearly older, and also sported a mustache and graying hair. His suit was expensive, and diamond cufflinks flashed in the light.

Captain Wheeler saluted smartly and snapped, "Good day, General Shafter, sir!"

The general waved a hand in a weak imitation of a salute in return. "Hello, Captain Wheeler," he replied somewhat disinterestedly. And then, on impulse, looked quickly at the captain and said, "By the way—tell General Wheeler that I need to see him. Something must be done about the mess down at the port. This is getting out of hand. Nobody can get anything done. Men and material keep coming in, and nothing is going out. This is turning into a disaster."

"Yes sir, General Shafter, sir," was Captain Wheeler's emphatic reply. "Where shall I tell him to find you, sir?"

"I'll be in the officers' lounge, with Mr. Plant here. We'll have some drinks, and he can dine with us later, if Mr. Plant does not object."

"It would be my pleasure!" exclaimed Plant. "I've been looking forward to meeting the illustrious General Wheeler! That is an excellent suggestion!"

At that point, the elevator reached the ground floor. Shafter and Plant made their way across the crowded lobby, beset by greeters, journalists, and officers at every slow and painful step. Captain Wheeler turned to Walker. "Come with me to the front desk where I can call up to Father's room and give him General Shafter's message. Then I'll take you to get enlisted."

Before Walker could even ask what he meant by 'call up to the room,' the captain was already gone around the corner and Walker had to hurry to catch up again. At the desk, Joe said he'd like to call Room 522. The clerk placed on the counter a contraption that Walker recognized from newspaper pictures as a telephone, and inserted the end of its cable into one of many connecting plugs on a switchboard.

"Just turn the crank two or three times to ring the room, sir," the clerk directed.

Joe spoke into the mouthpiece, repeating General Shafter's request to meet with General Wheeler in the officers' lounge. After a short pause, during which Walker recognized General Wheeler's voice and rapid speech emanating from the earphone, Joe ended the conversation with a "Yes sir," and placed the earphone back on its hook on the stand. Nodding to the clerk, he turned and indicated that Walker should follow him as he headed toward the door.

"That was a telephone, wasn't it?" queried Walker. "I've seen them in the newspaper and read about them. Can you really talk to someone far off with it?

"As a matter of fact, you can," said Joe with a one-sided smile. "Have you really never seen one in person? Surely, they have telephones in Decatur? They've been around for several years."

"Oh, they probably do, but I haven't seen them. There isn't one at Pond Spring."

"No, of course not." he laughed. Then he continued in a more sociable tone, "This is one of the first hotels in America to have telephones in the rooms, so it's something special. It's also one of only a few to have an elevator. You wouldn't expect to find such a luxurious hotel in a place like Tampa, but Henry Plant built it about ten years ago and it attracts a lot of important people."

"Plant? Was he the man on the elevator?"

"Yes, that was him. They say he spent three million dollars building this hotel, and that he and his wife traveled all over Europe buying artwork to furnish it. And he's very well connected—the army is using Tampa as a staging ground for the invasion of Cuba because he arranged it in Washington. I'm afraid it's not going well, though."

"That's what I gathered from what General Shafter was saying. The town does seem to be rather overcrowded with all the soldiers and trains." Walker thought for a minute and then added hesitantly, "Can General Wheeler do anything about it?"

"If anybody can, he can do it," Joe said with a note of pride in his voice. "On the other hand, General Shafter is in charge of this operation, so it's his responsibility in the end."

"What's wrong with General Shafter's leg? Was he wounded in action?"

"Gout."

Leaving the hotel they walked briskly through the brutal hundred-degree heat of the afternoon, thankful for the luxuriant gardens of the hotel grounds and the shade created by the trees. They left the shade behind when crossing a golf course, and then passed tennis courts and a bowling alley—these sights were all firsts for Walker.

They were both sweating when they arrived at the army administrative offices, set up in a large tent on the other side of the palatial hotel grounds. In only a few minutes, Walker was enlisted into the army and was issued a blue woolen uniform and a pair of boots. He rolled his civilian clothes into a bundle and strapped his belt around it.

"Well, Private Garrett!" smiled Captain Joe. "Now how do you feel?"

"I feel really good!" grinned Walker. "At last, I'm really in the army!"

The captain's face turned serious. "There are a few things you need to know, now that you are officially enlisted and in uniform. First, you never address an officer without saying 'sir' first and also ending with 'sir.' You also must salute an officer when addressing him. Otherwise, you can get into a lot of trouble."

"Right," nodded Walker, and then suddenly realizing the meaning of Joe's words, snapped to attention and saluted crisply. "Sir! Yes sir!" he corrected himself.

"That's much better, Private. Now, let's go get something to eat."

4

CUBA BOUND

Walker opened his eyes slowly, stretching his arms and arching his back. Sunlight was peeping through a gap in the draped windows, creating a knife of light across the dark room. For a moment he was unsure where he was, and then he remembered—he was sleeping on a sofa in Captain Joe's hotel room. In Tampa, Florida. Every night for the past two weeks. His body and his mind ached.

Suddenly the drapes were flung open and sunlight flooded the room. Startled, Walker sat up, squinting to see Captain Joe standing by the window, already in uniform.

"Let's get moving, Private Garrett," he snapped. "Today we are going to Cuba!"

Walker sat stunned for a couple of seconds, unable to believe his ears. Then he leaped to his feet. "Do you mean it?" he gasped in excitement, eyes wide open now.

Captain Joe grinned in spite of himself. "Yes! The Spanish fleet has finally been spotted—Cervera is in the Santiago Harbor and the U.S. Navy has blockaded him there. The invasion is on!"

Walker leaped into the air, pumping his fist skyward. The day had finally come! The departure of the invasion force had been delayed for days, pending the location of the Spanish fleet, which had once been thought to be in position to intercept the invasion flotilla. This was the best possible news. He began hurriedly pulling on his uniform.

Captain Joe walked to the door. "Get dressed and wait for me," he said. "I'm going to Father's room to see if he has specific orders. We have a lot to do today."

Walker pulled on his boots and grabbed his hat. Wait? What torture! Every cell in his body cried out for action. He paced back and forth like a caged animal, his mind racing through a million thoughts at once.

Despite the inaction, a lot had happened for Walker during these two weeks. He had been waiting to be assigned to a military unit and join its camp. However, there did not seem to be a good option available, and so General Wheeler had simply assigned Walker to be an aide to Captain Joe. Walker was a little disappointed that he would not be part of a combat unit, but relieved that he would be near the General. Joe did not seem to be as pleased as Walker. In fact, he seemed rather embarrassed to have a raw recruit as his aide, and was frequently brusque in his treatment of Walker.

Walker spent a good bit of his time running errands for Captain Joe and the General. He became very familiar with the city of Tampa, its back streets and alleys, and the locations of the various military camps scattered about it. He delivered messages and orders for his commanders, spending most of each day in the saddle. When the river bridges were blocked with traffic, which was frequently, he would simply prod his horse down the bank and swim to the other side. His reliability and efficiency started to change Captain Joe's attitude toward Walker for the better.

One advantage of staying at the hotel was that writing materials were readily available. Walker had written two letters already, detailing his adventures and the marvelous sights he'd seen. In addition to so many other things, he had seen the famous Clara Barton, founder of the Red Cross, who was in charge of the military hospitals, and her assistant, Annie Wheeler, daughter of the General. He'd seen Theodore Roosevelt and the Rough Riders drilling near the hotel in their distinctive cowboy-style uniforms. Roosevelt looked very dashing in his expensively tailored Brooks Brothers outfit.

One of those letters had been mailed to his parents, and the other to Abigail Dancy. He had received no mail in return yet. He guessed that it was probably sitting in a mailbag in a boxcar on one of those many trains, stationary on the tracks around Tampa.

Then he spied the unfinished letter left lying on the desk. He had begun writing it to his parents last night and, too tired to finish it, had left it for today. He quickly folded it, put it into an envelope, and tucked it into the pocket of his blue uniform coat. Just then the door opened and Captain Joe stepped into the room.

"No time to waste, Garrett," he said urgently. "Grab your knapsack and follow me. Hustle!"

It was a hectic day. Almost thirty thousand men were trying to move down a single rail line to the port, nine miles away, with all their equipment. Even a novice like Walker could see that it was utter chaos. Looking about at the scene of confusion, he was thankful now that he was attached to General Wheeler and Captain Joe's staff, and that he was not one of the multitude of men anxiously running about looking for their places.

It literally took all night to get the ships loaded. Even then, thousands of men had to be left behind. A third of the Rough Riders did not make it onto their ship due to lack of space, and overall, about half of the soldiers in Tampa did not make the trip to Cuba. Walker saw many men weeping openly at being left behind. Only a few of the horses were taken, and only for the officers. Even the cavalry units would have to fight on foot, though two horses were loaded aboard ship for Roosevelt's use.

The thousand soldiers on board would have to share two latrines. The only sources of fresh air for the sleeping quarters came from a few small, round port windows. There were hardly any lights, and upon entering from above decks, it took a minute for his eyes to adjust to the darkness so that he could see to pick his way among the bunks. He hoped that the trip to Cuba would pass quickly—this did not promise to be a pleasant voyage.

By evening the air was slightly cooler, and the men thronged the deck, loath to go below until necessary. Many carried their meals out onto the deck to eat rather than endure the stifling heat inside. Supper consisted of hardtack crackers, canned beef, and an apple, with coffee for those who could get it. By the time the line of soldiers had moved enough for Walker to reach the kitchen's serving window, however, the coffee was all gone and he had to settle for water.

As he watched the setting sun turn the Gulf of Mexico blood red, he thought ahead to the eventual combat in Cuba and wondered how much real blood would be spilled. Picking his way along the deck, stepping over the sprawled bodies of lounging soldiers, he found a relatively isolated place to sit. Taking the unfinished letter from his coat pocket and rummaging in another pocket for his stub of a pencil, he added a few more carefully worded lines while the light lasted. When it became too dark to write he continued to sit and watch the movements of the water until the moon was high over-head, and then headed below deck to his bunk for the night.

Sleeping was extremely difficult. With hundreds of men crowded together and no movement of air, the bunkroom was stiflingly hot. An amazing variety of snoring sounds reverberated from every corner of the room. Occasionally someone would attempt to get out of his bunk and go to the latrine, upsetting other sleepers and drawing curses.

Not far from Walker's bunk was a tooth-grinder who made the most awful noise as he gritted his teeth in his sleep. After a while, a sleepless soldier had had all of it that he could take and cried out, "My God, man, will you stop it!" and flung his hat in the direction of the tooth-grinder. In the pitch blackness it struck the wrong man, who woke and sat up with a start, banging his head on the bunk above him, waking the three men sleeping there. In seconds there was a chorus of shouted curses and threats, aggravated by the voices of other men who were yelling for quiet. As the hubbub was subsid-ing, the tooth-grinder awakened and demanded to know what all the fuss was about. A barrage of hats sailed in his direction this time, along with more shouted epithets. Eventually things settled down enough that Walker fell asleep from sheer exhaustion.

The men on board were of two different military units: the First U.S. Volunteer Cavalry, better known as the Rough Riders, and the Tenth Cavalry, a black unit also called "Buffalo Soldiers," who had previously served on the western frontier fighting Indians. They were bunked separately from the mostly white Rough Riders, on a lower deck.

The Rough Riders were a fascinating mix of cowboys, Ivy League college athletes, Indians, and even a few millionaires who just wanted to be in the fight. Their casual conviviality drew Walker's interest, and he tried to join their groups and conversations. However, the blue army uniform which he'd been so proud to don marked him as an outsider. The Rough Riders wore brown khaki pants with leggings, a blue flannel shirt, and a handkerchief knotted around the neck. They were protective of their unique status and would have nothing to do with a regular army soldier. Walker found himself coming to despise his hot, woolen blue coat.

The Tenth Cavalry was a regular army unit, wearing the same uniform as Walker. However, these "Buffalo Soldiers" had been confronted with extreme prejudice and hostility from the white civilians and soldiers during their month in Tampa and were hardly inclined to welcome a white boy into their circle. Not that Walker actually wanted to socialize with the black soldiers—after all, whites and blacks did not mingle socially. He was not allowed in the officers' part of the ship, and Captain Joe did not require his services on board, so Walker was left to himself.

On the fourth day of the voyage Walker decided to pass some time by cleaning and oiling his weapons. Carrying his rifle and revolver out onto the main deck, he found a spot in the shade and sat down, placing a cleaning kit next to him. Immediately a Buffalo Soldier sat down next to him, also carrying a rifle.

"Say, you got enough oil for two? I sho' could use some. Mine is packed with the rest of the gear down below."

Walker, thankful for anyone to talk to, replied, "Got plenty. Help yourself."

"Much obliged." Walker watched him quickly and expertly dismantle the rifle and begin wiping its parts with the oily rag. The cavalryman had yellow corporal's stripes on his blue sleeves. He appeared to be only a little older than Walker himself, with brown skin and closely cropped hair.

"Say, you're pretty good at that," Walker commented. "How long you been in the army?"

"Fo' years," was his short reply, concentrating on his work.

"What kind of rifle is that, anyway? It doesn't look like the one they issued me." Walker leaned in to take a closer look at the Buffalo Soldier's rifle.

"This here's a good rifle," the cavalryman said with a smile of satisfaction. "It's a Krag-Jorgensen. Thirty caliber. Got a five-round magazine."

"Now that thing—" pointing at Walker's partially disassembled weapon—"That ain't worth a stinkin' cow pie. I wouldn't have one of them a'tall."

"Well, now," Walker objected defensively, "it's a forty-five caliber. That's a sight more effective than a little old thirty caliber!"

"Yes," agreed the other man, "but it's a single shot. Basically, it ain't nothing more than a modified Civil War musket. While you a-working that hammer to get another round loaded, I'll be pouring more lead into them stinkin' Span'ards. Three or four rounds of thirty is worth more than one of forty-five."

"I reckon that just means that I'll have to make my one shot count!" Walker grinned. "One bullseye with a forty-five is worth more than three misses with any caliber!"

The cavalryman laughed. "I got to hand it to you—for a volunteer that ain't never been in combat, you got spunk. Just don't be standing next to me when you shoot that thing."

"What do you mean?"

"Ain't you looked at your ammo? That rifle uses the same kind of black powder cartridges they been using ever since the Civil War.

When you pull that trigger, you gonna get a big cloud of smoke in front of yo' eyes. That means that you can't shoot again 'til it's gone, and while you a-waitin' to see the other feller again, he gon' be shooting the hell out of you 'cause he knows 'zactly where you are by that cloud of smoke."

"Don't everybody use the same kind of ammunition?" Walker asked in astonishment.

"Ha!" exclaimed the Buffalo Soldier, derisively. "Ain't you never heard of smokeless gunpowder? That's what us reg'lar troops use in these Krags. The Span'ards got it, too. The only reason you volunteers got these old black powder trapdoor rifles is 'cause they ain't got enough of these good ones to go around, and they got plenty of them old things that nobody wants anymore."

"So," he concluded, "you just be sure and stand somewhere's way off from me when you pull that trigger, 'cause you about to be a target for every Span'ard in Cuba."

Walker frowned. This was something he had not anticipated. He would have to talk to Captain Joe and the General about getting one of those Krag rifles before they reached Cuba.

They cleaned their rifles in silence for a few minutes, and then Walker spoke again.

"Say, where are you from?"

"I'm from Decatur, Alabama," replied the cavalryman. "But I been chasin' Injuns out in the Dakotas for the last fo' years. Ain't been back home since I left."

"Why, I'm from Decatur!" exclaimed Walker, with eyebrows raised in amazement. "Well, not exactly from Decatur, but from near there, just a few miles away. I live on General Wheeler's plantation at Pond Spring. My pa's the overseer there."

The Buffalo Soldier jerked as if he'd been slapped. Looking at Walker with a shocked expression on his face, he asked sharply, "What's yo' name?"

"Walker Garrett. What's yours?"

"Well. If that don't just beat all," the soldier murmured softly, almost to himself, still staring at Walker. "I've heard of you. My mama cooks for the Dancy family in Decatur. She told me about you staying at the house whilst you was at the 'cademy. She says you a nice boy."

"Beulah is your mama?" Walker could not believe his ears. "Why, Beulah is the best cook in Dixie! She fixed me some ham biscuits to bring on the trip down to Tampa! Daisy brought them to me at the train station in Decatur. I think the world of both of them. But I didn't even know Beulah had a son—" Walker stopped short, fearing that he was saying too much.

"No reason she should tell you 'bout me. I was gone to the army fo' you come to Decatur." The soldier continued looking intently at Walker, and said again, "Well, if it just don't beat all."

"What did you say your name was?" Walker asked.

"You don't even know my mama's last name, do you?" said the Buffalo Soldier, with a smile tinged with bitterness. "She's just 'Beulah' to you, ain't she?"

Walker was speechless. He did not know what to say—he didn't even know what to think. Was something wrong?

"Dixon. Corporal Dixon, that's my name." The cavalryman hefted his reassembled rifle. "Thanks for the oil." And he wended his way along the deck toward a cluster of Buffalo Soldiers without looking back.

Walker was puzzled and, for some reason, disturbed by the conversation. The fact that Corporal Dixon was Beulah's son was remarkable, but he was not sure what the cavalryman had meant about Walker's not knowing her last name. Putting that out of his mind for the time being, the most important thing to Walker now was to try to get his hands on one of those Krag rifles and some smokeless ammunition. He headed off in search of Captain Joe.

5

CUBA!

June 19, 1898
Dear Ma and Pa,

I hope this letter finds you doing well. I am fine, other than a little sea sickness. We have been at sea now for five days and we can see the mountains of Cuba in the distance. We will all be very happy to be off of this stinking ship. After hundreds of men have been sea sick for days, with only two latrines—you cannot imagine how foul a place this is. Last night a storm made us close the portholes in the sleeping quarters and we couldn't get any air to breathe. It was awful. We have had nothing to eat but hardtack, canned beef, and warm water since we boarded. And a few apples, at first. Anything would be better than this.

It has been pretty quiet mostly. I've seen porpoises, sharks, seagulls, and a few flying fish. That's all for now.

Your son,
Walker

Walker flicked the remaining inch-long stub of his pencil overboard and folded the letter into his pocket. He would give it to the postal clerk tomorrow, along with one to Abigail Dancy. That done, he felt finally ready for action. There was nothing else to do but wait. Three more days were to pass before the men would see combat.

The tension was building as the thirty-two transports and their escort of Navy vessels approached closer to land, and Walker and many of the soldiers spent more and more time cleaning and polishing their weapons.

The invasion force had sailed to the eastern side of Cuba, circling back under the southeastern tip of the island. The objective was the capture and destruction of the Spanish fleet, bottled up in the harbor of Santiago. The army's orders were to advance on Santiago by land and take the city, depriving the Spanish fleet of its harbor and forcing it to surrender or steam out of port and engage the American Navy.

On June 22 the order finally came for the men to go ashore. The place chosen for the landing was the beach by a tiny town called Daiquirí, which boasted only a couple dozen buildings and no wharves or piers—just sand. Beginning at daylight and lasting for about an hour, the big naval guns shelled the beach and the immediate area beyond it to make sure no hostile forces were waiting to attack. It was the first time Walker had heard such large cannons, and he was filled with excitement and awe. Even though the ships were several hundred yards away from the troop transports, the noise of the guns sounded louder than thunder and Walker could see the flames leaping from the huge barrels. The beach and the thickly forested area behind it erupted as sand and dirt were thrown into the air with each exploding shell.

There's no way anybody could survive that pounding! he grinned to himself. *Look out, Spaniards! Here we come!*

It had not occurred to Walker that the process of putting the men, horses, and equipment ashore would be a complicated and difficult process. In fact, it was as chaotic as the loading of the ships in Tampa, if not worse. Some of the equipment was simply tossed overboard to wash ashore with the tide. The men clambered down rope ladders to some small landing boats and, when they had approached to about a hundred yards from the beach, they climbed out and waded ashore in the heavy surf. Some of the men were put out of the boats too far from shore, and several drowned while trying to reach land. One of the small boats capsized, and two of the Buffalo Soldiers perished in the water.

The horses and mules were a special problem. After trying unsuccessfully to lower them over the side with a winch and cable, it was decided to push them overboard, just like the equipment. The horses were neighing— screaming, really—and Walker could not bear to watch. Amazingly most of the animals made it to the beach uninjured, though one of Roosevelt's horses was lost.

As horses, men, and boxes of supplies began to arrive on shore, Walker wondered how Wheeler and his staff were going to get their things together and corral their mounts. He suddenly realized that this was his responsibility—just as his father had seen to the needs of the General during The War, Walker would now do the same. For the next hour Walker ran along the beach and into the surf, dragging ashore saddles, rations, and whatever supplies he could get. He made a large pile near the tree line about two hundred feet from the water's edge. He tethered four horses in the shade and, finding some buckets among the gear littering the beach, went in search of some fresh water for them to drink.

He returned to find Wheeler, Captain Joe, and Major Payne standing by his pile of supplies.

"Who is stockpiling this equipment?" shouted the Major indignantly. "And these horses? General Wheeler and his staff have the first right to these things! Who is responsible for this?"

"Sir! I am, sir!" responded Walker. The officers turned in surprise and stared as he briskly emerged from the trees and set down two five-gallon buckets of water for the horses, who began slurping and gulping almost frantically.

"I've rounded up what supplies I could manage, including some rations, saddles, and oats for the horses. It should be enough for now, sir."

"Well done, Private Garrett!" cried the General. "You are certainly following in the footsteps of your father! He always took care of what was needed before anyone else even realized that we needed it. Keep it up and you'll do well indeed!"

"Thank you, sir," beamed Walker, standing straighter.

"Now," continued the General, "let's get those horses saddled as soon as they finish drinking. We need to scout the area before dark."

Wheeler walked down the beach, surveying the disorganized melee of thousands of men and tons of material. He constantly shook his head in disgust, ranting to no one in particular about how embarrassing it was. Major Payne walked at the General's side, a step behind, nodding his head in agreement. Captain Joe began to follow them, but first turned toward Walker and, with a raised eyebrow and a faint suggestion of a smile at the corner of his mouth, gave him a quick nod of approval. Walker grinned in response.

While General Wheeler and his party scouted the surrounding hills, Walker was hard at work in the camp that was slowly taking shape on the beach. By the time the General returned three hours later, Walker had set up his tent with cots, blankets, a field desk and chair, and a kerosene lantern. Walker himself would sleep on the ground with the other troops, and he positioned his bedroll near the General's tent in case he was needed.

Lieutenant Colonel Roosevelt joined Wheeler that evening and they studied a map, discussing plans for the next day. Upon arriving, Roosevelt had handed Walker a rifle and a bandolier of ammunition.

"Here you go, son," he said in his rapid, clipped speech. "You'll be putting this to good use soon."

Walker was about to reply that he already had a rifle when he realized that this was one of the new Krag-Jorgenson models. His mouth dropped open and he was speechless for a moment.

"Why, sir! Yes sir! Thank you, sir!" he stammered. Roosevelt waved his hand dismissively.

"Anything for General Wheeler's people. We need these in the hands of every soldier!"

"Excellent!" chirped the General briskly. "Private Garrett will certainly use it effectively. I taught him how to shoot, myself."

Supper that night was the same fare as they'd eaten on board the ship, but in the fresh air of the night it seemed like a banquet. All of the men were excited at the prospect of battle and, in small groups clustered along the beach, talked and laughed nervously. Walker slowly made his way toward the water, pausing on the periphery of the circles of squatting men to listen briefly.

"We'll be marching to Santiago tomorrah, for shuah," asserted a blue coated soldier with a Boston accent. "Box 'em up in the city and force 'em to surrendah."

"Yeah, and you can bet that them Span'ards'll be a-waitin' for us just over them thar hills," replied another, in a distinctly southern drawl. "We'll be a-fightin' all the way thar."

"No chance," disagreed a third man, in a Louisiana Cajun twang. "They let us land heah widdout puttin' up a fight, di'n they? They already be on the run."

Walker eventually reached the edge of the water. The surf was rolling in, running up to his boots and then rushing back out to sea. He stood, hands in pockets, and filled his lungs with the air which, after such long days on the cramped ship, smelled wonderful. The breeze coming in off the water was cool and refreshing, and it seemed that there were a million stars in the night sky. To be able to walk about freely on solid ground felt marvelously liberating.

"Long way from Pond Spring," spoke a voice from behind Walker. He jerked with a start and turned to face Corporal Dixon.

"Ain't that a fact!" he chuckled, embarrassed at having been surprised.

"Even further from the Dakotas," Dixon added. "And a hell of a lot warmer. This wool uniform is good in cold weather, but we ain't gonna see no cold weather down here."

"True," agreed Walker. "but at least we'll have shade. I've never seen such thick woods. We'll be marching in single file."

"That means easy pickin's for Spanish snipers. And you won't know where them bullets come from."

That reminded Walker of his new rifle.

"I've got a Krag now, too," he said proudly. "No smoke to give away my position. They won't know where these bullets come from, either!"

"You know why you got that rifle, don't you?" asked Dixon. His voice had a cold edge to it.

"What do you mean? Colonel Roosevelt gave it to me just a little while ago. It's a Rough Rider rifle."

"No, it ain't either. It's a Tenth Cavalry rifle. Our landing boat rolled and dumped us in the water. Two of our men drowned, and I barely made it to shore myself. Roosevelt sent one of his Rough Riders to dive down and get the rifles from those men that died. That's why you got that rifle."

Walker did not know what to say.

"I'm sorry—were they friends of yours?" It sounded trite and Walker immediately bit his lip.

Dixon stared stonily at Walker for several seconds.

"*Friends*?" he repeated with a curled lip. "No. They was my *brothers*. But you wouldn't understand that." And then he turned and walked away up the beach.

Walker felt confused as he watched Dixon pick his way toward the black soldiers' camp area. There was something about Dixon that disturbed him, but he couldn't put his finger on it. *Why does he dislike me so much?* he wondered under his breath. *I've never done anything to him.*

Noticing that some of the campfires were being extinguished, he realized that he'd better get back to his own place while there was still some light. The General's tent was dark, and the sound of light snoring could be heard. Walker unrolled his blanket and stretched out on the sand. It wasn't particularly comfortable, but after a week in cramped berths on the transport ship, anything was an improvement. He took off his jacket, rolled it up to use for a pillow, and was sound asleep in seconds.

A blood-curdling scream awakened Walker just after midnight. He abruptly sat upright, trying to organize his confused thoughts, when a second scream and then a third brought him to his feet. He grabbed his rifle and fumbled feverishly to load it. Other soldiers were also on their feet, shouting at the top of their lungs. Someone fanned a smoldering campfire into flame and lifted a torch overhead. It looked like the beach itself was crawling! Hundreds of soldiers began stomping the beach with their boots and pounding with the butts of their rifles. Walker realized groggily that the beach was covered with small, crawling creatures. After several minutes of vigorous and vocal combat the soldiers succeeded in killing or chasing away all of the creatures, and a measure of calm was restored.

Walker by now was standing in the middle of the beach camp. In the flickering light he squatted down to inspect the remains of one of the diminutive attackers. He lifted the weird creature by his thumb and index finger for a better look when suddenly it reached out with a claw and pinched his hand painfully. With a yell he dropped it, and then stomped it into the sand and ground it with his heel.

"What the heck is that?" he exclaimed.

"Crabs!" rasped a nearby voice. "There's hunnerds of 'em!"

"Hunnerds?" echoed another. "There's thousands!"

"Billy Sanders got his nose pinched half off!"

"This feller over here is gonna need stitches in his face."

"Well, this feller over here is gonna need stitches in his *butt!*"

This led to a round of laughs mingled with curses as the men cautiously returned to their blankets, checking carefully for more of the unwelcome pests. Some of the smaller crabs were only four or five inches long, but Walker saw a few that were much larger, with pincers that could do real damage to a sleeping man. Settling back down to sleep, he decided that it would be wise, despite the warmth of the night, to cover his face with part of the blanket and to wear his boots. Closing his tired eyes once again, he reflected that he was not very impressed with Cuba so far.

6

FIRST BLOOD

The tree root caught Walker's boot, almost tripping him, just as a leafy branch released by the soldier in front of him snapped back and slapped him in the face. Gritting his teeth, he shifted his rifle strap on his shoulder and picked his feet up higher as he pushed on into the dense jungle.

"I thought this was supposed to be a road," he muttered.

"I'd call it a pig trail, myself," growled a voice from behind.

This was the second day since the landing, and the men had been advancing single file as rapidly as possible through the almost impenetrable, hot, humid, green wilderness. The air was full of the calls of colorful, exotic birds and other creatures. The only other sounds were those of the tramping of many feet along the trail and the clinking of canteen cups against scabbards and bandolier belts. The heat was so oppressive that the blue wool uniform was becoming intolerable, and Walker was beginning to envy the Rough Riders their lighter khakis. Some of the men were so overcome that they fell out of line and collapsed in exhaustion until they could rejoin the march.

He bumped into the back of the man in front of him for what must have been the tenth time as the line again came to a brief halt for some unexplained reason. The man behind bumped into Walker, and so forth back down the line. Walker could feel rivulets of sweat running down inside his jacket as he adjusted his collar, but as mosquitoes hovered in front of his face, he remembered again why he had turned up his collar—to keep them off his neck—and turned it back up again.

"Garrett! Private Garrett!" a voice called from toward the front of the line. "Get up here! On the double! General Wheeler wants you!"

Walker squeezed past the men in the line, brushing against the leaves, vines, and tree trunks, hastening forward. Suddenly a man struck Walker sharply on the back of his right shoulder as he passed. Walker stopped in surprise and turned toward the man, who pointed at the ground at Walker's feet. Looking down, he saw the largest spider he had ever seen—a black, hairy monster measuring at least six inches across its leg span.

"Tarantula!" the man croaked, as he stomped on the spider. "On your back!"

Walker could hardly speak, he was so stunned at the size of the creature. A bite from a spider that size could surely be fatal!

"Thanks!" was all he could manage. The man nodded once.

Reaching the front of the line, he saw the white-bearded General standing next to a dark-skinned man in shabby, baggy clothes. Wheeler motioned for Walker to approach.

"This is José," said the General. "He's Cuban. He tells us that the Spanish army is not far away. I want you to go with him to see for yourself and report back to me." He extended a pair of binoculars to Walker, who took them and looped the leather strap around his neck.

"Yes sir!" exclaimed Walker, relieved at the opportunity to do something besides hike in the green hell of the jungle. Turning to José he nodded and said, "Lead the way!"

José hesitated, looking confused, and turned back toward the General, who turned to look expectantly at another soldier beside him. The soldier spoke to José in Spanish, and then José's expression changed. He smiled, nodded rapidly, and gestured to Walker to follow him as he hurried off into the undergrowth. Walker, realizing that he and José could not communicate verbally, looked at Wheeler for a second with wide eyes, not sure what to do, but then immediately turned and plunged into the jungle to catch up with José. He would figure out something.

They spent an hour hurrying along narrow trails, climbing hills, wading streams. The pace was a quick trot and, while Walker was straining to keep up, it was a welcome change from the miserable marching of the past two days. When the undergrowth was impenetrable, José quickly hacked a path through it with a machete. It was the only thing José carried, and Walker wondered why a rebel soldier would not have a gun. He assumed that José must not be a real rebel fighter, but a servant, aide, or other menial worker. Remembering that he also was an aide to Captain Wheeler, he quickly reminded himself that he was armed and equipped for battle—a real soldier.

After a lengthy, steep climb, they clambered over some large rocks and arrived at a promontory overlooking a verdant, green valley. After two days without even seeing the sun, Walker was glad to feel its rays again, despite the heat. Having left the ubiquitous mosquitoes in the dense forest, he unbuttoned the collar of his jacket and took a deep breath of the cooler mountain air. Taking a drink of lukewarm water from his canteen, he removed his hat, wiped the sweat from his brow and surveyed the panoramic vista before him.

José crouched behind a boulder and gestured to Walker to join him. He pointed down to the right at a lower hill more than a half mile away, where a large blockhouse was plain to see. Noticing movement around the structure, Walker raised the binoculars for a better look. Spanish soldiers in light colored uniforms and broad brimmed hats were busily digging trenches and dragging logs to construct ramparts. They were clearly preparing defenses. Walker studied the site for several minutes, noting the absence of artillery or Gatling guns. The men appeared to be armed only with rifles. He estimated that there were at least two hundred troops.

José watched closely as Walker made his examination of the Spanish position. When Walker lowered the binoculars, José cleared his throat and leaned over toward Walker.

"Por favor?" He reached a tentative hand toward Walker, pointing to the binoculars. He pretended to hold binoculars to his eyes and looked toward the blockhouse.

"You want to take a look?" Walker lifted the strap from around his neck and held it out to him. José nodded rapidly, as if he understood Walker's words. His expression was almost childlike with delight and anticipation. When he looked toward the blockhouse he gasped in amazement, followed for a long moment by ooh's and ah's of pleasure and wonder. He returned the binoculars to Walker with a simple but earnest, "Gracias!"

José then tapped Walker on the shoulder and pointed down below the blockhouse into the bottom of the valley where a long crease wound through the thick foliage.

"Camino!" He moved his arm, pointing in a long arc from the left to the right, east to west, describing a path. Pointing further to the west, into the distance, he added, "Las Guásimas! El camino hacia Las Guásimas!" Nodding as if agreeing with himself, he looked expectantly at Walker to see his reaction. Walker's expression made it clear that he had no idea what José was saying, and José furrowed his brow and rubbed his chin for several seconds. Then, his countenance brightened and he tried again.

"Americanos!" He pointed eastward and pretended to march, swinging his arms back and forth in an exaggerated motion while stomping his feet in rhythm. He pointed again, and repeated "Americanos!" He then swept his arm rightward, tracing the faint line through the valley floor and said again, "El camino!" And finally, pointing toward the western end of the valley, added, "Las Guásimas! El camino hacia Las Guásimas!" He proudly repeated, looking at Walker with a triumphant smile.

"Las Guásimas?" echoed Walker, shaking his head and spreading his hands. "What is Las Guásimas?"

José put his fingertips to his temples and made an expression of bewilderment. Glancing about, he quickly stepped over to a patch of dirt and, picking up a small rock, began to draw. He drew a long line and on either side of it sketched several small rectangles. Around these boxes he added stick figures that were obviously people, some large and some small. On one of the rectangles he drew a Christian cross symbol. Pointing to the sketch, José repeated, "Las Guásimas!"

Walker stared at the drawing for several seconds, thinking hard.

"Oh! I see!" Walker then exclaimed in relief. "The Americans are marching on the road through this valley toward the town of Las Guásimas, and the Spanish are preparing to attack them! I must tell General Wheeler immediately! Let's get going!"

José grinned broadly, nodding vigorously and clapping his hands in delight that Walker had finally understood. Picking up his rifle and knapsack, Walker began hurrying back down the steep trail toward the dense jungle. José quickly passed him to take the lead, machete in hand, and they plunged into the shadowy green maze.

Hurrying down the rough stones of a dry creek bed, Walker missed a step and almost fell. Steadying himself with a hand on a protruding tree root, he looked up to see José dart to the right of a thorny thicket that blocked their path. Walker felt sure that the most direct course lay to the left of the thicket, so he bounded over the stones in that direction, smiling to himself, thinking that he would come out ahead of José.

To his surprise, when he stumbled through a wall of vines and leafy branches, he found himself standing in a wide section of the trail where the trees left a gap for the sunlight to penetrate to the forest floor. Looking to his right to see if José had reached the trail yet, he was stunned to see instead three Spanish soldiers, dressed in loose-fitting, pinstriped outfits, layered with leather belts, ammunition pouches, and bandoliers of cartridges, staring back at him with shocked expressions.

Immediately all four men leaped into fevered action. Walker unslung the rifle from his shoulder and worked the bolt back and forward to chamber a round. Before he could even shoulder the weapon, however, one of the Spaniards had raised a pistol and aimed straight at Walker. Suddenly the foliage beside the soldier burst apart and José sprang into the trail, bringing his machete down in a flashing arc as he grunted loudly with the exertion. The severed hand of the soldier, still grasping the pistol, dropped to the ground as blood spurted from the stump of his wrist. A second soldier, standing just behind the other, uttered an involuntary cry of surprise, his eyes and mouth opening wide. José, never pausing, pivoted and brought the machete upward in a backhand swing, slashing the throat of the soldier, whose cry ended in a gurgle as blood spewed forth, drenching the back of his handless comrade. The third Spaniard, pistol in hand, instantly turned and ran frantically up the trail. José reached behind his neck into the collar of his baggy shirt and drew out a nine-inch-long knife which he expertly threw, its blade flashing in the sunlight until it buried itself into the back of the fleeing man. The first soldier still stood in his tracks, staring horrified at his hand on the ground as blood gushed from his wrist. He grasped his wrist with his other hand, trying to stanch the flow, but then his eyes widened and his lips parted as he fell forward on his face. Walker saw José pull the blade of his machete from the man's back as he fell.

"Perros!" José hissed at the man lying at his feet, and spat.

Walker stood immobilized, his rifle still in his hands. Then, remembering to breathe, he noisily filled his lungs with air. His legs suddenly felt weak. José gave him a questioning look as if to say, "Are you alright?" and bent to wipe his machete blade on the uniform of one of the fallen Spaniards. He hurried up the trail to retrieve his knife.

Walker slowly approached the bodies. He had never seen anyone killed before, and he was feeling a bit dazed. He realized that José had saved his life, and it occurred to him that he was much less of a warrior than José. He felt a burning sense of shame that the dark little man in baggy clothes, without even a firearm, had so clearly demonstrated his superiority, but also thankful that José had been there.

He stooped to pick up the dead Spaniard's pistol, prying the clinched fingers loose and letting the hand drop to the ground with a soft thud. Inspecting the gun, he read aloud the stamped letters on the barrel: "Mauser, 7.63." Walker had never seen a weapon like this. Unlike the revolvers he had practiced shooting at Pond Spring, it had no cylinder for the cartridges, but a square box in front of the trigger appeared to serve that purpose. The barrel was about six inches long, half the total length of the pistol. The wooden handle was round, like a broom handle.

"So strange!" he breathed in wonderment.

He pulled the ammunition pouch from the man's body. It was a bandolier bag with a shoulder strap, and by its weight Walker estimated that it held about thirty cartridges. There was a large, fresh blood stain on the strap, but Walker draped it over his own head anyway, hanging it over his right shoulder, and adjusted it to ride at his left hip.

"Americano!" José hissed, crouching over the third soldier's body, knife in hand.

"Soldados!" He pointed up the trail, cupping his hand to his ear. Walker listened and then heard the sound of marching feet and the rhythmic ringing of metal against metal. More Spanish soldiers were coming. José ran back to Walker and, gesturing to him to follow, disappeared into the tangled undergrowth again. Walker shoved the pistol into his belt and followed.

7

———

FIRST BATTLE

"Let's go, boys! We've got the damn Yankees on the run again!" shouted General Wheeler, saber in hand. Walker had never seen the white-bearded legend so animated. His eyes were spitting fire, and it was plain to see that he was ecstatic to be on a battlefield again.

"Yankees?" echoed a soldier to Walker's left. "What war does he think this is, anyway?"

Just then a bullet whistled past the man's ear, slapping audibly through leaves and snapping small limbs. Ducking reflexively, he added, "And I don't think we've got them on the run, either!"

Walker resented the man's apparent disrespect for the General and wanted to reply, but more bullets were snapping through the brush and he decided that could wait.

"Return fire!" shouted Colonel Leonard Wood, leader of the Rough Riders.

"I can't see what to shoot at," muttered a soldier. "Where are they?"

Walker remembered what Corporal Dixon had said about the Spanish rifles using smokeless gunpowder, and this gave him an idea.

He wriggled on his belly through the grass and vines toward General Wheeler. He found the General standing with Captain Joe and a group of officers in a small grove of palm trees about fifty yards behind the front line. The General was gesturing with both hands and speaking rapidly, with frustration in his voice.

"Our men have got to return fire!" he barked. "We cannot continue simply sitting here in the bushes doing nothing! We are taking casualties every minute!"

"But the men can't see what to shoot at," objected one. "And our rifles give away our position by their smoke!"

"General Wheeler, sir!" interjected Walker. "I think I know a way to turn the tables on the Spaniards! We can use our black powder rifles to cover our troop movements and flank them."

"Private Garrett!" snapped a familiar voice. It was Major Payne. " Learn your place, boy! This is a council of officers, and we don't need any input from a private!"

"Not so fast there, Major Payne," intervened Wheeler in a calmer tone of voice. "I'd like to hear what Private Garrett has to say."

Turning to Walker, he said, "Speak up! We don't have time to waste."

"Yes sir!" And Walker quickly laid out his idea. The regular army soldiers would fire from concealment, not aiming their fire at any specific target or exposing themselves to enemy fire. The white smoke they produced would draw the fire of the Spanish force. Meanwhile, the Rough Riders would steal around to the left, outflanking the Spanish position, and the Tenth Cavalry—the Buffalo Soldiers—would do the same to the right, catching the Spanish in a crossfire. These two units each carried the newer Krag rifles, which used smokeless gunpowder. When they reached their positions and began to fire upon the Spanish, the Spanish would not be able to detect their location.

"We can give them a dose of their own medicine, sir!" he finished.

Roosevelt, who was peering around a palm tree trying to spot the enemy position, suddenly began to sputter and sneeze violently. A bullet had penetrated completely through the tree trunk, filling the Rough Rider's ear and nose with sawdust and shavings. Had he not been leaning to the side of the tree, he would have been killed. The need for immediate action seemed even more urgent.

General Wheeler instantly gave the orders. Wood and Roosevelt were to take their men flanking to the left, and Lieutenant Pershing would take his to the right.

"Garrett!"

"Yes sir, General Wheeler!"

"Go with Lieutenant Pershing. Take the binoculars and see if you can spot those Spaniards. We've got to give them some heat!"

The square-jawed, mustached Pershing motioned for Walker to follow him and they hurried away, crouching as they ran, using every tree for protection. Walker, having just come through this terrain with José, took the lead as they made a loop far to the east in order to stay within the tree line and escape the detection of the Spanish forces. Turning northward, they crawled on their bellies through the grass and bushes, finally arriving at an elevated position slightly higher than that held by the Spanish.

"There they are, sir!" Walker exclaimed, pointing. His sharp eyes had detected the light straw hats of the Spanish soldiers some six hundred yards away without the need of binoculars. But something was odd.

The white smoke produced by the American regulars could be clearly seen coming from the trees to the south of the Spanish position, but the Spanish soldiers appeared to be firing toward the west. Raising the binoculars, Walker scanned the area beyond the Spanish troops.

"Sir!" he gasped, extending the binoculars to Lieutenant Pershing. "Look over there! The Rough Riders are pinned down out there in the grassy area! They're getting shot to pieces!"

Pershing grabbed the binoculars and took a quick look. Without a second's hesitation he immediately turned to the five hundred black soldiers scattered along the ridge and shouted, "Open fire! Aim toward those white hats on yonder hill! Adjust your sights for six hundred yards!"

The Tenth Cavalry promptly unleashed a hailstorm of fire upon the Spanish position. The first rounds fell short, but the men quickly found the range and the Spanish suddenly found themselves being subjected to terrific pressure. The rifles used by the Tenth were the smokeless Krags, and the Spanish, thinking that the American troops were all using the black powder weapons, were confused as to the source of the fire. Excited movements could be seen in their lines as they moved and shifted, trying to find safety. The Rough Riders, no longer receiving such intense fire, rose from the grass and advanced toward the Spanish, firing as they came.

Seeing this, Pershing shouted, "Advance! Keep firing!" And the men of the Tenth rose as one and began to move down from the ridge toward the Spanish. Almost immediately, the soldiers emerged from the trees and, with their rifles belching white smoke, joined the three-pronged advance.

A bright flash caught Walker's eye—General Wheeler was waving his saber over his head, leading the charge! Filled with pride and excitement, Walker spontaneously threw back his head and let go with a shrill, spine-tingling "rebel yell"—the battle cry that had been the trademark of the gray soldiers of the Civil War. He fired a round toward the milling mass of Spanish soldiers and worked the bolt to prepare another shot while running down the slope.

By the time the American forces converged at the position held by the Spanish army, there was no one left there. The enemy had disappeared into the jungle, withdrawing toward the city of Santiago. Left behind were a half-dozen lifeless bodies sprawled in the grass, splotched with red. Their weapons, hats, and other equipment quickly became souvenirs for the excited American soldiers who swarmed over the area, waving their guns and talking loudly about their victory. Walker saw Colonel Roosevelt hurrying back and forth, slapping his men on the back and barking his congratulations.

"Well, well, well," said a familiar voice from behind Walker.

"Looks like them white boys won themselves a big victory. Can't wait for the folks back home to read all about it in the newspapers."

Turning, Walker raised an eyebrow at Corporal Dixon.

"What do you mean, 'the white boys won the victory?' You fellows did your part too. In fact, if we hadn't jumped on the Spanish when we did, the Rough Riders might have been massacred."

Dixon nodded. "And do you think that's gonna be in the newspapers?"

"Why wouldn't it?"

Dixon shook his head in exasperation. "You don't know nothin', do you? Do you really think colored soldiers are gon' be given credit for saving white boys' hides, even if it's true?"

Walker shrugged and spread his hands. "Well, they ought to," he said, without conviction. "If it's the truth."

"You know it's the truth," retorted Dixon. "And besides, what the hell was that scream you did when we was going down the ridge? That was the craziest thing I ever heard."

"That was the 'rebel yell,'" grinned Walker. "That's how the Confederate soldiers yelled when they charged across the battlefield in the Civil War!"

"Uh-huh," Dixon scoffed, his eyes narrowing. "And how'd that turn out for 'em?"

Walker literally gasped at these words. He stammered and tried to frame a response, but Dixon simply turned and walked away. Walker was furious. *How dare he mock the soldiers in gray!* Glaring at Dixon's back, Walker decided that he definitely did not like the corporal.

"Private Garrett!" Walker turned to see who was calling him. It was Captain Joe waving at him to come. He hurried over to find him with Pershing, Payne, and General Wheeler gathered in a small circle. They all looked at Walker as he approached.

"Well done, boy!" beamed the General. "Your idea worked like a charm!"

"The First Cavalry performed magnificently!" boomed Roosevelt. "The field report must give them credit for the victory!" Roosevelt could always be counted on to praise his Rough Riders as if they were the only troops present.

"Overall we lost seventeen men killed, and several dozen wounded," Major Payne averred. "From the looks of things here, the Spaniards lost no more than seven. I don't know if we can call this a victory or not!"

"The Spanish retreated and we have the ground!" snapped Wheeler. "It's a victory just the same as Sharpsburg in '62!" He was referring to a Civil War battle in which Lee's Confederate army retreated, despite having inflicted heavy losses on its Union opponent, thereby suffering a costly defeat. Major Payne opened his mouth as if about to reply, but then abruptly shut it, his nostrils flaring as he took a deep breath and then slowly exhaled.

"We must pursue them while they are retreating!" asserted Wheeler. "We don't want to make the same mistake as McClellan at Sharpsburg! Let's get the men formed up to march. On to Santiago!" And with that the wiry general scurried off, snapping orders right and left as he went.

Colonel Wood arrived to the group just as Wheeler was leaving. Hearing Wheeler's last words, he stroked his chin and said cautiously, "I think we would be wise to consult with General Shafter about our next move. After all, he is the commanding officer of this expedition."

"Then you'd better talk to General Wheeler right now, sir," advised Payne. "He's ready to march straight to Santiago!"

Saluting the officers, Walker withdrew and mingled with the hundreds of soldiers. He joined a group that was collecting the bodies of the dead and wounded. Payne had been correct—there were soon seventeen dead soldiers lying in a row on the hillside. Seeing so many dead Americans was more than Walker could comprehend at the moment, so he focused his mind on the task of moving the bodies. More than fifty were wounded, but many of them were able to walk on their own. A pack train of mules arrived a couple of hours later, bringing fresh supplies, and they were used to send the most seriously injured men back to the field hospital at Siboney, on the coast. Walker received a bandage for a cut on his hand, inflicted by a tall, razor-sharp sword of grass. Many of the men had received similar cuts, and painful stab wounds from the prickly cacti that lined the trails.

Walker saw some uniformed men setting up a six-foot post and connecting a long wire to its top. Next to the post they put a table and a familiar looking contraption, which they connected to the end of the wire. Approaching closer for a better look, he suddenly realized that the contraption was a telephone. He observed that the wire, wrapped in black rubber, stretched all the way to the tree line, where it disappeared into the jungle.

"We have a telephone—*here*?" he asked, in a tone of amazement.

"Matter of fact, we do," replied one of the men dryly. "One of the marvels of modern science comes to the battlefield."

"Civil War generals usually had their own telegraph lines and operators," challenged Walker. "This isn't that much different."

"True," admitted the other, "but it *is* different. And it's *better*. General Wheeler and General Shafter can talk to each other now, just like they were both sitting right here."

"I'll grant you that," conceded Walker. "Back home in Alabama, it's fifteen miles to the nearest telephone. And now we have one right here in Cuba!"

Within minutes, General Wheeler was seated at the table engaged in a vigorous discussion with General Shafter, who was back on the coast. It was obvious that Wheeler was not at all pleased.

Turning away, Walker bumped into Captain Joe.

"Joe! I mean, Sir! Captain Wheeler!" Walker cleared his throat to hide his embarrassment. "Why is the General so upset?"

Captain Joe returned Walker's salute. "I don't think General Shafter is happy that Pa fought a battle while he was still at Siboney. He's ordering us to remain here until he arrives to take command."

"Remain here!" Walker exclaimed. "Sir! The Spaniards are retreating toward Santiago! We should be chasing after them!"

"This is the army, Private Garrett," said Captain Joe in a steely tone of voice. "In the army, you obey orders. Period. End of discussion. So, find a good place for your bed roll. We are going to be here for a few days. I suggest a spot in the middle of the camp so the land crabs, snakes, scorpions, and tarantulas don't get to you."

"Or the buzzards," breathed Walker to himself, gazing skyward at the dozens of black specters circling endlessly. A sudden shiver passed over him, and he grabbed his bedroll and began to look for a good location.

8

SAN JUAN HILL

June 30, 1898

Dear Abigail,

I apologize for not having written in a while, but we've been very busy here in Cuba. We fought a battle just two days after landing. General Wheeler sent me to help move our wounded men back to the field hospital here on the coast. Along the way, we were fired upon by some Spanish snipers who were hiding up in the trees. We could hear them making bird calls to each other as signals, and I was able to spot a couple and shoot them. Most of the men in the hospital have fever, not combat wounds. The canned meat they give us is usually spoiled, and eating it can make you very sick.

I met a Corporal Dixon. He is Beulah's son. Please tell her that her son is well. Thank you for the crochet piece. It means a lot to me. I'll write again when I can.

Yours truly,
Pvt. Walker Garrett

W alker looked with pride at the signature. It sounded so official and military! Abigail would know that he was not just "Walker Garrett" anymore, but "*Private* Walker Garrett." He felt sure that she would be impressed.

When he returned to Las Guásimas from Siboney, the troops had moved further inland. Part of the force had split off and taken a more northerly route toward Santiago, passing through the town of El Caney. Walker's unit had taken the southerly route which led over a steep hill, called San Juan Hill. A detachment of Cuban fighters circled around to the western side of Santiago, completing the encirclement of the port city. Everyone could sense that a major action was about to begin.

Walker was summoned to General Wheeler's tent. When he arrived, the General was involved in a discussion with General Shafter and Colonels Wood and Roosevelt. He glanced casually around the interior of the tent, which was shared by Wheeler and Roosevelt. Lying on Roosevelt's iron cot was a book with a ribbon place-marker about midway in the book. Walker picked up the book and read the title: *Superiorite des Anglo-Saxons*.

"And just what do you think you are doing, Private Garrett?" It was Captain Joe, frowning with arms crossed.

"Nothing!" stammered Walker. Surprised and embarrassed, he quickly put the book back down. "I was ordered to come to the General's tent. I just wanted to see what book Colonel Roosevelt was reading, that's all, sir."

Captain Joe stepped over to the cot and bent to see the title.

"What language is that?" Walker asked.

"It's French," replied Joe. "It means 'The Superiority of the Anglo-Saxons,' which refers to the English people."

"Why would a Frenchman write a book about the superiority of the English?"

Captain Joe shrugged. "The sun never sets on the British Empire. They are the most powerful and wealthy country in the world. I suppose that the Frenchman is just recognizing the obvious."

Walker scratched his head, and looked confused.

"Are you saying that Britain is better than the United States?" he asked incredulously.

"Not necessarily," laughed Captain Joe. "Anglo-Saxons are the white, English-speaking people of the world, and that includes the United States."

"Oh!" exclaimed Walker, relieved. "That's good!" Then, in a tone of respect, he added, "Colonel Roosevelt must be a really smart man to be able to read French."

Before Captain Joe could respond, General Wheeler darted into the tent and both of them snapped to attention and saluted. With a casual wave of his hand, the General addressed Walker.

"Lieutenant Pershing has requested that you accompany him again today. Evidently you impressed him at Las Guásimas. Your friend José is here also. Take him and lead Pershing over to that hill yonder and support the regulars, who will be advancing up this hill. Don't let the Spanish see you coming." Wheeler pointed toward the hills and then exited the tent at his usual brisk pace, leaving Walker saluting the air.

"Well, get going, Private Garrett!" snapped Captain Joe, and Walker left the tent at a run.

Lieutenant Pershing and his company were ready to go. José greeted Walker with a grin and "Buenos días, mi amigo!" Walker noted that José again carried only a machete, but this time he did not fail to respect its capabilities. The men of the Tenth Cavalry rose from their resting positions and, without a word, quickly formed into two lines. Pershing silently motioned for José and Walker to take the lead, and they headed into the brush.

After pushing through the thick vegetation for about a half-mile, they stood on the banks of a small river. The San Juan River was about fifty yards across, with a slow, swirling current. Upstream to the right Walker could see small waterfalls. Under other circumstances he would have found it very pleasant, but at the moment he hesitated, unsure what to do next. José solved that problem by promptly stepping into the river and wading through the waist-deep water. Walker followed, and the Tenth was soon in the river.

No sooner had they left the safety of the trees than rifle shots rang out and bullets began popping in the water around them. No one needed to be told to hurry. Holding their rifles above their heads and zigzagging as they went, five hundred men churned the water as they strained toward the safety of the far bank. Reaching the other side, Walker turned to see Lieutenant Pershing, and Corporal Dixon right behind him. He saw three men suddenly go down in the river as the water turned red around them.

"Anderson!" shouted Corporal Dixon. "Hurry up!" Anderson, a short, wiry man, was struggling in the water, which reached his chest. His eyes were wide with fear. Bullets were striking the water within inches of his shoulders, and one snatched the blue cap off his head. He reached for the hat as it floated on the water, and he cried out in pain as another bullet struck his arm.

"Forget the hat!" screamed Dixon. "Get out of the river!"

Suddenly, dropping his rifle to the ground, Corporal Dixon leaped into the water and splashed toward him.

"Dixon!" bellowed Pershing. "What the hell are you doing? Are you crazy?"

Reaching Anderson, Dixon grabbed him by the shirt collar and began to drag him toward the bank. Bullets rained down around them as Walker watched, frozen. As the pair approached the river bank two other soldiers jumped into the river and helped drag them to safety.

"Medic!" shouted one of the men. "We need a medic over here right now!"

The regimental surgeon appeared almost immediately and began to examine two wounds on Corporal Dixon's left arm and side.

"Not me!" gasped Dixon, out of breath, pointing to Anderson. "Take care of him first! I can wait."

As the doctor cleaned and wrapped the bullet wounds of both men, Walker heard a sound like distant thunder. The sky was clear and blue, however, with no dark clouds in sight.

Turning to Pershing he asked, "Sir, what is that noise? Is that artillery?"

Pershing nodded. "That's a three-inch Hotchkiss gun. Our men are attacking the Spanish at El Caney, a few miles north of here."

As the unit stood, ready to advance into the thick jungle again, Walker looked back at the river. Six bodies were floating slowly away toward a bend in the river. Pershing, reading Walker's thoughts, said brusquely, "We'll have to recover them later. Right now we have a battle to fight."

The trees along the river bank provided protection for the men for only a short distance, and then they were forced to crawl on their bellies through the tall, thick grass. Rifle and artillery fire filled the air with a constant, deafening roar. Hundreds of Spanish bullets ripped through the tall grass viciously. The situation was rapidly becoming desperate.

Lieutenant Pershing raised his head for a quick look around. Quickly assessing the few options available, he made an immediate decision. Standing suddenly, he shouted, "Men of the Tenth! Advance!" As one man the entire company rose up from the grass and began to climb the slope, firing as they went. Walker was taken aback by the foolhardy and reckless command, but he too then rose to his feet. Without even consciously thinking about it, he screamed out the "rebel yell," and knees pumping, he charged upward.

As he passed by Dixon the corporal snapped, "You crazy screaming rebel! You ain't gonna get to the top of this hill before me!" And Dixon began sprinting shoulder to shoulder with Walker. Seeing the two forge ahead, the rest of the company gave out a shout as if with a single voice and five hundred men rushed up the hill, unmindful of the hail of bullets.

To their left Roosevelt was leading the Rough Riders in a similar charge up the hill. It became a race to see which unit would reach the top first. The Rough Riders encountered several strands of barbed wire which had been stretched across the field by the Spanish as part of their defense. As they stopped to cut the wires, the Tenth surged ahead, reaching the Spanish lines as the Spanish soldiers hurriedly retreated beyond a yellow stucco blockhouse.

The troops in the blockhouse were all that remained to be conquered on the hilltop. Three dozen Spanish soldiers inside kept up a constant fire, preventing a frontal assault by the Americans. Walker and the rest of the men crouched in the Spanish rifle pits, unable to advance further. The trenches were littered with the bodies of the soldiers killed by the American artillery barrage. Unlike men killed by rifle bullets, the men struck down by the shrapnel shells were ripped apart and almost unrecognizable. Walker felt sick to his stomach as he straddled what was, only moments earlier, a living man.

He felt a touch on his shoulder and flinched—it was José, motioning him to follow. Half crawling down the trench, they reached the far side of the blockhouse. José pointed to a low stone wall, beside which was a tree with spreading limbs, casting a broad shade. He pointed vigorously at a gaping hole in the red tile roof, caused by an artillery round. Walker did not need to understand José's excited staccato explanation to realize the opportunity this presented. He gestured to the soldiers nearest him and pointed to the tree and motioned to them to follow.

Walker and José, followed by two dozen Buffalo Soldiers, crept quickly from the trench to the house. There was only one window on this end of the house, and the soldiers inside were preoccupied with the assault force in front of them, so they were able to reach the shaded corner without being seen.

Leaning his rifle against the side of the house, Walker pulled the Mauser pistol from his belt and cocked the hammer. The soldiers laid aside their rifles also, after removing the bayonets, and several produced revolvers. José brandished his machete.

It was an easy step to the top of the stone wall, and from there to a horizontal tree limb, and from there to the roof. Only a couple at a time could go through the roof hole. Walker edged up to the hole, crouching low to avoid being seen by the occupants.

"You ain't going in b'fore me," hissed a voice. Corporal Dixon scuttled quickly up to the hole.

"Says who?" retorted Walker, and with an ear-splitting yell he leaped into the darkness. Dixon, giving out his own scream, was hardly an instant behind. Each of the men followed, screaming and shouting. Even José produced a falsetto war cry as he disappeared through the hole.

Walker hit the floor and rolled out of the bright circle of light, coming up on his knees, pistol in hand. As the Spanish soldiers turned from the windows in shock, Walker opened fire, knowing that he had to keep them occupied while the rest of the men plummeted through the hole and found their feet. Fortunately, the Mauser pistol he had taken from the dead soldier a week earlier had a ten-round magazine, and he sprayed bullets left and right as fast as he could. Dixon, with his Army-issued Colt .38 six-shooter, did the same.

The brawl that raged inside the house was a mass of confusion. The floor beneath the hole in the roof was illuminated, but in contrast the rest of the room was comparatively gloomy and dark. At first Walker and the others relied on seeing the outlines of the Spanish soldiers against the windows behind them, until their eyes adjusted to the dim light.

Hearing shouts from the other rooms of the house, Walker knew they were about to be greatly outnumbered. His pistol was out of bullets, so he crouched over the body of one of the slain Spanish soldiers and pulled the pistol from the man's belt. Letting go with another ear-splitting "rebel yell," he leaped to the wall at one side of the room, and as Spanish soldiers came running into the room past him, he fired at them in succession, sending several to the floor. He felt the wind of a bullet pass close to his face and smash into the adobe wall just six inches away, blinding one eye with dust and powder. Throwing his empty pistol into the face of a soldier, he sprang forward and drove his bayonet into him, up to the hilt. As the man fell with the bayonet still in his side, Walker relieved him of his pistol. Looking about the room for more targets, gun in his extended hand, he realized that all of the Spanish soldiers were down and only Americans were standing.

"Hold fire!" cried Corporal Dixon hoarsely. In the quiet that followed, only the heavy breathing of the men standing and the groans of the wounded could be heard.

"You men alright?" came a call from outside a window. The American unit nearest the house had taken advantage of the melee inside to advance to the house itself, and now bayoneted rifles protruded into the room through each window.

"We've got some men down," croaked Dixon. "But the Span'ards are all down."

The house was quickly filled with American soldiers. They searched the other rooms and examined the fallen bodies to see which were still alive and which were Americans.

"This one's ours."

"This one's alive."

"This one's dead."

The bodies of the dead were lifted and carried outside. Feeling suddenly weak, Walker sagged against the wall and slid to his knees.

"You hurt?" It was Colonel Roosevelt, standing next to him.

"No sir—I've just got some dirt in my eye. I'm alright," Walker replied.

"What's all this blood, if you've just got dirt in your eye?" snapped Roosevelt.

Walker looked at his arms. Feeling a pain in his left shoulder, he saw a hole in the jacket. Pulling it open with his other hand, he saw bright red on the shirt and skin. The blood had run down his arm and was dripping from his hand.

"I must have got hit," he mumbled.

"Get outside, and the medics will take care of you!"

Outside, Walker joined a group of a dozen men being bandaged. Almost all of them were Tenth Cavalry regulars. They were joined by José, who had lost part of a finger on his left hand, and displayed his white bandage proudly.

"You boys did good work today!" boomed Colonel Roosevelt, his head bobbing vigorously as he looked around the circle of men. "Going in through that hole in the roof was the epitome of bravery and martial courage! Colonel Wood, the Rough Riders, and I all want to thank you for helping us win the victory!" He raised a fist into the air as he spoke the last words, and giving a last bobbing nod of his head, turned and began giving orders to the other men to dig trenches in case of a counterattack by the Spanish.

"What does 'epitome' mean?" wondered one of the men aloud. "And 'martial courage?'"

Dixon spat on the ground. "Helping *them* win the victory? *We* won the victory! And without much help from them!"

"The United States won the victory," Walker said, grimacing as the medic applied a cleaning solution to his wounded shoulder. "We all won it together."

The arrival of Lieutenant Pershing cut short the talking.

"Simply marvelous!" he exclaimed. "I'm proud of the way you fellows fought today. We lost six good men, but your action saved the lives of many more."

Turning to Walker, he then added, "Going in through the roof was a brilliant stratagem! I'm putting your name in for a promotion, Garrett. That was real soldiering!"

Walker opened his mouth to say that it was actually José's idea, but Pershing was already striding away. Walker's hand, which he had pointed toward José, dropped to his side. He glanced toward José, who understood none of what had transpired.

"You're no better'n Roosevelt," sneered Dixon. "Taking credit for another man's work. That's the way you white boys get ahead, ain't it?"

"That's not true!" Walker argued angrily. "I was going to tell him it was José's idea."

"Was. Going. To tell him." Dixon repeated the words slowly, with emphasis. Then he turned his back and said to the rest of the Tenth, "Let's go pay respects to our brothers." They left Walker alone with José and a Cherokee Rough Rider who had cut his hand on some barbed wire while coming up the hill. That soldier glanced awkwardly at Walker, and then he too walked away.

José sensed that something had happened, and he looked at Walker with confusion and concern written on his face. Walker wracked his brain for a way to communicate. Finally, he pointed to the blockhouse and drawing on the few Spanish words he had learned, said to José, "Gracias, amigo!" José grinned in delight, waved his bandaged hand over his head and gave a quick falsetto whoop, and then threw back his head and laughed. Walker could not help but laugh with him, and put his arm around José's shoulders.

"Bueno amigo!" beamed José.

9

SANTIAGO

July 16, 1898

Dear Ma and Pa,

Thank you for your letter which I received last week. It made me feel like I was home again. Give old Duke a good head scratch for me. Things here have settled down a good bit. The Spanish finally surrendered Santiago and the war here is over. Captain Joe and I took down the Spanish flag over the fort and raised Old Glory! I was so proud! It is good that we did not have to storm the city, because it is walled and well-defended. With so many of our men sick with the fever, we would have had a hard time fighting another battle. I don't know what happens next, but I'll write again when I can.

Your son,

Walker

P.S. I am now Private First Class! I get to wear an infantry insignia on my collar!

After dropping the letter into the outgoing mail box outside the U. S. Army headquarters in Santiago, Walker wandered slowly down the crooked streets of the city, eventually reaching the harbor. The seafront was dominated by the enormous stone fortress, San Pedro de la Roca, which was two hundred years old. It had once guarded the city against the attacks of pirates, but more recently served as a prison. This Walker had learned by listening to the conversations of General Wheeler and Colonel Roosevelt. Sitting in the shade at the base of the castle, he gazed out toward the open sea. The seagulls were wheeling and calling overhead, and he listened to the rhythmic sound of the water lapping at the piers. Several hundred yards away, almost to the open sea, was the half-submerged wreckage of a Spanish warship—a reminder of the violence that had so recently disrupted this bucolic scene.

Reaching into his jacket he pulled out a small, thin packet tied with string. Four letters, written on small sheets of plain paper in tiny script—all that Walker had received from home. He read the letters in order, as always, pausing frequently to close his eyes and savor the pictures in his mind. Before retying the bundle, he took one more small envelope and held it in his hands, staring at it as if reading through the yellow paper. From it he pulled out a white, crocheted square, with the red heart and blue ribbon. Raising it to his face he inhaled as if breathing the scent. Walker had written Abigail three letters, full of details of his experiences. He had received nothing in return, so far. Perhaps she was still not feeling well? Perhaps her letters had gotten lost in the mail? Perhaps his letters had not reached her? Walker heaved a deep sigh, and tucked the packet away.

"Señor Walker!" He heard the call of a familiar voice, but looked about and could not place its source.

"Señor Walker!" This time he looked up and saw José waving his wide brimmed, floppy hat, leaning over the castle wall some fifty feet above him. José rattled off a rapid string of Spanish, none of which Walker understood, but he did understand José's vigorous pointing at him followed by an open-handed gesture. Evidently José wanted him to stay there and wait for him. José disappeared, and in a few minutes reappeared, running breathlessly from around a corner and stopped, panting, by Walker's side. José's high pitched chattering in Spanish, interrupted every few words by his gasping for breath, combined with frantic hand movements were too much for Walker.

He placed his hands on José's shoulders, looked him squarely in the eyes, and said in slow, firm tones, "José! Easy! Slow down! Catch your breath and tell me what is wrong."

José nodded as if he understood, and stopped talking and took two deep breaths. Then, as he opened his mouth to speak again, suddenly smacked himself on the forehead with the palm of his hand and cried, "Ola!" Digging urgently in his pants pocket he produced a folded note, which he thrust at Walker and made excited gestures for him to read it.

Walker recognized the neat, compact handwriting immediately as that of General Wheeler. In characteristically few words the General directed Walker to go with José to a nearby reconcentrado camp and help him take his family back to their home. Walker remembered reading in the newspapers about the reconcentrado camps—terrible places where the Spanish army, led by General "Butcher" Weyler, had confined hundreds of thousands of Cuban civilians in horrific conditions. Many thousands had died of starvation and disease. José's family was in a reconcentrado camp?

Walker looked slowly up from the paper to meet José's anguished eyes. José was anxiously gripping his hat, unable to stand still.

"Well, what are we waiting for?" said Walker grimly. "Let's get going!"

"Bueno amigo!" cried José. "Gracias!" And the two ran together up the rough cobblestone streets.

The village was seven miles from Santiago. Walker was glad that he had obtained a horse from the army corral—permitted only after Walker showed the handwritten note signed by General Wheeler. The guards had refused to provide a mount for José, so they had ridden together, José behind Walker.

Along the way, Walker noticed with concern that there were no villagers to be seen. Huts were empty and fields untended. A heavy silence hung over the countryside, and it seemed that even the animals were in hiding. Topping a small rise in the rutted, narrow road, Walker caught sight of the rooftops of a village in the distance. He also noted that several buzzards were circling overhead. He shrugged. Buzzards were everywhere in Cuba.

Descending the slope he lost sight of the village until, rounding a curve a half mile later, they were suddenly there. There had been a fence and a gate, but these were leaning half over, and they pushed their way in easily and proceeded down the main street.

If you could call it a street. It was so crooked that Walker could not see a hundred yards ahead. The buildings were decrepit, many roofless, with doors standing open. At first he could see and hear no one, but then they passed several bodies of men and women lying along the side of the street, apparently dead. Their emaciated bodies struck Walker speechless. José was murmuring under his breath in Spanish, punctuated with what sounded to Walker like sobs. In a moment José slipped from the horse to bend over a body, touching its head and calling softly. No response.

Walker dismounted and followed José up the street. The horse was snorting and tossing his head at the smells emanating from the buildings. It was all that Walker could do to keep from vomiting.

Reaching a small plaza in the center of the village, they came upon a group of about a hundred huddled villagers sitting on the ground. Some were rocking back and forth. Two bony women were holding limp babies in their laps. Walker could hear a low, moaning sound rising from the group. Two buzzards had descended from their circling to perch on an adjacent rooftop, from which they surveyed the scene with great interest.

With an agonized cry José suddenly leaped into the group, stepping over several hunched figures to kneel and tenderly embrace one of the living skeletons. While José was kissing the figure's cheeks and speaking to her in a low but excited voice, Walker hurriedly fetched a canteen of water from the saddle.

He lifted the canteen to the chapped lips of one after another.

Some accepted eagerly, while others seemed unable to swallow. When his supply of water was exhausted, he motioned to José. José nodded, and gently lifted the frail woman in his arms. He gestured to Walker and turned his eyes to another small figure lying next to the woman. Walker lifted this girl as gently as possible, hearing a painful moan escape her lips. She looked to be no more than seven. They stepped carefully over the bodies, returning to the horse. The low moaning sound was louder now, and there were croaking cries. They walked past the horse, and it turned and followed them, apparently glad to be leaving the ghastly scene.

Walker and José carried their burdens all the way back to Santiago, stopping only once to rest. Walker wished that he had saved some of the water for themselves, but remembering the gaunt and listless wretches who had gratefully swallowed a single mouthful, he felt guilty for the thought. As they walked, José talked to the two in gentle tones. Walker could not understand what he was saying, but it was not hard to guess. He learned that the woman in José's arms was his wife, Maria, and the girl carried by Walker was his daughter, Isabella. He learned that there had also been a son, Manuel, who had died in the village. José wept openly as they walked. Maria occasionally responded with low, almost inaudible whispers. Isabella made no response.

Upon reaching Santiago both men were exhausted from the long trek. Nevertheless, they did not stop until they reached the U.S. Army medical center which had been set up in the Santiago hospital. At the front door stood two American soldiers with rifles slung over their shoulders. Walker led the way up the dozen steps to stand before them.

"These two women need help immediately," he said earnestly. "They were in a reconcentrado camp a few miles away, and are almost dead. Where do we take them for treatment?"

"Not here," replied one of the soldiers, casually. "You'll have to find somewhere else."

"But they need help right now!" exclaimed Walker. "They are almost dead, and can't live much longer without help!"

"Too bad. This hospital is only for white American soldiers. There is a medical clinic for colored soldiers down near the waterfront. Maybe you could try there."

"But they're not soldiers!" cried Walker, furiously. "They are civilians! They're *people*! This is the wife and daughter of this man—" he nodded toward José—"who has been fighting with us against the Spanish! He even got wounded at San Juan Hill! We have to help him and his family!"

"Sorry, soldier," the guard said, his voice becoming harder. "Take these darkies to the colored clinic, or find a Cuban doctor. If you don't get out of here now, we will have to arrest you."

Walker stepped back, speechless. He turned to José, trying to think of something to say. José's face was full of anguish, and his eyes wide with confusion. Walker could find no words. Shaking his head, he went back down the steps with the frail Isabella in his arms. At the bottom, he turned and looked back up at José, who was still standing before the two guards. Motioning with his head for José to follow him, he backed slowly away from the hospital. José's mouth hung open as he gaped at Walker, disbelieving, and with a single, wide-eyed look at the two guards, he hesitantly followed Walker.

As they hurried down the narrow alleys toward the waterfront, Walker could hear José behind him, talking to himself. He understood some words, like medico, familia, and Dios. He wished that he could explain to José why his family could not be treated at the white soldiers' hospital, but realized that he really had no explanation. *This can't be right,* he thought. *I must tell General Wheeler.*

Upon reaching the waterfront, he looked right and left. To the left he saw a group of colored soldiers leaning against a wall, smoking. He hurried toward them.

"Can you fellows tell me where the colored soldiers' clinic is?" he called.

The soldiers stopped talking and gave each other puzzled looks. One of them, whose back was toward Walker, turned around. It was Corporal Dixon.

"Dixon!" exclaimed Walker, in relief. "These two people need medical attention right away! Where is the clinic?"

"Well, if it isn't Private First Class Garrett," drawled Dixon, with something less than pleasure in his voice. "Why are you bringing these folks to the colored clinic instead of the white boys' hospital up town?"

"They won't accept them at the hospital! They said 'no darkies.' Can you believe it?"

There were spontaneous snorts and guffaws from the group. One actually doubled over, laughing.

"Can I *believe* it?" Dixon's voice was incredulous. "Why, *no!* It's positively unbelievable that the white folks are refusing to treat a darky! I've never heard of such an outrage in all my life!" He made an angry face and held up a clenched fist.

At this, the group of soldiers completely lost all composure. Two got down on their knees, they were laughing so hard. They scarcely had breath enough to echo Dixon's words—"Unbelievable! Outrage! Never!" Several were wiping tears from their eyes.

"This is serious," Walker insisted. He could hardly comprehend their response.

"Of course it is," agreed Dixon, magnanimously. Bowing and sweeping his arm gallantly to point down the street, he added, "Second alley. Second door on the right. You can't miss it."

Giving a quick nod to José, Walker hurried past the still-laughing soldiers. At the second alley he turned left, away from the harbor. He saw a line of black soldiers leading to the second door on the right. Walker went to the front of the line, found the door open, and went in. He heard muttering from the soldiers as he pushed past them, but paid no attention. The small room contained six wooden chairs, all occupied by bandaged soldiers. Others stood, or sat on the floor.

"Can I get some help for these two people?" Walker called out, hoping that a doctor or nurse would hear him. Sure enough, a white doctor appeared from an adjacent room, followed by a young female Cuban nurse.

"What are you doing here?" he asked Walker.

Walker explained that the two females were José's family, from a reconcentrado camp, and that the white hospital had turned them away.

"They need help immediately," he begged.

"This one doesn't," said the doctor, pointing to Isabella. "She's dead."

The doctor leaned over Maria, pulling up her eyelid to check her eyes, and feeling for a pulse.

"This one won't last the night," he asserted flatly. "Nothing I can do for either of them." And with that he turned and went back into the other room.

The Cuban nurse, with sympathy in her eyes and in a soft voice, quickly told José what the doctor had said, and then just as quickly hurried to the other room to answer the doctor's summons.

Walker stepped slowly to the doorway after them.

"What do I do with her body?" he asked helplessly.

The doctor pointed in no particular direction. "Next alley. First door on the left."

It turned out to be a morgue. Dead bodies lay in rows on the floor. A sweaty, black attendant with rolled sleeves, pointed to the end of a short row: "Put 'em there."

"That one's not dead," Walker objected. The attendant shrugged.

"Bring 'er back when she is," he said with a one-sided grin, and went on with his work.

He gently laid Isabella's body at the end of the row. José handed Maria to Walker and then knelt over Isabella. His grieving cries were so intense that Walker had to step outside the door, partly to give José privacy, and partly because his own emotions were overwhelming him.

Outside the door he was surprised to see Corporal Dixon, apparently waiting for him. They stood in silence for a moment.

"You two carried them all the way back to town?" asked Dixon.

Walker nodded, his eyes wearily closed.

After another moment's silence, Dixon spoke again.

"There's a colored doctor over near the Tenth's campsite. He's not really a doctor, but he's pretty good. You can take her there."

Walker nodded again. "Thanks," was all he could say.

The colored "doctor"—actually a former barber—shook his head when he saw Maria, but allowed them to place her on an empty cot under the tent.

"We'll do what we can," he said, "but I can't promise anything."

José sat down on the ground beside the cot with a pail of water and a cloth which he used to gently bathe her face and moisten her tongue.

Walker could not bring himself to leave him there. He'd had nothing to eat since breakfast, and it was rapidly getting dark. Nevertheless he lay down on the ground at the edge of the tent, a few feet away from José and Maria. When he finally fell asleep, José was still kneeling by her side, murmuring softly and dabbing her face with the cloth.

A boot in his ribs awakened him roughly the next morning. It was daylight already. He rubbed his eyes and saw Corporal Dixon standing over him. He quickly looked towards Maria's cot, but it was empty and José was gone.

Jumping to his feet, he asked, "Where is José? and Maria?"

The colored physician spoke from a few feet away: "The woman died during the night. The Cuban fellow left. Must have been two, three hours ago."

"He went to the white soldiers' hospital," said Dixon.

"To the white hospital?" exclaimed Walker. "Why?"

"He attacked the guards with a machete. Killed one of 'em. The other one ran his bayonet through him, but not b'fore he was seriously wounded himself."

"No! That can't be right!" gasped Walker. "Not José!"

"Yes. José."

"Where is he? I have to go to him." Walker was stunned.

Dixon fixed his eyes on Walker's, and pointed. "Third alley past the fish wharf. First door on the left. I wouldn't go, if I was you."

Turning to walk away, Dixon looked back at Walker and said, without emotion, "Welcome to the colored man's world."

10

———

HALFWAY AROUND THE WORLD

November 11, 1898
Dear Ma and Pa,

I hope this finds you both doing well. I miss you and look forward to the day when I can see you again. I have just learned that I am to be leaving Cuba, and am glad of it. I thought we were coming to liberate Cuba, not to occupy it. I have had enough of tarantulas, scorpions, land crabs, and buzzards, not to mention the fevers that still plague our men. Thank goodness we have Clara Barton and Annie Wheeler to help nurse the men through it. Otherwise, we might all be dead.

I am sorry to disappoint you, but I am not returning home just yet. General Wheeler has been reassigned to the Philippines—it seems that the situation there has taken a turn for the worse, and the President wants him to go straighten things out. The General has asked me and Captain Joe and Annie to go with him, and of course, we all agreed. I'm not really sure where that place is, but I will write you as soon as I can. By the way—I forgot to tell you that I have been awarded a Citation Star medal for the fighting at San Juan Hill last July. The General himself pinned it on me!

Your son,

Walker

As the steamer pulled away from the dock at Santiago, Walker stood at the railing and watched as the old fortress, crooked alleys, and red-tiled roofs grew smaller. The emerald green hills embracing the city looked beautiful at a distance, but Walker now knew that under the lush canopy was a dangerous and deadly world. He reached inside his blue jacket to run his fingers along the smooth wooden handle of a machete, hanging from a strap over his shoulder. It had belonged to José. The memory of his friend filled Walker with sadness as he remembered how José had saved his life more than once. The sound of José's laughter, and of his weeping, filled Walker's head.

His churning thoughts and emotions were interrupted by a familiar voice.

"Well bless my soul if it ain't Private First Class Garrett! I was hoping I'd seen the last of you." It was Corporal Dixon, sounding none too pleased, with his hat pushed back and thumbs hooked into his belt.

"What are you doing here? I didn't know the Tenth was being sent to the Philippines!"

"Neither did I, 'til yesterday. 'Parently they want some *real* soldiers over there, so we can win this war." Dixon paused, with a slight curl to his upper lip as he gazed unblinking at Walker. "So why are *you* on this boat?"

"General Wheeler has been reassigned to the Philippines," answered Walker, missing the insult. "Captain Joe—uh, Captain Wheeler and I are going with him."

"General Wheeler do get around, don't he?"

This sounded slightly disrespectful to Walker. Raising his voice, he replied tersely, "The General is the best commander this army has, and if his country needs him in the Philippines, he is ready to go."

"Humph," snorted Dixon. "And where was he when his country needed him to help preserve the Union? Don't seem like such a all-fired patriot to me."

Walker stepped forward, fists clenched. He would have sailed into Dixon had not Captain Joe Wheeler suddenly emerged from the officers' quarters doorway.

"Garrett!" he barked.

"Yes sir!" replied Walker, snapping to attention and saluting briskly.

"General Wheeler's things need to be put away, and his maps and books set up on the desk in his cabin. Now!"

"Yes sir!" Walker saluted again, and quickly brushed past Dixon and ducked through the doorway into the dark interior. He would deal with Dixon later, he thought grimly.

Having neatly arranged the General's cabin, Walker decided to find the Philippines on a map. He was so absorbed in the maps that he did not hear the light-footed General enter the room.

"So, Mr. Garrett," he said in his abrupt manner of speaking. "Have you located the Philippine Islands yet?"

Walker leaped to his feet, face turning crimson. He snapped to attention and saluted so sharply that he almost hit himself in the eye.

"Sir! No sir! I mean, I apologize for looking at your maps, sir." He was stammering as he searched for more words, but the General waved him off with a short laugh.

"Quite all right, my boy," he chuckled. "I was planning to get the maps out myself. Let's take a look, shall we?" And he drew a second chair to the table and motioned for Walker to sit back down.

The General pointed to the southeast coast of Cuba, where Santiago was perched, and with his finger traced the route they would follow to the southwest to Panama.

"That's about 700 nautical miles," he explained, as Walker nodded. "We are not making top speed—less than 200 knots per day, so it will take us almost four days."

"But sir, I thought we were going to the Philippines, not to Panama." Walker was confused and a little embarrassed, thinking that the General had made a mistake.

"Quite right!" Wheeler laughed again. "This is only the beginning of this trip, my boy! We are going halfway around the world!"

Over the next hour Walker was treated to a geography lesson like nothing he had ever heard in school. The General described how some of the gold-seekers in 1849 had followed this same route to Panama, hiked across the isthmus to the Pacific side, and sailed north to California. Spreading another large map on the table, his finger then traced a path across the Pacific to the Hawaiian Islands, and he told proudly how the United States, just a few months earlier, had annexed the islands to bring democracy and Christianity to the people.

Finally, unrolling yet another map, he showed Walker the Philippine Islands. He pointed out the location of the great victory won by Commodore Dewey at the outset of the war with Spain. The Spanish, quickly defeated, had agreed to hand over the Philippines to the United States, and the U.S. intended to help the people there in the same way that it was helping the Cubans and Hawaiians, he explained.

"Why are we sending more troops to the Philippines if the war is over?" asked Walker. "It seems that our job there is done and finished."

The General heaved a deep sigh and slowly shook his head. "Yes, it should be that way." He spoke slowly this time, with a tone of sadness. "But some of the Filipino people don't want us to help them. They want us to leave the country to them—and they with no experience at self-government! It would be irresponsible of us to leave now, after winning for them the chance to have a better life. Why, it would be as if, after defeating the Spanish at Santiago, we had pulled up and left Cuba overnight, leaving the people there with no leadership and no government system in place. Anarchy! That's what would have happened. They would have been worse off than if we'd never gone to Cuba in the first place. Why, certainly it would be easier for us to just leave, but we have a Christian duty to perform for these people, even if they don't understand it. They'll understand eventually, and they'll thank us then."

"I see," murmured Walker, his brow wrinkled as he absorbed this information.

Sensing his uncertainty, General Wheeler reached into his shoulder bag lying on the cot and pulled out a newspaper. He slapped it down on top of the map authoritatively, and pointed to the masthead.

"*The New York Sun*!" he announced, almost triumphantly. "Delivered just before we weighed anchor in Santiago. Look here—" and he quickly flipped to an inside page.

"You've heard of Rudyard Kipling, haven't you?" And without stopping for an answer, he sped onward. "This is his greatest poem yet! Written about our mission in the Philippines! Read this and you will understand what we're about here, my boy!" And he pushed the newspaper over in front of Walker and gestured with his hand as if to say, "Go on! Read it yourself!"

"The White Man's Burden: The United States and the Philippine Islands," began Walker, somewhat hesitantly. Haltingly, he read the entire poem aloud, with the General occasionally helping with an awkward phrase.

"I'm usually a pretty good reader," he said, embarrassed at his difficulties. "This is rather strange, though. It's hard for me to understand what he is saying."

"Yes, it is a bit stiff," agreed the General, nodding. "But the message is the important thing. That's what you have to understand. Let's look at it again."

"'Take up the White Man's burden—send forth the best ye breed.' That means to send out the best young men we've got—young men like you, Walker—to help the poor, oppressed people of the world."

"'Your new-caught, sullen peoples, half devil and half child.' That's the Cuban people, the Hawaiian people, and the Filipinos. They're like children. They need Christianity to drive the devil out of them."

As the General proceeded through the poem, he pointed to each line with his finger, read it aloud, and with a piercing gaze at Walker, explained the meaning. Walker could only listen and nod, glancing quickly at the General's intense face, but mostly focusing on the lines of print.

"'The cry of hosts ye humour (Ah slowly) to the light:

'Why brought ye us from bondage, Our loved Egyptian night?'"

"Do you recognize what he means there, Walker? It's a Biblical reference."

"No sir." Walker blinked twice and shook his head slowly.

"Think! You know the story of how the Israelites, after being led out of slavery in Egypt, complained at Moses and wished they were back in Egypt?"

"Yes sir. I do."

"That's like what's happening in Cuba, Hawaii, and the Philippines. We liberated them, brought them good government, Christianity, modern medicine. Unfortunately, some of them don't seem to appreciate it. That's why we can't abandon them. We must do our duty."

Walker continued to nod.

"Think of it like this," the General enthused. "Suppose you have a sick child. The child needs medicine, but doesn't want to swallow it. What do you do? Let the child have its way, and perhaps die from sickness? Of course not! You make him take the medicine because you know it is for the best. You are helping the child, even if you have to pin him down and force the medicine down his throat. That's what we are doing. Giving the Cubans, the Filipinos and others, medicine! Someday they will thank us for it. But for now, we must do our duty whether they like it or not."

"Yes sir," beamed Walker. "Now I see it clear. Thank you for explaining it to me. Now it makes perfect sense."

"Of course it does!" The General's eyes twinkled with pleasure. "And you, my boy, get to be part of it! This is a wonderful adventure you are having, and wonderful things you are doing for people all over the world. You should be proud!"

"Yes sir," Walker said earnestly. "I am!"

"Oh my!" exclaimed the General suddenly, with his pocket watch in hand. "I didn't know it was this late! Hurry along to the mess hall or you'll miss your supper!"

Walker hurried along the deck toward the mess hall. At the entrance, there was a group of black soldiers from the Tenth Cavalry Regiment. They parted somewhat grudgingly to let him pass. Reaching the doorway, he paused and turned.

"Why are y'all waiting out here? Why aren't you inside eating?"

There was silence, and the group stared at Walker as if he had two heads.

Walker blinked in sudden realization, and ducked into the mess hall without speaking another word. He took his plate to a table and sat by himself, ate quickly, and then left just as quickly. As he exited he saw that there was a long line of the black soldiers still waiting to enter the mess hall. He turned and went in the other direction.

That evening Walker went to the bow of the ship and stood at the railing, facing toward the open sea. The deck beneath his feet rose and fell rhythmically as the ship plowed through the dark waters, and the stiff breeze made his uniform flap about him and ruffled his hair. He watched the tropical crescent moon move slowly across the black sky, and marveled at the fantastic array of stars that twinkled brightly.

In his mind he repeated the words of the poem by Kipling, and the General's explanation of how all of this was to liberate oppressed people. *That must be true,* he reasoned, *but then, why don't I feel good about it? I guess that's why it's called 'the white man's burden,'* he mused. *If it was easy or pleasant, it wouldn't be a burden. It's duty, like the General said. But,* said a voice in the back of his mind, *if we are bringing modern medicine to the people like the General said, why did José's family have to die without treatment?* Heaving a deep sigh, and with one last look upward at the starry heavens, he turned and slowly made his way to his bunk.

In the evening of the fourth day after leaving Santiago, the ship dropped anchor off the east coast of Panama, at the port city of

Colón. They spent one more night on the gently rolling ship, and early the next morning three hundred soldiers began carrying their packs down the gangway to the dock. Walker couldn't help but remember the chaos and confusion of the landing at Daiquirí, just a few months earlier. It seemed like a lifetime ago! It took only a couple of hours for all the men to reach the wharf and fall into lines, ready to move.

Walker was contemplating the coming fifty-mile march through the jungle-covered hills, and he was surprised when the column of marching soldiers arrived at a two-story brick train station. The sign in front said, in faded red letters, "Panama Railroad, 1849." Finding Captain Joe, he asked, "Sir, I thought we were marching across to the Pacific side?"

"Oh, no! That would be awful!" chuckled the captain. Pointing to the sign, he added, "This railroad has been here for half a century, built by Americans around the time of the California Gold Rush. We'll be looking at the Pacific Ocean in a few hours."

"What a relief!" exclaimed Walker. "I was dreading that march!"

As it turned out, the railroad station master had not been told that three hundred American soldiers wanted to travel to the other side of the country. Walker could see the General arguing and gesturing with the man inside the station door. After several minutes of this, General Wheeler stomped back out to the waiting soldiers with even more than his usual quickness, clearly displeased, shaking his head and muttering to himself. He conferred briefly with Captain Joe, who in turn gathered the lieutenants to give instructions. Within a few minutes the two columns of men were led around the station house to the platform by the tracks. They were told to drop their packs and find shade—they would be here for at least two hours while railroad cars were rounded up.

The soldiers of the Tenth sprawled under the palm trees a short distance from the station, while the white soldiers took shelter from the hot sun on the station platform and in the interior. The humidity was oppressive, and as the sky began to fill with dark clouds, the air seemed to grow heavier. Thunder rumbled in the distance.

Walker wandered into the station house in search of a drink of water. He found a hand-operated pump and sink in a washroom, and filled his canteen. The fresh water tasted good. He leaned against the doorway in the entrance facing Front Street and casually watched the slow-moving traffic. He could see almost all the way to the wharf.

A small, barefoot boy approached him.

"Te gustaría comprar una naranja?" the boy asked.

His months in Cuba had given Walker plenty of time to acquire a small vocabulary of Spanish. Besides, since the boy was holding out a bag of oranges toward Walker, it was not exactly difficult to grasp his meaning.

"Cuánto cuesta?" Walker responded. *How much*?

As he reached into his pocket for some coins, Walker suddenly realized that he had only a little American money and a few Cuban pesos. He showed the boy the coins. The boy grinned delightedly and quickly snatched all of the coins, dropped the bag of oranges, and ran out the door into the street.

Walker gaped incredulously as the boy darted through an opening in a fence and disappeared. Picking up the bag of oranges he saw that there were about seven or eight, plump and ripe. He shrugged and began to peel one of them. He had never eaten an orange before, and the tangy scent tickled his nose.

He heard behind him the sound of someone trying unsuccessfully to stifle a laugh. Glancing over his shoulder he saw a short, darkly tanned white man in a rumpled white suit, open collared shirt, and a white straw hat.

"Welcome to Panama!" he grinned, extending his arm in a grand gesture. "I hope you like oranges!"

"I've never had an orange, actually," Walker said. "Would you like one?"

"No, gracias," he laughed again. "I have an orange tree of my own."

"Let me introduce myself," he went on, stepping toward Walker and doffing his hat with a barely perceptible bow. "I am Monsieur

Victor Baptiste Moreau, of the great nation of France. I have lived here in Panama for fifteen years."

"I am Private First Class Walker Garrett, of the U.S. Army, First Volunteer Regiment and I just got here," returned Walker, politely touching the brim of his hat. "Why has a Frenchman lived in Panama for fifteen years?"

"I see that you do not know the history of this part of the world," smiled Moreau. "We French came here almost twenty years ago to build a canal connecting the two oceans, but the unhealthy climate defeated us. When the rest went home, I stayed. I own a hotel here in Colón, and another in Panama City, on the Pacific side. Life is good!

"And, may I ask," he continued, "why is a young American soldier here in Panama with his regiment? I thought you were all in Cuba and Puerto Rico."

"We were," said Walker. "But we're on our way to the Philippines. There's fighting there, too."

"Ah, yes," Moreau nodded. "Those troublesome Filipinos, seeking freedom and independence. You'll have to do something about that."

Walker, oblivious to the sarcasm, gave a nod. "Yes, our help is needed to liberate them from Spanish oppression. It's our duty to help people who want to be free."

At this Moreau suddenly bent double and exploded with what sounded like a violent cough. Back upright, he fanned his red face with his hat and cleared his throat loudly.

"My!" exclaimed Walker. "You should see a doctor about that."

"Mon Dieu!" wheezed Moreau. "I shall. As soon as we get to Panama City. My doctor is waiting at the wharf."

Walker thought this sounded rather strange, but chose to ignore it. Having finished peeling the orange, he hesitated, trying to decide how to eat it. He opened his mouth to bite it as if it were an apple, and Moreau quickly raised his palm toward Walker and, laughing, said, "Mon Dieu! No, no, no!"

He showed Walker how to pull the orange apart and separate the sections to eat one at a time. Putting the first section into his mouth, Walker began to chew. He grunted in surprise and his eyebrows came together, as if in concentration. He chewed slowly, and then spat two seeds into the nearby bushes.

"So! How do you like Panamanian oranges?"

"Amazing. Really juicy. Sweet. I like it!" Walker ate another section, savoring the experience.

"What part of the United States are you from?" asked Moreau, in a friendly tone.

"Alabama. It's one of the southern states."

"Ah, yes. The southern states—the ones that tried to separate from the others. The ones that fought to keep slaves. How do you feel about wearing the blue uniform now, and having colored soldiers at your side?"

Walker's eyes narrowed and he would have snapped an irritated retort, but he had another orange section in his mouth at the moment. Moreau waited patiently until he had swallowed it and spat out another seed.

"That was in the past. We are all Americans together now. Some of the men in the regiment are from northern states, some from western, eastern, southern—why, our general was a Confederate war hero. We're one country, united."

"Quite so, quite so," murmured Moreau. "I meant no offense. But, do you think the colored troops feel the same way? Please pardon my curiosity! I couldn't help but notice that they are separated from the white soldiers."

"That's just because they like to be with each other. Nobody told them to separate. We fight together. I fought in battles in Cuba with the colored soldiers. We get along just fine."

"How do you like having colored officers giving you orders?" Walker couldn't tell if Moreau was serious or teasing.

"You obviously don't know the history of *my* part of the world," Walker replied evenly. "White soldiers do not have colored officers. The colored soldiers have *white* officers. That's the way that works best." Walker's tone indicated that, as far as he was concerned, the matter was settled.

"I see, I see," said Moreau quickly, smoothly. "I am sure that they are very useful, as they always have been."

"That's right," said Walker, again missing the sarcasm completely.

"In fact," continued Moreau, "without colored workers, this railroad could not have been built. Irish and Chinese laborers were brought in, but they died like flies. It is said that each crosstie of the railroad track represents a life lost in the building of it. Only the West Indian blacks could tolerate the conditions here."

"It couldn't have been that hard," objected Walker. "Why, it's less than fifty miles to the Pacific Ocean. In America, we lay that much track in less than a month, and nobody dies."

"Oh, my young friend! This is nothing like what you are used to in the United States. Did you know that there are over three hundred bridges on this railroad line of less than fifty miles? And in November it rains hard almost every day, and tropical fevers are impossible to avoid."

"We just came from Cuba, so we know all about the tropical fevers." Walker was becoming annoyed. "And crabs, scorpions, spiders, snakes—this is not new to us."

"Of course! Of course!" Moreau held up his hands as if in surrender. "And six-meter-long boas that can squeeze a man to death and swallow him whole! There are no surprises for you here—except your first orange, of course!" Both Walker and Moreau laughed, and then were quiet for a moment.

Abruptly, Moreau extended his hand and said, "The train is being brought up to the platform now and I must board. Perhaps I'll see you in Panama City later today! But if not, bon voyage to the Philippines!"

"Thank you," replied Walker, shaking his hand warmly. Wanting to show off his limited Spanish vocabulary, he added, "Buen—buen—" he searched for the right word.

"Buen viaje!" Moreau doffed his hat again.

"Buen viaje!" Walker repeated quickly, and again touched the brim of his hat. *Good trip.*

Walker rejoined the soldiers as a small engine pulled cars up to the platform. He stared at the locomotive and laughed. It didn't even have a cab for the engineer, and only four wheels. Turning to a fellow soldier, he joked, "That little engine can't possibly pull a train all the way to the Pacific!"

"We'll get halfway up the hill and then roll right back down here again," laughed the other. Guffaws and laughs were heard from the rest of the company as they picked up their packs and rifles.

The tiny engine chugged past the platform, towing a few cars behind. Walker noted with concern that there was only one passenger car, two open-door freight cars, and five flatcars.

"Where are we supposed to ride?" he said to no one in particular.

At that instant, as if in answer to his question, Captain Joe shouted to the men to board the train. The sergeants ordered their men to the flatcars, and some to the boxcars. Walker found himself sitting on a flatcar with about forty other soldiers crowded closely together. His legs dangled off the side and he leaned back slightly, resting on his pack. General Wheeler and the other officers all sat in the passenger car with a dozen civilians. The rest of the soldiers climbed into the boxcars.

"I always wanted to be a hobo," said a man behind Walker. The men couldn't help but laugh at that. The laughter was cut short by an ear-splitting roar of thunder which rumbled and banged across the sky for several seconds. A sudden cool breeze swept through, just as the first large drops of rain began falling.

Another man spoke up, disgustedly, "*I* never wanted to be a hobo."

To which another added, "I'd rather be in the boxcar now." A few men actually jumped from the flatcars and ran up to the boxcars and climbed in. The last two to reach the boxcar, however, were waved off with jeers and hoots.

"No more room!"

"You need a bath! Stay out in the rain!"

"Go back to Cuba!"

"Go back to Kansas!"

A short, rather anemic toot of the steam whistle signaled that the train was leaving the station. Amid laughter from the boxcars, the forlorn pair of soldiers ran back to the flatcars just as the wheels began to turn slowly. The rain began descending in torrents, and though the men had donned ponchos, they were of little help. All were soaked to the skin within seconds. The train gradually picked up a bit more speed until it was moving at about fifteen miles per hour, which made the deluge seem even more overwhelming.

The downpour lasted about an hour. When it finally stopped, Walker raised his head and pushed back the dripping poncho. He was surprised to see that the dense green vegetation was so close to the track that he could almost reach out and touch the wet, hanging vines. Steam rose from the train, from the jungle, and from the men themselves. Walker leaned out and looked forward up the track, but could see nothing but fog and steam. There was nothing to do but sit and be miserable. There was no talking. No sound but the slow, rhythmic clacking of the wheels on the rails and the faint chugging of the little engine up ahead. They passed numerous boxcars and flatcars abandoned on sidings, covered with vines and small trees. Nature ruled here.

The track followed the path of a winding river. Walker caught only occasional glimpses of it through the trees, but eventually the train crossed the river on an iron bridge several hundred feet long and the men were treated to a beautiful and peaceful scene of a tropical paradise. The clouds parted briefly, and a brilliant sunbeam cut through the fog and reflected off the water below. If he had not been stiff and wet, he would have enjoyed the view.

After another hour they emerged from the steamy jungle at the crest of a high hill. A deep cut had been made through the hill for the railroad, and the slopes beside the track rose fifty feet or more. As they began a very gradual descent the high slopes diminished until it was possible to see some of the countryside. Walker stood up to stretch his legs and thought that he saw the Pacific Ocean in the distance. The rocking of the flatcar made standing up risky, though, so he sat back down.

For the first time since they had come ashore that morning, the sun came out and the temperature began to rise. The men stuffed their ponchos back into their knapsacks and began stretching, a few here or there standing briefly. By the time the little train had descended from the mountain and began passing through the outskirts of a city, the men were mostly dry and in somewhat better spirits. When the train groaned to a halt at the station, the men silently formed into marching lines and began the trek to the wharf. The men who had been in the boxcars appeared to be actually wetter than those who had ridden the flatcars. The rain had found its way into the boxcars, but the sun had not.

As they passed an aged hotel, Walker saw the sign over the entrance: Hôtel à Panamá. He recognized Monsieur Victor Baptiste Moreau standing on the front porch, watching the soldiers pass. They each politely lifted their hats with a nod.

"Bon voyage, Monsieur Garrett!" he called. "May you help the Filipinos find freedom and independence!"

"Thank you!" responded Walker. "I thought you were going to see your doctor at the wharf?"

Moreau laughed.

"I can see him from here. It is well enough!" And with that he turned and disappeared into the hotel.

Walker wondered what on earth he could mean. Looking ahead he could just make out the two smokestacks of the waiting ship which would take them to the Philippines, and a fluttering United States flag. "Nobody could see a doctor at the wharf from here," he muttered.

It was a couple of hours before the ship was ready to weigh anchor. While the soldiers were stowing their weapons and packs in their quarters, the cooks managed to put together a lunch of bread, fish, and fruit which they had obtained from a local market. The sun was making the metal deck too hot for comfort, so Walker crawled into a shaded area under a tarpaulin-draped lifeboat to eat. To his great surprise he discovered that General Wheeler was already there, sitting cross-legged and washing his food down with swallows of water from his canteen.

"Oh! General Wheeler!" he exclaimed. "Sir! I didn't know you were here! I'll go and—"

"Sit down, Garrett!" the old general waved his hand dismissively. "There's not a lot of shade to be had. And there won't be much until we reach Hawaii a week from now."

"Hawaii? Where is that? I thought we were going to the Philippines, sir!"

"Hawaii's on the way, near the middle of the ocean—remember? I showed you on the map. We'll stop there to refuel and restock supplies. Besides, there could be a bit of trouble going on there which requires our attention. Shouldn't take long."

They ate in silence for a few minutes. The tarp was raised briefly and Captain Joe slid under it to join them in the shade. There was a light breeze coming in from the water, making the heat somewhat more tolerable. Walker reached into his bag of oranges and offered one to each, which they accepted with enthusiasm.

"Where did you get these?" asked Captain Joe.

Walker told them how the small boy had taken his money, dropped the bag, and dashed away down the street. They all laughed. Then Walker summarized his conversation with the Frenchman.

"He said he would see his doctor at the wharf when he got to Panama City, but when I saw him standing on the hotel front porch and reminded him, he said he could see his doctor from there. That seemed very strange. All I could see at the wharf were the smokestacks of this ship. Nobody could have seen a doctor at the wharf from there."

The General and Captain Joe exchanged frowning looks. Captain Joe cleared his throat.

"Walker, I think this ship is the doctor he was referring to. It wasn't his throat or a cough which was bothering him—it was *us*. He didn't like having American soldiers in town. The ship is his doctor because it will take us away, and then he will feel better."

The General nodded. "I think that's right, Joseph. Even though the French attempt to dig a canal across Panama failed, some of them still think they own this area. They have a treaty that says they can still build the canal, even if they aren't going to do it, and they don't like seeing Americans here. After all, we built the railroad, and their half-dug canal is covered in vines and swamps. I think they resent us for that."

Walker reflected on that for a moment. "Will we ever build a canal here?" he asked. "It seems like a good idea to me. Look how long it took the *Oregon* to reach Cuba from San Francisco last spring—sixty-seven days! A canal through Panama would cut that in half!"

"Less than half," corrected Captain Joe. "It would take less than a month with a canal."

"Rest assured that our leaders in Washington are thinking the same thing," nodded General Wheeler. "I had the same discussion with Lieutenant Colonel Roosevelt. He is determined that the United States will finish the job the French began here. And I'm sure that he will do it! He's a man of action, and when he says he is going to do a thing, it gets done!

"Mark my words," he intoned solemnly, "Theodore Roosevelt will make history! He will be president someday, and the world will never be the same!" He gave Walker and Captain Joe a fiery, penetrating glare as if to emphasize his words.

Walker's eyes widened. He felt excited to think that he actually knew and had spoken with such great men as General Wheeler and Colonel Roosevelt. Suddenly he felt dwarfed by the realization that he stood at the brink of a new era and sat silently, lost in thought. The General and Captain Joe continued talking, but Walker's mind was far away.

11

HAWAII

It was an uneventful seventeen-day voyage to Hawaii on the slow troop transport. By the time it arrived at the port of Honolulu in early December, Walker was so tired of the constantly undulating ocean waves that he said a silent prayer of thanks for the sight of dry land. When he went ashore, his sea legs were unsteady under him and he nearly fell down three times before he even reached the dock. It was the same for the other soldiers, and they couldn't help but laugh at each other's drunken staggers. By the time they reached the barracks they were fairly well adjusted, though it would take another day to be completely comfortable walking on solid land.

Upon reaching the single-story barracks the men entered to see that their bunks were in a large room, double-stacked with lower and upper bunks. Walker quickly tossed his duffle bag onto a lower cot just inside the door and hurried to the adjacent officers' quarters to unpack General Wheeler's trunk. He knew the General would want immediate access to his books and maps.

Upon returning to the barracks, Walker was struck by the quiet in the room. Looking around, he understood why. The white and black soldiers were bunked in the same room. The whites had claimed bunks at the far side of the room, away from the main doors and large windows which would admit heat. The black soldiers of the Tenth occupied the front portion, and both sides of the room were nervously quiet, whispering and glancing furtively at each other. Walker's duffle bag, on a cot near the entrance, was surrounded by the soldiers of the Tenth. It was evident that all of the other bunks were occupied, so Walker stood there awkwardly, studying his duffle bag, unsure what to do next.

"Looks like you lucked out, Alabama boy. You on the good side of the room!" Walker's head jerked up to see Corporal Dixon's face grinning at him from the upper bunk. Walker was speechless. Dixon rolled onto his back and laughed out loud, joined by a few others around them.

"A bunk's a bunk," Walker retorted, finally finding his voice. He sat down on the cot and began unlacing his boots while Dixon laughed again, even harder than before. Reaching down, he snatched Walker's hat off his head and sailed it across the room with a loud whoop.

Walker leaped to his feet, his face flushing with anger. Grabbing Dixon's hat, he sent it flying out the door into the street.

"Keep your hands off my stuff!" he hissed furiously.

Dixon sat up, dangling his legs off the side of the bunk. Still laughing, he reached out with both hands and ruffled Walker's hair, making it into a disheveled mess. "Does that include yo' *hair*, Alabama boy?"

Walker completely lost his temper at that, and grabbing Dixon by the arms he pulled him off the bunk. The two began wrestling, rolling on the floor, thrashing violently. The room was instantly in an uproar. All of the men ran toward the struggling combatants, encircling them and shouting excitedly.

"Whup 'im good, Dixon!"

"Get him 'round the throat, Garrett! Choke 'im down!"

"Don't let 'im get on top o'you! Hit 'im!"

Suddenly the noise ceased abruptly. The cheering men all straightened and stood at attention, with arms frozen in stiff salutes. On the floor, Walker and Dixon were still straining at each other with all their might, grimacing and grunting. Then, noticing the silence around them, they looked up. General Wheeler was standing there, watching with arms folded and one raised eyebrow.

The two wrestlers scrambled to their feet and stood at attention, breathing hard and saluting.

"General Wheeler! Sir!" began Walker in a panic, dabbing blood from his nose.

The General simply held out his arm, with his palm facing toward Walker. Walker shut his mouth and swallowed hard.

Ten seconds passed. The General pulled a hat from behind his back and studied it with interest. Looking at the two men as if trying to determine who owned the hat, he extended it toward Dixon.

"I believe this is yours, Corporal." Dixon accepted it wordlessly.

"The rest of you men, go back to your bunks—and stay there," snapped the General. "And you two—" he paused, "Come with me." His tone sounded ominous. He whirled smartly and marched out the door. Dixon and Walker followed, with eyes fixed straight ahead.

The trio marched briskly past the officers' quarters to the mess hall, past the front doors, around the corner to the back of the building and into the kitchen. The kitchen door was open, as were the windows. It was soon clear why—the room was hot, with stoves boiling water in large pots.

"I've brought you some help!" announced the General to the cooking staff. Turning to the two soldiers, he snapped, "Can I trust you two to not fight in here?"

"Yes sir, General, sir!" They replied in unison.

The General paused at the door to turn and say, "I want to see both of you in my quarters after you're done here." And he was gone before they could repeat their "Yes sir!"

"I don't know what you fellers have done, and I don't care," drawled a burly, shirtless, red-headed cook. "I want one o' you to get on that pile of 'taters, and t'other cuttin' up these here onions." He extended a tattooed arm, holding two knives in his hand.

"I'll take the 'taters," said Dixon quickly, and taking the proffered knife, dragged a stool and a bucket over to the large pile of potatoes and began peeling them. Glaring at Dixon, Walker took the other knife and prepared to begin slicing the onions. Holding them at arm's length so that they wouldn't bring tears to his eyes, he tried to cut one in half.

"That ain't never gonna do!" growled the cook. "Put that pan in your lap and get on with it, soldier!"

Walker could feel the pungent scent of the onions working its way up his nose, through his sinuses, and then, it seemed, to the center of his brain. He began wheezing loudly and jerking his head to the side to breathe untainted air. He tried turning his face upward and his eyes downward, but only sliced his finger with the sharp blade.

"Don't you go getting' blood on my onions!" shouted the cook. Grabbing a dirty rag from the table he wrapped it around Walker's finger and tied it tightly. "Now get to work, 'fore I tie one 'round your neck!"

Walker could hear a snorting laugh from the direction of Dixon and the potato pile, but ignored it. He found that if he clenched his teeth and sucked air into his mouth and exhaled through his nose, the fumes of the onions were less potent.

They finally finished their tasks. Both had long since shed their shirts, like the rest of the kitchen crew. Stepping outside into the cool breeze they stretched their arms and twisted their aching backs.

"I hope I never see another onion for the rest of my life," groaned Walker.

"I wouldn't mind some mashed 'taters," opined Dixon. "Next week."

For a moment both watched the sun descending behind some palm trees. The air seemed a tiny bit cooler, and the flag on the mast of their ship in the distance fluttered weakly in the breeze. *This is much better than Cuba or Panama,* Walker thought. *I'm glad we're annexing Hawaii, and not those places.*

Dixon must have been thinking the same thing. "I think I could kind of like this place," he said.

"Well," said Walker quietly, "Let's go see the General." It was a silent walk back to the officers' quarters, where Walker tapped lightly at General Wheeler's door.

"Come in!" came Wheeler's voice.

The two stepped hesitantly into the small, outer office where the General sat at a desk, papers spread before him. He sniffed the air as if detecting an unpleasant odor, and then turning to face them, pointed toward the door.

"You men smell like sweat and onions," he frowned. "Let's do this out there."

Walker and Dixon stood at attention on the boarded sidewalk while the General simply glared at them for a long minute.

"You men fought the Spanish together in Cuba. Now you're fighting each other? And for what reason?"

"Sir," said Dixon humbly. "It was nothing. Just a little horseplay that got out of hand. It won't happen again, sir."

"Is that right, Garrett? 'A little horseplay that got out of hand?'"

"Yes sir, General Wheeler. It won't happen again, sir."

Another long pause.

"L. G. Dixon. That's what it said in your hat band. What does L. G. stand for? 'Large'? You look more like a medium, to me."

"Sir, it don't stand for nuthin'. That's what my mama named me. I just go by Dixon, sir."

"Hmph," snorted the General. "Initials have to stand for something. Doesn't matter, though, I reckon."

Turning to Walker, he said, "Your father would be ashamed if he knew you were brawling in the barracks with another American soldier. He was a soldier's soldier. Never would he have done such a thing."

Walker dropped his head. "Please, sir," he entreated earnestly, "don't tell my pa. I'll slice onions every day. Just don't tell him about this. Please!"

Turning back to Dixon, Wheeler raised his voice to a higher pitch. "And what about your father, Corporal Dixon? What would he think of you now?"

"Ain't got no pa," murmured Dixon softly. "Just my ma."

"Nonsense! Everybody's got a father."

Dixon shrugged and said nothing.

The General spun about and walked away for several steps, stood with his back to them briefly, and then turned and came back to stand in front of them.

"Here is what you will do. You will each write a letter to the other man's parents, explaining why they should be proud of their son. You, Garrett, will write to Dixon's mother, and you, Dixon, will write to Garrett's father. You will do this and bring the letters to me by this time tomorrow. Understood?"

"Yes sir!" they chorused.

"Now, go get yourselves cleaned up and ready for chow. Dismissed!"

When they were a safe distance away and the General could not hear them, Walker exclaimed, "I can't believe he's letting us off so easy! I just knew we were going to be demoted or locked in the brig!"

"Don't seem so easy to me," Dixon hissed. "How am I going to write a letter like that? I'd rather slice onions for a month."

"Just say what you told the General. That it was just horseplay that got out of hand."

"I doubt that will be enough to satisfy him. I can tell that he wants us to say something good. That devious little man has a mean streak."

"A mean streak!" Walker almost shouted, aghast. "Devious! Why General Wheeler is the—"

"Oh, shut up!" Dixon cut him off. "Just you write your letter and I'll write mine, and hope it passes inspection—'cause you know, sure as hell he's going to read 'em."

Walker sputtered angrily and glared at Dixon, but held his tongue. *He's probably right,* he thought. *These letters better be good.*

That evening about eight o'clock Captain Joe stepped into the dimly lit barracks, accompanied by a lieutenant of the Tenth Cavalry. "Lieutenant Washington's platoon—outside now! Leave your rifles—bring only your sidearms." Turning to Walker, he continued, "Private Garrett, you're with me. Let's go."

Once outside the men formed into four rows, with a squad of

eight soldiers per row. Captain Joe stood with the lieutenant in front of them and Walker stood behind the captain, feeling awkward and out of place.

"Men, our job tonight is only to keep the peace," began Captain Joe. "We are going to the dock, where Hawaii's former queen—Liliuokalani—is returning tonight from exile to attend the annexation ceremony in a few days. We don't expect any trouble, but some of the locals may get excited and want to make a demonstration. If things get out of hand we will intervene, but we will not use force unless absolutely necessary. Do not draw your weapons unless told to do so by your commander. Keep your eyes and ears open!"

Upon reaching the harbor they found that a sizable crowd had already gathered, waiting patiently for their queen. The four squads of soldiers were stationed around the perimeter, while Captain Joe directed Walker and Lieutenant Washington to follow him as he slowly made his way to the dock. They stood among the native Hawaiians at the edge of the crowd. It was eerily quiet, and Walker felt uneasy.

The moon was full, and he had never seen such brilliant moonlight. It was almost like day. Gazing about, he was struck by the tropical beauty of the place. The distant mountains beyond Honolulu seemed close enough to reach out and touch. The surf was gently curling on the beach, and the few ships in the harbor were silhouetted against a sky that seemed silver rather than blue or black.

"Sir, when is the queen's ship going to arrive?" he whispered to Captain Joe.

"That's it right there," he whispered in reply, pointing. "The *Gaelic*."

As if on cue, the stolid figure of the aging queen suddenly appeared on the deck, and Walker felt the energy of the crowd begin to rise. She slowly descended the gangplank to the dock, leaning heavily on the arm of a white-bearded man at her side. It seemed as if the crowd was holding its collective breath—there was absolutely no sound, and Walker could even hear the soft footsteps of the two as they reached the dock.

Suddenly a piercing wailing sound arose. A single old woman, with gray hair and dark, wrinkled skin, began to chant, swaying back and forth, with arms and eyes raised toward the sky. Walker could understand none of the words, and wasn't even sure that there *were* words. The quavering voice gradually became louder and higher, with intensifying emotion. Walker felt a tingling sensation on the back of his neck, and he stared breathlessly at the old woman as she sang her wild, plaintive song. The others in the crowd did not appear to be surprised or concerned at all, and Walker wondered if this was some kind of tradition. The queen did not acknowledge the wailing, but went to a waiting carriage and was taken away. The song stopped, and the crowd began to disperse.

A hand suddenly grasped Walker's shoulder, violently startling him back to his senses. It was Captain Joe. "Private Garrett!" he hissed. "Come on! I've told you three times already!"

Dazed and embarrassed, Walker followed and they rejoined the platoon under a stand of palm trees a short distance from the harbor.

"Well done, men!" said Captain Joe quietly. "Now it's back to the barracks for a good night's sleep. We have a full day tomorrow."

As the men filed back into the barrack, Walker lingered at the rear, hesitating.

"Something bothering you, Private Garrett?" asked Captain Joe.

"Yes sir," replied Walker. "Can I talk to you for a minute, sir?"

"Very well. What's on your mind?"

"Well, sir, I was wondering why you took soldiers from the Tenth and not from the First. And I was also wondering why you took me with you, sir."

Captain Joe chuckled. Folding his arms across his chest, he looked at Walker with a slight smile. "Father is right. You *are* observant and inquisitive." With a jerk of his head, he motioned to Walker to step away from the barrack. Moving beyond the rectangle of light coming from the doorway, he turned to Walker.

"Describe the crowd at the dock tonight."

"Well, sir, they were quiet and well-behaved. Except for that one old woman who sang that strange song, nobody else made a noise."

"True, but what did you see when you looked at them?"

Walker was a little confused at the probing. "There were two or three hundred men and women. No small children."

Obviously still not satisfied, Captain Joe paused a moment and then asked, "What kind of people were they?"

"Hawaiians, sir."

"And what do Hawaiians look like?"

"Well, sir, they're brown. Some lighter, some darker. They have black hair, except the old ones sometimes have gray hair. They wear simple, plain clothing. They seem to like flowers. They usually smile a lot, but not tonight."

Captain Joe nodded approvingly. "And if you were going to use soldiers to keep control of a big crowd of unhappy, brown Hawaiians, which soldiers would you take—the Tenth, or the First?"

Walker thought silently for a moment. "You mean, sir, that our dark-skinned soldiers are more accepted by the dark-skinned Hawaiians, and are less likely to have problems than white-skinned soldiers?"

"Exactly."

"I wouldn't have thought of that, sir. But don't you think that white-skinned soldiers would be seen as more official, and would get more respect and cooperation from the Hawaiians?"

"You might think so, but it's not necessarily true. In some parts of the world, white people are not always respected by darker people. They don't like our dominance and our superiority. Our presence could provoke resistance. No need to cause trouble if we can avoid it."

"I see, sir. Is that why the Tenth is being sent to the Philippines?"

Captain Joe smiled, giving Walker an approving look. "I think you're catching on!"

"And one last thing, sir. Why did you take me along with you?"

"Frankly, it wasn't my idea. Father—General Wheeler—told me to take you so that you would witness this event. He sees potential in you, Garrett, and he wants you to learn from all of these experiences. He thinks that you will do important things when you get back home. This is a training ground for you."

Walker was speechless. He was completely unprepared to hear or absorb a statement like that. He stood paralyzed.

"So!" concluded Captain Joe. "That answers that. Let's get to bed." And he briskly walked away. After a moment, Walker slowly returned to the bunkroom.

Following breakfast the next morning Walker obtained a sheet of paper and a pencil from the quartermaster and went back into the mess hall to write his letter. Dixon was across the room at another table, also writing. There was another black soldier with him, wearing glasses and speaking in a northern accent.

"S-o-l-d-i-e-r."

"You're crazy. That can't be how you spell 'soldier.' It don't sound nuthin' like that. It should be s-o-l-j-e-r."

"That's how you spell it. Trust me."

Seeing Walker, the two lowered their voices to an indistinguishable murmur. Walker could hear the pencil on the paper. Heaving a sigh, he began to work on his own letter. It took half an hour. He found that it was not difficult to write to Beulah. He was even glad of the chance to please her by telling her what a fine soldier her son was. He sent his greetings to Daisy, and also mentioned Abigail and the rest of the Dancy family.

They finished at the same time, both standing up and noisily scraping their chairs on the wooden floor. Without speaking to each other they walked to the officers' quarters and knocked on the frame of the open door. The General came to the door. He took the letters from their hands and said, "Wait out here," and retired to the interior to read them.

They waited for several minutes.

"Them letters weren't that long," fretted Dixon. "He must not like 'em."

The General returned to the doorway and gave them both a penetrating stare. After several seconds of silence, he nodded. "Very well. I hope you've learned your lesson."

"Yes sir!"

"Make sure this doesn't happen again, or the outcome will be much less pleasant." And then he disappeared into the room again. Walker and Dixon saluted the empty doorway and hesitantly backed away.

"Well, I guess that's that," breathed Walker.

"I sure hope so," returned Dixon. He then strode away without looking back.

12

THE ANNEXATION

December 12, 1898

Dear Walker,

Please forgive me for not having written sooner. I spent the summer with relatives in Charleston, and the fall with other relatives in Richmond, so it was not until I returned home for Christmas that I saw the letters you had written. They certainly portray a different view of the war than what we read in the newspapers! Beulah asked me to thank you for the letter you wrote about her son and what a fine soldier he is. It made her so happy and proud! And Father said for you to give his regards to General Wheeler. We continue to pray for the safety of all our men in uniform. I would write more but I must get ready for this evening's Christmas party.

With kindest regards,

Abigail Dancy

Walker folded the letter for the hundredth time and slipped it back into his breast pocket, next to the crocheted square. It was a relief to know that the long silence from Abigail was not due to disinterest—she simply hadn't been receiving his letters. "I would write more," she had said! Walker wasn't sure why she hadn't just waited until the next day to write more, but he decided that it was the thought that counted most—she probably wanted to get her letter in the mail right away. His thoughts were interrupted by the command to form up the line. The annexation ceremony was about to begin.

The Iolani Palace was a beautiful, two-story structure with a large wrap-around porch on both floors. Nestled in a grove of palm trees which swayed gracefully in the breeze, the white plaster exterior gleamed brilliantly in the bright sunshine. Flanking it were the fantastic banyan trees, with their curtains of aerial roots creating an other-worldly aspect to the vibrant, green grounds.

A large wooden platform had been built in front of the palace, extending from the first-floor level, decorated with small flags and lined with rows of chairs for the officials and invited guests. A prominent chair was reserved for the former queen, but it would remain conspicuously empty during the annexation ceremony. In fact, no native Hawaiians attended the ceremony— only white Hawaiians and Americans participated.

There were speeches, and a lengthy prayer by the local Methodist minister. The president of Hawaii, Sanford B. Dole, spoke briefly. The Hawaiian flag was lowered and the "Stars and Stripes" was raised. Salutes were fired, and the Hawaiian band—or at least, those members of it who were willing to attend—played the Hawaiian national song, "Hawaii Ponoi." An American military band from the USS *Philadelphia*, recently arrived from San Diego, played the "Star Spangled Banner." And then it was over. Hawaii belonged to the United States.

It had been a peaceful day, with no demonstrations or trouble from the native population. In fact, Walker was struck by the complete absence of natives on the street as he followed the General and Captain Joe from the palace to Washington Place, the home of the former queen. It was practically across the street from the palace, and half of the troops under General Wheeler's command had been stationed around it throughout the annexation ceremony to make sure the queen was safe and no disruptions occurred.

The house was large, white, and square, surrounded with tall trees and gardens. Like the palace, it was two stories tall, with pillared porches encircling it on both levels. It resembled some fancy antebellum plantation homes Walker had seen in pictures, and reminded him a little of Pond Spring, but larger and much more ornate.

They climbed the three steps to the porch and approached the front door, which was attended by a black-uniformed native doorman. He silently opened the door and gestured for them to enter. Respectfully removing their hats, the three entered the main hall.

The floor was tiled with large black and white squares, and at the end of the hall Walker saw a beautiful spiraling staircase with no visible supports and graceful, wrought iron railings.

"Beautiful!" he murmured in admiration. His eyes quickly scanned the walls, taking in the paintings, decorations, and other furnishings. He was impressed.

Queen Liliuokalani was sitting in a brilliantly decorated reception room on a low, stylish sofa, with a grand piano behind her. There were many of her Hawaiian subjects lying on the floor or kneeling before her with expressions of sorrow and grief. It was like a funeral scene. Seeing the General at the door she impassively motioned for him to come in, and the captain followed him. Walker, however, felt intimidated by the gravity of the moment and took a step backward. As he did so, he bumped into a man behind him.

Turning quickly, he exclaimed in a hoarse whisper, "Oh, excuse me, sir! I didn't know you were there!" He recognized the white-bearded man who had assisted the queen from the ship to her carriage a few nights before.

"Quite all right," the man said politely, and moved to enter the reception room, but seeing the General and the Captain, he hesitated, and then also took a step back.

"I'll let the Queen have a private audience with the American officers," he murmured, and stepped back to the middle of the hallway, away from the door. Walker followed, sensing an opportunity to ask a few questions.

"Hello, sir. My name is Walker Garrett and I'm a Private First Class in the United States Army." He extended his hand and tried to smile.

The white-bearded man looked rather coolly into Walker's eyes for several seconds, and then, without smiling, reached to give Walker's hand a brief shake. "Good day to you, Private First Class Walker Garrett, of the United States Army. I am Archibald Cleghorn, the Governor of this island of Oahu."

"Oh—I—I didn't know—" Walker stammered, flustered. "I didn't know you were important—I mean, I didn't know there was a governor. Just a queen!"

Cleghorn glared at Walker with arched eyebrows, and then he shook his head as if in disbelief. "You don't know anything about Hawaii, do you?" he asked, with a note of anger. "Yes, we have a governor. No, we do *not* have a queen—we have a *former* queen. And now we will have a territorial governor over all of the Hawaiian Islands, appointed by the United States Congress."

He continued to glare at Walker, who stood speechless, his hat in his hands and his cheeks reddening with embarrassment. Cleghorn then, as if regretting his outburst, gestured amicably and in a softer voice said, "What's done is done. There's no going back, now." He grimaced and sighed. "So, my boy, you're a long way from home, aren't you?"

"Yes sir, a long way. I left home over six months ago. Seems like years."

"I'm sure it does. So, what do you think of Hawaii? Do you like it?"

"Oh, it's very beautiful here, sir! Much better than Cuba!"

"Ah, Cuba! I'm sure that was unpleasant business. You're a bit young for war, aren't you—Private First Class Garrett?"

"No sir! I'm nineteen, sir!"

"Nineteen! Well, I suppose you *are* a man, then." If there was sarcasm, Walker did not notice it. He smiled, beamed, and nodded.

"Sir, may I ask a question?"

"Certainly, and I'll do my best to answer it for you." Cleghorn pulled a watch from his vest pocket by its chain, glanced at it, and pushed it back into the pocket. "Go ahead."

"We were sent here to keep the peace and put down any disturbances or disruptions to the annexation ceremony. Why are the Hawaiians unhappy about becoming part of the United States? It's the greatest country in the world, and I think they should want to be annexed. We bring democracy and a constitution, progress and prosperity. Why don't they want that?"

Cleghorn cleared his throat. He turned his chin upward and ran his finger around between his neck and shirt collar, adjusted his coat on his shoulders, and blew a big breath out with a whistling sound through pursed lips. He then cleared his throat again. Finally, in a strained but controlled voice, he spoke.

"Young man, you have much to learn. First, Hawaii already *has* a constitution. It was written in 1840 by the Hawaiian people, for themselves. It provided for elections of representatives and for the equal rights of the people. And no slavery! That was twenty-five years before your country abolished that desecration, and only after a bloody civil war was fought over it. Hawaii became a republic several years ago. We don't need the United States to bring us a constitution and democracy. In fact, it is Americans like Mr. Dole who have restricted the right to vote to wealthy people like themselves, even if not citizens of Hawaii. Does the United States allow non-citizens to vote in its elections? I think not! And when Queen Liliuokalani attempted to correct this, she was forcibly overthrown and imprisoned for months in the palace until she abdicated and left the country."

Walker blinked. "I didn't know all that, sir."

Cleghorn steamed on: "Secondly—progress and prosperity? Annexation will bring prosperity alright—to the landowners who are already wealthy. Annexation will allow the plantation owners here to sell their sugar in the United States without having to deal with the burden of tariffs. And as for *progress*, our Iolani Palace had electric lights and telephones before your White House. What progress can you offer us?"

Without waiting for a reply, he continued: "And *third*—the Hawaiian people have expressed their opposition to this annexation repeatedly and clearly. Petitions signed by over twenty thousand native Hawaiians were presented to Congress, all to no avail." He paused, peering intently into Walker's eyes. "Doesn't the Declaration of Independence say that 'governments derive their just powers from the consent of the governed?'"

"Yes sir. It does, sir."

"Have you read the Queen's proclamation of opposition to the annexation?"

"No sir. I have not, sir."

"Of course not! The Hawaiian people do not consent to be governed by the United States, but what does that matter?" Cleghorn spread his hands wide with raised eyebrows, as if waiting for an answer that did not come.

"You see, Garrett, my boy," he sighed resignedly, "the United States does not bring a constitution, democracy, progress, or prosperity to Hawaii. It merely seizes these islands for reasons of its own, the most important of which is naval power in the Pacific. That damned book by your Captain Mahan is at the root of all this. Your government wants control of this outpost before some other country gets it first. It is Hawaii's misfortune that its people are few, poor, and weak. That they love peace, music, and laughter."

A rumble of thunder suddenly rattled the windows of the building and instantly came the patter of raindrops on the roof and outside walkways.

"Look!" He extended his arm to point. "Even the heavens are weeping for poor Hawaii today!" Cleghorn heaved a mighty sigh, and folded his arms across his chest, and gazed sadly out at the falling rain.

Walker fidgeted with his hat and shifted awkwardly in his boots, not knowing what to say or do. Luckily, General Wheeler and Captain Joe came out of the reception room at that moment and turned toward the front door.

Walker hastily backed toward them, making a feeble parting gesture with his hat, and said, "Thank you, Governor Cleghorn. That was very—very – interesting, sir. And—and—" he floundered—"and Merry Christmas!" With that he turned and almost ran out the door onto the front porch to catch up with the Wheelers as they marched unflinchingly into the rain.

13

EXPANDING AN EMPIRE

December 25, 1898
Dear Ma and Pa,

Greetings and Merry Christmas from Hawaii! I hope that you are doing well. We are leaving Hawaii tomorrow for the Philippines. We will probably be at sea for four weeks. I do not look forward to that. Thank you for your letter I received last week and the socks. I really needed them. It is good to hear news from home and I wish that I could be there with you for Christmas. I dream about your good cooking, Mother! I will write again when we get to the Philippines. The General sends his regards to you both.
Your son,
Walker

As Walker's ship steamed out of the harbor toward the open sea it was joined by two other troop transport ships and a U.S. Navy cruiser, the *Charleston*. Walker stood at the stern railing, rising and falling as the ship rode the ocean swells, and watched as the islands faded into the distance and disappeared. He reflected on his conversation with Governor Cleghorn and remembered the sadness of Queen Liliuokalani and the Hawaiian people. The eerie, wailing song of the woman at the dock that night came back to his mind and sent a chill up his spine. *People just don't understand what we are doing,* he frowned. *We are only trying to help them. Eventually they will understand, and things will be better.*

As soon as the ships were well out to sea, the *Charleston* changed course and headed northwest instead of due west. The change was noticed, and rumors began to spread among the troops that they were heading to some secret Spanish island fortress for a battle. Before long the *Charleston* stopped and signaled to the transports for the officers to join Captain Glass for a conference. A boat was lowered over the side of the ship, and General Wheeler and the naval officers were rowed to the *Charleston* to meet with Glass and the other army and navy commanders. Upon their return the news was announced that their new destination was the island of Guam, a Spanish possession which lay between Hawaii and the Philippines. None of the men had ever heard of Guam, so speculation began anew about the difficulty of the task ahead, and this filled the next two weeks as they crept across the Pacific Ocean toward their objective. The men's expectation that they would meet stiff resistance was reinforced as the *Charleston*'s gunners began taking target practice at crates dropped overboard by the transports.

The excitement on board the transports rose to a fever pitch as the island of Guam came into view. The ships circled the island's southern end, staying several miles away. Coming up the western side of the island toward Agana, the capital city and main harbor, the *Charleston* moved in closer while the troop ships stayed a mile out to sea. Walker and hundreds of other soldiers lined the railing, watching to see what would happen.

Behind the harbor was an old fortress. Walker did not see any activity around it or on its walls. No artillery was visible. Everything was very quiet. He saw a small group of people further down the beach who appeared to be watching the ships.

Then the guns of the *Charleston* roared—not once, nor twice, but thirteen times. The artillery shells pounded into the old fortress, sending up great clouds of dust. Still no activity could be seen at the fortress, and no shots were fired in return. It was strangely quiet.

A few of the spectators on the beach pushed a small boat into the water and rowed toward the *Charleston*. Walker learned later that these included the Spanish officer in charge of the port, who, upon reaching the warship, apologized for not replying to its salute, explaining that they had no gunpowder. They asked to borrow some gunpowder so that they might provide a more appropriate welcome to the visitors. They were quite surprised to learn that it was not a social call or a salute, but that their country and the United States were at war. After being interrogated about the island's defenses, they were released so that they might inform their governor of the situation.

That evening General Wheeler summoned Walker to his cabin. He had just received an account of the day's developments from Captain Glass, with the additional news that a meeting was to take place the next morning on the beach with the governor of Guam at eight o'clock. Captain Glass wanted an army commander to be present at that meeting, and requested that General Wheeler attend. The General agreed, and decided to take Captain Joe and Walker with him. To Walker's surprise, the General also ordered Corporal Dixon to accompany them in the boat.

And so it was that Walker and Dixon arrived on the beach of Guam, splashing ashore and helping pull the boat up onto the sand so that the officers could step out without wetting their uniforms. However, General Wheeler, never one to shy away from the action, spryly hopped from the boat and got to the beach before them, wet to the knees, but unconcerned.

Suspecting a trick, Captain Glass did not go ashore himself, but sent Lieutenant William Brauner to represent him to the governor. The small group advanced to meet the governor and his advisors. After somewhat tense greetings had been exchanged via translators, Brauner handed the governor a letter from Captain Glass.

"Governor Marina," said Brauner in an even, but civil tone, "this is Captain Glass's ultimatum demanding the complete surrender of the island and all of its defenses. You have one half hour to reply before we land troops on your beach and begin shelling your fortifications."

Nervously clearing his throat, Governor Marina bowed quickly and motioned to his advisors to follow him. They retired to a small boatshed on the edge of the beach, and closed the door.

Walker and Dixon stood a few yards behind the Lieutenant and General Wheeler, silently watching. The sailors retired to their boat and lounged casually, talking quietly. A group of dark-skinned natives in military uniforms stood in a loosely ordered formation between the Americans and the boatshed. They appeared to be intently watching Walker and Dixon as they whispered together.

A man in a white shirt and wearing a straw hat strolled over to General Wheeler. Doffing his hat, he introduced himself in English. Walker heard him say that he was José Portusach, the brother of one of the key advisors to the Governor. Walker noted that he had served as translator for the Lieutenant and Governor earlier.

"It strikes me as rather odd that you have come ashore with only four sailors and two soldiers," he said, stroking his chin thoughtfully. "You can see that you are greatly outnumbered here. What is to keep us from taking all of you prisoner and holding you as hostages?"

To Walker's surprise, General Wheeler laughed out loud and slapped his knee.

"My dear Señor Portusach!" he exclaimed, gesturing broadly out to sea where the three troop ships and the cruiser loomed. "Do you really think that would be a wise thing to attempt? I think the outcome would be inevitable, don't you?"

"But General! Would your ships attack if their commanders and men were being held here?" Portusach's smile seemed to suggest that this was merely a speculative discussion, but Walker thought that the look in his eyes did not reflect the same harmless intent.

"Señor." The General's voice was now more serious, but still friendly. "First, you should note that our commander is still on the cruiser. Captain Glass did not trust your Governor, and sent his lieutenant instead. Second, a state of war already exists between your country and mine, and if you take us prisoner you are obligated to treat us as prisoners of war, which precludes your abusing any of your prisoners, even when you are attacked. If you should do so, you would face the prospect of execution as a war criminal. Third, you have barely fifty Spanish troops and a like number of Chamorros, whose loyalty is uncertain. We have two thousand soldiers aboard those ships, and they would like nothing better than to come ashore. Think carefully before you attempt such a misguided and foolish action. I fail to see how it could possibly ameliorate your present situation."

Portusach raised both hands in a gesture suggesting that nothing of the sort had even crossed his mind. "Let me assure you, my dear General, that—"

The General interrupted brusquely. "I am not your 'dear General,' Señor Portusach. I am here to effect the surrender of your forces and to establish American sovereignty over this island—without bloodshed if possible, but if not, then by any means necessary. We are prepared to do what has to be done."

Portusach's face and body seemed to slump. He made a wry expression, and shrugged. He doffed his hat again and, bowing ever so slightly, turned and strolled back to the small group of civilians, who seemed eager to hear the report of his conversation.

They were then approached by a Spanish officer who detached himself from the ranks of the Chamorro troops and came toward them somewhat hesitantly. "I speak leetle English," he began, holding his thumb and forefinger close together to show how little. Clearing his throat, and saying "Ah" frequently, he continued.

"You have many men?" he asked, pointing to the ships.

"Yes," replied the General. Taking his saber, he wrote "2000" in the sand.

The officer's eyebrows rose and he murmured, "Oh!" and exhaled loudly.

"You have many like these?" He pointed to Walker and Dixon.

"Yes. All of them are like these. What do you mean?"

"We have seen, ah, yellow hair, but we have not seen, ah, the black man. The black man we have not seen. The Chamorros are, ah, afraid of him."

"Tell them we have many black soldiers like him on the ships. They are powerful soldiers. You should be afraid." Walker admired how the General was playing upon the fears of the native troops. He suppressed a smile.

"But—" the officer's brow was creased with his efforts, "is it not true, ah, that the black man in America was, ah, a servant many years? And now you give black man a gun?"

Walker's head jerked visibly. *What kind of thinking is this? Obviously, this Spaniard knows nothing of American society!*

There was a brief moment of silence. And then General Wheeler said in a soft tone of voice, "Perhaps it would be best if I let Corporal Dixon answer that question." Turning to Dixon, he said, "Corporal?" and gestured toward the officer, indicating that Dixon was to address the Spaniard.

The officer fixed his unblinking eyes on Dixon, who cleared his throat and shifted his feet uneasily. He spoke slowly.

"Yes, it's true that black people like me were slaves in America— for over two hundred years. It took a war to set us free. Many men died in that war. Some died fighting *for* our freedom, and some died fighting *against* it." Here Dixon coughed and cleared his throat again, realizing suddenly that he was speaking in the presence of a former Confederate general.

"Black men also fought in that war," he continued, "and freedom won. And since that time, we black people have made America our country too. Black men are in the government, in the businesses, and in the army. We're Americans too. So, yes, black men have guns. We use them against America's enemies." Dixon paused, and then added, "Does that answer your question?"

The Spaniard nodded hesitantly. "Yes. I think I understand. Gracias." He backed away a few steps, and then, as he was turning, he stopped and looked at Dixon with a penetrating gaze.

"Is really true?" he asked, with a note of doubt in his voice.

Dixon's voice was low and controlled, his face expressionless. "Yes, it's true." He then turned away to stare out toward the ships in the harbor, and slowly walked a few steps down the beach toward the water.

Walker stood frozen, trying to grasp what he had just heard. He was about to ask the General a question when Governor Marina and his advisors emerged from the boatshed, and the General and Captain Joe went over to stand beside Lieutenant Brauner.

"Just in time," remarked the lieutenant, holding his pocket watch. "Twenty-nine minutes."

The governor handed the lieutenant a letter addressed to Captain Glass. The lieutenant immediately broke the seal and opened the letter, ignoring the objections of the governor. Looking up from the letter, Brauner announced in an authoritative voice, "Gentlemen, you are now my prisoners; you will have to repair to the *Charleston* with me."

This produced a loud outcry of dissent from the governor and his group. "Treachery! You came under a flag of truce! We cannot go aboard your ship! What about our families? We have no time to pack!"

Brauner replied coolly, "This letter of yours tenders an offer of complete surrender, so I have the right to make any demand I wish. Write letters to your families and have your necessary things sent to the ship. You will be going with us to Manila. Also, I want all of your Spanish and Chamorro troops ready to surrender their weapons by four o'clock this afternoon."

The governor and his advisors appeared devastated. Their shoulders slumped and their heads hung down as they moved to the boat. Walker looked toward the Chamorros to see how they were reacting. He was surprised to see grins and laughs. They seemed quite pleased. Remembering how the Cuban people had fought for freedom from Spanish control, Walker wondered if anyone liked the Spanish.

They will be happy now that they are under the United States flag, he said to himself. Then he remembered how the Hawaiian people had felt about the raising of the "Stars and Stripes" over their islands, and he began to feel confused. He felt a need to talk with the General. General Wheeler always explained things so clearly, and Walker had many questions to ask.

As Lieutenant Brauner returned to the *Charleston* with his prisoners, General Wheeler motioned to Walker and Dixon to follow him. He beckoned to the Spanish officer who had spoken with them earlier, and ordered him to guide them to the old Spanish fort which overlooked the harbor. "We'll need five horses," demanded the General. "Can you get five horses?"

"Si—yes—I can, ah, five horses, ah, I will have. Please come!" And he led them from the beach up a palm tree-lined dirt road toward the town. The Chamorro troops watched curiously as they passed, and then followed them at a distance.

The dirt road continued through the town and beyond. The small, neat houses had thatched roofs, and some were built on stone pillars which elevated them several feet above the ground. Their guide did not even attempt to inquire for horses in the village, apparently knowing it would be in vain.

Eventually, after walking about two miles on the sandy road, the officer produced one horse, one donkey, and a cart pulled by a water buffalo with immense horns. General Wheeler mounted the horse, Captain Joe the donkey, and Walker and Dixon seated themselves in the back of the cart, while the Spaniard sat in the driver's seat almost touching the buffalo's tail. This did not appreciably increase their rate of travel, but it was better than walking.

Sitting at the back of the cart with their legs dangling, facing toward the rear, Walker and Dixon watched the Chamorro troops, who still followed them at a distance of about a hundred yards. The troops were joined by a dozen or more curious children who skipped and ran alongside them, talking and laughing.

"They all seem pretty happy that the Spanish are leaving," Walker commented. "Apparently they are like the Cubans and Filipinos— they all want to be free, and they want the United States to liberate them."

Dixon coughed once, and then said nothing.

"Well?" prodded Walker. "Isn't that right? We're liberating all of these people from the Spanish, and they're grateful to us for it."

"You forgot to mention the Hawaiians," Dixon said quietly.

Walker bristled. "They will change their minds when they see how much better things are with American rule," he argued. "They will be much better off, and then they will be glad to be part of the United States!"

"Of course," replied Dixon calmly. "I'm sure you're right."

Dixon's quiet serenity only made Walker more irritated. "You don't really believe it, do you?" he demanded. "All that talk about how America is your country now, and 'freedom won.' America brought freedom to colored people, and just like that, it is bringing freedom to these people too. You know it's true! Why won't you just admit it?"

Dixon inhaled deeply, and then exhaled a long breath through pursed lips. Then he spoke. "Yes, Private First Class Garrett. It's true. America will bring freedom to these people in just the same way it brought freedom to the slaves. They will have the same rights, freedoms, and opportunities that the black man in America has today. Now, if you're done talking, I think I'll walk a bit more."

And with that, he hopped off the cart. Waiting until the cart had traveled twenty or thirty yards further up the road, he turned and began to follow. Thumbs hooked in his belt, and his hat pushed onto the back of his head, he whistled "Dixie" as he strolled along.

This was more than Walker could endure, so he turned and clambered into the front seat beside the officer. The seat was just wide enough for two, and Walker began to put his limited Spanish vocabulary to work. They carried on a fractured bilingual conversation until they reached the old fort at the summit of a hill overlooking Agana.

It didn't take much time for General Wheeler and Captain Joe to size up the fort. It was little more than a ruin. The few artillery pieces were obsolete and useless. It was not worth the gunpowder it would take to destroy it. Within minutes of arriving they were on their way back down the hill.

They stopped in an open air market in the town to purchase something to eat, but the Chamorros would not accept anything as payment—they insisted on giving them bread, fruit, and bowls of rice and grated coconut. It was Walker's first taste of coconut, besides some other fruits he couldn't identify.

By the time they returned to the beach, Captain Glass had come ashore with a company of Marines and a military band. The Marines raised the U.S. flag while the band played the "Star Spangled Banner." They then lowered the flag, folded it, and took it back to the *Charleston* with them. The Chamorro soldiers cut their buttons from their jackets and gave them to the Americans as souvenirs, smiling and saying "Gracias!" as they did so. Walker accepted five. Dixon seemed especially popular, pocketing more than twenty buttons.

They made it back to their ship just in time to eat supper, or "evening mess," as the soldiers termed it. Walker was still so full of bread, rice, and fruit, he really wasn't hungry. After eating a few bites, he went outside and stood at the bow railing for an hour, watching the beautiful ocean sunset. As he made his way toward his bunk below deck, he passed General Wheeler's stateroom. The door was open and the General was sitting at his desk with an open book.

Walker tapped lightly at the door and asked, "General Wheeler? Excuse me, sir, but may I ask you a question?"

"Of course, Walker! Come in. Take a seat." The General seemed relieved to have a diversion. "My! What a day we've had!" the General beamed. "We've made history today, Walker! The next generation will be reading about this in their history books. And you were here, helping make it happen!"

"Yes sir! It's all really amazing. I'm not sure I can absorb it all yet, sir."

"Amazing indeed! There's been nothing like it in our country's proud history! We're changing the world, Walker! For the better!"

"Yes sir, I know we are, sir. And I'm proud to be an American."

"So—what's this question you want to ask me?"

"It's about something Dixon said this morning, sir. He said that since the Civil War, black people were in the government, in the businesses, and in the army. I know coloreds are in the army, and I suppose that some do own businesses in the colored neighborhoods, but is it true that they are in the government? I've never seen a colored man in any political office."

"Hmph." The General leaned back in his chair and intertwined his fingers across his stomach as he studied Walker for a moment. "When you were in the Academy in Decatur, they didn't teach you about the Reconstruction times, did they?"

"Yes sir! We learned how the carpetbaggers and scalawags took advantage of the white people to fill their own pockets, and how the Ku Klux Klan and other patriotic southern groups tried to keep the peace and bring justice. The colored people were used by the Republican carpetbaggers to keep them in power. I know all about Reconstruction!"

"I see," the General mused, stroking his beard. "You didn't learn anything about Hiram Revels, Blanche Bruce, Benjamin Turner, or Pinckney Pinchback, did you?"

"No sir, I never heard of them."

"During Reconstruction, Revels and Bruce served in the U.S. Senate, Turner served in the House from a district in south Alabama, and Pinchback was the governor of Louisiana. They were all colored. There were several others who served in the House of Representatives. There were dozens of colored men, mostly former slaves, who were elected to state legislatures during Reconstruction. In fact, blacks were a majority in the South Carolina state legislature for a short while."

"You don't mean it!" Walker exclaimed without thinking, and then stammered, "I mean—sir, I mean—" He couldn't finish the sentence.

"Yes, Walker. I *do* mean it," the General smiled in amusement. "I suppose I shouldn't be surprised that you have not heard about these things. Schools generally don't teach the present very well. They do much better on the history of past times. But it's true. Colored people have been very active in government since the War, though not so much since Reconstruction ended, about twenty years ago. Dixon told the truth."

Walker scratched his head in puzzlement. "But sir," he asked hesitantly, "why were the coloreds in government then, but not now?"

"Voting rights, Walker. Voting rights. The Fifteenth Amendment gave black men the right to vote, and that's why so many were elected to office during Reconstruction. However, when Reconstruction ended in 1877, they began to lose that right across the South, thanks to state laws that prevented them from voting."

"But—sir—how could state laws prevent them from voting if the Constitution said they *could* vote?"

The General nodded his approval at Walker's question. "There are ways. The most common are poll taxes and literacy tests. An uneducated black man won't be able to pass the literacy test, and if he does, there's still the poll tax. Most blacks can't afford to pay to vote. Legally, they still have the *right* to vote, but they can't *exercise* that right if they can't qualify and meet the conditions required by the states. Black voting has been pretty much eliminated, and as a result, no colored men sit in legislatures or in Congress now."

"But—sir—there are a lot of white people who are uneducated and poor, and they still manage to vote. Why don't those laws keep them from voting?"

The General nodded again, this time with a one-sided smile. "Have you ever heard of what's called 'the grandfather clause?' Most of the former Confederate states added it to their state constitutions after Reconstruction. It says that if your ancestors were eligible to vote before Reconstruction, then you can vote too—without having to pass a literacy test or pay the poll tax. That exemption allows poor, illiterate whites to vote."

Walker stared, speechless. Finally, after a long moment of silence, he asked earnestly, "Do you think that's right, General Wheeler, sir?"

The General paused for another long moment of silence. When he spoke, it was not in his usual rapid-fire style, but with deliberate slowness, as he chose his words carefully. "Walker, we've both seen the bravery and resourcefulness of black soldiers on the battlefield. They fight just as well as any white soldiers. Without them we might not have taken San Juan Hill. Those men deserve the right to vote."

Here the General paused reflectively, and then continued. "However, the white population, at least in the South, is not ready for this.

If black men began to vote and elect black representatives, it might inflame white hostility and we might have night riders in white hoods burning crosses across the South again. Whatever you may have heard about the Klan enforcing order and justice, they also killed and terrorized a great many people, both black and white. We don't want to go back to that.

Wheeler sighed pensively. "So, how can this situation be resolved?" he asked rhetorically with an expansive gesture. Answering his own question, he concluded, "It will take time. We must be patient, and I believe that, eventually, when the memories and passions of The War have subsided, and when slavery lies in the distant historical past, reasonable and fair-minded white men will recognize that the black man—"

A sudden knock at the door stopped the General mid-sentence.

"Enter!"

Captain Joe stuck his head in.

"Orders just in from Captain Glass—we raise anchor and set sail for Manila within the hour, sir!"

"Excellent!" the General enthused, rising from his chair. "It's time to get back to our real mission!" Turning to Walker, he gave a quick nod. "Walker, we'll have to continue this discussion later. I'm glad to see that you are listening and thinking. You are learning things here that you wouldn't have learned at home in Alabama. Keep it up, my boy! And off to quarters with you!"

Walker made his way to the white soldiers' quarters and found his bunk in the semi-darkness. He lay awake for a long time, thinking about what the General had said, and also about what Dixon had said earlier. The things the General had told him were too much for Walker to absorb at once. Finally, weary and confused, he decided that the General was right—it would take time and patience for the situation to work itself out. For now, it was best to let things be as they were. He had an uneasy feeling that this was not really a proper conclusion, but since he could not conceive of a better one, he sighed, wadded up his pillow under his head, and surrendered to dreamless sleep.

14

MANILA!

February 2, 1899
Dear Ma and Pa,

    I hope you are doing well. I would love to see the farm again. I guess it is getting close to time for spring planting in a few weeks, so I know Pa will be busy. We will be going ashore in Manila tomorrow. It will be good to be back on land. They say this is the coldest month of the year here, but it is almost 90 degrees. At least it is not raining. I think I should have joined the Navy instead of the Army, since I have spent so much time on ships at sea. It is a long way across the Pacific Ocean. I spent most of the voyage in General Wheeler's quarters, reading his books. I understand that there is fighting in the Philippines, though I don't know why, since the Spanish have already been defeated and the islands are ours now. I promise to be careful and write when I can.
    Your son,
    Walker

Walker's first sight of the Philippines reminded him of Cuba, Panama, and every other tropical vista he had seen over the past months. The distant hills were covered with dark green foliage, and he imagined that he could almost hear the now-familiar sounds of the birds and insects, even before he reached land. The city of Manila sprawled along the shoreline for nearly a mile, embracing the mouth of a river which emptied into the bay. Walker was surprised at the size of the city and the bulk of the imposing Spanish fort to the right of the mouth of the river, on its south bank. His sharp eyes could see that some of the buildings in the crowded city center were at least three stories tall, and he could make out the steeples and towers of several formidable churches. The harbor was sprinkled with small fishing boats and barges, pushed slowly by pole-wielding boatmen. It was such a peaceful scene that he found it difficult to imagine that a war could be going on. The presence of several United States warships was the only discordant note in the almost pastoral setting.

Once ashore, the men had no sooner gotten settled into their barracks in the old Spanish fort than the officers ordered them to assemble in the courtyard. Walker stood stiffly in formation with the others, staring straight ahead. A small cluster of people across the courtyard were talking actively, but he could not make out what they were saying. He saw General Wheeler, his daughter Annie and Captain Joe, and to his surprise recognized Major Payne and Lieutenant Pershing, whom he had not seen since Cuba. There were three other officers with them, and a large, heavy-set man in a suit, who was doing most of the talking. The group abruptly turned and came toward the formation of soldiers.

General Wheeler stepped forward and spoke. His high-pitched voice rang out in the courtyard as he paced along the line of men. "I hope you men got plenty of rest and sleep on the ship these past weeks, because we are about to see a lot of action. The Filipino insurgents are organized and armed, and they don't recognize our authority here. We are going to have to show them who's in charge, beginning right now. Our commanding officer is Major General Otis." General Wheeler gestured toward General Otis, and stepped back as Otis stepped forward.

"Welcome to the Philippines," rasped the gray-haired general. His bushy gray whiskers drooped down on each side of his face like a pair of wings, reminding Walker of pictures he'd seen of Civil War General Ambrose E. Burnsides, whose famous whiskers had become immortalized as "sideburns." Otis's whiskers vibrated when he talked, and Walker struggled to keep his mind focused on the general's words.

"Last night the Filipinos opened fire on American troops without provocation. Battle has begun. The Filipino leader, Emilio Aguinaldo, claims that it was accidental, but the fighting, having begun, must go on to the grim end. The battle is heating up as we speak, and there is no time to waste. Your officers will give you your assignments. Remember the flag you fly, and acquit yourselves like true American soldiers!"

The old general spun about and marched away, disappearing through a doorway across the courtyard. Then, the obese man in the suit stepped forward almost tentatively and, raising a soft, plump hand as if calling for attention, spoke in a calm, measured voice. "Gentlemen, let me also welcome you to the Philippines. I am Judge William Howard Taft, head of the Philippine Commission. I am the civil authority here in the islands, representing the President of the United States, William McKinley." Pausing for effect, his hand still raised, he went on. "It is highly regrettable that violence has been initiated. We have no wish to have conflict with the Filipino people, and our hope is that peace can be restored quickly, with the least possible loss of life."

Listening to the man's deep voice and slow, carefully enunciated words, Walker couldn't help thinking that he had never seen such a fat man. *He must weigh well over three hundred pounds,* he thought. He became focused on watching the man's double chin shake and the upturned ends of his mustache bounce as his head moved with each word.

"President McKinley has announced a policy of 'benevolent assimilation,'" Taft went on. "This means that we want to befriend the Filipino people, and show them that we mean them only good, and no harm. So, as you go forth to maintain order, remember that we are here not to oppress or punish, but as the President himself said, to 'civilize and Christianize' the Filipinos." Judge Taft gazed serenely about at the soldiers for a long moment as if letting his words sink in. Finally lowering his hand, he nodded to General Wheeler and turned and ambled off to disappear through the same doorway as Otis and the others.

As soon as Taft was out of sight, General Wheeler gave a signal and Major Payne, Captain Joe, and Lieutenant Pershing all began barking orders. Within seconds, all of the men were running for their equipment, passing out rifles, ammunition, canteens, and knapsacks. They left the courtyard at a double-time trot, having fixed bayonets on the rifles and draped bandoliers of bullets over their shoulders.

Captain Joe ordered Walker to go with Pershing, who commanded the men of the Tenth. They hurried along the south bank of the river, heading east, away from the harbor. The river was widest near the mouth—almost two hundred yards across, Walker estimated. As they approached an impressive stone bridge, he noticed a sign that said "Rio Pasig."

Shots suddenly rang out from across the river, and Walker heard the whistling sound of bullets passing close by. The column of men was exposed to enemy fire with nowhere to take shelter, so Pershing shouted and waved his arm toward the bridge. The men ran to the bridge and, turning onto it, began to run across it toward the source of the shots, with the lieutenant leading the way. The iron side rails afforded some protection as they crouched while running, but bullets were ringing loudly off the railings and lamp posts, much too close for comfort. Two men were hit and went down on the wooden flooring.

Pershing immediately ordered the men to return fire. While the men in the front half of the column were blazing away with their rifles resting on the railings or shooting between them, Pershing brought the rear half forward, and when they reached the front they stopped and began shooting while the others advanced past them. Thus, in this leap-frog manner, they crossed the bridge. By the time they reached the other side, the Filipino attackers had retreated up one of the many canals that emptied into the river.

Civilian traffic on the bridge had panicked. Men and women ran in both directions, women screaming and men shouting. Carriages drawn by horses and carts by oxen were jerked about wildly as the animals lunged out of control, but it did not appear to Walker that any people or animals were hit by bullets. Things calmed down almost immediately as soon as the shooting stopped. Boatmen reappeared from under the arched roofs of their wide, flat-bottomed cascos and began plying their oars to get away from the scene as quickly as possible. Walker noticed the body of a white-clad Filipino floating face down in the river, drifting slowly with the current, a red stain in the middle of his shirt. Taking cartridges from his bandolier, he reloaded his rifle.

Pershing divided the men into two columns and sent them up one of the canals, one column on each side. Buildings and residences hugged the canals tightly, leaving little room for the men to maneuver. Walker soon saw the brilliance of Pershing's tactic, for as insurgents opened fire on the men on one side of the canal, the soldiers on the other side would return the fire and silence the shooters. They faced constant attacks as they advanced all the way to the outskirts of the city, turned, and came back following a different canal. It was slow work, and by the time they returned to the old fortress the sun was going down. Four men were helped to the infirmary.

The city streets were swarming with American soldiers. Walker hadn't realized how many of them were present in and around Manila, but there were thousands. A steady rain of gunshots could be heard in the distance, to the north and south mainly, and they continued into the night. When crossing back over the bridge on the return to the fortress Walker had noticed several more white-clad Filipinos floating in the river. Pedestrians and boatmen were nowhere to be seen. Except for American soldiers, the city seemed to be empty.

"This isn't just an insurrection," he breathed to himself. "It's a war!"

Upon reaching the mess hall Walker found that the white soldiers had already eaten, and he and the black soldiers of the Tenth were the last to be fed. Most of the white soldiers continued to sit at the tables and talk, however, leaving few seats available for the latecomers. Lieutenant Pershing took his food and went to a table of white officers in the corner. Officers' tables had chairs, while the rest had benches.

Walker looked around for an empty place. The only one he saw was next to Corporal Dixon at a table of soldiers of the Tenth. Conversation at the table quieted abruptly when Walker stopped at the bench, plate and cup in hand.

"Is this place taken?" he asked.

There was an awkward silence, broken by Dixon. "Ain't there no seats with the white boys?"

"Never mind," said Walker, turning away. "I'll go outside."

"Hell, Garrett—sit down," snapped a sergeant gruffly. "You fought with us all day, you might as well eat with us."

"But don't let it go to your head," cracked Dixon. Loud guffaws exploded all around the table, with one man nearly choking on his food, which only added to the levity. One of the men scooted over to make more room, and stifling the urge to make a retort to Dixon, Walker took his seat and kept silent. As conversation resumed, Walker dug into the fried fish and rice, stewed tomatoes, and boiled eggs, washing it down with gulps of cool water. He casually listened as they talked about the day's events.

"Say, did y'all see anything funny about that river today?

"Yeah—they's some really big white fish floatin' in it." More guffaws.

"No, really. Y'all see which way they were floating?"

"Yeah—face down!" More laughing.

"But which *direction* were they going when we went cross the bridge the first time? I'll tell you—they were going east. Away from the harbor. Going inland."

"Inland? You sure about that?"

"Hunnerd percent sure. But when we came back across it later, the bodies were floating west—toward the harbor. Opposite to what they was, earlier."

"That can't be right. A river can't change direction like that."

"I know what I saw. Didn't anybody else see it?" There was a quiet pause as eyes turned up and down the table.

"I did," said Walker. "I didn't realize it at the time, but now that you mention it, they were floating east in the morning and west in the evening."

"That's true," seconded Dixon in a surprised tone, and others along the table began to nod in agreement. "How can that happen? That can't happen, can it?"

"How can what happen?" The voice had a slight Spanish accent. Walker and the others turned toward the end of the table to see a dark-skinned, young Filipino man wearing a tan suit, white shirt with unbuttoned collar and loosened necktie, holding his straw hat in hand.

As they studied him for several seconds, he smiled and repeated his question. "How can what happen, señores?"

Dixon spoke—"How can the river flow east in the morning and west in the evening?"

"Ah!" he smiled, nodding. "It's very simple, really. The Rio Pasig is not really a river in the usual sense of the word. It is—how do you say in English?—I think it is 'estuary.' It connects the harbor of Manila with the bay. The current flows from the harbor to the bay when the tide is high, and when the tide goes out, it flows the other direction."

A chorus of delighted exclamations broke out along the table as those who had claimed to observe the reversal of the current laughingly jeered at those who had denied it.

"The bay—that's Laguna de Bay?" queried Walker. "About fifteen miles from the harbor?"

"Si! Yes, señor! How do you know of our country?"

"I saw a map on the ship, on the way here. You sure do have a lot of islands in your country!"

The dark man smiled almost apologetically. "We are a country of islands," he agreed. "The Philippines are over seven thousand islands. You are on the island of Luzon, the largest of the islands."

"Seven thousand!" Walker's jaw dropped, and the table erupted in more exclamations of disbelief. "How can you keep up with all of them?"

He laughed easily. "We don't have to. Only about two thousand are inhabited, and most are very small. Some are not even named. Almost two hundred languages are spoken here, so it is a very difficult country to govern. The Spanish tried for almost four hundred years. I think the United States wants to try now." He spread his hands with raised eyebrows as if to say, 'Who knows?'

"Two thousand inhabited islands!" breathed Walker in amazement.

"Two hundred languages!" echoed Dixon.

"And who might you be, sir?" interjected the sergeant.

The Filipino gave a quick bow and a wave of his hat. "I am Emilio Jacinto, and I am a writer for one of the newspapers here—*El Diario de Manila*."

"Emilio? Are you the one who is leading the insurrection?"

"No no, señor!" he exclaimed in dismay, raising his hands as if to repudiate the very idea. "That is Emilio *Aguinaldo*. I am not that Emilio! I am only a simple journalist! Those are his men you have been fighting against today. You have killed many—several hundred, I hear. I think the insurrection cannot last long. You are too strong for us—for the forces of Aguinaldo, I mean." He seemed embarrassed at his slip.

"I came to speak to some of your officers to get information for my newspaper," he explained. "So now I will be on my way. Buenas noches, señores!" And with a smile and another bow, he turned toward the exit. Behind him the soldiers buzzed with animated discussion about the things he had said.

Walker's cup rang with a metallic, hollow sound as he set it back on the table.

"Hold your cup out, Garrett." said the sergeant, lifting the tin pitcher of water. "You did good work today. I saw you get three of them rascals."

Walker extended his cup to be filled. "Thank you," he said, appreciative of the compliment.

"Lawdy mercy!" exclaimed Dixon loudly, with an exaggerated drawl. "I never heard a Alabama white boy say 'thank you' to a darky befo'!"

The table fell silent as Walker rose to his feet. Looking Dixon in the eye, he replied, "I said 'thank you' to a *sergeant*. Color don't matter." Draining the cup in a single draught and tossing it onto the table with a clang, he walked out the door into the twilight of the courtyard. Not a word was spoken as he left.

Once outside he exhaled heavily and shook his head as if to clear his mind. *Why is Dixon always trying to get under my skin?* he fumed. *One of these days, he's going to go too far.* Scowling, he stood still and gazed up into the starry night sky. The moon began to emerge from behind some clouds, filling the courtyard with a soft glow. Walker felt his tension releasing as he began to relax.

A soft "ahem" from behind Walker startled him. Whirling about he saw the Filipino who had spoken with them at the table. Stepping slowly from the darker shadows along the periphery of the courtyard, the young man gestured with open hands as if to show that he was not armed.

"May we talk?" he asked in a friendly tone of voice.

"What do you want to talk about?" replied Walker cautiously.

"Is it true what I hear, that you Americans are planning to stay here and rule this country, even though the Filipino people would prefer to govern themselves?"

"It's not a conquest," growled Walker defensively. "President McKinley calls it 'benevolent assimilation.' He says we are going to 'civilize and Christianize' the Filipinos. We're here to help."

The young man stood silently for a moment, absorbing Walker's words. "Did you see the large churches in the city?" he asked. "We've been Christians for four hundred years—since before your country was settled by Europeans. Do you see our harbor? The boats and ships? We trade with all parts of the world. We have presses, foundries, mines—we make our own things. Do you know that we have seven daily newspapers, besides others? And universities, colleges, seminaries—our oldest school was founded in 1611—the University of Santo Tomas. And we have five hospitals. We began vaccinating against smallpox a century ago."

Emilio paused for several seconds, reflectively. "Why do you think that we need to be civilized and Christianized?"

Walker felt confused. He couldn't think of anything to say.

Cocking his head to one side, Emilio asked softly, "Will you 'civilize and Christianize' us with your *guns*?"

After several seconds of silence, Emilio gestured helplessly, turned, and slowly walked away. Walker stood motionless, struggling with conflicting emotions. The Filipino's words reminded him of the conversation he'd had with the governor in Hawaii. Troubled, he headed slowly toward the soldiers' barracks.

He noticed that the light was on in General Wheeler's quarters. "General Wheeler, sir, is there anything I can do for you before lights out?"

"Thank you, Walker, but I think I have everything I need for the moment." The General looked up from the maps on his desktop to study Walker through his small spectacles. "I hear that you fellows ran into some resistance today. How did it go?"

"Very well, sir. Lieutenant Pershing handled the situation perfectly. We crossed the bridge over the Rio Pasig and pushed the rebels all the way to the outskirts of the city. Only four of our men were wounded, none killed. We got several of the Filipinos."

"Excellent work! You've become a real combat veteran, Walker my boy. The closer the bullets come, the braver it makes you. You know, I had sixteen horses shot from under me during the War. Was wounded twice. You get used to it, after a while."

"Yes sir." Walker paused, hesitating. "General Wheeler, sir, did you know that the Rio Pasig is not really a river, but an estuary connecting to the inland bay? The current flows east in the morning when the tide comes in, and west in the evening when the tide goes out."

The General looked quizzically at Walker for a few seconds. "That is very interesting, Walker. Yes, that is what the map shows. It is good that you have realized this—it could come in handy at some point. A soldier must always know his surroundings. The lay of the land. Knowledge is an important weapon. Indispensable." And then, after another short pause, "Was there something you wanted to ask?"

Walker took a deep breath and scratched his head. "Yes sir. There is something from this morning that has been bothering me."

Wheeler gestured to the empty chair, and Walker sat lightly on the edge of the seat, hat in hand.

"Sir, this morning General Otis said that, now that fighting has begun, it must continue to 'the grim end.' Those were his words. But Judge Taft said the President had announced a policy of 'benevolent assimilation.' He said we were to 'befriend the Filipinos.' Those were *his* words. General Otis is the military commander here, and Mr. Taft is the political official in charge. It doesn't sound to me like they are reading from the same page, if I may say so, sir. I'm confused."

Wheeler chuckled and leaned back in his chair, taking off his glasses. "Ah, Walker my boy," he exclaimed. "Welcome to the world of politicians and generals! With all due respect to the President and the Judge, politicians can be counted on to say what they want people to hear—or at least, what they *think* the people want to hear, and military leaders can be counted on to say what the facts are. That doesn't mean that the politicians are lying—by no means! They say what they want things to be, even if things aren't that way in reality. A general doesn't have the luxury of indulging in wishful thinking. He has to deal with the situation on the ground at the moment. That's why General Otis and the Judge appear to be at odds. They're just talking about two different things!"

Walker nodded slowly. "I think I understand, sir. And when President McKinley says we're here to 'civilize and Christianize' the

Filipinos—even though they already have churches, schools, hospitals, and newspapers—he wants the American people to believe that we are here to help the Filipinos, even if that's not the real reason. Is that right?"

The general grunted in surprise and squinted at Walker, reaching for his glasses again. Tugging at his beard, he spoke softly. "So, Walker, you have been giving this some thought, haven't you? What do *you* think is the reason we are here, if not to help the Filipinos?"

"Well, sir, I was remembering the poem we read, on the ship when we left Cuba. The one by Rudyard Kipling—"The White Man's Burden"—do you remember it, sir?"

"Oh yes! Very well! I'm pleased that you remember it also!"

"Well, I think the Cubans did need our help, and it was our responsibility to help them. But I'm not so sure the Hawaiians or the Filipinos do need our help. A man at the Queen's house in Hawaii mentioned a book by an American named Mahan and said it was why we were taking over. I noticed that you have this book on your shelf when I was setting up your office onboard the ship, so I read a little of it now and then when I had time. *The Influence of Sea Power Upon History*. It says that we should take control of certain places in the world so that our Navy can have coaling stations—it's important for our national security. Is that why we want to control Hawaii and the Philippines? To have naval bases in these places? And in Guam?"

The general grunted again, and continued stroking his white beard, giving Walker a penetrating stare for a long moment. Walker began to feel uncomfortable, and wondered if he had said something wrong. He was about to apologize when General Wheeler finally spoke.

"The Spanish have ruled Cuba, Guam, and the Philippines for four hundred years. These people have had no experience in governing themselves. For us to liberate them from Spanish misrule and then abandon them to their own devices would be irresponsible and unchristian. Anarchy would prevail, and they would be worse off than before. It is understandable that some of them want to be independent immediately, but they are not ready for that. They would not have gained their freedom without our assistance, and they can't keep it without our assistance, either." General Wheeler nodded in a fatherly manner. "Have no doubt, Walker, my boy, that we are doing the right thing. You can trust that your leaders in Washington are going to give these peoples what they really need."

There was a brief moment of silence as Walker nodded thoughtfully.

"So!" the General exclaimed abruptly. "Is there anything else you wanted to ask?"

"No sir, General Wheeler." Walker rose to his feet, hat in hand. "Thank you, sir. You always explain things so clearly. I really appreciate it, sir!"

"Well, then," the General smiled indulgently, "You get a good night's sleep. It will be another busy day tomorrow!"

15

"NO MERCY!"

The rest break was over and it was time to get back on the trail. Walker rose stiffly to his feet and grunted as he shouldered the heavy pack. Pushing his sweaty hat to the back of his head, he picked up his rifle and moved into line. Dense foliage bracketed the narrow trail as it twisted its way through the jungle. He hardly noticed the ubiquitous singing of birds and chattering calls of monkeys anymore.

Having established military control over the city of Manila, the U.S. Army was extending its reach into the countryside. The rebel forces had withdrawn north of the city and were regrouping under the cover of the dense tropical forest. General Wheeler had been given command of a regiment to push northward and outflank the retreating insurgents, cutting off their path of escape. Speed was of the essence, and they were moving as fast as they could on the narrow roads and trails through the forests and fields of the countryside.

The sky was cloudy, which was a good thing since it kept the afternoon sun from baking them in the heat. Even though it was April, the temperature each day reached nearly ninety degrees. Walker was thankful that it was the dry season. By summer it would rain constantly, and would be even hotter.

When I get back to Alabama, he thought to himself, *I'll never complain about the weather again.*

At that instant one of the soldiers just behind Walker spoke up. "When I get back to Michigan," he said loudly, "I'll never complain about the weather again!" And then he added, "Nor about having to walk two miles to town for a sack of flour!"

"Soldier! Are you hot and tired?"

No one had heard the approach of General Wheeler. The noises of the marching soldiers had drowned out the sounds of his horse's hooves, which were muffled by the grass alongside the path.

"N-n-no s-sir!" stammered the shocked soldier. "I'm just fine, General Wheeler, sir! I didn't know you were—"

"Give me that pack." The spry old general bounded from the saddle. Grasping the backpack, he shouldered it and handed the reins to the soldier.

"Get on the horse!" he ordered, as he began marching briskly up the line.

"On your feet, men!" he shouted. "No time to waste! Get moving! Follow me!"

The soldier stood paralyzed for a few seconds, looking helplessly at the other men marching past him. General Wheeler was already thirty yards away and moving to the front of the line. Reluctantly he put his foot into the stirrup and swung into the saddle.

Walker heaved a big sigh of relief that he had not spoken his thoughts out loud. He made a mental note to never complain about anything again—at least not without first checking to see if General Wheeler was nearby.

The column snaked its way through the thinning trees into an area of open fields. A small village stood about a quarter-mile ahead, on the banks of a large creek. The huts were raised on stilts several feet above the ground. Goats, cows, carabao, and chickens were scattered about. Children skipped and played between the huts, and some women were washing clothes at the creek. Walker noticed that no men were present. It struck him as odd that the men were not working in the fields or gardens, and he began to have an uneasy feeling that something was not right.

Apparently General Wheeler thought this looked suspicious also, and without a word raised his arm, signaling the column to halt. No one spoke as they stood motionlessly for a long moment, looking curiously about. Only the occasional bleating of a goat, clucking of a chicken, or laugh of a child broke the silence.

Suddenly the quietness exploded with a barrage of gunshots coming from the trees beyond the creek. The first soldier to fall was the man on the General's horse, who was knocked from the saddle as if hit with a club, dead before he hit the ground. Several other men went down, some silently and others with shouts of surprise and cries of pain.

"Get down!" came General Wheeler's screaming command. "Return fire!"

It was bedlam. Everyone was shouting, it seemed, and the incoming bullets were kicking up dust in front and among them. Walker hit the dirt on his stomach and worked the bolt back and forth to chamber a round in his rifle. He could not actually see the shooters among the trees, but he instinctively guessed that they would be positioned on the left side of the trunks, assuming that they were probably right-handed. He began firing just to the left of the trunks, aiming shoulder height. He could see a couple of men stumble and fall backward, their lightly colored clothing visible now in the shadows. Suffering casualties apparently frightened the other rebels, and they began to withdraw deeper into the trees. The movement made them easier to identify, however, and the soldiers quickly cut down several more.

"Advance!" General Wheeler rose to his feet, pistol in hand, and began to run toward the creek. Walker and the others sprinted to keep up. He continued to fire into the trees as he ran, without attempting to aim. Other soldiers stopped to fire, and then ran a short distance before stopping to fire again.

The attackers were now in full retreat. Reaching the bank of the creek ahead of the others, Walker knelt and aimed at a fleeing figure in the distant underbrush. Just as he squeezed the trigger, something hot sliced through his left side, just above his belt. He didn't fall down, but he knew he'd been hit by a bullet. He felt a burning sensation as blood ran down over his belt and stained his trousers almost halfway to his knee.

General Wheeler assigned some soldiers to take a position in the trees on the far side of the creek in case the rebels decided to make a second attack. Walker and some other men were ordered back to the road to take care of their fallen comrades. The rest entered the village, rifles at the ready, and began to search the huts.

Three of the soldiers were dead and a dozen were wounded, a couple seriously enough to need a doctor right away. When General Wheeler returned from the village with a carabao-drawn cart, the dead men and the wounded who were unable to walk were put into the cart. They headed back toward Manila with a small escort force while the rest of the men formed up the line and pushed on.

Chained to the cart and walking behind it were three captured rebels who had been wounded and unable to escape. They limped and stumbled along, obviously suffering, but no one cared. They had revealed nothing under interrogation, despite being treated roughly. Walker had heard shots from within the trees across the creek, and later learned from some other soldiers that they had dispatched a few captured rebel fighters. He wondered if General Wheeler was aware of this.

There was no more talking or joking among the men as they marched. Everyone was deadly serious, studying every tree, bush, and ridge. Walker's bullet wound had been cleaned and bandaged by the medic, but it still burned painfully and throbbed with each step.

Later that afternoon as they were filing along a trail through dense jungle growth, they were suddenly fired upon by riflemen concealed behind some large rocks ahead.

"Take cover!" shouted a sergeant. The men dove from the trail into the underbrush. Immediately screams were heard. Sharpened bamboo stakes had been driven into the ground alongside the trail, hidden by the dense growth, and the ambush had been for the purpose of making the men dive onto the stakes. Walker narrowly missed landing on a stake which sliced through his sleeve and cut a gash above his eyebrow. The gunshots ceased almost immediately, having accomplished their purpose.

Some of the screams that Walker heard did not sound human. He suddenly recognized the terrified, frantic neighing of a horse. General Wheeler had spurred his horse off the trail when the shooting started, and the animal had pierced a hoof with one of the bamboo stakes. The General had no choice but to put him out of his pain. A pistol shot rang out, and the agonized screams ceased.

Walker felt anger rising in his heart. These rebels were like nothing he'd experienced before. *They deserve no mercy*, he thought. His eyes narrowed and he clenched his jaw as blood trickled down the side of his face. He pushed more cartridges into the rifle magazine and checked his pistol.

"No mercy!" he scowled under his breath. Then he remembered the shooting of the captured rebels earlier in the day. He hesitated, and gave his head a quick shake as if trying to clear his mind. Taking a deep breath, he scowled again.

"No mercy!" This time louder. The soldier next to him heard, nodded, and repeated it more loudly. In a moment, the soldiers up and down the line were growling the words, almost in a chant.

"No mercy!"

"No mercy!"

"No mercy!"

16

CHASING AGUINALDO

Walker fanned himself with his hat as General Wheeler stood in front of a map hanging on the wall of his office, hands on hips. He had drawn a line running northwest from Manila along the western side of a large swamp, and another line running due north on the eastern side of the swamp. Once past the swamp region, the western line bent to the northeast and converged with the other line in the highlands of the interior. The General nodded silently to himself as he studied it, tracing the lines with his finger, deep in thought.

"Shall I go get the officers for a briefing, sir?" asked Captain Joe quietly, standing a few feet behind his father.

Startled, the General jerked and turned quickly. "Yes! Have them here at fourteen hundred hours. We have a lot to do before sunrise tomorrow morning!" And then he turned back to the map, placing his finger on the lines again.

Walker followed Captain Joe into the yard, placing his broad-brimmed, sweat-stained, khaki hat on his head, in deference to the blazing tropical sun.

"Captain Wheeler, sir—what were those lines on the map? Are we heading out on a march, sir?"

"That is correct, Private Garrett," replied Captain Joe in a tone that suggested that he did not care to explain further.

"We're going after Aguinaldo, aren't we, sir?" Walker asked anyway.

Wheeler slowed his brisk pace and glanced sideways at Walker with a frown. Hesitating, he finally decided to give in to Walker's curiosity. "You saw the two lines on the map?"

"Yes sir. One to the west and one to the east."

"MacArthur's division is the western line. That's us. Lawton is the eastern line. We meet up at San Isidro, where Aguinaldo has moved his capital. If we can get there before the rains start, we just might close down this war for good."

"With the General leading the way, I know we can do it, Captain Joe!" blurted Walker excitedly, forgetting to say 'sir.'

Wheeler cleared his throat. "The General isn't exactly 'leading the way,' Walker. Actually, we're bringing up the rear. Our job is to make sure the other brigades get the supplies and equipment they need to do the fighting."

Walker's eyes widened and he took a step back, shaking his head. "They can't do that! The General isn't going to like that not one bit—sir!"

"Well, the General is a soldier, and soldiers follow orders. That's what you do in the army, Private Garrett. Like it or not, we will do our duty and do it right."

The Captain continued across the yard toward the officers' quarters. Walker stood for a moment in the heat of the sun, letting the news he had just received sink in. Heaving a troubled sigh he headed toward the barracks, sure that this was not going to go well.

The next morning it became clear that the weather was not going to cooperate. The air felt heavy, and the smell of rain was unmistakable. Dark clouds covered the sky and thunder rumbled in the distance, growing steadily closer. By the time the supply wagons were loaded and the soldiers were formed into their marching ranks, the storm arrived. Lightning illuminated the old fortress like noon day and torrents of rain descended at a sharp angle, while thunder crashed continuously with such deafening noise that the battle-hardened horses began to panic, and had to be led back into their stalls. Even after the worst had passed, the heavy rain persisted until midday and did not finally stop until late afternoon. General MacArthur and General Lawton decided to postpone the expedition until the next day, rather than get such a late start.

In fact, the unseasonable downpours became a daily plague for an entire week. The roads were completely washed out, leaving only a sea of mud to indicate where they had been. Nevertheless, as soon as the rains subsided the march began, and two columns of soldiers slowly snaked their way into the countryside, one heading north and the other northwest.

Struggling through the deep mud, MacArthur's division covered only about seven miles that day. The Filipino forces had destroyed the railroad and bridges as they retreated, which added to their difficulties. Reaching the town of Calumpit by late afternoon, the column was stopped by a damaged railroad bridge over the Pampanga River. The swollen river was more than a hundred yards across, and the insurgents had fortified the far end of the bridge. They also had established entrenched positions along the north bank of the river. General Arthur MacArthur, General Wheeler, and a group of other officers gathered to discuss the situation. They talked and argued until sunset without coming up with a plan, and the men began looking for a dry place to unroll their bedrolls for the night.

As darkness fell, Captain Joe found Walker, who had just finished tethering the General's horse and setting up the General's tent and cot. "Garrett," he motioned with his hand, "you're wanted in the meeting."

"Yes sir, Captain Wheeler! What meeting is that, sir?"

"*What* meeting?" the captain echoed in disbelief. "It's *the* meeting. The one with General MacArthur, General Wheeler, Colonel Funston—and all of the other officers! Get over there, on the double! They're waiting on you!"

Walker trotted off in the direction in which Captain Joe had pointed and found the officers standing in a small grove of trees. His mind was racing as he approached. *What on earth could all these generals and officers want with me? Am I in some kind of trouble?* He tried in vain to think of anything he had done that would account for this summons.

"Sirs—Private First Class Walker Garrett reporting for duty, sir!"

"At ease, Garrett," said General MacArthur gruffly. "General Wheeler speaks very highly of you. We have a mission that you may choose to accept or decline. It is extremely hazardous, and I am not ordering you to undertake it. I will let Colonel Funston describe it, since it is his idea."

"I accept the mission, sir!" responded Walker, snapping back to attention with a crisp salute.

A contemptuous snort from his left caught Walker's ear. He glanced quickly and saw Major Payne turn his back and walk away, shaking his head.

Colonel Frederick Funston stepped forward. He was surprisingly short at only five feet four inches, weighing a little over a hundred pounds, with a short dark beard. He was only in his mid-thirties, but had already earned a reputation for bravery while fighting in Cuba, becoming known among the men as "Fearless Freddie." He looked Walker in the eye as he spoke.

"Garrett, we need someone to inspect that bridge. It may be our only way across this river. We need to know how badly it is damaged, and whether it can be crossed or not. The only way to do this is to crawl along the underside of the bridge in the darkness, all the way to the other side. You'll have to be perfectly quiet to avoid detection by their sentries. One slip and you will fall forty feet into the river, and sure death. I would go myself, but General MacArthur won't allow an officer to risk his life in this way. It is your choice. Will you accept this mission?"

"Sir—I accept the mission, sir!" Walker repeated, saluting again.

Funston nodded once. "Follow me!" He said tersely, striding briskly toward the river, more than a quarter-mile away.

As Walker stepped forward to follow him, General Wheeler placed a hand on his shoulder. "I have confidence in you, Private

Garrett," he said. "This is very dangerous. I know you can do it." He squeezed Walker's shoulder and gave him a slap on the back.

"Thank you, sir," mumbled Walker, a little embarrassed, and then hurried to catch up with Colonel Funston.

Reaching the river they lay on their stomachs in the high grass fifty yards from the end of the bridge. There was no moon, and the far side of the river was shrouded in blackness. *Good thing*, thought Walker. *They'll be less likely to see me.* Funston was whispering instructions to Walker and pointing in the general direction of the river, but Walker was only partly listening. Removing his shirt, boots, socks, and hat, he crawled toward the bridge, staying close to the railroad track.

Slipping down the bank beside the bridge, he crouched beneath it, looking up at the girders and wooden crossbeams. The bridge was very sturdily constructed in order to bear the weight of trains. Strong H-beams bordered each side, bracketing the heavy wooden crossties. For additional support there were smaller iron I-beams crisscrossing under the wooden ties, forming a zig-zag pattern the length of the bridge. These I-beams had a flange, or lip, which could be used for handholds.

Reaching up with both hands, he gripped the flange of an I-beam and swung his legs upward to hook his heels onto the flange, hanging by his all-fours. Moving like a large inch-worm, he walked his hands forward one at a time and followed with his feet. Reaching the side of the deck, he had to twist sharply as he moved to the next beam, angling in the opposite direction.

It was slow going, and the heavy humidity of the stagnant night air didn't help. He frequently had to wipe his sweaty hands on his pants, one at a time, to keep from losing his grip on the iron beams. After what seemed an eternity Walker looked back and was dismayed to realize that he was barely halfway across. He made the mistake of looking down. It seemed so far down to the fast-flowing black current below that he immediately started to get dizzy. He focused his mind on the task of creeping along the beams, and moved on.

Suddenly he could see stars—lots of them. He strained his eyes in the darkness and saw that several of the crossties were missing from the deck of the bridge. There were no rails overhead. The insurgents had dismantled the bridge, and the destruction was more extensive as he advanced further across. By the time Walker reached the other side of the river there were no crossties at all, and even some of the iron beams had been removed, preventing him from reaching the bank.

He hung suspended from an I-beam for a couple of minutes. A few yards away there were some rebel sentries, and he could hear their voices as they talked. They seemed calm, not nervous or fearful, occasionally laughing softly. Walker's Spanish was not good enough to understand all that they said, but he did catch the names of Luna, the Filipino general in command, and Pilar, who was apparently another general. He clearly heard one man ask his comrades if the Americans would try to cross the bridge, and another laughed and said he hoped so.

Walker decided it was time to make his way back. Inching backward was more difficult and time-consuming, and his hands and shoulders were nearing exhaustion. He dropped his feet down and, reversing his grip on the beam to turn himself around, swung his legs back up and again hooked his heels onto the flange. Now able to move in a headfirst direction again, he made better progress. By the time he reached the other side of the river he had been gone for two hours and was drenched in sweat, his hands and shoulders beginning to cramp.

He crawled back up the bank to the grassy area where he had left Colonel Funston. No one was there, but his things were, so he pulled his socks and boots back on and headed for the grove. He found the officers lounging around a small campfire, smoking pipes and cigars. When he stepped into the firelight glistening with sweat and carrying his shirt, his hat pushed to the back of his head, they appeared startled at first, but then immediately rose to their feet.

"Private First Class Garrett reporting, sirs." He gave a tired, shaky salute.

"Garrett! Don't you know better than to present yourself to your commanders half-dressed! Get your uniform on!" It was Major Payne, standing at Walker's elbow. Walker smelled liquor on Payne's breath.

"What did you find, Private Garrett?" asked General MacArthur.

"Sir, the bridge is in pretty bad shape," Walker began, and proceeded to describe carefully all that he had seen and heard while he slowly donned his shirt. He was so exhausted that his hands trembled as he buttoned it. When he finished making his report there was a brief moment of silence, broken by Colonel Funston.

"Well, taking the bridge by direct assault is obviously not an option," he scowled as he spat into the campfire.

"So, it's Luna," observed MacArthur. "He's second only to Aguinaldo in the command structure. That means we're facing a major Insurgent force. Resistance will be stout."

"Maybe we can outflank them," suggested one officer. "Cross the river above or below them, and hit them from behind."

"There aren't any other bridges near here, and the river isn't fordable," countered another.

As the discussion continued, Walker saluted once more and slowly backed out of the circle into the shadows. He was turning to leave when General Wheeler again put a hand on his shoulder and squeezed it.

"Walker, my boy," he said softly, "You did me proud tonight. Your father would be proud of you, too. You are a real soldier, young man."

"Thank you, sir," was all Walker could say, and gave a heartfelt salute. The General saluted in response. As the words sank in, he felt almost overwhelmed. By the time he reached his bedroll and stretched out, he could only stare up into the starry sky and repeat the General's words to himself over and over until he fell asleep.

The next morning the sun came out from behind the clouds and lifted the spirits of the men, who had seen nothing but rain for more than a week. However, this also meant that it would be a very hot day, and everyone knew that whatever action was planned would have to be done early.

Once again Walker was summoned by General MacArthur. When he arrived, he saw the same group of generals and officers as the night before. He felt a sinking feeling in his stomach, wondering if another dangerous assignment was coming his way. He was not wrong.

Upon reaching the circle of officers he was surprised to see none other than Corporal Dixon among them. Their eyes met as Walker joined the group. He raised an eyebrow questioningly, but Dixon merely shrugged in reply. They stood side by side, waiting.

"At ease, men," said MacArthur, casually. He began to pace back and forth with his hands clasped behind his back, deep in thought. Then he turned to face them with furrowed brows.

"The problem is simple," he said. "We need to get across this river, but we can't use the bridge and we can't ford it." He heaved a deep breath, as if reluctant to go on. "Colonel Funston has proposed a solution, but it is extremely dangerous. We need two fearless men who are good swimmers." He paused briefly. "I'll let the colonel explain his plan."

The diminutive young colonel stepped forward energetically. With his animated gestures and quick, bobbing nods of his head for emphasis, he reminded Walker of Colonel Roosevelt.

"Like the general said, we need two good swimmers. The river is wide and swift. You will have a rope tied around your waist, and you will tie that rope to something solid on the other side. We will then use those ropes to ferry rafts of soldiers across the river."

"Uh, sir," interrupted Dixon hesitantly, "Ain't the Filipinos likely goin' to be shootin' at us?"

"We'll have a hundred rifles covering you, keeping the Insurgents down in their trenches. You'll be as safe as we can make it."

That did not sound very reassuring, but both men saluted and agreed to do it.

"Excellent!" enthused the colonel. "Let's get going! Follow me!" And he left the circle at a trot, motioning for them to follow.

Moments later they were crouching naked in the brush along the river bank, with long, rough ropes knotted around their waists.

"We got to be the stupidest soldiers in this army," scowled Dixon, under his breath.

"That's a long way across," Walker said uneasily. "And the current's fast. And these ropes are gonna get pretty heavy before we get to the other side."

"Don't worry, though," said Dixon sarcastically. "They won't be shootin' at us. They'll be down in their trenches."

Walker exhaled nervously. "We are definitely the stupidest soldiers in this army," he agreed.

Suddenly a hundred rifles opened fire from behind them, unleashing a constant stream of bullets upon the Insurgents entrenched on the far side of the river. This was the signal for Walker and Dixon to sprint down the bank and plunge into the water. Walker swam harder than ever before in his life, sucking in deep breaths of air at every other stroke. He could feel the rope's weight increase, the farther he swam. The two of them stayed even as far as the middle of the river, when Dixon began to forge slightly ahead. Enemy bullets began to strike the water around them, and when one grazed Walker's thigh, he intensified his efforts and drew even with Dixon.

Both of them were slowing, struggling desperately to keep afloat as they dragged the thick lengths of rope through the water. Finally their feet touched ground on the other side and they scrambled up the bank, bleeding and slipping in the mud as they crawled toward the enemy trench. Despite the supporting fire from the American side, bullets continued to strike near them, splattering them with mud.

Dixon suddenly scooped up a double handful of the mud, compressed it into a ball between his hands and hurled it into the trench. Walker followed his example, and the two launched a dozen mud balls into the enemy position. The few Filipinos remaining in the trench were apparently shocked and confused by this strange assault, and turned and fled into the underbrush.

Tying their ropes to the sturdy wooden posts which anchored the battlements of the trenches, they waved to signal that the ropes were secured. Funston's men had dragged an improvised raft to the river and, using the ropes, eight men on the raft began to pull themselves across, hand over hand. Colonel Funston was on the first crossing, and after the raft made several trips there were soon fifty or more men across the river.

As they disrupted the Insurgent position along the bank, more soldiers crossed, and by midday the defense of the bridge had completely broken down. The troops began crossing the bridge in single-file, walking on the long beams on the edge of the deck.

By mid-afternoon it was too hot for military action, and things quieted down as the men on both sides sought respite from the sun in the cooler shade. Walker and Dixon, having washed off the mud in the river and dressed again with their wounds bandaged, were sitting under a tree, leaning against the trunk, drinking water from their canteens.

"Where'd you learn to swim like that?" asked Walker.

"I didn't," replied Dixon. "Never swam a river in my life."

Walker stared in disbelief. "Then why didn't you say so? Why did you jump in that river with a rope tied to you if you couldn't swim?"

"I didn't say I couldn't *swim*. I'm just not a *good* swimmer. I don't know who recommended me for this, but in the army you don't say 'no.'

"Besides," he continued, "I wasn't going to let you be the big hero while I'm just standing on the river bank. If you can do it, I can do it."

"There they are!" a voice sounded a short distance away, and they looked up to see a group heading toward them. They realized that the man in front was General MacArthur and immediately jumped to their feet, standing at attention and holding a stiff salute.

"At ease, men," said MacArthur, with a wave of his hand. "I just want to personally tell you both how impressed I am with what you did this morning. I wasn't at all sure that you would make it, but you did a superb job. That was real bravery! You'll both be getting a medal for this!"

"Evans!" barked the general, over his shoulder. An aide stepped forward.

"Yes sir!"

"Give me two of those cigars!"

Turning back to Walker and Dixon, he handed each of them a

long, fat cigar. "Straight from Cuba! El Supremo! You've earned it, men! Enjoy!" And then MacArthur strode off through the trees, followed by the group. General Wheeler was not among them, Walker noted, though he did get a brief, baleful glare from Major Payne.

After they had gone, Dixon laughed scornfully. "Don't that beat all! Man gets a rope tied 'round him, half drowned in a river, shot two or three times, and what does he get for it? A cigar!"

"And a medal," Walker reminded him, holding the cigar under his nose and inhaling.

"I'll trade you my medal for your cigar," Dixon scoffed.

"Nah," said Walker, as he examined the cigar. "I ain't never smoked one of these before. I want to see what it's like."

"Don't enjoy it too much, 'cause you can't afford these. A dozen of 'em would take your whole month's pay. Make that two month's pay."

"My goodness!" exclaimed Walker, with a big grin. "Got to find me a match!" And he limped away, cigar clamped between his teeth.

Walker momentarily returned with borrowed matches, only to find Dixon blowing a cloud of smoke up into the air. Leaning against the tree trunk, he gazed smugly at Walker's surprised expression.

"Why didn't you say you had matches?" Walker demanded indignantly.

"You didn't ask," Dixon smirked. Walker rolled his eyes, struck a match, and took his place leaning against the tree, taking a deep draw on the cigar. Dixon chuckled as Walker began to cough and wheeze, smoke coming from his mouth and nostrils. Soon, Walker joined him, red-faced, laughing and coughing at the same time.

Sunrise the next day found General Wheeler and a small company of soldiers inspecting the railroad tracks northward from the Pampanga River. There were several rivers and streams in the immediate area, and thanks to the heavy rains there was extensive flooding across the flat, low country. The men were soon wading in murky, knee-deep water. They could see green hills in the distance, but the water around them was getting progressively deeper as they drew closer to the Tarlac River. Before long it was almost waist-deep, and they could no longer see the rails or roadbed beneath their feet.

They knew they were very close to the river when they saw the superstructure of a bridge above the water. Judging from the angles of the visible ironwork, General Wheeler estimated that the track lay about eight feet beneath the surface of the water.

"We need to know if the rails are still intact," declared the General. "I will do the inspection myself." He dismounted, stepping from the stirrup onto a big rock. He handed Walker the reins and began unbuttoning his field jacket.

"Sir," objected Walker, "Let me do it. I'm a good swimmer."

The General gave Walker a piercing look. "I'm perfectly capable of doing it myself, Private Garrett, but thank you for the offer."

There was a touch of irritation in his voice, which Walker did not fail to notice. He reddened as he saluted. "Yes sir!"

The General handed Walker his hat and jacket. Then he removed his belt with its holstered revolver, which Walker draped over his shoulder. To his surprise, the General continued disrobing until he was completely nude and Walker held all of his clothes, including his boots and hat.

Wheeler waded into the deepening water, and when it reached his chest he launched forward, diving down. His bare white feet flashed briefly into view, and then he was gone. The men stood silently, staring at the placid surface of the water, waiting for the General to reappear. After a long minute Walker became concerned. He turned toward Captain Joe.

"I'm going after him, sir. Something must be wrong."

Captain Joe merely grinned and pointed toward the bridge.

Walker turned back to see the General swimming toward them from more than fifty yards away. Wide-eyed, he shook his head in disbelief.

"Never underestimate the General!" laughed Captain Joe.

"Utterly useless!" fumed General Wheeler, his beard dripping as he walked in waist-deep water. "By the time these flood waters recede enough for us to use this bridge, the war will be over! We'll have to find another way to move supplies to the front lines." Once again back in his uniform, he rode past the men, waving his arm for them to follow.

Before they had gone twenty yards the General stopped short and pointed off to his left. A veritable forest of bamboo stood tall and green, some with trunks almost a foot in diameter.

"That's *it*!" he exclaimed excitedly. "We'll build our own bridge out of that bamboo! We'll come back tomorrow with axes, saws, and ropes and get to work!" Spurring his horse, he splashed away at a gallop, leaving the men to slosh through the brackish water back to camp.

After evening mess Walker gathered all of the tools and equipment they would need for the next day's work building the bamboo bridge. Piling it into a wagon, he leaned against it, pulled a half-smoked cigar from his pocket and rummaged for a match. Before he could light it, however, he heard his name called by a feminine voice. He was so surprised that he almost dropped the cigar, fumbling it like a juggler and, catching it in both hands, tucked it quickly back into his pocket. Turning, he saw Annie Wheeler in her nurse's apron, hand over her mouth as her shoulders shook with silent laughter.

"Why, Walker Garrett!" she exclaimed with mock severity. "I didn't know you smoked cigars!"

Blushing, Walker lowered his eyes. "I don't, Miss Annie," he said meekly. "It's my first. General MacArthur gave it to me for swimming the river, and I've been working on it for two days now."

"So, how do you like it?"

"Well-l-l-," Walker replied hesitantly, drawing out the word at length. "Can't say that I do, actually. It makes me feel like I'm swimming in the river again. I'm determined to finish it, but I don't reckon I'll smoke another one any time soon."

"I think that would be wise," she smiled. Then she added, "Father wants to see you now."

"Yes ma'am, I'll be right there."

The General was sitting on a canvas chair in his tent, and Captain Joe was seated on a three-legged stool. Annie sat on her father's cot. A small lantern illuminated the cozy scene, as twilight descended rapidly. When Walker arrived Captain Joe moved quickly to sit beside Annie, and gestured to Walker to take the stool. Feeling somewhat awkward at sitting in the General's presence, Walker held his hat by the brim in both hands and sat stiffly erect, as if still standing at attention.

"At ease, Walker," said the General, with a wry smile. "We're all family here."

"How is that leg wound healing, Walker?" asked Annie. "Are you keeping it clean, with fresh bandages?"

"Yes ma'am," he replied. "It don't hurt too much."

"I hear that you got one of General MacArthur's special cigars," commented Captain Joe. "How do you like that?"

"It's, ah, very interesting, sir," said Walker carefully. "I may finish it in a couple of days."

The three Wheelers laughed together in a friendly way, and Walker forced a chuckle, ducking his head modestly.

"Walker, I asked you to come because I have some news to give you," spoke General Wheeler, in a serious tone. "After we finish that bamboo bridge, I am returning home to the States. Annie and Joe are going with me."

He paused to let his words sink in, as Walker sat speechless. He blinked, uncomprehendingly.

"I've done all that I can do here," he went on. "I'm being relegated to supply train work, behind the scenes, away from combat. But I'm a soldier, and soldiers fight. Anyone can deliver supplies. If my commanders don't want me to fight, then I'll go back home, back to Congress, and carry on the fight from there."

"But sir!" exclaimed Walker, finding his voice. "They can't do that! Why, you're the—"

"Yes, Walker," interrupted the General. "Yes, they *can* do that. And there's nothing I can do about it. But I'm at peace with it. I have important work to do at home, and good Lord willing, I can still make a difference. So, that's the way it is."

Walker heaved a deep breath and bit his lip. "I will miss you, sir," he said earnestly.

"Ah, Walker," returned the General, with genuine warmth. "I am proud to have been your commanding officer for almost two years. You've become a stellar soldier, and I will enjoy telling your parents all about your adventures! I know you will have many more! You're not just a fine lad, anymore—you've become a *man!*"

"Thank you, sir," Walker said and shifted his weight, about to rise to his feet.

"There's one more thing I wanted to say to you before you go," said Wheeler, quickly extending his hand, palm out. Walker relaxed back onto the stool.

"Yes sir?"

"This war is changing, Walker, and not in a good way. The Insurgents have given up on fighting a conventional battlefield war, and are adopting guerrilla tactics. Hit and run. Ambushes. Scorched earth. We've already seen some of this, you know. It's going to get much, much worse." He paused and sighed, shaking his head as if deeply troubled.

"It reminds me of Lee's surrender at Appomattox, in '65. We were worn down, trapped. We told General Lee that we would disband the army and carry on the fight on the highways and byways, to the last man. He said 'No.' He said the people had suffered enough and it was time for the war to end. 'There is only one thing left for me to do, and I would rather die a thousand deaths than do it, but I must go and see Grant.' I'll always remember those words."

Walker sat, mesmerized. Stories about the War always captivated his imagination. He was thrilled to hear the recounting of those days by someone who was there in person. The four of them sat quietly for a moment, lost in the reverie of that hallowed memory.

"If Aguinaldo had the wisdom and character of 'Old Marse Robert,'" Wheeler continued, "He would realize the agony he is perpetrating upon his country, and he would just go ahead and surrender. It's going to be like Sherman's march through Georgia all over again, but worse. If Union soldiers did those terrible things to their own countrymen, think what our soldiers will do to these dark-skinned foreigners. It is going to be hell."

Pausing again for effect, the General leaned forward and fixed his piercing eyes on Walker. "Stay above it, Walker. Don't descend into the depths of depravity, no matter what others around you do. Remember who you are. Remember the 'white man's burden.' Don't hurt civilians, and don't hurt their women and their children. A true son of the South is always a gentleman, and you must carry that standard high! Never let it fall—never let your honor be sullied! Conduct yourself so that your ancestors and your descendants will be proud of you!"

Standing suddenly, the General put his hand on Walker's shoulder. "Will you do that, Walker Garrett? Can I count on you? Can your country count on you?"

Walker stood also. "Yes sir!" he choked out the words, saluting smartly. "You can count on me, sir!"

"I know I can, Walker," said Wheeler, returning the salute. "I know I can."

Walker sensed that the meeting was over, and he stepped carefully backward from the tent, turning to find his way in the darkness back to his place. When he was a short distance away, he turned to look back. The three figures were silhouetted against the tent by the lantern light. It seemed to him an almost holy scene, timeless and unforgettable. He gazed on it for a moment before trudging on through the trees, carefully stepping over the prone bodies of sleeping men.

Stretching out on his blanket on the ground, Walker arranged some of his gear under his head as a pillow and pulled his hat down over his eyes. Reflecting over the General's words he realized he was not entirely sure what he had committed to, or what the General could count on him for, but he felt he had been given a sacred commission of some sort. He hoped he was up to it.

17

———

CALAMBA, PART 1

July 20, 1899
Dear Ma and Pa,

Thank you for the long letter. It made me feel like I was home again. I'm sorry to hear that old Duke died. He treed his share of squirrels, for sure. I know you were happy to see General Wheeler again. I hated to see him and Captain Joe leave. Thank you for the pocket knife. I have a machete from Cuba, but it's too big to trim my fingernails and toe nails, so the pocket knife will come in real handy.

I'm glad to hear that you enjoyed the letter about me from Corporal Dixon. His mother is Beulah, the cook for the Dancy family in Decatur. I couldn't say why he wrote the letter, but he's a good soldier. I don't know when I'll get back home. It doesn't look like the war will end here any time soon if we don't find that fellow Aguinaldo. We're looking for him high and low. Wish us luck!

Your son,
Walker

The rainy season had arrived in earnest, and the temperatures were climbing higher each day. This did nothing to help the mood of the soldiers as the fighting intensified, and the guerilla tactics employed by the Filipinos kept everyone's nerves on edge. The thousand infantrymen had come by water from Manila on the Rio Pasig in several broad, flat-bottomed cascos to the Laguna de Bay. The gunboats *Napindan* and *Oeste* towed them the twenty miles across the bay to the town of Calamba.

The bay, really a large inland lake, was dotted with small fishing boats, their single sails filling with the warm breeze as the fishermen headed for land with their morning catch. It would be raining again by afternoon.

"Paddles!" came the shouted order from the gunboat.

"Lock and load!" came a raspy voice from the middle of the boat, as the men along the sides raised oars and began to row the boats toward shore. The air was filled with the sounds of rifles being loaded, chambered, and cocked. Every eye was trained on the shoreline and the village just beyond, watching for any suspicious movements.

Reaching shallow water, the men jumped over the sides of the cascos and began wading ashore. Immediately the sound of firing rifles exploded from the village and bullets began splatting in the water around them. Insurgent fighters came pouring out of the houses along the dock, advancing and firing as they came. The *Oeste* and *Napindan* returned fire with their small cannons and a Gatling gun. A few of the rebels fell to the ground.

The soldier in front of Walker was struck squarely in the head, and a shower of blood and brains sprayed Walker's face. He frantically tried to wipe the blood from his eyes with one hand while holding his rifle above the water with the other, when a man behind Walker, hit by a bullet in the shoulder, fell off balance and accidentally fired his rifle. The bullet cut a groove through the edge of Walker's left ear and nicked his eyebrow. Jerking his head reflexively to the right he almost fell, but managed to stay on his feet and keep moving forward.

Reaching thigh-deep water he raised his rifle and scanned the beach for targets. The enemy fighters were beginning to withdraw toward the buildings, firing as they retreated. Walker aimed carefully and squeezed off three shots, scoring hits with all three. He would have done more, but many of his fellow soldiers were in front of him and were reaching the beach, and he couldn't chance hitting them.

As the Americans splashed ashore, the last of the insurgents disappeared into the alleys and doorways. Walker, full of blood lust, never slowed down. Screaming the "rebel yell," he sprinted in the direction of the retreating attackers, and the other men took up the yelling and followed. They pursued the Filipinos through the town. It was dangerous, deadly fighting. The enemy withdrew in an orderly fashion, inflicting casualties and forcing their pursuers to move carefully and slowly. In two hours the town was cleared of the rebels, who took cover on a nearby mountain. Mt. Makiling was a thickly forested, extinct volcano, rising about three thousand feet from the bayside. It did not seem prudent to pursue them further, so the troops pulled back into the town.

Brigadier General Hall set up his headquarters in the church building on the main square, and summoned his officers for a meeting. Meanwhile the troops spread out and began to patrol the streets, watching for any sign of rebel presence. Walker, carrying his rifle at the ready, advanced cautiously up a small, dirt sidestreet. It was no more than a dozen feet wide, lined with single-story adobe buildings. He paused at the intersection of another small street, peering carefully in all directions.

"Is it safe to come out now?" A feminine voice spoke anxiously from a doorway behind Walker.

Shocked to encounter an English-speaking woman in such a place, Walker whirled about and stood speechless for several seconds. His wide eyes stared at the young, blonde woman in a crisp white blouse and dark blue skirt.

"Well? Is it?" She repeated the question with a raised eyebrow.

Finding his voice, Walker stammered, stumbling over the words. "Who the—what the—who are—Good Lord, woman! Who are you, and what are you doing here?"

She drew herself up with hands on her hips and said proudly, "I am a school teacher, sent here by the United States government to educate these poor Filipino children! So, who are you and what are *you* doing here?" The last words rang out with a challenging edge.

The question caught Walker so off guard that, again, he had no words. A familiar voice spoke from a few feet away.

"We are American soldiers, sent here by the United States government to keep the peace so you can do your school teaching." Dixon, doffing his hat, added, "Corporal Dixon, ma'am."

"And I'm Private First Class Garrett. Walker Garrett." Walker touched the brim of his hat, with a polite nod.

"Well, gentlemen, my name is Harriet Franklin. And I can tell you that your services are not needed here. This place has been perfectly peaceful ever since we got here six months ago, until this morning when you arrived and shot the place up like it was Gettysburg, Dodge City, or something. Please go back go to wherever you came from and tell your officers that no soldiers are needed in Calamba."

"Who is 'we'?" asked Dixon.

"We are the 'Thomasites,' as they call us, because we came over on the *Thomas*. There are over five hundred of us teachers here on Luzon. We are giving the Filipinos a chance at a real education. This building is our school, and we have five teachers here in Calamba. The others are inside with the children, who have been frightened out of their wits by all the shooting. How long are you planning to be here? We'd like to get back to work."

"What are you teaching them, ma'am?" asked Dixon.

"The three R's—reading, writing, and arithmetic!" She said it as if they should have known already. "And democracy!" she added. "We must teach them to practice democracy."

"Reading and writing," repeated Walker. "In English or Spanish?"

"Why, in English, of course!" she exclaimed, amazed that he should have to ask.

"Oh." said Walker. "Of course."

"How long are you going to be here?" She repeated the question a little louder. "You are not needed here, and we have important work to do."

"I don't know how long we will be here," said Walker apologetically. "But I need to come into your school building and look around. There could be—"

"Absolutely not!" She cut him off short. "I will not have a soldier with a gun and blood all over his face poking around in my school and scaring the children all over again!"

Walker blinked. "Blood all over my face?" He reached up and touched his cheek and looked at his finger. He licked his finger and rubbed his cheek and looked at it again.

"Walker Garrett! You've got blood all down your cheek, in your eyebrows, around your eyes, and down the side of your neck! It's even in your hair! Did you take a bath in blood? You look horrible!"

"Uh, sorry. I didn't know," he mumbled, dropping his head and turning slightly as if to hide that side of his face. His demeanor was so meek, almost ashamed, that she immediately touched his arm sympathetically.

"Step in here. Let me get some of that blood off you." Harriet stepped back into the dark interior, gesturing abruptly for him to follow.

Walker saw empty rooms, but no children, or anyone else, for that matter. The building appeared to be deserted. Reaching a sunlit interior courtyard, she stopped and turned. Frowning at his rifle, she pointed to the floor beside the doorway and said, "Stand there!"

Producing a rough, irregularly shaped sponge from a bucket of water, she began to scrub his face and neck.

"Walker Garrett! Do you realize that you've been shot in the ear? My goodness! A piece of your ear is missing!"

Walker reached up to feel his left ear, but Harriet knocked his hand away. "Don't touch that! Your hands are dirty! You should never touch an open wound without washing your hands first. It's unsanitary!"

"Where are the children?" Walker asked, to change the subject. "You said they were inside."

"They are on the other side of the building, away from the street," she replied. "The other teachers are with them."

At that moment, as if on cue, a young man with a thin, short beard and wispy mustache appeared in a doorway on the other side of the courtyard.

"Is everything alright, Harriet?" he asked.

"Yes, the shooting has stopped. I'm just patching up this soldier. They'll be moving on shortly. Tell the children not to worry."

Turning back to Walker, she said, "You seem awfully young to be a soldier, Walker. How old are you?"

"I'm nineteen," he said. "That's old enough to fight." And then he added, "How old are you? You seem awfully young to be teaching school in a remote village on the other side of the world in the middle of a war."

She laughed softly, wrapping a strip of linen around his head and over his ear. "I'm twenty-one, Walker. I'm a graduate of the Vermont Normal Institute, and teaching here is my calling. I wouldn't be anywhere else in the world, war or no war. These villagers are good people. Hard working, decent people. I'm going to do all I can to help them."

"But the rebels are not good, hard working, decent people," argued Walker. "They kill and torture people, ambush our patrols, and boobytrap the trails. I don't think you are safe here. You and the other teachers need to return to Manila, at least until this war is over."

"No, Walker," she said, tying a knot in the linen strip to hold it in place. "I'm not going anywhere. But thank you for your concern. I really think this place would be peaceful if you soldiers would just stay away. If you weren't here, the rebels wouldn't be 'rebels.' They would be fishermen, farmers, cobblers, and bakers. Don't take it personally, Walker—you are obviously a good person—but you and the other soldiers—you are the problem, not the solution."

Walker felt as if he had been slapped. He recoiled a step back and fixed his eyes on hers. Before he could find the words to reply, his name was called from the street.

"Garrett!" It was Dixon. "Get out here!"

Placing his sweaty, blood-spattered hat back on his head, Walker gave a quick nod and turned to go.

"Wait!" she said suddenly. Reaching behind her neck, she unfastened a fine silver chain and pulled it free. There was a small, silver cross on it. Stepping close to Walker, she reached up and fastened it around his neck. "You need protection, Walker. May God be with you."

"Thank you," he mumbled awkwardly, tucking the cross into the neck of his shirt.

"I'll pray for you, Walker Garrett!" called Harriet, as he strode away.

18

CALAMBA, PART 2

The rest of the day was spent establishing a defensive perimeter around the town, posting sentries, and setting up camp along the beach. The villagers gradually began to reappear, and the central market square became active again by afternoon. By evening a sense of normalcy had begun to return. Walker sat on the beach eating his supper from a tin pan, when he heard his name called.

"Garrett!" It was Dixon, about thirty yards away. "Captain Pershing wants to see us. Now." Without waiting he turned and headed toward the officers' tent, a short distance down the beach.

The sides of the tent were raised and fastened to the frame to allow the breeze to blow through. Inside the tent Walker could see a table at which two uniformed men were seated. To his surprise there was also a woman and a small boy, who appeared to be about ten or twelve years old. The men were Generals Hall and Lawton, and the others were Lawton's wife and son. Captain Pershing stood to one side, and beside him was Major Payne.

"Well, lo and behold, if it isn't Private Garrett," remarked Major Payne icily. "You're a long way from home, boy."

"Yes sir, I am. But it's Private First Class now, sir."

"Congratulations on the promotion. You're clearly on your way up the ladder." The sarcasm was unmistakable.

Walker fixed his eyes on Major Payne's for a couple of seconds before replying. "Thank you, sir."

"General Hall, sir, and General Lawton—these are the two men I was telling you about." Captain Pershing stepped around the table, gesturing with his hand toward Walker and Dixon. "Two of my finest soldiers—they're perfect for the mission, sirs."

"Are you gonna kill the jungle darkies?" piped up the boy.

"Manley!" exclaimed the woman, darting a quick, embarrassed glance at Dixon, who remained expressionless. "Mind your manners!"

"That's what everybody calls them, mother. And 'jungle n----rs.'"

"That's enough of that, young man!" she snapped, slamming her drinking glass onto the metal table with a loud noise. "I will *not* have you talking like that!"

"Let's continue this conversation over in my tent," said General Lawton, standing up abruptly.

The mother and son continued arguing in the officers' tent behind them as the group walked away to the general's private tent.

Once there, Major Payne chuckled heartily. "You've got a fine boy there, General Lawton, sir! He knows that our n----rs can whup their n----rs any day of the week, yes indeed!"

It may have been the major's words or just that Walker disliked him so intensely, but Walker felt anger rising in his chest and he spoke before he could restrain himself.

"Major Payne, sir, the men of the Tenth are not n----rs. They are soldiers of the United States Army and have earned the respect of any man in uniform. They are some of the best we've got." And then he remembered to add, "Sir."

"How dare you—" Major Payne began furiously, reddening and his upper lip curling.

"I agree with Garrett, Major, sir," interjected Captain Pershing firmly. "The Tenth is my regiment, and I'm proud of their work. Let's not disrespect them, sir."

"I haven't disrespected anybody!" snapped Payne, with clenched fists. "And I will not be spoken to like this by subordinates!" Turning to the two generals, he spread his hands. "Sirs! I insist that these men be disciplined! This kind of insubordination cannot be tolerated in an army!"

"Quite right, but we'll deal with that later, Major Payne," replied Hall gruffly. "Right now we've got a thousand rebels on a mountain looking down on us, and we've got to do something about it. File a report with my staff, and we'll get to it as soon as this is over."

"Sir!" Major Payne saluted sharply. "If you don't mind, sir, I'll go and oversee the water curing of those prisoners. They may have more information to give." And taking his leave, the major stormed out of the tent.

The awkward silence that followed was broken by General Lawton commenting wryly, "I'll have to have a talk with that boy of mine. See what a mess he started!"

"Oh, leave the boy alone, Henry. He's alright," intoned General Hall. "It's good for him to be exposed to the real world like this. How many twelve-year old boys have a chance to be in the thick of a battle halfway around the world? He's just growing up."

"Thanks, Robert. I suppose you're right."

"So! We'll deal with all that later," said Hall, giving the three of them a stern look. "But right now we need to know where those rebels are hiding and what they are planning to do."

"And we want you two men to find out," added Lawton. "Do you think you can do that?"

"What did you have in mind, sir?" asked Dixon, still standing at attention.

Before they could answer, the evening air was split by a blood-curdling scream coming from the direction in which Major Payne had disappeared.

The two generals chuckled.

"That water cure really makes 'em sing, doesn't it?" grinned Hall.

"Nobody does it better than Payne," chimed in Lawton. "They won't be thirsty again for a month of Sundays!"

Another scream. It was clear that someone was in extreme agony. After that, there were no more screams, but the sounds of choking and strangling were hard to ignore.

"We've got two Macabebe scouts who are going to lead you up the mountain," explained Hall, returning to the subject. "You are to find out exactly where the rebels are hiding, and see if you can determine what their intentions are."

"Are they retreating? Organizing for a counter-attack? Circling our position? Digging in?" Lawton ticked off the possibilities on his fingers as he talked.

"This is the same thing you did in Cuba, Garrett," added Pershing. "It was very useful information that you brought back. We might not have won that fight at Las Guásimas without it."

Walker nodded, his mind going back to José and remembering his laugh. He pressed his elbow against the machete under his jacket, hanging from the strap over his shoulder.

"Do we need our rifles, sir?" asked Dixon.

"No," said Pershing. "It will be dark, anyway. Just your sidearms will do."

"Yes sir. When do we leave, sir?"

"Right now," said Hall. "The scouts are right behind you."

Two lean, dark Filipinos had somehow silently materialized just a few feet behind them. Wearing loose, light clothing, with a cartridge belt hanging over one shoulder and across the chest, they were both barefoot, with wide straw hats. Both carried short repeating rifles, with lever action. They were clearly not regular troops.

"Garrett—you go with Miguel," ordered Pershing, pointing. "Dixon, go with Lobo."

As they turned to go, Pershing stopped them with a hanging, "And—"

They paused.

"I don't have to tell you what will happen if the rebels capture you. If they don't kill you, you'll wish they had."

"Yes sir."

As they left the beachfront Walker heard the strangling, choking sounds again, but more loudly. He noticed a group of soldiers under a nearby tent, gathered around what appeared to be two or three men prostrate on the ground, and someone—it looked like Major Payne, he thought—was pouring a bucket of water over the face of one of them. He could hear groaning, coughing, and gagging sounds.

"Those prisoners probably wish we'd killed them, too," commented Dixon. "That's not what I call 'benevolent assimilation.'"

They hurried through the narrow, winding streets of Calamba. There were cobblestones in the central square, but mostly dirt in the rest of the town. The official buildings in the center had tile roofs, but the smaller structures were all thatched. As they went past the doorway of the improvised school, Walker peered into the dusky interior, but did not see Harriet. He wondered how a young woman from Vermont could bring herself to live like this. It seemed so strange, somehow, but he couldn't help but feel admiration for her courage and selflessness.

Leaving the town they passed through scrub brush for a short distance, went through a field of high grass, and then reached the trees. As the road split, Miguel led Walker to the left, and Lobo and Dixon went to the right. The fading twilight was even darker in the forest, and Walker was glad that Miguel was wearing light-colored clothing, making him easier to see. The dirt road soon narrowed to a rutted path, and then to a single-file trail. They splashed across several small streams.

The trail began to climb, at first gradually and then more steeply, with zigzagging switchbacks. As they ascended, the path became increasingly rocky and the jungle growth overhung the trail, blocking out the moonlight except for occasional gaps in the foliage. Walker tripped over tree roots and rocks, and wondered how Miguel managed to keep such a quick pace without shoes to protect his feet.

Miguel suddenly stopped and held up his hand to signal silence. Walker then realized that the steady background noise of the tropical birds and monkeys had ceased. He could hardly hear over the sound of his own heavy breathing and the pounding of his heart, but then he heard it, too—the tread of many feet ahead of them. They were very close and coming quickly. Miguel gestured urgently to get off the trail, and the two of them slipped into the underbrush. Miguel pointed to a nearby tree and whispered loudly, "Trepar!" *Climb!* Grasping a stout vine and planting a foot against the trunk of a tree, he disappeared up into the foliage.

Walker stepped up onto an outcropping of rock and, jumping up, grabbed a limb of the tree Miguel had indicated. He scrambled onto the limb, and feeling his way in the semidarkness, climbed up several feet higher and positioned himself behind the trunk, away from the trail where rebel soldiers were already beginning to file past.

He stood with his feet on a sturdy limb and his left arm raised, holding onto a smaller limb above his head. Something suddenly seized his left arm above the elbow, gripping it tightly. He could feel sharp teeth piercing into his bicep and a heavy, sinuous form sliding over his shoulder, passing behind his neck, around his side, and beginning to encircle his hips. He realized in horror that he was being attacked by a huge snake—undoubtedly one of the giant pythons he had heard about.

The creature's weight was astonishing—at least two hundred pounds. He could feel that its girth was larger than one of his thighs. He realized that he had to do something quickly. His right arm was still free, so he reached inside his jacket and pulled the machete from its scabbard. Thankfully, he had spent an hour with a whetstone sharpening the blade to a razor's edge in preparation for the expedition to Calamba.

The rebel force was still passing down the trail just a few feet away and Walker hesitated, not wanting to create a disturbance that would attract their attention. However, as the snake continued to encircle his body and tighten its coils, he knew that he had to act or it would be too late.

Putting the edge of the blade against the thick sinew that wrapped around his torso, he began to saw frantically. Blood spurted upward, spraying Walker's neck and face. The python hissed through its clenched jaws, and the enveloping coils tightened even more. Walker was barely able to draw breath. In desperation he turned the blade upward and, releasing his grip on the limb and twisting his arm to bring the snake's head closer, he drove the point into the beast, just below and behind the head. Hot blood gushed into his face and down his chest. He shoved the blade with all his strength, slicing deeply into the neck. Still it refused to release its bite. Walker sawed into it again, and on the third thrust severed the monster's head. Even more blood spurted out onto Walker, running down his neck, chest, and back. He could smell its stinking odor and would have vomited, had he been able.

The snake's headless body thrashed silently, the severed neck flailing against Walker's back and side. The encircling coils did not immediately relax, but flexed spasmodically, squeezing the air out of Walker's lungs. On the verge of unconsciousness, he jabbed at the massive body with the tip of the machete, and it gradually began to slide downward. Finally able to draw a deep breath again, he clung to the tree, shaking. By the time the last of the rebels had disappeared down the trail, Walker had steadied himself.

"Americano!" Whispered loudly. It was Miguel. He was standing in the trail, motioning for Walker to come.

"I'm – coming!" gasped Walker.

He moved so slowly, however, that Miguel grew impatient. "Americano! Date prisa!" *Hurry up.* Miguel stepped onto the boulder at the foot of the tree and looked up to see what was taking Walker so long. Just at that moment, the massive body of the python fell to the ground, almost landing on him. Miguel stifled a scream and leaped backward into the trail, falling to the ground in terror. He grabbed his rifle and levered a round into the chamber, raising it to his shoulder.

"Don't shoot! No disparar!" cried Walker hoarsely. "It's dead! Está muerto!"

Miguel kept his rifle trained on the mass of the snake's still-twitching body, tense and ready to shoot, and looking nervously left and right as if expecting to see more snakes. "Por Dios!" he kept muttering. *My God!*

Reaching the ground, Walker found that his legs would hardly function. He staggered through the leafy vines along the trail's edge, and collapsed to his knees next to Miguel. He gasped loudly for air, bending forward with his head almost touching the ground.

Miguel reached down to help him to his feet, taking him by his left arm. The huge snake's foot-long head was still attached to Walker's arm, its jaws not having relaxed their grip, and Miguel's hand was placed on the head. The Filipino literally went airborne, uttering an inhuman exclamation and dancing a dozen feet away before getting control of himself.

"Shhh!" hissed Walker. The rebels weren't that far away yet, and they could not afford to be heard. He tried to pry the snake's jaws loose with his other hand, but they were firmly fixed. The eyes seemed to still be alive, glowing in the moonlight. His arm was aching and beginning to throb with pain.

"Por favor!" He reached toward Miguel and gestured to the snake's head.

At first shaking his head vigorously, Miguel reluctantly approached. Moaning with trepidation, he took hold of the jaws with both hands. It took all his strength, but he was able to separate them enough that Walker could pull his arm free. The jaws snapped back closed as soon as he released them, and Miguel dropped the head to the ground and kicked it into the bushes. Walker groaned and rubbed his arm, which was bloody all the way down to his wrist.

"Gracias, amigo."

Miguel couldn't stand still, pacing nervously and muttering to himself, continuously wiping his hands on his pants. He plainly wanted to get away from that place as quickly as possible.

It took a couple of minutes before Walker felt ready to get moving again. They stood indecisively in the trail for a moment, looking uncertainly in both directions. It didn't seem to make any sense to follow the rebels down the mountain, so they turned and continued on their way upward.

It turned out that they didn't need to go all the way to the top. Reaching a level clearing, they saw a pile of supplies—baskets, boxes, and rolls of blankets. Walker guessed that the rebels had left their food and extra ammunition at their camp while making their attack.

He was about to walk out into the clearing when Miguel grabbed his arm and pulled him back into the shadows, pointing. Then Walker saw the guards—two of them. On the far side of the pile of supplies, they stood smoking cigarettes and talking quietly.

Walker unsheathed the machete and motioned for Miguel to follow. Lying on the ground, he crawled toward them, taking advantage of the moon being behind some clouds for a few minutes. Reaching a stack of boxes immediately behind the two men, he rose to a crouch, gripping the handle of the bloody machete. Miguel produced a knife, which he held by the blade.

As the two watchmen laughed at some joke, Walker dashed around the boxes, raising the machete overhead. Miguel threw his knife, and the blade buried itself in the back of one of the men, who staggered a couple of steps forward before falling on his face. The other man whirled about, eyes and mouth wide open, just as Walker's machete descended. It was over in a matter of seconds. Miguel retrieved his knife, and nodded to Walker.

"Tagalog," he said distastefully, gesturing toward the bodies with a curled upper lip.

Walker stared down at the lifeless, still body at his feet. He had shot enemy soldiers in combat, but killing a man with a blade, up close and face to face—it was different. He looked at the machete, dripping red in the moonlight and realized, almost in surprise, that it was his own hand gripping the handle. The reality of what had happened was beginning to sink in when he heard branches snapping and the sound of approaching steps. He pulled his Mauser and cocked it, and Miguel shouldered his rifle.

"Easy there, Garrett!" It was Dixon. "Hold your fire!" He and Lobo emerged from the jungle on the far side of the small clearing and joined them. Surveying the scene, Dixon nudged one of the bodies with the toe of his boot. "Nice work. Quiet, too." He nodded his approval. "So where did all the rebels go?"

"We met them going down the trail. Barely got into the trees and avoided being seen. They must be going down to attack the town again. Once they were past us, there was nothing we could do about it, so we came on up here. I hope our sentries are paying attention."

"We need to get down there as fast as we can," said Dixon. "We'll go back down the trail Lobo and me just came up, and try to get ahead of them."

They scrambled down the rugged trail at maximum speed, slapping vines and limbs out of their way, and nearly tripping over rocks and roots. Going down was much faster than the ascent, to be sure. They did not stop to rest until they reached the edge of the tree line, looking out over the flat grassland stretching toward the town, less than a quarter-mile away. They had made good time—the rebels had not yet begun their attack.

Standing back in the shadows, they scoured the area for a sign that the rebels were there. As the moon came out from behind a cloud, they all at the same time saw the line of men crouching and moving slowly forward at the edge of the town, silhouetted against the adobe wall of a thatched house.

Walker immediately grabbed the rifle from Miguel's hands and fired a shot into the air. Jerking the lever down and up, he fired a second, and then a third. After a few seconds of stunned silence, the rebels, realizing that the element of surprise had been lost, rose up with a shout and charged into the town, running down the streets toward the waterfront. A staccato rattle of gun shots burst forth. Walker was not sure who was doing the shooting, but he hoped that it wasn't only the rebels.

A sizable detachment, however, had turned toward the sound of the shots behind them and began to return fire. Bullets flew around the four men, thudding into trees and ripping through the vines and leaves. Walker heard one whistle within an inch of his ear, and dropped reflexively to one knee. They retreated hastily back up the trail, darting from tree to tree for cover. They did not fire any more shots toward the rebels to avoid giving away their position, but the rebels, naturally assuming that their attackers were on the main trail, began advancing directly toward them.

"Miguel! Lobo!" cried Walker, searching his limited Spanish

vocabulary. "Hierba! Pronto!" *Grass—quickly!* The two Macabebes led the way, scrambling off the trail into the near total darkness of the jungle midnight. They moved at a right angle to the advance of the rebel force and, partially hidden by a ground swell and the short scrub brush, they crawled from the trees into the waist-high grass.

They wriggled on their stomachs as quickly as possible, getting away from the mouth of the trail and the edge of the forest. They had crawled about fifty yards when he heard Miguel hiss.

"Parar!" *Halt.*

The ground beneath them was very wet and muddy, and stank of stagnant water. He jerked involuntarily when a large rat ran across his back. It was running in Dixon's direction, and in a few seconds he heard the surprised squeal of the rat and a burst of expletives from Dixon.

"Shhh!" hissed one of the Macabebes.

"Shhh yourself," he heard Dixon mutter.

They lay in the muck for several minutes without moving. The sound of gunfire from the town was constant, and it was plain that a battle was raging fiercely. Walker very slowly raised his head until he could just peek through the tips of the grass. He saw a few shadowy figures in the distant trees, milling about, and could hear their voices as they talked. He saw more figures join them, apparently having returned from advancing some distance up the trail, and then the group of about forty men headed back toward Calamba at a fast trot.

They resumed crawling through the grass until they reached the other side of the field. Crouching, they ran to the nearest building—a small, thatched, adobe house. Carefully rounding the corner, they began stealthily making their way toward the sounds of the battle near the waterfront. The street was deserted, but the air was full of the barking of dogs, along with the constant gunfire.

Before they reached the waterfront, however, the gunfire began to diminish. The rebels, having failed to achieve the advantage of surprise, were being repulsed. After only about fifteen minutes of combat, they began withdrawing back up the narrow, twisting streets of the town. Reaching an angle in the street, Walker, Dixon, and the two scouts unexpectedly came face to face with several dozen of them, separated by less than thirty yards.

All four of them promptly opened fire into the mass of men, who were closely confined in the narrow street. Aiming was not necessary. Walker and Dixon each emptied their pistols, while Miguel and Lobo's rifles emitted rapid, deafening booms. It was a complete shock to the rebels, who were caught completely unprepared for a rear attack. Shouting in fear and confusion, some tried to turn and run back toward the waterfront, but they collided with those still coming behind them, sending many sprawling to the ground. Chaos reigned.

"In here!" shouted Dixon, pointing to an alley just behind them. They ran into the alley, hurriedly reloading their weapons. At the other end of the alley was a street parallel to the one they had just left, but it was also full of rebels who were running from the battle zone. It appeared that the four were trapped between two numerically superior enemy forces. The overhanging thatched roofs blocked out the limited moonlight, making it almost impossible to see anything.

Pressing his back against the adobe wall, Walker felt it give way slightly. Realizing that he was leaning against a wooden door, he gave a powerful backward kick and smashed the door open. All four quickly ducked into the interior, which was completely black and unlit. From somewhere in the darkness, he heard a suppressed cry of fear. He thought it sounded like it came from an adjacent room. Stepping carefully in the darkness toward the sound, he reached out a hand and found a doorway.

"Over here!" he hissed, not bothering to try to use Spanish. It wasn't necessary—all three shuffled quickly to him, and they moved into the interior of the building just as they heard the sound of rebels in the alley. It sounded like a whole company of fighters were gathered outside the exterior door. They each cocked their weapons, ready for a desperate shoot-out in the dark.

Just then, however, there was a sharp, whistling sound in the sky above and suddenly a terrific explosion knocked them to the floor. A shell fired from the *Napindan* had struck the building just across the alley, blasting its adobe walls into rubble and pulverizing the rebels in the alley with the shards. The exterior wall of the building Walker and the others occupied buckled, and the thatch from the roof crashed down, burying the rebels. A cloud of dust filled the air.

The streets on both sides of the destroyed building were partially blocked with the debris. A cacophony of yelling and shouting ensued as injured men were helped to their feet, and the tightly packed mass was immobilized. There was another sharp whistling sound, and thirty yards further up the street another explosion sent shrapnel, brick, and men flying in all directions. The shouting intensified, with wild gestures and arm-waving. Many of the rebels, in total disarray, raced down the side alleys to get to parallel streets to continue their retreat toward the mountain.

Shells from the two gunboats' cannons continued to rain down upon the streets of Calamba at the rate of about four per minute. The destinations of the projectiles were unpredictable, but they tended to reach further inland with each shot, chasing the fleeing rebels out of the town and into the jungle.

"I think it's clear now," Walker said to Dixon.

"Let's get out of here," agreed Dixon.

"You're Americans?" an incredulous female voice burst out in the darkness.

"Who are you?" asked Walker, shocked.

A match was struck by someone on the far side of the room, and in its bright glow they saw five white Americans huddled in the corner—two women and three men. One of the men held the match to a candle, and it cast a flickering light across the room.

"Harriet!" cried out Walker in amazement. "This is the school building?" In the darkness, he had not recognized it.

Before she could reply, however, a barefoot, dust-covered rebel soldier staggered into the room, having survived the shell blast in the alley.

"Libertad!" he cried hoarsely, as he fired his rifle at the teacher holding the candle. The bullet passed through him and also struck the woman standing behind him. They both fell backward into the corner and the candle, dropping to the floor, was almost extinguished. The rebel had quickly cocked the rifle to fire again when he was hit by a hail of bullets from all four of the scouting party. His body was thrown against the wall and he dropped the rifle, which discharged when it hit the floor.

Harriet was knocked off her feet by the impact of the bullet.

"No! Harriet!" cried out one of the teachers, in horror. It was the young man with the wispy mustache whom Walker had seen earlier. He snatched up the candle and knelt over her. The candlelight revealed the red stain spreading on her white blouse. The other teacher, kneeling beside their two wounded colleagues, called their names in anguish.

"Vera! Andrew!" he begged. "Speak to me!"

Walker and Dixon sprang to their aid. They had seen enough bullet wounds to know how serious it was. Unfortunately, the first bullet had gone through the chests of the two victims—the bleeding was severe and there was bloody froth on their lips. There was nothing that could be done—they did not last long. Harriet was already dead when Walker touched her neck to feel her pulse. He stroked her golden hair gently.

"I'm sorry," he said to the young man. He was too stunned to say more. The other man simply stared, wide-eyed and speechless.

Miguel and Lobo slipped back through the doorway to see if there were any other rebel survivors, and shortly there were three more gunshots. They returned and gave a silent nod.

"We need to get these bodies back down to the camp," said Dixon to Walker. "You and I can each take one, and you two" —pointing to the two teachers— "can take one together."

Dixon grasped the body of the dead male teacher and hoisted it over his shoulder. Walker bent over Harriet's body, but the young man quickly held up his hand in protest.

"I'll carry Harriet," he insisted.

Walker lifted the body of the other woman, and the remaining teacher carried the candle. It was like a bizarre funeral procession under the moonlight. They headed slowly down the street with their burdens, Miguel and Lobo keeping a careful watch for threats. About halfway to the town square, they met a contingent of U.S. soldiers advancing up the street in pursuit of the rebels. The soldiers stepped aside and allowed the funereal march to pass in silence. Several of the men removed their hats as a show of respect for the deceased. They were not used to seeing dead, bloodied white women.

Reaching the bivouac area at the beach, they found the tent where the dead and wounded were gathered. There were seven soldiers' bodies lying in a row on the ground, covered by blankets. All of the soldiers in the area stopped what they were doing and watched quietly as they placed the three teachers' bodies in the row and draped blankets over them. Then, without speaking to anyone, Walker slowly walked to where his bedroll lay on the ground, and stretched out on it. Lying face down, he suddenly could not hold back the tears, and silently wept for the deaths of the three teachers, and especially for Harriet.

He pulled the silver cross from his shirt neck and felt it between his fingers. "You need something to protect you," she had said. *Maybe she should have kept it for herself,* he thought, as his tears ran down into the blanket. He had barely even met her, but he grieved her loss.

Suddenly he felt very lonely and far from home. *Maybe Harriet was right— maybe we shouldn't be here. 'Benevolent assimilation' indeed,* he thought, scornfully. *These people don't deserve our help. She came here to make things better, but now her body lies over there under a blanket.* A heavy wave of sadness came over him, and he just couldn't think about it anymore. Walker closed his eyes, and his exhausted mind and body surrendered to a deep sleep.

19

PAYNE'S REVENGE

The sun was peeking over the mountain, sending its first rays of the day down upon the town of Calamba when Walker awoke to the bugler blowing reveille the next morning. The camp was soon busy with soldiers breaking down tents and packing equipment for transport.

He climbed stiffly to his feet and stretched, wincing at the soreness in his left arm, which reminded him of last night's encounter with the python. Glancing down at himself, he saw that he was caked with mud and blood. He could even feel it in his hair. He would have to wash in the bay, he thought, and let the sun dry him.

He grabbed his mess kit from his knapsack and headed over to where the cooks had prepared steaming caldrons of beans and rice. He spied Miguel and Lobo sitting on the sand, still covered in dried mud and looking rather out of place.

"Hambriento?" he asked, patting his stomach. *Hungry?* They looked at each other awkwardly, and then nodded together.

"Ven!" he said, beckoning and pointing toward the chow line. *Come!* They rose, and with their rifles slung over their shoulders, followed Walker.

"That sure does smell good!" he said, holding out his tin pan to receive a large dipperful of the mixture plopped unceremoniously by the burly cook.

"These two fellas here," he gestured toward the Macabebes, "they saved us from the surprise attack last night. They could use a little grub, too."

"We don't feed their kind," scowled the cook, turning his head to spit on the ground. "They can git their own, some'ere's else."

"I said they saved us last night," protested Walker. "Without them, we'd have a lot of dead soldiers around here this morning."

"And *I* said we don't feed their kind," repeated the cook. "Tell 'em to move along, 'fore I reach for Old Faithful there—" he nodded toward a large butcher knife lying on the table.

"Let me explain myself a little more clearly," said Walker quietly. He pulled the Mauser from his belt, cocked the hammer, pointed it at Old Faithful, and pulled the trigger. The gun roared and Old Faithful flew off the table in two pieces, the handle striking the cook in the groin and the blade narrowly missing his head. Every soldier within a hundred feet turned to watch.

"Listen up," Walker said tersely. "You're gonna take two of them pans," pointing with the pistol at a stack of mess pans, "and you're gonna fill them with that grub—" pointing with the pistol at the cauldron, "and you're gonna do it *now*, or—" and he pointed the barrel at the cook, who was holding his hands over the place where the handle had hit him—"or I'll shoot both of your hands and you'll be peeling 'taters with your teeth for the next month or two."

"Garrett! What the hell are you doing?" It was Captain Pershing, striding rapidly toward them.

"Sir, I'm just getting some breakfast for Miguel and Lobo here, seeing as how they saved our skins from the surprise attack last night. Seems the least we can do, sir."

"I tole him we don't feed—" began the wide-eyed cook, painfully standing up almost straight.

"Two pans!" snapped Pershing. "Fill 'em full. And put a spoon in 'em."

"Yessir!" replied the cook, and quickly obeyed the order.

Pershing himself handed the plates to the two scouts. With a quick nod, he said, "Gracias, amigos!"

They both responded with "Gracias!" and walked away slowly, wolfing down the food.

"Garrett! Follow me!" snapped Pershing. "We have business to attend to."

When they were some distance away, Pershing stopped and turned to Walker. "Finish eating," he said, as he disapprovingly looked Walker up and down. "And then tell me what happened last night."

Pershing waited patiently until Walker finished giving his account of the night's developments. His expression showed his amazement at the python attack, the close call with the artillery shell, and the murder of the teachers by the rebel. Walker was careful to give credit to the Macabebes for their work. He did not know that Pershing had already heard a report from Miguel and Lobo and knew the details.

"Remarkable," Pershing commented thoughtfully, and then, giving Walker a penetrating gaze, repeated himself—"Remarkable."

"You've got a bit of a problem, Garrett," he went on. "Hall and Lawton have returned to the gunboats and are preparing for the return to Manila. They've left Payne in charge on shore, and he wants to see you about your disrespectful comments last evening. I don't know what he has in mind, but I'm sure it won't be pleasant. What-ever you do, keep your mouth shut except to say 'yes sir.' I can't help you this time. I may even be in some trouble, myself."

"Yes sir," responded Walker.

They found Payne standing by the small dock along the shore-line. He was cursing and shouting orders to the soldiers as they broke down the officer tents, apparently making the most of his newfound authority. Walker and Pershing stood a few feet away, waiting. Payne ignored them for several minutes, but finally, tired of shouting and having exhausted his vocabulary of profanity, he turned to face them.

He paced slowly toward them and stopped in front of Walker, hands on hips. "Soldier, you are filthy!" he snarled, shouting the final word.

"Yes sir," said Walker calmly, saluting.

"You are a disgrace to your uniform!" he continued, at high volume. Soldiers working around them stopped what they were doing to watch. "I can barely even *see* your uniform!"

"Yes sir," said Walker again, standing at attention.

"That may be good enough for Alabama, but it's not good enough for the United States Army!" Payne was beginning to get warmed up, pacing back and forth in front of Walker, waving his arms and pointing in Walker's face as he shouted. He employed all of his profanity again, and added a few other choice expressions for additional color. Walker continued to stand stiffly, allowing no expression or reaction to cross his face.

A sizable crowd of spectator soldiers gathered as the tirade lasted fully ten minutes. Payne's voice was becoming hoarse and his face red, with veins standing out on his neck and forehead. Finally noticing the audience, he whirled around with arms spread wide and screamed, "Get back to work! You lazy bunch of gawkers!" He added a stream of obscenities for emphasis, and the men hastily dispersed in all directions.

Turning back to Walker he stood for a moment, glaring and breathing hard. Removing his hat, he wiped the sweat from his brow with a handkerchief. Meticulously refolding the handkerchief, he returned it to his pocket. Finally he spoke, this time in a normal voice.

"Garrett, we've got seven dead soldiers over there under those blankets, and three dead civilians. They're starting to smell. You're going to move those bodies to one of those cascos, and then you're going to paddle it to Manila today, by yourself." Stepping close to Walker and putting his face only inches away from Walker's face, he hissed, "Think you can do that, soldier?"

"Yes sir," said Walker, unflinching. "It will be an honor to escort the bodies of our brave soldiers and those courageous teachers who died serving their country. Thank you, sir." And then he saluted crisply, for good measure.

Payne's eyes narrowed to slits, his lip curled and his face reddened again. He inhaled deeply, as if about to launch into another screaming tirade.

"Major Payne, sir!" cut in Captain Pershing. "How about if I assign Corporal Dixon to assist in moving the bodies, so that they won't fall into the water? It would be an indignity for them to—"

"Who's in charge here, Captain Pershing?" roared Payne. He was so angry he could hardly speak.

"You are, sir," replied Pershing coolly.

"And don't you forget it, Captain! I said he's to move them himself, and that's what he will do—unless you want to help him yourself, Captain?"

"Yes sir," Pershing spoke softly. "I'll do that, sir."

The two locked eyes for several seconds before Major Payne furiously wheeled about and stormed off to shout and curse at some soldiers down the beach.

Pershing turned to Walker and said matter-of-factly, "You get the heads and I'll get the feet."

Together they carried the ten bodies to the casco. Even with the broad, flat-bottomed boat pulled up to the shore line, they still had to wade more than knee-deep into the water, depositing their heavy burdens carefully. They climbed into the boat to arrange the bodies three abreast, with four across the broader midsection, overlapping the heads and feet. Walker took advantage of the opportunity to put his head underwater, washing most of the mud and blood off his face.

"Well, that's an improvement, somewhat," remarked Pershing.

"Thank you, sir."

"You've got four oars," Pershing noted dryly, pointing into the boat. "If you wear one out, at least you've got three spares."

"No sir," came a voice from the shore. It was Corporal Dixon. "Two spares."

He splashed into the water, climbed over the side of the casco into the stern, and picked up one of the oars.

"Major Payne's orders are for Garrett to row the boat to Manila by himself, Corporal Dixon," said Pershing.

"Yes sir," said Dixon respectfully. "But it's near forty miles and there are hostiles along the way. It's a suicide mission for one man alone. I'll deal with whatever the major wants to do to me, but this is a two-man job."

"Three!" came another voice from the shore. The young teacher with the wispy mustache waded into the bay and climbed into the bow. "I'm in," he declared, and picked up one of the oars, studying it as if figuring out how to use it.

Miguel and Lobo appeared out of nowhere and helped Walker push the boat off, and then climbed in. Miguel took the second oar in the stern, next to Dixon, leaning his rifle against the side. Lobo crouched midway with his rifle at the ready.

Pershing surveyed the group and then cleared his throat. "Don't wear those oars out— you don't have any spares."

"Yes sir," said Walker, saluting.

"Forty miles against the current— it's going to be a very long and difficult day."

"Not too bad, sir! The current goes out in the afternoon, with the tide. That will make things a lot easier."

"Very well, Garrett," said Pershing, with a tone of surprise. "I'll see you all in Manila, then. Good luck!"

They paddled out into Laguna de Bay and turned the casco north by northwest. It was more than twenty miles to the Rio Pasig in a straight line and, with only four oars, progress was slow. It was still several hours until the tide would begin to flow out toward Manila Bay. Payne had been right— the bodies were beginning to smell. The hot sun was making the odor worse by the hour, and Walker felt guilty for thinking it, but he was glad he was in the bow and not in the stern of the boat.

Walker was not in the mood to talk, so he paddled silently and steadily, favoring his bruised and sore left arm. As they left the town and the gunboats behind, the only sounds were that of the water lapping against the sides of the casco, and the soft splashing of the oars. There came a distant rumbling of thunder, and they could see dark clouds on the horizon.

"It will rain this afternoon," remarked the teacher. "It usually does, this time of year."

"Should cool things down a little," Walker said, wiping sweat from his brow.

"I could use a bath 'bout now," called Dixon, from the rear of the boat.

"You'll get a good one, soon," the teacher called back. And then it was silent paddling again for a long period.

"I could use a drink of water 'bout now, too," Dixon called again, breaking the silence. "Wish we'd brung some canteens."

They heard a sound like that of thunder again, but coming from behind them.

"El barcos!" cried Lobo, pointing toward the rear. *The boats!*

It was the two gunboats, the *Napindan* and *Oeste*, their steam engines grumbling as black smoke rose from their stacks. They were crowded with officers, and the soldiers were crammed into the long string of cascos being towed behind. The *Oeste* chugged past them first, setting their small boat to bobbing in its widening wake. The soldiers being towed behind it began to whoop and wave their hats, some saluting as they glided past. It was hard to understand what they were saying, but Walker caught the word 'python' several times. Apparently the story about the previous night's adventure had gotten around. As the last casco in the line passed them, the soldiers flung several canteens of water toward them. They fell short, but Lobo dove overboard and retrieved them. The paddlers waved and shouted their thanks.

As the *Napindan* cruised past, Walker noticed Major Payne standing at the side railing, glaring at them. *Uh-oh*, thought Walker. *He's going to be fit to be tied, seeing that I'm not paddling this boat by myself. He'll probably explode when we get to Manila.*

The soldiers in the cascos behind the *Napindan* threw more canteens and a couple of knapsacks, all of which were fetched by Lobo. They found that the knapsacks contained fruit and hardtack. There were more salutes, whoops and waves, and shouts of "Python Man!"

The last two boats in the line were occupied by the soldiers of the Tenth. Sitting in the bow of the first boat was Captain Pershing, his eyes fixed straight ahead. *Why isn't he on the gunboat with the other officers?* wondered Walker. And then it dawned on him that Pershing was not the kind of officer who would enjoy privileges denied to his men. The Tenth Cavalry Regiment was his command, and he would always be found with his men.

As the last casco moved past them, one of the men stood up in the back of the boat and whirled something twice around his head, flinging it toward them. It was a canteen full of water, but with a rope tied to it. The other end of the rope was tied to the rear of their casco. The soldiers made urgent signs that they were to tie it to their boat. It fell about ten feet short, but right next to Lobo, who quickly threw it to Walker.

Time was of the essence, as the gunboat was plowing the swells beyond them and was pulling rapidly away. Walker untied the rope from the ring of the canteen and looped it twice around the cross board on which they sat in the bow.

"Tie that!" he rasped at the teacher, who frantically knotted it in a clumsy but serviceable knot. Walker ripped off his shirt and used it to grip the rope tightly, bracing his feet against the hull of the bow. With no time to spare— the rope immediately began to tighten, pulling through Walker's hands which, even though protected by the shirt, became very hot. He grunted loudly with the exertion as he gripped the rope and strained against the hull, forcing the boat to slowly accelerate, helped along by vigorous paddling by Dixon and Miguel. When all of the slack in the rope was gone, the rope snapped out of Walker's hands and the boat jerked forward.

Walker held his breath, fearing that the board would break under the sudden strain or that the knot would slip, but they both held firm. The casco moved smoothly and briskly into line with the others. He looked back to see Lobo, grinning and dripping wet, having just clambered back into the midsection of the boat. All five of them raised their arms and whooped in celebration, and Walker pumped his fist in the air. The soldiers of the Tenth were just as excited, laughing and cheering for them.

He put his hands into the water to cool them, and then put his shirt back on. It was almost in shreds, and his hands were beet red. *There will be blisters by evening*, he thought. *But they'll be worth it.*

They laid the oars aside and relaxed. Passing a canteen to each man, they helped themselves to the fruit and hardtack.

"Good job!" Walker said to the teacher. "That knot did the trick."

"Good job, yourself," he replied, peeling a banana. "If you hadn't done that with the rope, that board would have snapped in two and we'd be sitting back there in the bay with four oars."

"We'll probably catch hell for this in Manila," called Dixon.

"I'll be a buck private again by morning, probably," Walker called back.

Their conversation was interrupted by a loud crash of thunder, followed by a long series of rumbling, banging sounds in the black clouds above, fading into the distance. The sun was suddenly blocked by the massive dark cloud, and a cool breeze blew briskly over them, making the hair on the back of Walker's neck stand up.

"Here it comes!" yelled the teacher.

"I wish they'd put some ponchos in them knapsacks," shouted Dixon, as the downpour swept across the water like a gray curtain and enveloped them in a drenching rain. The thunder was continuous and deafening, punctuated with brilliant lightning flashes which crackled ominously across the sky. There was nothing to do but sit and endure it. The deluge lasted for more than two hours, until the naval procession completed its crossing of Laguna de Bay and was entering the Rio Pasig.

The reappearance of the sun made it seem as if there had been no rain storm at all. Steam rose from their clothes, and from the neat rows of bodies. The rain had suppressed the odor, but it now returned. There were several inches of water standing in the boat, but there was nothing to bail it out with, so they rode onward with the water sloshing back and forth as the boat bobbed along.

"What's your name, Teacher?" asked Walker. "I'm Walker Garrett."

"Douglas Franklin," he replied. "Harriet is— was— my sister."

"Oh!" was all Walker could say. That was not at all what he had expected. He managed to add, "Sorry— that's awful— I mean, it's terrible to lose your sister. I'm sorry."

"You have no idea how terrible it is," Franklin said, his head drooping. "I don't know how I'm going to tell our mother. She didn't want us to come here, but I promised I would take care of Harriet. I guaranteed that she would come home safe and sound. And now—" he glanced over his shoulder at the bodies lying under the wet blankets and winced as if in physical pain. He sighed heavily, and did not finish the sentence.

"It wasn't your fault," began Walker, trying to console him.

"Fault!" exclaimed Franklin in amazement. "What difference does it make whose fault it is? My beautiful, sweet, kind, loving sister is dead! We will never again hear the sound of her laughter, the angelic notes of her singing hymns in church, the wisdom of her prayers. She was making a difference in the world, ministering to these poor children, and now this! Who cares whose *fault* it is?"

"Yes, of course— I didn't mean— I just— you are quite, uh, right — it's terrible, just terrible—" Walker was fumbling for thoughts and words.

"In fact, if it's anybody's fault, it's yours!" accused Franklin, turning to glare angrily at Walker.

"Mine!" exclaimed Walker in shock, spreading his hands in innocence. "What did I do to cause her death?"

"Maybe not you personally, but you are a U.S. soldier and it's the U.S. policy of imperialism, forcing our country's rule upon the Filipinos, that led to this. Didn't you hear what the rebel shouted as he shot Vera and Andrew? He shouted 'Libertad!' That means Liberty! These three wonderful teachers were killed because the Filipinos want to be free, and the U.S. Army won't let them. It's like Harriet told you— the rebels wouldn't be rebels if you weren't here. If it's anybody's fault, it's the army, and you're part of the army, Garrett. You helped kill Harriet, Vera, and Andrew."

Walker seriously considered punching Franklin in the face. He clenched his fists and shifted his weight on the board, turning toward the other man. Before he could act, however, a voice spoke from the rear of the boat.

"You're just as guilty, Franklin!" called Dixon.

"What?" exploded Franklin, twisting about to glare at Dixon. "What kind of ridiculous statement is that? You don't know what you are talking about!"

"Think about it," said Dixon, evenly and firmly. "Military and political control over a country is one thing, but church and family is even more important. These folks is Catholic and speak Spanish. You teachers was taking their children and teaching 'em English, and diff'rent religious ideas. It wasn't no accident that that rebel shot teachers instead of soldiers. You all are just as much the enemy to the Filipinos as us soldiers are. Maybe more. If there's fault to be had here, there's 'nuff to go around for everybody."

"Preposterous!" Franklin almost screamed the word. "We are here to help these people! We are not the enemy!"

"Tell that to the Filipinos," mocked Dixon. "They decide who's the enemy. And it looks like you all's on the list, whether you like it or not."

Franklin leaped to his feet and whirled about, pointing his finger at Dixon. "How dare you— a Negro— judge me!" he cried passionately. "My grandparents were abolitionists. My parents went south and taught in the Freedman's Bureau schools after the war, before their school was burned down by the Ku Klux Klan. They named me for Frederick Douglass, and Harriet for both Harriet Beecher Stowe and Harriet Tubman. For three generations, we Franklins have spent our lives fighting for justice for your people!

"You, on the other hand, are a hypocrite!" he continued furiously. "As soon as you had freedom for yourself, what did you do? You joined the army and went off to the Plains to kill the Indians and imprison the survivors on barren reservations. Hundreds of thousands of Union soldiers died fighting for your freedom, but you take up arms to deny it to the Indians, and now to the Filipinos. That is the worst sort of hypocrisy!" Finished, he glared triumphantly at Dixon.

"If you really believe in justice for colored people," replied Dixon, "I guess you'll be giving your land back to the Injuns when you get back home. Right?"

Franklin gasped wordlessly and gave his head a shake as if trying to clear his thoughts. He was clearly dumbfounded.

"I'm sorry your sister and your two friends are dead," Dixon went on. "We lost seven of ours. Y'all chose to be here. Us— not so much. But we got a job to do, and we're doing it. Truth be told, your job and ours ain't all that much differ'nt. We both forcing American ways down the throats of people that don't want it.

Gesturing toward the blanket-covered bodies, he shook his head. "Being a winner is better'n being a loser, but winning costs something, too. And sometimes you wonder if it's worth it."

There was an awkward silence when Dixon finished. And then, with perfect timing the casco jerked, pulled into a curve of the winding river. Franklin, facing the rear of the boat, was unprepared for it and lost his balance, falling helplessly over the side into the river with a loud splash. Lobo reached out and grabbed his arm as the boat moved past him, helping Franklin back into the boat. Franklin spoke a few words to Lobo in Spanish, and Lobo then moved carefully over the bodies to the bow and took the seat next to Walker. Franklin took Lobo's seat in the midsection and sat alone for the rest of the trip. No one spoke.

Traveling on the Pasig was slower than crossing the bay due to the extremely circuitous route of the river, snaking its way fifteen miles to Manila. Its width varied from about seventy-five yards at its narrowest, to as much as two hundred yards as it neared the Bay of Manila. The banks were lined with huts, vegetable gardens and fields, and the ever-present dense jungle. As soon as the flotilla began to pass, all of the Filipinos hurried into the huts or forest, and by the time Walker's boat finally glided past at the end of the procession, there was no one to be seen. Even the animals were taken into hiding. It was eerie, he thought, like ghost-towns.

It was late afternoon when they finally arrived at the harbor in Manila, and in the hustle and bustle of moving the men and gear from the boats to the fort, Walker lost contact with Franklin. He caught a final glimpse of him following a cart bearing the bodies of the three slain teachers. Walker never saw him again.

Walker just had time to wash up and put on clean clothes before reporting to the mess hall for supper. When he arrived he found the men of the Tenth standing in a group outside the door while white troops filed in. Walker started to join the line of white soldiers, but then, before his eyes he saw again the sight of Captain Pershing sitting in the bow of the casco with his regiment, declining to enjoy the more comfortable gunboat with the other officers. He stopped abruptly, apologized to the man who bumped into him from behind, and stepped aside. He casually strolled past the group of black soldiers and took his place at the end of their line.

One of the sergeants walked back to where Walker stood. "What are you doing back here, Garrett?"

"I'm with my unit, sergeant— where I belong."

"The other whites in our unit are already in there eating."

"Yes, sergeant, but I'm not an officer. I know my place."

The sergeant looked intently at Walker for several seconds before turning away and going back to his place up the line.

"I hear we got snake meat for supper!" called out a soldier, provoking laughs and mock screams of "No!" up the line, as some of the men turned to look at Walker, grinning.

"I'd rather have snake meat for supper, than be a snake's meat for supper!" rejoined Walker. The whole company burst into loud hoots and laughs, some clapping their approval.

"Alright, men! Let's go!" It was Captain Pershing, standing at the entrance with Miguel and Lobo behind him. The captain had a small paper-wrapped bundle under his arm. As the Tenth filed rapidly into the mess hall, each man saluted the captain, who held a stiff salute until the last man had entered.

Pershing and the two Macabebes went to the front of the line. The cook was the same man who was in Calamba earlier that morning.

He glared at Pershing and the Filipinos, jutting his jaw forward like a bulldog.

"Three!" said Pershing, with his thumb indicating himself and the two scouts. When the cook did not move immediately, he added, "Before I bring Private Garrett over here."

The cook blinked, scowled, and snapped at his line servers, "Three! Load 'em up!" The line of waiting soldiers erupted in a loud cheer, causing everyone in the room to turn and look.

They made their way to the far end of the large hall to some empty tables and benches. Pershing seated himself at the head of one of the tables, placing the bundle on the floor beside him, and directed Miguel and Lobo to sit at each side. As the Tenth filled the benches, Pershing motioned for Dixon to take a seat next to them, and then Walker also.

At the conclusion of the meal, Pershing stood and called for the men's attention. The tables became quiet and everyone turned to face the captain.

"I congratulate you all on a job well done," he began. "The Tenth Cavalry performed its assigned tasks in the usual exemplary way. We are fortunate that none of our number were killed, and only three were wounded. Only one of the wounded is serious enough to require hospitalization, and that is Sergeant Harris. He is expected to fully recover, but it will take several weeks, and he may have to return to the States. I encourage you to find time to go by the medical ward and visit him. In the meantime, we are short a sergeant."

Pershing picked up the bundle from the floor and took from it a uniform shirt with sergeant stripes on the sleeves, holding it up for all to see. "To fill that position we need a man of courage, skill, and leadership ability, and who enjoys the confidence and respect of the unit. There is no one who demonstrates these qualities more than Corporal L. G. Dixon."

Dixon's jaw dropped, as the room was again filled with cheering and applause. Some of the men banged on the tables and stomped their feet, whooping. A couple scampered over to thump Dixon on the back, then hurried back to their seats.

Pershing motioned Dixon to stand. Handing him the shirt, he said, "Sergeant Dixon, you've earned this promotion, and I know you'll do us proud." More cheers and applause followed.

"Now, this leaves us short a corporal," continued Pershing, pulling another shirt from the paper. He held up this shirt, showing the corporal's stripes on the sleeves. "For this position we need a man of courage and fighting ability, one who is loyal to our unit, is cool in a crisis, and who enjoys the respect of our men. Many of you fit this description, but one soldier stands out with distinction. Our new corporal is—" he paused ever so briefly— "our own regimental snake-charmer and boat-paddler-in-chief, Private First-Class Walker Garrett."

There was a brief second of silence, as if the men weren't sure how to respond, but then the cheering and applause burst out, gaining in volume with more whooping, table-banging, foot-stomping, and back-thumping.

When all was quiet again, Pershing concluded his remarks. "I'm proud to be the commander of such a fine outfit as this. Tomorrow we resume patrols in the countryside, so get a good night's sleep. Dixon and Garrett— I need to see you before you leave."

As the men rose, gathered their plates and headed for the exit, Dixon and Walker, along with Miguel and Lobo, waited for Pershing. He motioned them to come closer, and then, quietly, in a tone of confidentiality, the captain spoke.

"There's been an unexpected development," he said. "A courier for Aguinaldo has been captured and we may have a chance to find where he is hiding out. The courier was carrying a coded message asking for reinforcements to be sent to Aguinaldo's camp. General MacArthur has approved a plan proposed by Major General Funston to exploit this opportunity, but it is very dangerous. He proposes to use Macabebe scouts, posing as the reinforcements. He and some other American soldiers will pretend to be prisoners, and the Macabebes will take them to the camp. I've recommended Miguel and Lobo to lead the Macabebes— they're the best scouts we've got. They have asked that you two go with them. They trust you. You don't have to accept this assignment. It's highly unusual to detach soldiers from their unit for a secret mission like this, but this could be a big opportunity. The decision is yours.

"One of the benefits of accepting," Pershing added wryly, with a grim twinkle in his eye, "is that you would leave tonight, before Major Payne can track you down."

"Count me in, Captain!" responded Walker instantly.

"I'm on board, too, Captain, sir!" seconded Dixon.

"I thought so," nodded Pershing. "Get your gear and get down to the dock. The boat leaves on the hour."

20

EN ROUTE TO CASIGURAN

The USS *Vicksburg* was a three-masted gunboat, capable of using sails or steam power. Boasting twelve cannons—the largest being four-inchers firing a thirty-three pound shell—and with a new air-cooled Colt-Browning machine gun, it was well-equipped for dealing with the lightly-armed rebel forces. Steaming out of the Manila harbor that night under the hazy aura of a tropical moon, it turned south, and by sun-up was heading east through the Verde Island Passage. It would take two and a half days to reach Casiguran Bay on the eastern shore of Luzon.

On board, besides the crew, were eighty Macabebe scouts and newly-promoted Major General Frederick Funston, with a half-dozen American officers and soldiers. Conditions were crowded, and most of the men preferred to lounge on the deck to take advantage of the cooler night air. During the day they sought the interior shade to escape the blazing sun.

At the end of the first full day, as the sun was setting, the captain shut down the steam engine and the crew unfurled the sails. It was the first time that Walker had actually been on a sailing ship, and the beauty of the sails as they filled with the wind took his breath away.

As he stood on the deck looking upward at the billowing canvas, one of the young crew members, apparently about Walker's own age, slapped him on the back.

"Quite a sight, ain't it!"

"Yes, it is! I've never seen sails up close like this before. It's really beautiful!"

"Want to see 'em even closer? I'm about to head up to the crow's nest." He gestured to a telescope slung over his shoulder by a strap. "You can come along if you want."

"You mean up there?" Walker gasped in disbelief, pointing to the perch high on the forward mast.

The sailor laughed. "Kinda scary the first time, but once you get up there, you'll love it."

"Alright, let's go," Walker agreed, taking a deep breath. "You lead the way and I'll follow."

The sailor scampered up the rigging like a monkey. Walker tried to keep up, but as he climbed higher above the deck and looked down, he froze. Gripping the ropes tightly, he climbed slowly, step by step. Looking up, he saw the sailor already in the lookout station, grinning down at him. Gritting his teeth, he pushed himself to go faster. The massive sails seemed so much larger now that he was up in the midst of them, and the flapping and popping noises they made in the wind were much louder than he had expected. The ship's rising and falling motion, combined with rolling side to side, gave him the sensation of falling as his weight shifted uncontrollably and the rigging swayed with him. It was quite terrifying, actually, and more than once he thought that he would fall to his death. He clambered awkwardly into the cage at last, and sat down on the flooring, gasping for breath.

"That's the way ever'body does it, first time!" grinned the sailor. "I'm kinda s'prised you made it at all. Not bad for a soldier!"

The sailor scanned the horizon with the telescope, standing with feet spread and swaying easily as the ship rolled and rocked. Walker slowly and carefully rose to his feet, holding onto the mast, the wind ruffling his hair. The view was gorgeous. There was a golden glow in the sky, and the setting sun created brilliant red and purple colors in the clouds and across the water. Islands were visible in the distance on both sides, and flocks of birds could be seen. He saw a school of porpoises not far from the ship, arcing their way through the water. Walker was mesmerized by the beauty of it all, the silence broken only by the cracking sounds of the sails.

"What's your name, sailor?"

"Seaman George Watkins. Yours?"

"Priv— I mean, Corporal Walker Garrett." Walker pointed to the telescope. "What are you looking for, Watkins? The Filipino rebels don't have any ships. There's no threats to be watching out for, are there?"

"Not really. Just following regulations, mainly. But it never hurts to be on the safe side. Don't want to be s'prised, y'know." Watkins handed the telescope to Walker. "Have a look! Face the bow and brace your feet like this. Then you can use both hands on the scope."

Walker found that putting his back against the mast and spreading his feet widely gave him enough stability that he could free his hands. He spent several minutes inspecting the distant islands, the birds in flight, the porpoises, and the clouds.

"We better head back down now," said Watkins. "It gets dark fast when the sun sets, and you don't want to be climbing down that rigging in the dark."

The descent was not quite as challenging for Walker as the ascent, though his heart was still in his throat for part of the way. Watkins was waiting for him when he finally reached the deck. The deck had never seemed like such a stable place to him before, but now it was almost as good as solid ground. He heaved a sigh of relief as he let go of the rigging.

Watkins clapped him on the back again. "Well done, Garrett! Come back tomorrow and we'll do it again!" And without further ado, he disappeared through a doorway.

"Well, Corporal Garrett, you are a man of surprises."

Walker turned to face Dixon. "You should try it. It's really beautiful up there when the sun is setting."

"Ain't no way I'm climbing up them ropes. If God had a-wanted me to climb up a bunch of ropes to a bucket like that, he woulda give me a tail."

"It was pretty scary," admitted Walker, "but I think it wouldn't be so bad the second time. I think I'll take him up on that offer to do it again tomorrow."

"Help yo' self. If you don't make it, I'll write 'nother letter home for you."

"Be sure and tell 'em I made corporal."

Dixon laughed. And then he became serious. "You got any letter-writin' things, like paper, pencil, and all that?" he asked, seeming a little self-conscious. "I need to write my mama and my sister. Been a long time."

"Sure, Sarge. I'll get it for you after supper."

As Walker watched Dixon walk away, he thought it seemed that Dixon was less hostile than he'd been in the past. He wondered if it was just his imagination.

After eating, Walker stepped into the bunk room to get the writing materials from his pack. To his surprise he found Dixon already lying in his hammock with one leg hanging out, toes on the floor, gently rocking the hammock from side to side.

"You feelin' alright, Dixon?"

"Yeah, I'm fine," he replied, a bit startled. "Just thinkin'."

"What's that you've got there?"

"This?" He held up a small object he'd been holding. It was a white, crocheted square with a red heart, and a blue ribbon tied in a bow.

"Just a little somethin' Daisy sent me. She crochets these little things and sells them. This one has a heart in it—" he held it out for Walker to see. Walker took it and studied it closely.

"She made these to sell for Valentine's Day. She makes 'em with stars for Christmas, and crosses for Easter. Sells 'em for a dime apiece. Says she's already saved near five dollahs."

Walker slowly handed it back. "That's amazing. Daisy is a really sweet girl."

"And smart, too," added Dixon. "She's growing up into a mighty fine young lady. I hope she can make a good life for herself. Maybe get married and have her own house. Move up north somewheres. I don't know."

"Yeah, hope so," Walker said gruffly, clearing his throat. "Here's a couple sheets of paper and a pencil. Just toss it on my hammock when you're done with it."

Walker went back out to the deck and stood by the rail, watching the last rays of the sun disappear behind the ocean's horizon. Reaching into the breast pocket over his heart, he took out the creased yellow envelope and held up the crocheted square between his fingers to catch the dim light. He felt disturbed and sad at the same time. He struggled to sort out his feelings.

So, Abigail Dancy didn't really make this herself, after all. She bought it from Daisy for ten cents, and told me it was her own work. I've been a fool, thinking that she cared about me. Her, a girl from a wealthy, important family. Me, a boy from the country, son of a plantation overseer. What was I thinking? That probably explains why I've gotten only short notes from her. Why did I waste my time writing her all those letters? I've been such a fool.

Walker grimaced and shook his head. He slipped the crocheted square back into the envelope. Holding it out over the railing, he contemplated it briefly, and then let it fall into the ocean swells below.

It was as if a piece of himself had been tossed aside, and he suddenly felt deflated. Realizing that there wasn't someone special on the other side of the world who was thinking about him made him feel painfully alone. He reached into the neck of his shirt and pulled out the silver chain with the small, silver cross. His thoughts went back to Harriet, and he remembered the way it felt when she fastened the chain around his neck. He had hardly met her, but he still felt her loss keenly. Somehow she seemed more real and alive to him than Abigail Dancy. Leaning on the railing with both hands, staring out at the ocean, he scowled, beginning to feel angry.

Abruptly he turned and walked aimlessly down the deck, staggering unsteadily as the ship rolled. With one particularly strong roll, he careened against the side of the ship and almost fell into an open doorway. There was an immediate chorus of voices shouting his name— "Wolka! Wolka!" It was the Macabebe scouts, sitting on the floor among the swinging hammocks. There were a few naked light bulbs dangling from the ceiling, and he could see that they were playing some kind of game.

He stepped into the room and they all clapped and hooted their approval. Miguel motioned for him to sit next to him, and with words and signs explained that they were having a wrestling contest. Two Macabebes faced each other on their knees, stripped to the waist, hands on each other's shoulders. At a signal they began to strain and grunt, while those watching cheered for one or the other. Eventually one would be toppled to the floor and the contest was over, and two more men took their positions.

"Wolka! Wolka!" some of the men began to chant, and the rest of the group took it up. Miguel grinned and punched Walker in the shoulder, pointing to the open space where the wrestling took place.

After first waving his hands and shaking his head, Walker could see that there was no getting out of it, so he crawled out to the middle of the area. More cheers erupted. He found himself facing the huskiest Filipino of all, a short, stocky, muscular man. Shirts removed, they gripped each other's shoulders, awaiting the signal. The noise inside the room was almost deafening.

Miguel slapped the steel floor with his palm, and the match was on. Walker was almost toppled within seconds, but was able to keep his knees under him by sliding them along the floor and twisting his torso. The sturdy Filipino had a lower center of gravity, but Walker's longer arms gave him a leverage advantage. After an exhaustingly long minute of straining, Walker drew closer to his opponent and, with his left arm, pushed hard to the right. The man braced himself on his left knee, resisting the pressure, when suddenly Walker reversed, throwing all his strength into his right arm with a leftward shove. The Macabebe couldn't compensate in time and lost his balance, falling to the floor amid explosive cheering and shouting from the crowd.

Walker grabbed the man's hand and pulled him back up. Leaning in with hands clasped, they slapped each other on the shoulder.

"Muy bueno!" They shook hands, and Walker grabbed his shirt and stood up. There were calls for another match, but he waved them off this time and headed for the deck outside. It was stiflingly hot in the room, and he was glistening with sweat.

Stepping through the doorway into the fresh air, he almost ran into Lieutenant Hazzard, one of the officers on General Funston's staff.

"What's going on in there, Corporal?"

"Sir! Just a little fun, sir. The Macabebes are having a wrestling contest."

"Why are you so sweaty? Were you wrestling, too?"

"Yes sir, just one match, sir." Walker added, "I won, sir."

"Damn sure better have won!" exclaimed the lieutenant. "Can't have the darkies thinking they're better than us! Got to keep 'em in their place!"

"They're on our side, sir," said Walker, "and it's just a friendly game."

"Nothing is 'just a friendly game,' soldier!" snapped the officer. "They may be on our side for now, but they're just Filipinos under the skin. Mark my words, someday we'll have to shoot them, same as we shoot the others!"

"But sir," protested Walker. "We're trusting these men with our lives on this mission. There's seven of us and eighty of them, and we'll be in the jungle together for days. I don't think—"

"Don't think *what*, Corporal?" rasped the lieutenant, putting his face close to Walker's in a threatening manner. "Do you think they're helping us out of the goodness of their hearts? They'll be our allies as long as it serves their interests. And when it doesn't—" he drew a quick line across his throat. "Be ready, soldier!"

"Yes sir," responded Walker softly. "I'll be ready, sir."

Lieutenant Hazzard turned and staggered like a drunkard along the rolling deck until he reached the officers' quarters, and then lunged through the doorway, closing the door behind him. Walker stood for a moment, gazing out to sea, and then turned and went back into the crowded, steamy bunk room and joined in the clapping and cheering for the wrestlers.

21

AGUINALDO

It was nighttime on the third day of the voyage when they finally reached their destination at Casiguran Bay, and they rowed to shore in small boats in the dark. Ahead of them lay a ninety-mile march up the east coast of the island to the village of Palanan, in the mountains of Isabella Province. The march was expected to take seven days, but each man was issued only three days' rations and ammunition for his rifle. They hired a local man to guide them. He was told that these were reinforcements requested by Aguinaldo, along with some important American prisoners. He seemed quite happy to see Americans as prisoners, and enthusiastically agreed to lead the way.

The Macabebes wore the uniforms of the insurgent forces, as did Dixon, whose brown skin matched that of the Filipinos well. The white Americans, including General Funston, all wore the uniforms of infantry privates, pretending to be prisoners.

The roads were increasingly rugged, and after the midpoint of the journey, nonexistent. They forded streams, climbed steep cliffs, and sometimes had to wade out into the ocean to get around massive boulders or mangrove thickets. It was the most difficult terrain on the island of Luzon.

There were no tents, of course. Each man slept on the ground, with only a blanket. Unfortunately it rained frequently, so the ground was always wet. The conditions were absolutely miserable. Walker slept poorly, unable to put his nighttime battle with the python out of his mind. The serpent's teeth marks were still visible in his bruised upper left arm. Even while clambering over rocks and following Miguel on the narrow trails, he constantly surveyed the trees overhead for any sign of jungle predators.

They eventually left the coast and turned inland, climbing into the higher elevations as they drew closer to the village of Palanan. They cut back to two meals a day to conserve their rations and even resorted to eating snails, but still ran out of food by the sixth day. Finally, weak from lack of food, they could go no further. They collapsed to the ground, exhausted.

Funston summoned Miguel and Lobo, careful to escape the notice of the guide. Dixon and Walker accompanied them to hear what the general had to say.

"We aren't going to make it without help," he gasped, sitting with his back against a tree. "You two—" pointing to the Macabebes, "You take the guide and go to Aguinaldo and ask for assistance. Ask him to send food. Tell him you are bringing prisoners and reinforcements."

One of the other Filipinos translated, and Miguel and Lobo then talked to each other in low but animated voices. It was clear that they were not enthusiastic about the assignment, but they nodded their consent and, taking the guide, disappeared into the dense forest. It would take several hours for them to reach the village and return down the mountain with the aid, if Aguinaldo did send anything. The survival of the company depended on their bringing food soon.

All of the men sprawled alongside the trail. No one spoke. Walker looked carefully about for snakes, and chose a resting place as far away from trees and bushes as possible so that he could see anything that approached. A stout stick in his hand, he sat on a rock, his head swiveling slowly from side to side as he kept watch.

"You just like a long-tailed cat in a room full of rocking chairs," said Dixon, clapping Walker on the back. Walker, startled, leaped off his perch and whirled about.

"Don't sneak up on me like that!" he hissed furiously. "I could have knocked your head off!"

Dixon stepped back and held up both hands in innocence. "Don't go swinging that thing at me. I ain't no snake."

Walker heaved a deep breath, trying to relax. "I can't get that off my mind," he said apologetically. "You don't know how big that snake was. His head was that long—" he held up his hands more than a foot apart.

"I can't even imagine it," said Dixon, shaking his head. "I woulda just died right there on the spot."

"If I hadn't had that machete I wouldn't be here today."

"Well, I don't think no snake is goin' to come in here in the middle of almost ninety men to get his supper. You can relax, Corporal Garrett."

"That's true," Walker conceded and lay down on the damp ground, looking up into the lofty branches at the distant fragments of blue sky.

Dixon took a seat on the rock and pushed his hat onto the back of his head, scratching the week's worth of beard stubble covering his cheeks.

"What do you think of what Funston is doing?" he asked quietly, glancing about to make sure no Americans were within earshot.

"What do you mean?"

"Think about it. Aguinaldo is the enemy. We are about to attack his camp and try to capture him, which is perfectly alright in a war, except that our men are wearing enemy uniforms. And now here we are, starving and begging him to send us food to save our lives. Are we going to eat the food he sends, and then attack his camp? That don't seem quite right, to me. You don't bite the hand that feeds you."

"Well, it's— " began Walker. "It's like— I think— You don't— I mean—" And then he fell silent, his brow furrowed in thought. After a long moment, he finally sat up and said in exasperation, "Dang it Dixon, why do you always think of things like this?"

"Things like what's fair, right, and decent?"

"Yeah!" retorted Walker, and then realized what he'd said. "No!" he quickly added. Then, confused, he scowled and slammed the stick on the ground. "Hell. I don't know anything anymore. I'm just a mess. Double hell."

"Yo' mama wouldn't like hearing you talk like that, Corporal Garrett."

"Mama ain't here, Sergeant Dixon," he snapped, and then added, "fortunately."

"If my mama was here, she'd know how to fix this mess," Dixon chuckled.

"Yes, she would," agreed Walker. "She'd have 'em all sitting at a table together eatin' collard greens, cornbread, peas, and fried okra." They laughed, somewhat ruefully.

"I'm thinking of taking up smoking," said Walker. "Mama wouldn't like that, neither."

"I tried it. Waste of money," opined Dixon. "Why don't you take up drinkin' instead? At least that way you can have fun, 'cept you don't remember it later, and you feel like hell."

"Oh yes, that sounds much better," said Walker sarcastically. "Sign me up for that."

They were silent for a while, and then Walker spoke. "I don't guess there's nothing we can do about it," he said slowly. "If Aguinaldo sends food, I'm sure going to eat it. And if Funston has the Macs attack and capture him, I don't see what I can do. I'm not even sure why I'm here."

"I'll eat it too," said Dixon. "But I don't think this plan is going to work. This whole expedition has been a disaster from the beginning. Three days' rations for a seven-day march through the most God-awful country you ever saw? You got to be kidding. And I ain't ever eatin' another snail long as I live, even if I starve to death."

He shook his head pessimistically. "Mark my words, Garrett—justice is not on our side here. We don't deserve to win this thing, and odds are neither of us will live to tell the tale. If you ever see yo' mama again, you'll know it's God's doin'. It ain't in our hands no more." He then strolled away to find a comfortable spot under a small tree, where he curled up to sleep. Walker resumed his seat on the rock, stick in hand, scanning in all directions.

Darkness came quickly when the sun set. Walker had begun to wonder if Miguel and Lobo would ever return when suddenly there came a shout from the trail above them. Everyone rose to their feet, shouldering rifles and cocking revolvers. The three men staggered into view through the foliage carrying large bags of rice and leather skins of water. In their weakened condition it was a miracle they had made it at all.

Hoarse shouts of joy went up from parched, dry throats, and there was a mad rush to the bags of food. By the time the rice had been consumed it was completely black under the jungle canopy. Walker couldn't see his own hand in front of his face. With a full stomach and tired, aching muscles, he couldn't help relaxing, despite still feeling a need to surveille the area. Before long, he dropped off into the deepest sleep he had experienced since the fight with the python, and didn't wake until morning.

The next day they finally reached their destination. The small village of Palanan was pleasantly situated on the banks of the Palanan River, a rain-swollen stream about a hundred yards wide. The village consisted of a main street and several side streets, the main house serving as Aguinaldo's headquarters. The previous day had been Aguinaldo's birthday and there were festive decorations, arches, and two bandstands still there from the celebration.

There was only one small boat, so it took a while for the party to cross the river. During that process, Miguel, Lobo, Dixon, and a group of Macabebes went up to the main house where Aguinaldo stood at a window watching the crossing. The Macabebes kept Aguinaldo and his officers distracted by telling a long and detailed story about how they had fought a battle with the American forces and captured their prisoners. There was much laughing and nodding.

When the entire force was finally across the river, they lined up in formation. Aguinaldo's personal security force of about twenty men had already formed a line in front of the main house to welcome the new arrivals. Funston shouted a prearranged signal and the Macabebes raised their rifles and opened fire upon the insurgents. Several fell to the ground and the others, in shock and panic, turned and ran. A few fired wild shots as they fled.

Walker, Funston, and the other American officers sprinted toward the house. Gunshots were heard from inside the building, and an Insurgent officer leaped from a window and ran for the river, with two Macabebes in pursuit. Walker caught a glimpse of Aguinaldo's face through the window as he shouted commands to his troops, and saw Dixon wrestle him away. Arriving in the room, Walker saw two Insurgents lying dead, and the others disarmed and unresisting. Dixon lay atop Aguinaldo, pinning him to the floor, which had probably saved the rebel leader's life. Funston announced to Aguinaldo that he was now a prisoner of the United States Army, and even without translation the Filipino understood, and hung his head dejectedly.

Aguinaldo's soldiers and the villagers had all fled, leaving behind a large supply of food which was left over from the previous day's festivities. The Americans and Macabebes feasted royally, celebrating their victory. Lieutenant Mitchell had brought a camera and went about taking pictures of everyone and everything.

The weary Americans and Filipinos rested in the village for the next two nights, and on the third day, having eaten all of the food, they began their return march to the coast. It was all downhill so it was a much easier trek than the ascent, and the Macabebes talked, sang, and laughed along the way. Walker noticed that Dixon, who brought up the rear of the column, kept turning to look intently behind them as if expecting to see something. However, it was an uneventful march and they reached the coast about noon. The *Vicksburg* arrived shortly thereafter, summoned by signal fires on the beach, and by late afternoon they were all aboard and underway, heading back to Manila.

With daylight almost gone, Walker spied Dixon at the railing, staring back in the direction of Palanan Bay. Joining him, they stood for a while without talking.

"I noticed that on the way down the mountain this morning, you kept looking back," commented Walker. "You weren't expecting to see anything, were you?"

"Naw," drawled Dixon, almost too casually. "Just habit."

Walker nodded and wondered why he felt sure Dixon was not telling him the truth. After a pause, he queried, "Really?"

It was Dixon's turn to pause. "Fagen was there."

"Fagen? I've heard that name. Who's Fagen?"

Dixon glared at him with narrowed eyes. "Ever'body's heard of Fagen! Black soldier who went over to the Filipino side. A genius at guerilla warfare. Been giving the U.S. fits for the past year. He even captured a boatload of our weapons and ammo not long ago. Funston's offering a six-hunnerd doller reward for him, dead or alive."

"An American soldier went over to fight for the rebels?" echoed Walker in amazement. "How is that possible?"

Dixon snorted loudly. "Easy!" he snapped. "'Specially for a black soldier. We get treated like dirt, just like the Filipinos. The whites call us and them both n----rs. Fagen's not the only one, neither. Lots of blacks— and some whites, too— have gone over t'other side."

Walker was at a loss for words, and took a moment to process this new information. He shook his head slowly and ran his hand through his hair. "You say he— that Fagen— was there? At Palanan?"

Dixon nodded. "He was in the jungle, just out of sight. Called me over to talk yesterday. Tried to get me to go with him. Said I'd be an officer in the Filipino army. Get me a Filipino wife."

Walker gasped audibly. "Why didn't he attack?"

"His men had all run away. He was rounding up a new force. If we'd stayed there another day, we'd prob'ly got attacked. That's why I kept lookin' back'ards all the way down the mountain. I figured he'd try to rescue Aguinaldo."

"Why didn't you shoot him? Six hundred dollars is a lot of money."

Dixon's lip curled as he glared at Walker. "Just when I start thinkin' you might be all right, you go and say something stupid like that." He shook his head. "I couldn't no more shoot him than I could shoot Lobo, 'less it was self-defense. He's a brother. I don't agree with his choice, but I understand it. You never will."

Walker was stunned. How could Dixon understand the defector's action? It was more than he could comprehend. He raised his eyes to the darkening sky as if seeking divine insight, and saw the lookout nest high on the foremast. Suddenly it seemed like the ideal place to do some serious thinking. Grasping the rigging, he climbed quickly up and found it empty.

Bracing his back against the steel mast he gazed out across the calm sea, feeling its serenity slowly creeping into his agitated mind and soul. The sun went completely down, leaving a brilliant red and purple glow in the western sky, until blackness took over. Walker had seen the nighttime sky many times, but at sea it seemed even more breathtaking. There was nothing to block one's view from one horizon to the other, and the stars were inconceivably numerous. The moon began to rise in the east, its soft, luminous glow reflected in the glassy surface of the water. Walker felt transported to another world, suspended between heaven and earth. The slow undulations of the ship's motion had a hypnotic effect, and as his tension subsided he had the sensation of floating through the air, as if he were leaving Earth behind and falling upward into the heavens beyond. This sense of ethereal detachment lasted for a long while, and Walker was slipping into a trance-like state.

"Garrett!" It was Seaman Watkins, sticking his head through the opening in the floor of the lookout nest. "What are you doing up here? You trying to escape?" He laughed at his own joke.

"It's a thought," replied Walker, jolted back to reality.

Watkins climbed into the perch and stood alongside Walker with folded arms. He took a deep breath and let it out slowly— "Really nice up here at nighttime, ain't it?"

"Very nice indeed," agreed Walker. "It takes away all the bad feelings and gives you peace."

"When I'm up here at night looking up at the stars I realize how small I am, and how big the Universe is. It helps me stop worrying about the little cares and concerns that bother me. When I go back down, I can be calm and easy."

"I see what you mean," Walker murmured, gazing up into the starry heavens again. "We're just a speck down here. How important can we be, anyway?"

They swayed gently in the bucket for several minutes, each immersed in his own thoughts. Walker suddenly felt a need to ask a question. "Do y'all have any colored sailors?"

"Sure! We've got about a dozen or so. They work in the galley, laundry, and engine room, below decks."

"None of them work on deck, in the rigging, manning the guns—nothing like the white sailors do?"

"Oh, no," Watkins laughed. "Colored sailors never do those things. They don't have the training for it. They do those other things so that us white sailors are free to handle the more important jobs."

"But they could be trained to do those important jobs, couldn't they? I've spent a lot of time with black soldiers, and they're just as good as white soldiers. I would think that colored sailors could learn to do anything white sailors can."

"Garrett! What's got you thinking these kind of things? The colored sailors are happy doing what they do. No need for any change. Don't rock the boat!" And then he laughed and repeated the words— "Don't rock the boat!"— as if it was a funny joke.

"I don't know," said Walker slowly. "When I look up into that sky and realize what tiny specks we all are, I wonder if one speck is really any better than any other speck—white, black, brown specks. Maybe all specks really look the same from up there."

"I think you better head back down, Garrett! Being up here is giving you some really strange thoughts. Watch your step— it's a long way down!"

"Yeah," sighed Walker. "I have a lot of strange thoughts these days. There's a lot to think about."

Descending the rigging wasn't too bad, thanks to the brilliant moon, but it required several minutes of white-knuckle concentration until his feet were firmly planted on the deck again and he could exhale in relief.

Not ready to go to sleep yet, he decided to stroll around the ship. Reaching the bow, to his surprise he saw the Filipino rebel leader perched atop one of the big guns, staring out across the water. During the voyage Aguinaldo and his officers had the free run of the ship, and were treated more like guests than prisoners. The man seemed small and vulnerable. Walker stood awkwardly for a moment, fumbling for a few words in Spanish.

"Buenas noches, señor," he ventured. *Good evening, sir.*

"Buenas noches," responded Aguinaldo. The sadness in his voice was unmistakable. He glanced toward Walker, and then turned back to the sea.

"Ah, do you think that the war— la guerra— will end soon— termine pronto?"

Aguinaldo did not react immediately and Walker began to wonder if he had used the wrong words. Then the Filipino sighed and spoke softly, "No sé." *I don't know.*

Walker gathered that he really didn't want to talk about it, at least not to a common soldier who spoke limited Spanish, and after a moment of silence was about to walk away when the man spoke again.

"Eso espero." *I hope so.*

"Eso espero— también." *I hope so, too.* He ambled back toward the stern of the ship, leaving the forlorn captive to his self-imposed isolation.

During the two days of the voyage back to Manila, Walker had a lot of time to think. He didn't see much of Dixon but chatted frequently with Miguel, and enjoyed wrestling with the "Little Macs," as General Funston called them. He spent a good bit of time in the lookout nest, and there was also time to write another letter home, for the first time in weeks.

September 9, 1899
Dear Ma and Pa,

I hope this finds you both doing well. Thanks for keeping me caught up on all the news from home. It's almost like being there. It's the rainy season here, so it's very wet and hot, like usual.

A lot has happened here since I wrote last. I met some American schoolteachers and made friends with a couple of Filipino scouts. I got promoted to corporal, so now I have two stripes on my sleeves! I guess the biggest news is that we finally captured Emilio Aguinaldo, the rebel leader! In fact, I am on a ship with him right now, heading for Manila. He is a small man, very quiet, and doesn't speak English. He seems very sad, which I guess is understandable. I hope that this awful war will finally end, now that he is a prisoner. I look forward to coming home soon, hopefully.

Pa—you asked about Corporal Dixon, who wrote you the letter. He is now a sergeant. He is about four years older than me. We get along pretty well, most of the time. He is on the ship too, and we talk sometimes. He's a good soldier.

Give my best regards to the General if you see him. I wish he was still here.

Your son,
Walker

22

GOOD-BYE, PHILIPPINES

*H**e is truly the fattest man I have ever seen in my life,* thought Walker as he watched Judge William Howard Taft take the oath of office as the first civil governor of the Philippines. *I guess that's what eating a big steak for breakfast everyday does for you.*

The swearing-in of Taft was the climax of the program, conducted in the courtyard of the fortress in Manila. General Funston received a promotion to Brigadier General, and several soldiers were decorated with medals and ribbons for their accomplishments. Walker and Dixon each received ribbons for their participation in the capture of Aguinaldo, and Walker was also decorated with a medal for his wounds received at Calamba. Both finally received the medals promised by General MacArthur for the swimming of the Pampanga River several months earlier. The military band played some patriotic music as the audience of soldiers dispersed to return to their regular duties.

The honorees lingered, shaking hands and chatting pleasantly. The other soldiers wanted to hear Walker and Dixon tell about the Palanan expedition and about Walker's battle with the python. In a separate cluster, the officers and political figures carried on their own conversation. While Dixon was describing the treacherous march and the eating of snails, Walker inclined his ear toward the other group to pick up what they were saying.

"I told President McKinley that our little brown brothers are not ready for self-government," Taft said, shaking his head. "They will need fifty to a hundred years of close supervision to develop anything resembling Anglo-Saxon political principles and skills." He scraped under a fingernail with a pocketknife, and then continued. "They will need firm guidance every step of the way. The rebel leaders should be deported to Guam, and any Filipinos who refuse to lay down their arms should be treated as outlaws, subject to the severest penalties."

"Well, Governor," remonstrated General MacArthur, "sometimes the carrot works better than the stick. I think we can develop a better relationship with the Filipinos if we continue with the Benevolent Assimilation plan."

"That's where you're wrong, General," rebutted Taft, with a dismissive wave of his hand. "You have been much too merciful in commuting death sentences of these convicted Insurrectos. A firm hand is what is needed."

"I totally agree, Governor," chimed in Funston enthusiastically. "I personally strung up thirty-five Filipinos without trials and administered the water cure to many more. What's all the fuss about dispatching a few treacherous savages? If we'd done more of this from the beginning, the war would have ended sooner. And all those Americans who are criticizing the way we captured Aguinaldo and crying for peace should be dragged out of their homes and lynched."

"I think we may be sowing the seeds of future difficulties—" began MacArthur.

"Quite the contrary," interjected Taft. "Look at how many rebel leaders have surrendered since Aguinaldo was captured. The insurrection is dying, even as we speak. No, we must stay the course. A firm hand—that's what is needed here."

Walker was then drawn back into the soldiers' conversation as they clamored for a telling of the python battle. He elaborated the details of the grisly story as they walked toward the mess hall for lunch. He had told it so many times by now that he was getting pretty good at it. He held them spellbound, telling how he had sawed off its huge head with blood spurting into his face while trapped in its powerful coils.

Lunch that day was a special menu of roast pork, rice, and vegetables—a welcome change from the usual rice, beans, and hardtack. Each soldier received a cup of warm beer to go with their water—intended as a treat, but actually rather unappetizing. At a nearby table covered with a white tablecloth, Taft and the officers were having steak and potatoes with chilled wine, and pie for dessert. A white-jacketed Filipino attendant hovered about them, wine bottle in hand, to refill their glasses.

After the meal it was time to return to their separate units and get back to work. Exchanging friendly farewells, they broke up and hurried off. Dixon and Walker had to go several miles north of Manila to rejoin the Tenth, where it was assigned a district to patrol. The regiment had finally acquired horses, which greatly enhanced their ability to monitor their area.

"While we're here, let's see if we got any mail," suggested Dixon. "Won't have another chance for a while." They detoured past the mail room, where both of them were handed letters. Dixon's was from Daisy, and Walker had a letter from his mother, and– to his shock—one from Abigail Dancy. He tucked it quickly into his jacket out of sight, and carefully opened the one from his mother to read as they rode.

Dixon read his letter from Daisy, occasionally making thoughtful noises and grunts, some that sounded surprised and some that sounded disappointed.

"Mama and Daisy say tell you 'hello,'" he said without looking up. "They say they glad we're friends." At that, he snorted and gave his head a shake as if in disbelief, and then turned to Walker and said "Hell-l-l-o," drawing the word out so long that it seemed he would never get to the "o" syllable. It was Walker's turn to snort.

"I don't think that was quite what they had in mind."

"You don't know," replied Dixon dryly. "Take what you can git." Then he held up a crocheted square. This one was white with a red star in the middle and a green ribbon tied in a bow. "Daisy's making these for Christmas. Says she's already sold a couple dozen. Like it?"

"Yes, it's very pretty."

"Good. 'Cause she sent one to you, too." Dixon handed the delicately crocheted square to Walker. "Take good care of it."

"I certainly will! Daisy does beautiful work. I'll keep it in my pocket. Tell her I said thank you very much!"

As he read his mother's letter, Walker suddenly grunted in surprise and concern.

"Bad news?"

"I don't know. Ma says Pa had to go to the doctor. His heart was beating too fast and he fainted after church. She says he's doing better and taking it easy, but it don't sound good." He sighed heavily, and frowned. "I hope he's alright. This letter was written more than a month ago."

"Well, ain't no point in worrying 'bout it now. Whatever was going to happen has probably already happened."

"Oh, thanks," Walker scowled. "I feel lots better now."

They rode in silence for a few minutes, and then Walker casually asked Dixon, "What about your pa? I never heard you say anything about your father."

"Ain't nuthin' to say. Never was around. Never met 'im."

"Well, he had to be around if you've got a little sister. You must've been about twelve when Daisy was born."

"That wasn't my father. Mama married him when I was a kid. We didn't get along too good, anyway."

"I never met him when I was staying at the Dancys' house. Beulah never mentioned him. Neither did Daisy. What was—"

Dixon turned angrily on Walker. "It ain't none of your damned business, Corporal Garrett! Just leave it alone!"

"You're right. It's none of my business," Walker apologized, taken aback by the intensity of Dixon's reaction. For the rest of the way back to camp they each kept to their own thoughts.

Later that evening Walker found a private moment to read Abigail's letter. He gazed at the pale yellow envelope, his eyes tracing the graceful, flowing script. It was addressed to "Pfc. Walker Garrett," so she obviously had not heard of his promotion. He felt strangely detached as he contemplated the letter. A few weeks earlier he would have felt eager anticipation at opening it, but now he was only mildly curious—even a bit annoyed. His fingers told him that there was something besides a sheet of paper inside. He tapped it against his hand and then carefully tore off the end of the envelope.

Pulling the folded letter out and opening it, his eyebrows rose and he gave a short laugh when he saw what was inside. It was a white crocheted square with a red star in the middle, and a green ribbon tied in a bow. He shook his head incredulously. *Again?*

November 11, 1899

Dear Walker,

I hope this finds you well. It has been a long time since you've written, but I know you've been busy with the war. I saw that Aguinaldo was captured, and that you and Beulah's L. G. were there. It was very exciting to see your names in the newspaper. Everyone is talking about it. Do you think the war will end now? General Wheeler was here recently to visit. He spoke highly of you both.

I will be visiting relatives in Richmond and Charleston during the upcoming holiday season and may not write again for a while. I am still practicing my needlework, and am including a sample again. It is a Christmas design. I hope it gives you some pleasure and reminds you of home.

Kindest regards,

Abigail Dancy

Walker gritted his teeth as he folded the letter and put it back into the envelop. *How can it give me pleasure when I know that you are lying about having made it yourself? I know you bought it from Daisy for ten cents. And you saw my name in the newspaper? Surely, it would have said*

"Corporal Walker Garrett," not "Pfc." Apparently you didn't actually read it yourself. And you'll be too busy dancing at balls for the next two months to write another short note? Do you think I'm just a stupid country boy that you can play with, like a game?

Walker stepped over to the cooking hut, where there had been a campfire burning earlier. He held a corner of the yellow envelope to a glowing red coal and, when the flames began licking upward, dropped it onto the pile of smoking embers and walked away without looking back.

The next couple of days were filled with routine patrol duty. Almost every day a few rebels approached the camp to surrender. Their weapons were collected and they were escorted to a large stockade in Manila for processing. Most of the time was spent standing guard around the circumference of their assigned district. Captain Pershing or another officer visited the posts regularly to see how things were going, but overall it was dull and boring.

Since the Tenth was a black unit, Walker's official role was still that of an aide to the commanding officer, who in this case was Captain Pershing. He was relieved to be able to ride in the group with the captain to check on the outposts rather than to simply stand around, swatting flies and mosquitoes.

One afternoon as they paused to let the horses drink from a stream, Walker ventured to ask the captain a question. "Captain Pershing, sir," he began, "May I ask a question, sir?"

"Go ahead, Corporal Garrett."

"A couple of days ago when I was in Manila, I overheard part of a conversation between Governor Taft, General MacArthur, and General Funston. I wasn't eavesdropping, sir—they were standing right next to us."

Pershing said nothing, but gave Walker a quizzical look.

"The governor and General Funston were arguing that the Filipinos need a firm hand, and that we should treat the rebels harshly. General MacArthur was in favor of 'Benevolent Assimilation,' and said that harsh treatment would sow seeds for future problems. What do you think about that, sir?"

Pershing cleared his throat and looked away. The saddle leather creaked as the captain shifted his weight, and the other officers immediately became quiet. Walker suddenly feared that his question was inappropriate and that the captain would be angry with him. Then turning back toward Walker, he replied in a measured tone which clearly indicated that he was choosing his words carefully.

"We are in the army, Corporal Garrett. In the army there is a chain of command. It is our duty and responsibility to follow our commanders, and to not question their judgment. President McKinley is General MacArthur's commanding officer. General MacArthur is my commanding officer—and I am yours. President McKinley's policy is Benevolent Assimilation, and General MacArthur is supporting that, as he should. I support his position, as I should. If you think differently, you should keep it to yourself. What Governor Taft and General Funston think and say is not our concern."

"Yes sir, Captain Pershing. Thank you, sir." Walker felt somewhat rebuked by the captain's terse response, but at the same time felt relieved that the captain did not approve of the harsh approach favored by Taft and Funston. Or at least he didn't *seem* to approve of it. His words were almost lawyerly in their technical precision, yet Walker couldn't imagine Captain Pershing hanging rebels without trials, or administering the water cure. He always insisted that the rebels who surrendered to the Tenth be treated with respect and decency, fed and given medical care if they needed it, before being taken to the stockade.

"By the way, Captain Pershing, sir—whatever happened to Major Payne? I haven't seen him since Dixon and I got back from the Palanan expedition."

"Major Payne is in charge of the Manila stockade," said Pershing, in the same terse voice as before. "All of the surrendered rebels are under his authority."

Walker coughed and cleared his throat, and then said nothing. *I bet those rebels wouldn't be surrendering if they knew what they were in for*, he thought.

"I don't think he's ever heard of 'Benevolent Assimilation,'" grinned one of the lieutenants.

"He sure doesn't let any of them go thirsty," joked another, and the officers all broke out in laughter. Payne's frequent use of the water cure was well known. Walker did not laugh, nor did Captain Pershing.

"Enough of that!" Pershing snapped. "Let's get moving!" And they splashed across the stream and cantered up the narrow dirt road toward the next checkpoint.

Dixon was in charge of the squad at the next post. They had just accepted the surrender of a dozen ragged, barefoot, underfed Filipino rebels. The rebels had turned over five rifles, three revolvers, and thirty rounds of ammunition. All of the weapons were old and rusty. Walker couldn't help feeling pity for the men as he watched them sitting silently on the ground, heads down.

"Sergeant Dixon!"

"Yes sir, Captain?"

"Take two of your men and escort these prisoners to camp. Feed them, and then march them to the stockade in Manila. Corporal Garrett—ride back and tell Johnson to whip up some grub and have it ready when they get there in about an hour."

"Yes sir, Captain!" Walker saluted as he reined his horse about and galloped away.

Unlike the white cook who had objected to feeding the Filipino scouts even though they were allies, the cooks of the Tenth seemed to take pleasure in feeding the hungry rebels. Ever since his conversation with Dixon about the deserter, Fagen, Walker had noticed that the black soldiers seemed to have sympathy and pity for their opponents.

Thinking about what awaited these defeated men at the hands of Major Payne, he felt a sense of indignation, even anger. *I thought the White Man's Burden was about helping people, not crushing and destroying their souls. America can do better than this.* The thought surprised him, but once in his head he couldn't shake it. An idea began to form, and though it was rather shocking, he knew it was right. When the rebels finished eating, Walker volunteered to accompany Dixon to escort them to Manila.

"You?" scoffed Dixon, apparently in a foul mood. "I figured you'd want to ride 'round on that horse some more."

"I need the exercise," replied Walker offhandedly. "Besides, this is more important."

For an instant Walker thought Dixon was going to reject his offer, but then the sergeant shrugged, spat on the ground and said, "Hell— let's get going."

The prisoners' hands were tied behind their backs with short lengths of rope which were then tied together with a long rope. They walked single file, like links in a chain. Walker and Dixon, with rifles slung over their shoulders and wearing holstered .38 revolvers at their belts, brought up the rear.

Descending from the Batasan Hills to the northeast of Manila, Walker imagined that he could see Manila Bay in the distant haze, even though it was several miles away. They passed through small villages with children and chickens running in the streets. Every thatched-roof house had a neat vegetable garden next to it. A few adult figures could be seen in the adjacent fields, and the ever-present rainforest loomed nearby.

After they had marched for an hour, Walker decided to broach his idea.

"Major Payne is in charge of the stockade," commented Walker. "These fellows are in for a hard time. I've heard he likes to do the water cure on the prisoners."

Dixon did not respond.

"Now that they're defeated, surrendered, and disarmed, I don't see any reason to torture them that way," he ventured further.

Dixon still ignored him.

Frustrated at Dixon's silence, Walker raised his voice slightly. "I don't think it's right to treat people that way. We can do something about it."

"We can't do nuthin' about it," snapped Dixon, breaking his

silence. "We just do our job and leave the rest to them—" pointing toward Manila in the distance.

"Think about it," insisted Walker. "What if they never got to the stockade? Who would ever know?"

"What the hell are you talkin' about, Garrett? You been out in the sun too long?"

"Think about it," Walker repeated. "If they don't get to the stockade, nobody will miss them."

"I heard you the first time, Garrett!" Dixon seethed. "And I said there ain't nuthin' we can do about it!"

"Yes, there is!" Walker was getting angry now. *What's eating him?* he wondered.

"All we have to do is untie them and let them go home," he explained earnestly. "They don't have weapons or ammunition. They've surrendered. They don't want to fight anymore. Let's just turn them loose."

Dixon stared at him as if he'd sprouted horns and said in amazement, "You *have* been out in the sun too long."

Walker just looked at him intently, with a raised eyebrow.

"You're serious, ain't you?"

"Yes I am. Are you in, or not?"

Dixon stopped in the road. He put his hands on his hips and stared at Walker as if waiting to see what he was going to do. Walker decided to interpret that as permission to go ahead.

"Halt!" he shouted. "Parada! No vaya!" He wasn't sure if he was saying it correctly, but it didn't seem to matter—the line stopped. He walked to the front of the line and faced them.

"La paz! No Guerra! Ir casa!" He tried to say that the war was over and that they should all go home. "Comprehender?" he asked. The men only looked at him blankly.

Reaching under his jacket he pulled out José's machete and approached the prisoner in the front of the line. The man's eyes widened and he took a step back, his face showing fear. Walker put a hand on his shoulder and, turning him to the side, cut the rope that bound his hands. Stepping to the second man he did the same, and repeated it all the way down the line. The men stood still, rubbing their wrists and looking uncertain what to do.

"Go home," said Walker. "Casa. Tu casa." He waved his arm as if trying to scare off crows. "Adios!" Walker couldn't tell if they didn't understand him or just couldn't believe that they were being released.

"Let's go, Garrett," said Dixon. "They'll figure it out."

Coiling the long rope and draping it over his shoulder, Walker turned and began walking away with Dixon, back in the direction they had come. As they went around a bend in the dirt road they looked back and saw the men still standing there.

"Maybe they don't have nowhere to go home to," Dixon wondered aloud.

"Surely they'll figure out something," said Walker hopefully. "Anything's better than going to the stockade."

"Well, it's their problem now," said Dixon curtly. "They've got their chance. It's up to them to use it."

"What's eating you, Dixon? You've been riled up all day."

Dixon took a half-dozen more steps, and then stopped and turned toward Walker. "I found something of yours," he said coldly. Reaching into his pants pocket, he threw a small object against Walker's chest. Walker caught it with his hand against his shirt. "You must've lost it."

Walker held it up. It was a white crocheted square with a red star in the middle and a green ribbon, but it was badly scorched and blackened, and half gone.

"Your Christmas gift from Daisy!" Walker exclaimed. "What happened to it?"

"It ain't *mine*," snarled Dixon, pulling an identical but unblemished one from his breast pocket. "It's the one I gave *you* t'other night. You said you liked it and you'd keep it. Liar! If you didn't want it, you should've said so."

"Where did—how—I don't—" Walker stammered, confused.

"You don't remember throwing it in the cook-house campfire?" jeered Dixon, his lip curling in disgust. "Along with your other trash?"

Then it dawned on Walker what had happened. "No! Wait!" he exclaimed. "Look—!" And he pulled from his pocket a perfect white square with its green ribbon and red star. "This is the one you gave me! I have kept it, just like I said I would."

It was Dixon's turn to be confused. "Then where did this burnt one come from?"

"Did you see a scrap of yellow paper in the ashes along with it?"

"Yeah. Almost all burned up, but a little bit was left."

"That was the envelope with the letter sent to me by Abigail Dancy. She sent me one of Daisy's crocheted squares—but she said she made it herself. It's the second time she's done that. I can't believe she buys these from Daisy and claims she crocheted them. I hate being lied to like that, so I just threw it all in the campfire."

Dixon roared with laughter. "'Dancin' Dancy' sent *you* a letter?" He threw his head back and roared again. "You the last person on earth I would of thought she'd be writin' letters to!" He continued to laugh as if it was truly the funniest thing he had ever heard.

Walker was getting annoyed. "It's not *that* funny," he growled bitterly.

"Yes, it is! And I bet you been writin' letters back to her too, ain't you?" And he burst out in another peal of laughter.

Walker tossed the scorched fragment into the thorns beside the road and walked along in silence. Dixon tried to stifle his laughter, but failed every couple of minutes and shook in uncontrollable merriment.

"Seriously, Garrett, why would the daughter of the richest man in town be writing letters to a corporal in the Philippines? You can see there's something not right about that, can't you?"

"Yeah," muttered Walker, downcast. "I guess I always knew it was too good to be true."

"Too good to be true?" exclaimed Dixon, aghast. "What are you talkin' 'bout? Hell, Garrett—you're worth ten of her! All she ever does is dance and play the piano and wear fancy dresses. She'll never amount to anything but a rich man's wife, and do nuthin' but boss the servants 'round. Like she used to do Mama." This last was spoken with a flash of anger.

"'Dancin' Dancy'—that's what we used to call her." And Dixon gave an explosive "Bah!" and spat into the bushes. "Forget her. Don't waste your time thinkin' on her."

"Well," said Walker, "I did throw that into the campfire, you know."

"Took you long enough. How long you been away from there? Two years?"

"I reckon that's about right. Seems longer. A lot longer."

They walked in silence for a while. The return trip was mostly uphill, and they were glad for the shade of the trees. The camp with its makeshift huts came into view, and they paused to rest at the top of a rise. They didn't want to get back too soon and raise suspicions about how they had made the trip so quickly.

"Daisy's pa was lynched," Dixon said suddenly, as if it was something he needed to get off his chest. "He was accused of touching a white woman. They said he tried to rape her. It wasn't true, but it didn't matter. They dragged him out of the jail cell that night and strung 'im up from one of those big trees in the town square. Said he didn't deserve a trial. People posed for pictures with his naked body, hanging there on the rope. After the crowd left, me and some others cut 'im down and buried 'im. Mama told me to git out of town. Git as far away as I could. So I joined the army and went out West. Ain't been back since. Ain't ever going back, I don't reckon."

Walker was speechless. He wanted to say something, but could not find words. Finally, after a long minute he mumbled, "I'm sorry."

Dixon did not respond, but only gazed into the distance, beyond the hills.

"Funston bragged about how many he's hung without trials," Walker added.

"Yeah," said Dixon tersely. "Ain't no different here, 'cept that we the ones doing the lynching now."

Walker heaved a tired sigh. "I'm glad we let those men go."

Dixon turned and looked at Walker. "Garrett, you s'prise me, sometimes. Not often, but sometimes." And then he added, almost as an afterthought, "I'm glad, too."

They walked on to camp, arriving just in time for evening mess. Before the call to line up, one of the lieutenants ordered the two of them to come to Captain Pershing's quarters. He gave them a serious frown as they passed by him. Walker began to feel uneasy.

Pershing leaned back in his chair and studied them for a moment before speaking. His strong jaw and thick mustache gave him a stern visage under normal conditions, but now he appeared downright fierce, his eyes glaring balefully as he looked from one to the other.

"Tell me what happened this afternoon." He focused on Dixon.

"Sir, we brought some surrenders to camp, fed 'em, and marched 'em to the—" Here Dixon stopped. He cleared his throat, took a deep breath, and continued, "We, ah, I ordered Corporal Garrett to remove the ropes from their hands, and—"

"Sir, that's not quite correct. Sergeant Dixon did not order me to—"

"Sir," Dixon began to interrupt, "Sir, I was in charge, and —"

Pershing held up his hand, palm toward them, and they fell silent. "I don't care whose idea it was. Why did you do it?"

Both of them began talking energetically at the same time, gesturing and shaking their heads. In the torrent of words, "Payne," "water cure," "rebels," and "wrong" sounded prominently. At length they finally became quiet, and then both saluted and said a final, "Sir!"

Pershing simply stared at them without blinking. "You admit you violated orders?"

"Yes sir," replied Dixon, and Walker echoed him.

"Thank you. You are dismissed." He picked up a pen and began to write.

"Sir?"

"What is it, Garrett?"

"How did you know, sir?"

Without looking up Pershing replied gruffly, "I watched you from a ridge to your west."

Walker winced, and slowly followed Dixon out to the back of the chow line.

"I reckon we'll be the ones gone to the stockade now," breathed Dixon dejectedly.

"How stupid could I be? How stupid! How stupid!" Walker groaned aloud.

"No," said Dixon firmly. "It wasn't stupid—it was the right thing to do. We'll have to pay a price for it, but I'm still glad we did it. I'd do it again, ever'time."

"I wonder what it feels like to be water cured," Walker murmured, rubbing his temples.

Neither of them had much appetite, eating only about half of their meal. Walker felt sick to his stomach. It wasn't just the impending punishment that upset him, but more than that, he felt badly about having disappointed Captain Pershing. He could only imagine what the captain must think of him now.

As the men were returning their dishes and utensils to the kitchen, Lieutenant Draper shouted for them to assemble in the middle of the camp to hear an announcement from Captain Pershing. Walker and Dixon made eye contact. This did not sound good. *Here it comes,* thought Walker.

The soldiers sat or knelt on the ground as the captain stood before them, a piece of paper in his hand. His deep voice rang out over the group. "Any of you men ever been to China?" he asked.

Shorty Anderson's hand shot up, only to draw laughs and thrown hats.

"Where's China?" came a voice from the back.

"It's on the other side of the world!" came a reply.

"No, that's the United States!" More laughter and hand clapping. Even Walker had to grin at that one.

Pershing held up his hand for quiet.

"There's a rebellion taking place in China. Foreigners—diplomats, missionaries, businessmen, teachers—are being attacked and killed. Hundreds are barricaded in the capital city of Peking and are under siege at this very hour. An international force from a half-dozen countries is assembling to rescue them, and President McKinley wants American soldiers to participate. A contingent of Marines has already been sent, but it's not enough. Infantry and artillery regiments are being prepared to go. General MacArthur has been ordered to send all the men he can spare." He paused to let these words sink in, as his eyes moved over the group, man by man.

"He has decided to send the Ninth Infantry Regiment, and have the Ninth and Tenth Cavalry Regiments each contribute a squadron. Each company in the regiment will send a dozen soldiers. Our contingent will be led by Second Lieutenant McFarley. You will report in the morning, and board ship in Manila tomorrow. It is a voyage of about two thousand miles to the port of Taku, China. You'll be there in a little over a week, with luck.

"I will read the list of names now, in alphabetical order, but first let me say that it is with regret that I—that all of us in the Tenth— will say good-bye to you, and we all wish you well. It has been an honor and a privilege to be your commander, both in Cuba and here in the Philippines."

Holding up the piece of paper he began to read the names, pronouncing each loudly and clearly, pausing to allow for the response of clapping and calls of support from the group.

"Anderson!"

"Hey Shorty! It's back to China for you!" came a call, followed by laughter.

"Brown!"

"You can do it, Jesse!"

"Dixon!"

"Show them Chinese what a Buffalo Soldier is made of!"

"Garrett!"

"Snake Man! Give 'em hell, Snake Man!"

Walker did not hear the rest of the list. His numbed mind tried unsuccessfully to grasp the reality that he was about to ship out for China. He had been facing the prospect of Major Payne and the Manila stockade. Surely, this was a good thing? Or was he being punished?

When the list was finished, Pershing dismissed them. He then barked, "Dixon! Garrett! See me in my quarters, now!"

As they stood in front of the captain's collapsible camp desk for the second time in an hour, the two soldiers saluted.

"Yes sir, Captain Pershing." They spoke in quietly subdued voices.

The captain rose from his chair and walked slowly around the desk to stand directly in front of them, within an easy arm's reach. He sighed heavily as he glared at them in turn, hands clasped behind his back. Then he spoke in a surprisingly gentle tone.

"It didn't happen." He paused for several seconds. "Do you understand me?"

Neither replied, but only stared.

"It didn't happen," he repeated slowly, giving emphasis to each word. "And don't you ever let anything like it—ever—happen again. Do you understand me?"

"Yes sir!" They nodded vigorously, saluting.

He nodded curtly. "Get out of here. Go to China."

By the time he retraced his steps around the desk and took his seat, the two were gone into the night.

23

HELLO, CHINA

June 30, 1900

Dear Ma,

Your last letter broke my heart. I can't believe that Pa is gone. He was so strong and healthy when I left. It just doesn't seem possible that he is not there anymore. I wish I could come and comfort you, but I am on a ship bound for China. Americans there are in danger for their lives, and we have to save them. It is good of General Wheeler to let you stay on in the house at Pond Spring. He has always taken good care of us, and I know he will take care of you until I can get there. I am glad that Pa got to see the General one more time. As for your question about Corporal Dixon (he's Sergeant Dixon now), I don't know why Pa would have been concerned about us being friends. He's a good soldier and I trust him with my life. Don't worry about anything. I'll be praying for you, too.

Your son, with love,

Walker

Walker sadly folded the letter and slipped it through the slot in the mail room of the USS *Logan*. His mother's letter, which he had received just as he was boarding ship in Manila, had devastated him. To think that he would never see his father again was overwhelming. The ship had been at sea for three days now, and he had hardly left his berth below decks except to eat meals. He simply lay there in semi-darkness, reliving his memories of his father and their life together at Pond Spring, and wondering how his mother was coping with her loss. *She must be incredibly lonely*, he thought, sighing. *Her husband dead and her only child on the other side of the planet. At least she has the General, Annie, and the rest of the Wheeler family to lean on.*

Lost in such thoughts, he almost tripped while stepping through the hatch going out onto the deck. Stumbling forward as the ship suddenly rolled heavily, he barely caught himself on the railing to keep from falling overboard.

"Watch your step there, soldier!" yelled a crewman. "We ain't stoppin' to fish you out of the ocean, and you can't swim to China from here!"

Giving a wave of his hand, he turned to proceed down the deck, holding the railing to steady himself, as the ocean was becoming more turbulent. A sudden gust of wind caught his hat and would have blown it overboard had it not been secured under his chin by a loose cord.

"Storm rising!" shouted the crewman. "Everybody get below! Gonna get rough out here!"

Walker looked up at the sky, past the huge single smokestack. The sky was so dark that he could hardly see the black coal smoke belching from it. A magnificent flash of lightning illuminated the heavens, followed instantly by a loud crash of thunder. The soldiers needed no further encouragement to clear the decks and get below.

The wind was beginning to howl mournfully even as Walker descended the narrow steps to the bunkroom. The rising and falling of the ship's bow made it almost impossible to walk down the steps, and he lost his footing and fell the final few rungs, landing in an unceremonious heap at the bottom. He barely got to his feet in time to avoid being landed upon by three other soldiers who also came crashing down.

Reaching his hammock in the poorly lit bunkroom, he settled in for the ride. His berth was the lowest in a stack of three, which he preferred because he was able to put a foot down on the floor to reduce its swinging and swaying. He soon realized, however, that there was also a major disadvantage to having the bottom berth during a storm. The tossing and rolling of the ship soon made most of the soldiers seasick, and many of them vomited over the side of their hammocks. The bottom bunk caught the worst of all of it.

Walker heard the sounds of the men's distress and saw that he would have to take immediate action. Slipping out of his hammock, he flipped it upside down so that it faced the floor and crept down the narrow aisle to the bulkhead. Along the way his boot slipped in a puddle of vomit and he landed on one knee, but quickly moved on. Reaching the doorway, he squatted with his back to the wall. Below decks there was little air flow even at the doorway, but it was somewhat better than in the middle of the room.

It was a miserable night, with no sleep for anyone. Fortunately by morning the storm had passed and the sea was calm again. It was still raining, but otherwise a welcome respite from the agony of the past few hours. Emerging into the fresh air, Walker hunched his shoulders against the rain and, keeping close to the superstructure, staggered to the enlisted men's mess. The room was almost deserted and, with his bowl of oatmeal and a tin cup of coffee, he had a table to himself—for a few minutes, at least.

"Shoulda knowed I'd find you here." It was Dixon, sliding into the bench at the end of the table. "Don't know how I can eat after all that, but I'm gonna try." And he took a big bite of steaming oatmeal, only to spit it back into the bowl with a gasp. "Hot!" was all he could manage to say. Blowing energetically and waving the spoonful in the air as if that would help, he took a smaller bite and breathed noisily through his teeth as he chewed.

"Not too bad," he commented, and quickly finished the bowl.

"I've done my share of stable cleaning," Walker said, shaking his head, "but I never smelled anything as awful as that bunkroom this morning. I b'lieve I'd volunteer to go to hell before I'd do that again."

"That'd be a hard choice to make. Might have to flip a coin."

They sat quietly for several minutes, each absorbed in his own thoughts.

Dixon broke the silence. "Ain't seen much of you since we left port."

"Been keepin' to myself, I guess."

There was another lengthy silence, broken by Walker.

"I got another letter from home just before we shipped out. From mama." He hesitated, and Dixon, waiting, raised a questioning eyebrow.

"Pa died."

"Sorry to hear that. Can't say I know how you feel, seeing as I never had a daddy, but I reckon it must hurt."

"Yeah, it does. I'm the only child, so my mama's got nobody to look after her. General Wheeler's going to let her stay on at Pond Spring, so that's good."

"Nice of him."

Walker shot a quick look at Dixon to see if he was being sarcastic.

"No, I mean it. It's nice of him. Did I ever tell you that he helped my mama get her job cookin' for the Dancys?"

"He did? No, you never told me that! How did he know Beulah?"

"She used to cook for him at Pond Spring. I guess I didn't tell you that, either."

"Seriously? You're joking! That can't be true!"

"It's true, Garrett. That was before I was born, so I don't remember anything about it, myself. She's been with the Dancys for up'ards of twenty-five years or more. I figured that she would've told you, herself."

"No, she never said a word about it. Strange—I can't imagine why she wouldn't have told me."

Another silence lasted several minutes.

"Well, Corporal Garrett, I'm sorry for your loss."

"Thank you, Dixon. I appreciate that. I really do." Walker started to stand up and offer his hand to Dixon, but the other man was already walking away, so Walker shrugged and kept his seat.

Other soldiers were beginning to straggle into the room, looking disheveled and unwell. Listening to the others talk about how terrible the night had been somehow made him feel better, so he sat and listened. Besides, there was nowhere else to go, other than out into the rain or back to the nauseating bunkroom. He wished they were already in China.

Within a couple of days the men began to see a shoreline on the western horizon. They saw occasional Chinese fishing boats with ribbed, fan-like red and yellow sails. Some had three sails, and others only one. They were too far away for Walker to be able to get a good look at them, but they looked unusual and artistic in their design. He began to feel curious about China, wondering how it would be different from the Philippines and the other places he'd seen.

When the *Logan* finally stopped moving and dropped anchor, the first thing Walker noticed was that, unlike every other place he'd gone, there was no jungle forest to be seen. Taku was a well-developed seaport, and there were dozens of ships, flying the flags of many different countries. There were low hills in the distance, but human civilization was everywhere. It was clear that a lot of people lived here.

The Chinese forts guarding the harbor of Taku had already been captured by Western forces, so the ship was able to approach close enough that Walker could see the skyline of the city beyond the harbor. He observed that, unlike in Manila, there were no churches towering over the other buildings. The roof lines that stood out were different than anything he had ever seen—bright red tiles on a stair-stepping series of roof levels, with upward curling corners at the ends. Some roofs boasted green or black tiles, and some curved gracefully in flowing lines. Walker's eyebrows rose and his lips formed an "ooh" as he marveled. He wondered what kind of buildings these were—political, or perhaps religious? Or homes of the wealthy?

Captain Pershing had said that Chinese militants were killing foreigners, including missionaries, teachers, businessmen, and diplomats. Walker was puzzled. China looked like a very prosperous and civilized place. He could see beautiful buildings. How could it be that these people could also be so violent and ruthless as to kill people like missionaries and teachers? He remembered the Filipino rebel who shot Harriet and the other teachers in Calamba, and what Dixon had said about it in the casco. Maybe it was like that—the missionaries and teachers were seen as a threat to the Chinese way of life. Walker began to have the unpleasant thought that this was yet another repetition of the same kind of conflict he had seen several times already.

As the sun was setting, a small boat came out from the harbor to the *Logan*. A group of well-dressed women accompanied by a few children were taken on board and were quickly ushered to the best quarters available. They seemed relieved to be on the ship, and the children clung tightly to their mothers' hands as they hurried along the deck, staring at the soldiers with wide eyes. Some of the soldiers began to clap and cheer for them, and he heard the women's voices responding with "Thank you!" and "God bless you!" until they disappeared through a hatchway. A number of wounded soldiers were also brought aboard from the launch and taken to the ship's infirmary. A few of them were able to walk, but most were carried on stretchers with bandages on heads, arms, or legs. Some of them looked to be in pretty bad shape, and the watching soldiers were respectfully silent as they passed.

Seeing the fear and exhaustion in the faces of the children deeply affected Walker. *It's one thing to fight against foreign governments and businesses, but it's something entirely different to threaten women and children,* he thought. He began pacing back and forth, his fists clenched as he glared toward the harbor and the city beyond it. *How long are we going to sit here on this ship when there are innocent people in danger? We should be doing something!* He and the other soldiers became increasingly restless as they waited for action.

Early the next morning found Walker again standing at the railing, gazing across the harbor. He heard a light step behind him and, turning, encountered one of the women coming out onto the deck. She appeared to be about fifty years old, and had dark hair lightly streaked with gray at the temples arranged under a wide-brimmed straw hat, and wore a dark blue dress with a khaki jacket.

"Good morning, ma'am," said Walker, doffing his hat. "Welcome aboard! I hope you and the others slept well last night."

"Why, thank you, soldier!" she replied with a motherly smile. "Yes, in fact, I had the best night's sleep I've had in a month! But once you're awake, it's time to get up!"

"Yes ma'am. I know what you mean. I couldn't sleep any more either, thinking about how scared those children looked as they came on board last evening. I'm eager to get ashore and do something about it!"

"I know you will! Our men in Tientsin and Peking need all the help they can get. I am so glad to see all of you here, and I hope that more are on the way." Turning up her collar against the ocean breeze, she continued, "Can you show me the way to the dining room, or whatever you call it on a ship? I am half starved!"

"Yes ma'am, I'd be happy to. Right this way!"

She took his arm as they strolled up the deck. "What is your name, young man? Tell me about yourself."

"I'm Corporal Walker Garrett, ma'am. From Alabama. I've fought in Cuba and the Philippines, and was there for the annexations of Hawaii and Guam. It's been an interesting two years."

"My! I should think so! You certainly have some stories to tell!"

"Yes ma'am, I do." He considered telling her about his battle with the python, but decided that it might not be such a good idea right before breakfast.

"Well, my name is Anna Drew. My husband is Edward Bangs Drew, the American commissioner for the Imperial Chinese Customs Service in Tientsin. We've been living in China for more than twenty-five years, and I must admit that we did not see this Boxer uprising coming. It caught us completely unprepared, and I just hope it isn't too late."

Walker was about to ask "too late for what?" when they reached the entrance to the officers' mess hall. Not being an officer he stopped at the door, but Mrs. Drew insisted that he accompany her and show her how to get breakfast. He escorted her to the serving line where the kitchen staff welcomed her warmly and filled a big plate with scrambled eggs, bacon, fried potatoes, fresh bread, and a cherry pastry.

"And now a plate for my new friend, Corporal Walker!" she exclaimed.

"Thank you, Mrs. Drew," said Walker, politely not correcting her mistake on his name, "but I'm not an officer, and this is the officers' mess."

"Nonsense! We're Americans and we believe in democracy, don't we? I insist that you join me—it will be so nice to have someone to talk to during breakfast!"

Walker looked helplessly at the white aproned cook, unsure what to do.

"Here you go, Corporal Walker," the cook boomed, solving the problem for him. "Enjoy your breakfast, ma'am!"

They settled in at a small table with a white tablecloth, equipped with salt and pepper shakers. The coffee cups were ceramic, not tin. Walker felt very awkward—and excited. He hadn't eaten anything like this since he had left home.

"Thank you, ma'am," he mumbled. "This is really nice."

"What do the other soldiers have for breakfast?" she inquired.

"We have oatmeal, hardtack, and coffee, usually. And everything is tin—plates, spoons, cups. We sit on benches at long tables—no tablecloths. We're used to it."

"Well then," she said cheerfully, "This is your lucky day, isn't it?"

He tried to say "yes ma'am" but his mouth was full of eggs, and it sounded like a grunt. She hid a smile and ate quietly for a few minutes, letting him devour his special breakfast. He knew he was eating like a starved farmhand, but he couldn't help himself. He couldn't remember when food had tasted this good.

"You know, they've given me more food than I can eat," Mrs. Drew said in mock astonishment. "Can I give you some of mine? It would be a shame for it to go to waste!" And without waiting for an answer, she held her plate over his and raked some of the eggs, bacon, and fried potatoes onto his plate.

"Now, you clean your plate, young man!" she admonished him sternly.

And he did. He didn't stop until only the cherry pastry remained. Sighing with deep satisfaction, he looked up with some embarrassment. "I should be ashamed of myself for eating like a pig," he said apologetically, "but that was absolutely the most delicious meal I've eaten in two years! Thank you, ma'am!"

"I am so glad that you enjoyed it, Corporal Walker!"

Picking at the pastry in a more civilized manner, he asked, "What was it like for you in Taku, ma'am?"

"I actually live in Tientsin, a city about thirty miles up the Pei-Ho River from Taku. It is one of China's most important port cities, with more than a million people. Many foreign countries have offices there to manage their imports and exports. I suppose there might be as many as a thousand foreigners—Americans and Europeans."

"A million!" Walker's jaw dropped. "That's amazing!"

"Yes," she nodded, "a million is a very large city, even for China. Tientsin is actually two cities: the walled city proper, where all the Chinese live, and the foreign settlement about two miles away, which is where we live. It's much nicer there than in the walled city—clean and spacious. Many Chinese servants and tradespeople live there also.

"But to answer your question, the situation in Tientsin for us foreigners is very bad. Most of the women and children have had to evacuate. My own daughters have already gone to Nagasaki. The Chinese army is shelling us night and day from the walled city, and they and the Boxers are advancing closer and closer. We have soldiers and sailors there to defend us, but we desperately need more. They will be so happy to see you men!"

"We won't let nothing happen to your friends," Walker assured her confidently. "As soon as they let us off this ship, we'll be there in no time. There's more than a thousand soldiers aboard."

"That will be wonderful, Corporal Walker. But there are tens of thousands of the Chinese army and even more of the Boxers. That's why we need our American soldiers, along with the British, French, Italian, Russian, Japanese, German, and Austrian forces. It will take everyone working together to repel this attack."

Walker whistled softly in amazement. "I see what you mean. This is bigger than I realized."

"Oh, Corporal Walker! That's not the half of it! As soon as you rescue the international community in Tientsin, you have to go as quickly as possible to Peking, the capital city, which is almost a hundred miles further. The embassies there are under siege, and we don't even know if they are still alive! The situation is dire, and I'm afraid that you have a lot of dangerous fighting ahead of you!"

"Are the Chinese good fighters? Do they have modern weapons?"

"The army is fairly good, from what I hear. They have modern artillery and rifles which they've purchased from Western countries, and they know how to use them. The Boxers, however, prefer to use traditional weapons like swords, spears, knives and such, besides the traditional Chinese martial arts, which is why they are called 'Boxers.' They are a threat mainly because of their sheer numbers, but they must be taken seriously. They almost captured our railway station a few days ago, had not the Russian soldiers beaten them off."

"Why is this happening?" asked Walker. "I don't understand what they are fighting for—or against. Did we do something to antagonize them?"

Mrs. Drew sighed, and a troubled expression came over her face. "They believe that they are fighting for their way of life against foreigners who are corrupting their country. The Boxers are actually called the 'I Ho Ch'uan,' which means 'Society of Righteous and Harmonious Fists.' Their motto is 'Support the empire; destroy the foreigners.' They come from the common people, the peasants of the countryside. They have suffered greatly from floods and droughts and plagues of locusts in recent years. Our railroads and steamboats have taken the jobs away from many workers, and they hate our schools. They especially hate our missionaries."

"Why do they hate missionaries? They aren't hurting anybody."

"Buddhism is very deeply rooted in China. They say that when a man becomes a Christian, he ceases to be a Chinaman. Converts are called 'rice Christians' because it is said that they became Christians only to get food. The Boxers tell people that their traditional gods are angry and are punishing them with the bad weather and poor harvests. The Chinese Christians have become scapegoats for all of the problems afflicting the people, and thousands of them have been slaughtered across northern China. Hundreds of converts are sheltering in our foreign settlement in Tientsin. If the Boxers succeed in breaking through, there will be a terrible massacre!"

"We won't let that happen," said Walker grimly. "Killing innocent people ain't the way to solve problems. We'll just have to put a stop to that!"

"I hope and pray that you will, Corporal Walker," said Mrs. Drew fervently. "And I have one small favor to ask—when you get to Tientsin, I would appreciate it if you would find my husband and Lou Hoover and let them know that I am safe aboard the *Logan*. The Hoovers—Herbert and Lou—are staying in our house because theirs was not as safe from the artillery shells. Lou is my best friend in Tientsin, and she stayed behind to help with the wounded in our makeshift hospital. Her husband, Herbert, is a mining engineer who is helping with the barricades. Wonderful people!"

Before Walker could respond, a deep voice boomed from just a few steps away—

"Corporal! What are you doing in the officers' mess?"

It was Colonel Liscum, the commanding officer of the Ninth Infantry Regiment.

"Sir!" Walker jumped to his feet, saluting.

Mrs. Drew quickly rose, also. "Now officer, don't be angry at my young friend here. I insisted that he keep me company during break-fast, and he has been a perfect gentleman. If your other soldiers are as fine as this young man, then I know we are in good hands!"

Removing his hat and bowing graciously, Liscum introduced himself and apologized for his brusque entrance.

Seeing his chance to make an exit, Walker took a step back, and with a quick nod and gesture with his hat said, "Thank you, Mrs. Drew. I'll deliver your message, and I hope you get to see your children again real soon!" And with that he hurried out onto the deck.

I'm going to be an officer one of these days, he thought, as he leaned against the handrail. *Officers get the best of everything, and more pay, too. No more hardtack for breakfast when I'm an officer. And no more tin cups of coffee. Real plates and mugs, and bacon and eggs every morning!*

While imagining what it would be like to be an officer, Walker strolled back down the deck to the enlisted men's mess hall and stepped in for a second breakfast. The room was almost full, and it seemed that everyone was talking at once. Stuffing a handful of hard-tack crackers into his steaming bowl of oatmeal, he took a tin cup of coffee and made his way to one of the long, bare tables and slipped into the bench between two soldiers who were engaged in animated conversation with the others at the table. A naked light bulb over-head provided dim, flickering light.

"I hear we may have to fight our way into Tientsin," said one soldier with a Northwestern twang. "Them Boxers got the whole city surrounded!"

"It ain't jist Boxers," chimed in a Southerner. "The Chinese army is in on it, too, an' they got artill'ry."

"We can roust a whole army of Chinks," boasted a big Texan, with a slow drawl. "Them yella bellies ain't no match for the U.S. Army!"

"That's not what I heard," countered a bespectacled New Englander, ticking off his points on each finger as he made his argument. "A relief force of more than two thousand tried to get to Peking, and didn't make it. Almost got wiped out, and had to retreat. Got pinned down, had to be rescued themselves, and barely made it back to

Tientsin!" Out of fingers, he spread his hands as if to say, "So there it is."

"Vasn't dot relief expedition led by Admiral Seymour, mit men from der ships? Du can't 'spect sailors to make a man's verk! Let us real soldiers take over, und see vot happens!" This from a midwestern German immigrant, who thumped his brawny fist on the table for emphasis.

"I heered dere was a bunch of Russians in dat expedition," jeered a Cajun. "'Parently dem Russies don fight too good! We gon show 'em how, yessiree!"

Walker listened as the men talked excitedly, bragging about what they would do once on land, and claiming superiority for American soldiers over all the other nationalities. It occurred to him that he would have said the same things when he first landed in Cuba, two years ago. However, as he remembered how José had saved his life, and how Miguel and Lobo and the other Macabebes had made possible the capture of Aguinaldo, he couldn't help but be amused at the arrogance of some of the men. *The Chinese will be formidable opponents,* he thought, *and we better be thankful for all the help we can get.*

By the time he finished his oatmeal and coffee he was ready to leave, having heard as much as he cared to. He felt a need for quiet and solitude and, finding a relatively isolated perch on an upper deck near the stern, sat at the railing with his legs hanging over the side and gazed toward the Chinese shore. He knew that this might be his last chance to relax for a long time to come.

24

SAVING TIENTSIN

The barge was a steam-powered paddle-wheeler, and it churned the water of the river into a white froth as it slowly chugged its way upstream past Taku and into the countryside beyond. The river was over a thousand yards wide near its mouth, narrowing to about three hundred yards further inland. It was not a clean river, carrying a lot of silt in its brown current. As he studied the rice paddies and villages of adobe brick plastered with mud and grass, Walker thought, *This doesn't look all that different from the Philippines.* He was somewhat taken aback, however, by the sight of women and mules hitched to the same plow, pulling side by side.

He felt a poke in the back of his shoulder and then Dixon was standing next to him. Dixon pointed toward the river, wordlessly. Following the direction of his arm, Walker shaded his eyes, peering intently, and then noticed something floating in the water.

"What's that?" he asked, and then realized it was a dead body. It was swollen to twice normal size, face down, drifting slowly with the current. And then he saw others. There must have been a dozen bodies in the river within view at that moment. A cloud of black flies swarmed over each body.

"We goin' where they comin' from," Dixon muttered under his breath. "Ain't gonna be no Sunday school picnic."

Walker was about to reply when he saw something on the far river bank that caught his attention. Leaning forward to get a better look, he suddenly recoiled with a visceral grunt.

"Good Lord!" he exclaimed loudly, and all the soldiers within earshot turned to look. He simply pointed. It took a few seconds before they realized what it was—a bloated body that had washed ashore was being devoured by a pack of large dogs. The air was suddenly filled with profanities and exclamations of revulsion, and then all was silent as the men grasped the same thought that Dixon had just spoken. They were heading into a war zone, and it was going to be serious business.

The gravity of the situation was impressed upon them again when they reached Tientsin. The foreign settlement adjacent to the walled city was a fortified camp, ringed with barricades of boxes and bags of rice, wool, and other commodities, manned by hundreds of soldiers in a variety of uniforms. Smoke wafted skyward from ruined buildings, and rubble was scattered everywhere. Few windows were intact. There was an air of desperation, and the new arrivals were greeted with a sense of relief, but not with celebration.

They dropped their knapsacks and bedrolls on the grass in an open area under some trees. All around them Walker could hear a virtual Babel of languages—Russian, Japanese, French, Italian, and German. He observed the colorful uniforms of the French with their red pants, and Italian soldiers with their feathered plumes, and the simple, drab outfits of the British. Looking at himself and his American comrades, he decided that they were pretty drab and plain also. He noticed some turbaned troops not far away, and was intrigued by their dark skin. There was no time to investigate, however, because they were immediately ordered to the barricades to relieve other units that had been on the line for days and were near exhaustion.

It was a relatively quiet afternoon, except for about an hour during which the Chinese on the distant wall fired artillery shells into the settlement. Some of the shells exploded overhead, but most did not explode at all. *If they ever fix the problem with their artillery shells, we're going to be in trouble,* thought Walker.

The main threat to the troops and civilians was the hail of bullets that the Chinese army poured into the settlement daily. Their aim was usually high, fortunately, but many casualties were still being suffered. A makeshift hospital had been set up in a fancy building called the Tientsin Club, a brick two-story building with slender, white engaged columns. One of the men in the Tenth, standing only a few yards away from Walker, was struck in the leg by a bullet and fell with a surprised yelp. Blood quickly soaked his pants leg from the mid-thigh down to the knee.

"Get that man to the hospital!" shouted Lieutenant McFarley.

"I'll go, sir!" said Walker immediately. Leaning his rifle against the barricade of boxes and bags, he hurried over to the fallen soldier.

"Come on, Shorty," he said. "We'll get you taken care of in no time."

They hurried across the compound with Anderson hopping on one leg, his arm across Walker's shoulders. Reaching the Tientsin Club, they looked at the flight of steps leading to the entrance.

"I reckon there ain't but one way to do this," he said, and lifted Shorty in his arms. Luckily it was only a dozen steps to the top, and they then hobbled together into the interior.

"Put him over there," ordered a bespectacled, balding man wearing a white apron stained with blood with a stethoscope around his neck, as he gestured toward a rumpled blanket on the floor, half hidden behind a partition in the corner.

"What's wrong with right here?" asked Walker, pointing to an empty cot a few feet away.

"That's for whites," replied the doctor tersely, without turning.

Instantly Walker's mind flashed back to Cuba, and he remembered the soldiers turning away José's wife and daughter without treatment. Without a word, he hoisted Shorty over to the cot and eased him down onto it.

"I said put him over *there*," snapped the doctor irritably.

"No," said Walker, quietly defiant. Something in his tone made the doctor stop and turn. Their eyes met and the doctor blinked, taking a step back.

"He's staying right here, and you'll treat him just like the white soldiers."

"Now, see here—" the doctor began to sputter, reddening. He was interrupted by a pleasant, feminine voice from behind Walker.

"That will be just fine, soldier! We'll take good care of your friend. Just leave him right there. That will be alright, *won't it*, Doctor Peters?" The last part was spoken with emphasis.

Turning, Walker beheld a tall, attractive, dark-haired young woman carrying a basket of bandages, which she placed on a table. She smiled stiffly at Walker and the doctor in a way that seemed to say, "Mind your manners, boys."

The doctor inhaled and seemed about to emit a verbal blast, when he caught Walker's eye again and thought better of it. With a scowl he turned away, waving a hand dismissively. "Out of my hospital!" he snarled. He could be heard muttering under his breath as he strode away.

"I'll be back later to check on you," Walker said to Shorty.

"Thanks, Garrett. I'll be alright."

The young woman then spoke in Chinese, giving directions and beckoning with her hand. A Chinese nurse hurried over to Shorty's cot with a towel and a bucket of water, and began to cut away his pants leg.

As Walker descended the front steps heading back to his post, the young woman was right behind him, carrying an empty basket.

"Well, Garrett!" she said, with a note of surprise in her voice. "I gather that you're not much of a conformist, are you?"

Walker wasn't sure exactly what that meant, but he stopped and removed his hat respectfully, giving her a courtly nod. "Thank you for speaking up in there, ma'am. I won't let a good man be pushed aside and disrespected, no matter what color he is."

"That's a remarkable statement for someone with a Southern accent."

Walker shrugged. "He deserves to be treated like anybody else."

"I completely agree. The same for the Chinese—they get treated worse than anyone here, even though they are Christians and are working hard for us all. Their women are making the bandages that I bring to the hospital, and their men stacked all those boxes and bags to make the barricades. But because they are Chinese, nobody trusts them. My husband had to intervene to prevent a group of them from being flogged and perhaps even executed. Where would we be without them?"

She lifted a battered bicycle that was lying on the ground and set it on its wheels, hanging the empty basket on the handlebars and putting her foot on the pedal.

"You've got a flat tire," Walker said, pointing.

"Yes," she laughed. "A bullet punctured it as I was coming over. I'll have to borrow my husband's bicycle. This one rides pretty rough now!"

"How is it that you speak Chinese?" Walker knew he was being bothersome, but his curiosity demanded an answer.

"We have been in China for two years, and I'm good with languages. My husband, Herbert, has learned a lot of Chinese also, but he has less time for it."

"Herbert? Is that Herbert Hoover? And you're Lou?"

"Why, yes! How do you know of us?"

"Mrs. Anna Drew asked me to tell you that she is alright. She made it safe and sound to the *Logan*, an American ship in the Taku harbor, along with some other women and children. She wants me to tell her husband, too."

"Oh, that is good news! Thank you so much! Anna was an angel to us—we are staying in their house for the time being. I will be sure to pass that on to Edward, her husband. He will be so relieved."

She put her weight on the pedal and the bicycle began move briskly, the flat tire making it vibrate on the brick pavement. "Stay safe, Garrett!" she called over her shoulder.

Walker shook his head as he watched her pedal away, noticing for the first time the .38 revolver tucked into the back of her belt. *A bullet punctures her tire, and she still rides along as if nothing has happened,* he marveled. *She's braver than some soldiers.* Suddenly, for the first time in two years, he remembered the article he had read in the newspaper he'd found in the Birmingham train station—"Very few girls want to be left behind," it had said. "She wishes to be in the thick of the fight!" He remembered laughing at the idea then, but now, thinking of Harriet and watching Lou Hoover pedal her bicycle across the bullet-riddled settlement, he realized how wrong he had been. *I'll take the line alongside either of them anytime,* he thought. *They've got what it takes, as much as any man.*

Just before midnight the men at the barricade saw action. Most of them were sitting with their backs to the barrier, smoking and talking, while others took turns standing sentry duty. A few artillery shells exploded overhead, doing no real damage, and a storm of bullets peppered the barricade for several minutes.

"They're coming!" called out a sentry.

Everyone got to their feet and chambered rounds in their rifles as they took firing positions. As Walker peered over the pile of rice and peanut bags in front of him, he was shocked at what he saw. Under the dim light of the barely visible moon, the ground itself between the foreign settlement and the old city wall appeared to be alive and moving. Many thousands of Boxers were swarming toward them, the leaders already within four hundred yards of the barricade and coming quickly. The cacophony of sounds coming from the advancing horde was like that of a strong wind blowing through dry leaves, getting louder by the minute. He was mystified by the bright red lights he could see flickering among them as they advanced.

"Hold your fire until they are closer!" shouted a British officer. Walker tightened his finger on the trigger, looking down the barrel to find a target.

What he saw next was even more astonishing. The Boxers stopped advancing when they were within two hundred yards and began to leap into the air, twisting and gyrating as they swung swords and spears over their heads. Some fell to the earth and rolled about, then got back up to leap acrobatically again. He could see that the red lights were lanterns, and those carrying them joined in the leaping and wild dancing. Thousands of voices were raised in unnerving shrieks and shouts of "Sha! Sha!" which Walker later learned meant "Kill! Kill!" They appeared to be working themselves into a frenzy, and Walker sensed that a climax was imminent. He didn't have long to wait. The shrieking reached a crescendo of volume and pitch, and then the charge began.

"Fire!"

The rifles erupted in a deadly roar, and Boxers fell by the dozens. The avalanche came onward, oblivious to the hail of bullets. Walker fired as fast as he could, picking out the armed attackers rather than those carrying the red lanterns, who he thought were not a real threat. He realized soon, however, that the lanterns were not for illumination, but for starting fires. The lantern carriers threw their flaming censers onto the barricades, igniting the bags. The smoke obscured the soldiers' vision and allowed the sword-wielding attackers to reach the barrier. Some executed amazing leaps over the top, landing among the soldiers and slashing about with their long, curved blades. Soldiers were shouting frantically and Boxers were screaming, and with the gunfire, flames, and smoke, it was truly a scene from hell.

Walker's rifle was empty, so, dropping it, he pulled his pistol and fired almost point-blank at the invaders. He spied a figure atop the barricade swinging a red lantern and instantly emptied his gun, using both hands. The attacker crumpled, twisting and falling forward while the glowing lantern hit the ground, spreading fire in all directions. More Boxers were vaulting over the barricade, screaming as they came. Walker ripped off his jacket and snatched the machete free from its loop over his left shoulder, and also pulled his foot-long bayonet from its scabbard on his belt. The "rebel yell" instinctively came to his lips as he leaped forward, slashing madly right and left with both blades. It was more of a riot than a battle.

Fortunately, the Boxers who penetrated the defensive barrier were greatly outnumbered and the soldiers were able to defeat them after several minutes of desperate fighting. As the Boxers retreated under heavy fire, buckets of water were hurriedly brought to douse the flames and save the barricade. A half-dozen soldiers were killed and many more were wounded, some seriously.

Walker wiped the blood from his weapons on the clothing of a dead Boxer, and returned them to their sheaths. He retrieved his firearms, and as he began to reload them he noticed that his hands were shaking. He knelt on one knee to steady himself. Wiping what he thought was sweat from his forehead, his hand came away covered with blood. *When did that happen?* he wondered.

Suddenly Dixon was there, crouching beside him. "So, Garrett, was that more exciting than rasslin' with a python?"

"Lord a mercy!" breathed Walker in reply. "I've never seen nothin' like that. If they'd been carrying guns instead of swords and knives, they might of taken us."

"Probably so. We lost two killed and five wounded, counting you."

"Me? I ain't wounded."

"Then what's that blood all over you? Get over to the hospital and get cleaned up. And don't be gone long—they might come back."

At the hospital, Walker saw Lieutenant McFarley lying on a cot. His right arm was missing from the shoulder down, and he was moaning and crying out in pain. Doctor Peters gave him a syringe of some drug, and in a few minutes McFarley passed out. Lou Hoover and some Chinese women were busily taking care of wounded men, and there was no time for talk. After getting a bandage wrapped around his head, he headed back to the barricade.

It was quiet for the rest of the night. They threw the bodies of the Boxers back over the barricade. Walker lifted the shoulders of one of the red-clad bodies while another soldier lifted the feet. He realized that this was the one who had been holding the red lantern when he shot him. Taking a closer look, he was shocked to see that it was a young girl! He froze, mouth open, and almost dropped the body.

"What's the matter, Yank?" asked the other soldier, a Brit.

"This is a girl!" he exclaimed in amazement.

The Brit laughed. "Never seen a girl before?" he asked, derisively.

"Never killed one."

"Get used to it," the Brit scowled, becoming serious. "Those Red

Lanterns are all girls, and they're just as dangerous as the Boxers. Never hesitate to put lead through one of 'em or they'll get you, for sure."

"Who's in charge here?" asked an authoritative voice. It was Colonel Liscum, commander of the Ninth.

"Sir!" Walker snapped to attention, saluting briskly.

"Who's in charge of the Tenth squadron?" repeated the colonel.

"Lieutenant McFarley, sir! He's in the hospital—lost his arm last night!"

"Lost his *life*, you mean. He died this morning. Loss of blood. Who is second in command?"

"Sir? Dead?" Walker stammered, stunned. "I saw—he was—I'm sorry to hear that, sir!"

"Corporal, are you going to tell me who is in charge now, or should I ask somebody else?"

"Sorry, sir. McFarley was our only officer. The next highest ranking soldier in our unit would be Sergeant Dixon, sir. He's right over there."

Liscum glanced in the direction Walker pointed and then looked back at him, hands on hips, frowning.

"He's colored."

"Yes sir. He is colored, sir. Sort of a medium brown, I'd say, sir."

Liscum took a threatening step forward, his eyes spitting fire and his upper lip curling. "Would you like to be a private again, soldier? Don't give me any smart mouth!"

"No sir! Not at all, sir!" Walker saluted again, for good measure. "But Sergeant Dixon has been a soldier for eight years and has fought Indians on the plains, Spaniards in Cuba, and Filipinos in the Philippines. The men all respect him, sir, and he'll make an excellent leader."

"None of that matters to me, and I don't need your recommendation, Corporal. But you're clearly not officer material, so I guess it's got to be Dixon." He turned to go, and then stopped and looked back at Walker. "Get rid of these bodies. They stink."

"Yes sir!" Accompanied by another salute.

"By the way," said Liscum, turning back again. "You'll have to be reassigned to a different unit. We can't have a white soldier under a colored officer. It just wouldn't do."

"Sir!" objected Walker. "I've been attached to the Tenth since I left Florida in '98, first as an aide to Captain Joe Wheeler, then an aide to Captain Pershing, and then to Lieutenant McFarley. This unit is my home, and I would like to stay with these men, sir."

Liscum peered intently at Walker for a long second.

"Do you mean that you would be willing to take orders from a colored man, soldier?"

"Sir, I respect Sergeant Dixon and would have no problem taking orders from him."

Liscum squinted down his nose at Walker for several more seconds before responding. "Very well," he snapped, and turned abruptly away.

As he bent to lift the Red Lantern girl again, he noticed that the British soldier was staring at him with open mouth.

"You never seen a colonel before?" Walker said.

"I never saw a soldier get away with giving a colonel lip like that before. A British officer would've tossed you into the brig for that. You Yanks are pretty casual about discipline."

"We get the job done. That's what counts. Help me with this girl."

They tossed the body over the barricade. When the last of the bodies had been removed, the British soldier leaned against the wall and studied Walker.

"By the way, I've been wondering about your black soldiers. They used to be slaves, and now they fight under your flag, but in separate units. Their officers are always white. Is that what you mean by 'getting the job done?'"

"Well, they get the job done as well as anybody. There are some black officers, and in time there'll be a lot more."

The Brit lit a cigarette and grunted as if he didn't believe Walker.

"By the way," Walker continued, "I saw some dark-skinned soldiers in the bivouac area with a British flag, and I was wondering who they are."

"They're Sikhs, from India."

"So they're not British? Why do they carry a British flag?"

"They're British imperial troops. India is part of the British Empire."

"That means Britain conquered their country and rules over them, right? And don't they have white officers, too?"

"It's not the same thing, Yank! They have white officers because we Englishmen have the training to be officers, and they don't."

"Why don't they?"

"They're not cut out for it. Besides, no white man would take orders from a colored man. Would you really take orders from a colored officer?"

"I reckon I will, if Liscum puts Sergeant Dixon in charge of our unit. He's a first-rate soldier and the right man for the job."

"That's Second Lieutenant Dixon, thank you very much!" Walker turned to see Dixon walking up.

"My!" he exclaimed with a grin. Standing up stiffly, he saluted. "Sir!"

"At ease, Garrett," Dixon said, with a wry expression. "It's only temporary. I've been breveted a second lieutenant, and Jesse Brown's filling in at sergeant. They're giving me McFarley's jacket to wear, as soon as they get the blood washed out of it. Easier than cutting the shoulder straps off of it and sewing them onto mine, especially since I'll be a sergeant again, 'fore too long. It will have a hole in the shoulder—colored man's luck." He shrugged.

"Congratulations! What do you want us to do, Lieutenant Dixon?"

"We going to be relieved by the British Indian troops in a few minutes. As soon as they get here, we going to breakfast."

"Yes sir!" Walker saluted again. Dixon returned the salute and then continued down the barricade, speaking quietly with each of the men as he went.

After he was out of earshot, the British soldier shook his head in disbelief. "I don't believe what I just saw. It's just not natural."

"There's nobody I'd rather see with those shoulder straps. You know, you oughta get to know some of those Sikh fellows. They might change your mind about colored officers."

"Bah!" he spat, and with a disgusted look, turned and walked away.

The commanders of the different countries' military forces met that evening and decided that it was time to go on the offensive and attack the walled Chinese city to drive out the Boxers and Chinese army forces. The attack was planned for early the next morning.

The men arose in the dark at three a.m. to eat a quick breakfast and assemble in marching order. German and Russian troops were to attack the East Gate of the city while the British, French, Japanese, and Americans attacked the South Gate. The terrain was swampy, flat, and treeless, and crisscrossed with canals, causeways, and dikes, besides a few burial mounds. Both the native city and the foreign community were surrounded by a ten-foot-high mud wall which could be used for cover, but approaching the city gates under enemy fire would be very difficult. Getting through the massive gates would be even more difficult.

Led by Herbert Hoover, who knew the area well, they left the foreign settlement at three-thirty, exiting its southern gate and following the mud wall westward, using it for cover. Heavy rifle fire from the twenty-five-foot-high city wall kept the men low and hugging close to the mud wall. By five o'clock they had reached a position directly opposite the city's South Gate, but the next step would be the most difficult. They were still a thousand yards from the city gate, and a large swamp, a canal, and other obstacles blocked their path. Crossing this space under heavy fire without protective cover was going to be brutal. Nevertheless the order was given and the men scrambled through an opening in the wall, over a small bridge across a canal, and ran frantically toward anything that offered protection. After advancing about a hundred yards, most of the men lay face down in the mud against a dike in front of the swamp while the rest clustered behind grave mounds. The Chinese rifle fire was incessant and very accurate, so that putting one's head up was risky.

Several soldiers had already been hit. Things were not looking good, Walker thought.

The situation was dire. The men could not afford to stay where they were, but there was also no way to advance to a safer position closer to the city wall. It appeared that there was a better position to the right of them, and Colonel Liscum saw it.

"Ninth to the right!" shouted Liscum, jumping to his feet and waving his arm over his head. The battalion immediately sprang up and sprinted toward a low mud wall a hundred yards away. Unfortunately, just before they reached it they discovered that a small canal lay before them, with water too deep to wade and no bridge. They dove into the mud along the bank of the canal, gaining some limited protection from fire coming from the city wall, but now exposed to fire coming from their right. Liscum stood, pointing as he shouted an order. A bullet sent him toppling face down, dead.

"Keep down and return fire!" This time it was Lieutenant Dixon taking charge.

Walker slipped down the bank and crouched in waist-deep water to make himself a smaller target. He fired as rapidly as possible toward the Chinese troops who were shooting at them from a group of huts several hundred yards away. At that distance it was impossible to actually aim at a specific enemy soldier, but returning fire might help interfere with their accuracy. The Ninth was taking casualties at an alarming rate, but they could neither advance nor retreat without making things even worse.

The pressure on them eased slightly, thanks to the attacks by the other Allied forces. The German and Russian contingents were assaulting the East Gate of the city, supported by artillery fire from the foreign settlement. A lucky shot landed an artillery shell in the Chinese powder magazine causing a tremendous explosion which could be heard for more than a mile away, and a plume of smoke rose several hundred feet in the air. Japanese engineers repeatedly attempted to reach the South Gate to plant explosives, but were repulsed each time. On occasion they reached the wall itself and the

Chinese defenders, being unable to fire down upon them, threw stones and bricks down, driving the attackers away.

Finally, in the wee hours of the morning, a Japanese soldier succeeded in reaching the South Gate with an explosive charge. When it detonated the soldier was killed, but the outer gate was blown in. Reacting to the blast, the Japanese charged forward en masse. Placing ladders at the wall, several men scaled it and dropped down on the other side. The inner gate was quickly opened, and British and American soldiers joined the Japanese in rushing into the city. What followed was a desperate struggle by both sides in the darkness, illuminated only by the fires raging across the city.

Bayonets were the weapon of choice in the dark streets. The Chinese resisted tenaciously until a roaring crash signaled that the East Gate had also been breached. The Chinese forces immediately beat a hasty retreat, exiting the city at its North Gate. The street fighting had lasted one hour.

The Chinese civilian population frantically tried to escape out the North Gate also, but hundreds were trampled to death in the stampede, and the foreign troops made it worse by firing into the crowd, causing even more panic. A third of the city was on fire, the flammable housing materials having been set ablaze by the artillery shells during the previous day.

As the sun rose, Walker could hardly believe his eyes as he surveyed the scene. The streets were covered with dead bodies—both human and animal—and blood was everywhere. Corpses were piled several feet high in some places. Discipline broke down among the foreign troops and an orgy of looting began, and lasted most of the day. Soldiers broke into shops and homes, smashing porcelain and glassware, searching eagerly for gold, silver, or jewels. Any resistance by the Chinese civilians typically led to death at the end of a bayonet.

By mid-day the fires across the city had mostly been extinguished. Bodies were collected and piled for burning. The stench was overwhelming. Buzzards circled continuously overhead, and some descended to perch expectantly on the ornate rooftops of the surviving structures. This was carnage and destruction on a scale beyond anything Walker had yet seen. He stumbled aimlessly into a wide plaza littered with piles of bodies, pools of blood, and soldiers scurrying about with their hands full of stolen goods. Speechless, he gazed about, trying to comprehend what had happened to such a beautiful, prosperous, ancient city, in barely more than a day of battle. He could not absorb what his eyes beheld.

"Garrett! Are you deaf?" It was Dixon, fifty yards away. "Get over here!"

Dixon had rounded up the battered remains of the Tenth. "We're getting out of here. Heading back to camp. Nothin' for us to do here."

"Yes sir," said Walker, saluting tiredly. "Have you ever seen anything like this?"

"Don't want to see nothin' like this. Seen enough already."

No one spoke as they walked out of the city and made their way back to the bivouac area in the foreign settlement. Each man was almost completely covered in mud and blood, and many were limping or leaning on a fellow soldier for support. Having had hardly anything to eat since breakfast the previous day, they were famished, thirsty, and in need of medical attention. They would have only a few days to recover before an even more challenging mission awaited them—the march to Peking.

25

ON TO PEKING

Walker squinted up at the scorching sun and removed his hat to wipe the sweat from his brow. He stood on an elevated roadway snaking its way across the flat plain stretching toward Peking, flanked on both sides by fields of towering cornstalks. Shifting the weight of his heavy backpack, he thought, *I have never been so hot in all my life. This is like walking through a blast furnace.* The rest of the Tenth trudged up from the cornfield to the roadway, some kneeling and some leaning with hands on knees. No one spoke, but everyone was thinking the same thing.

It was two weeks since the fall of Tientsin, and news reports from Peking were dire—the international community there was not going to be able to hold out much longer. Despite the fact that less than half the desired number of troops were available for the rescue expedition, it was decided to start anyway. Therefore, approximately twenty-thousand men representing eight nations began to move northward up the Pei-Ho River toward the Chinese capital city, some eighty miles away.

Within two days after leaving Tientsin they had fought two battles against the Chinese army. The Japanese bore the brunt of the fighting, suffering the most casualties as the Chinese were driven back in retreat. No further battles occurred until they reached Peking a week later. The retreating Chinese breached the dikes along the river, flooding the countryside and making the march even more difficult for the invaders. Following the second battle some of the foreign units, including the French, decided to return to Tientsin. The relief expedition, however, continued onward.

"I don't know which is worse," said Dixon, "—being up on this blistering road, or fighting through that jungle of corn. I ain't never seen such corn. It's like a forest."

"You could get lost in there," added another man. "Can't see six feet in front of you."

"At least you can catch a breeze now and then up here," chimed in a third.

"Some fresh water would be a good thing," croaked another, as he drained the final drops from his canteen.

It was now August, and the heat was getting worse each day. Temperatures reached 105 in the shade. The road was littered with men who had passed out from the heat, foaming at the mouth, and a horse-drawn cart was piled with bodies of men who had died of heat exhaustion. The only real relief the men had from the heat of the day was at night when they would bathe in the waters of the Pei-Ho. One had to occasionally step aside to let a dead body float past, but no one seemed to mind. The soldiers even filled their canteens with the water without bothering to boil it. To sleep, they unrolled their blankets among the stiff cornstalks, too tired to clear them for a proper campsite.

When passing through villages the men would empty the wells, filling every container they could find. In one village they discovered a number of umbrellas, and those lucky enough to get one had some protection from the sun as they marched along. Eventually, however, sheer fatigue led them to discard them, to be claimed by other soldiers following behind. Walker, along with many other men, lined his hat with cornstalk leaves which hung halfway down his back. The flowing cornstalk leaves and colorful umbrellas made for a very unusual sight as the multinational army slowly made its way northward.

The Chinese villagers and townspeople typically fled at the approach of the foreign troops. Some women committed suicide rather than fall into the hands of the feared attackers. American and British soldiers, upon finding cringing, frightened people who had been unable to escape—usually the elderly—treated them humanely, providing food and medical care if needed. Walker observed that the Russians and Japanese, however, were more likely to shoot them or bayonet them.

"Why are they like that?" asked Walker, standing in the shade during a rest-break in a small village. "They seem to enjoy killing just for the sake of killing."

"Maybe has something to do with them living next door to China, 'stead of halfway 'round the world," replied Dixon. "Maybe they don't get along so good."

Walker thought about that for a moment. "I don't know," he said, skeptically. "Seems like it's more of a personal thing."

"If you was born a Russian," argued Dixon, "you think you would be diff'rent from them?"

"I can't say that I would," he admitted. "I still think it's a choice, but maybe we don't all see the same choices. Maybe you're right— maybe where we come from gives us our choices. But I still think a person *has* some choices. You can't just always take the bad ones and say you're not to blame. It's up to us to pick the best choices of the ones we've got. That's a personal thing."

Dixon laughed softly. "Remember that when you get back to Alabama, Garrett." He then called for the unit to resume the march. Walker stood for a long minute contemplating Dixon's final comment, and then joined the end of the line slowly heading out of the village.

Five more miserable days in the heat finally brought them to the outskirts of Peking. The expedition force had lost hundreds of men to heat exhaustion, and those who completed the trek were severely fatigued. The Chinese army had pulled back within the city walls, so the allies took a day to rest and reconnoiter the situation before beginning the assault.

Peking was a city of many walls. The newer, southern part of the city, known as the Chinese City, was encircled by a wall twenty feet high and thirty feet thick. The older, northern part of the city, called the Tartar City, was surrounded by the massive Tartar Wall—forty feet high and fifty feet wide across the top, with multi-story pagodas rising above its gates. Within it were the walls of the Imperial City, and inside that, the walled Forbidden City, where only the emperor's family was allowed. The walls and gates were manned by Chinese soldiers, armed with modern rifles and artillery.

The rescue force was advancing on the capital from the east, and each of the four national contingents was assigned a gate to attack. The Russians were to assault the gate on the northeast corner of the Tartar Wall, and the Japanese were assigned a gate a mile south of them. Another mile to the south, the Americans were to attack the Tungpienmen Gate at the juncture of the Tartar Wall and the Chinese City wall, and the British took the southernmost gate. The gates assigned to the American and British forces were closest to the foreign legations, but once through those gates they would have to then penetrate the Tartar Wall in order to reach the besieged defenders.

Each country's contingent wanted to be the first to reach the international community, and a competitive spirit imbued the soldiers and their commanders. The gate assigned to the Russian force was the farthest from the Legation Quarter, so, in the dark hours of the early morning, before the assault was scheduled to begin, the Russians marched south and attacked the Tungpienmen Gate, which was assigned to the Americans. This gate had appeared to be weakly defended and the Russians thought that they might be able to force their way through and achieve a quick victory. However, after breaching the outer gate with artillery, they were pinned down by heavy rifle fire from the top of the wall and were unable to advance further. This movement served mainly to irritate the other national units and precipitate a pell-mell rush by all parties to launch their attacks ahead of schedule.

Arriving at the Tungpienmen Gate the Americans found it clogged with Russian troops and equipment. Their commanding officer had been shot and they were disorganized, leaderless, and going nowhere. It was obvious that entering through this gate was not an option. As he gazed up at the massive wall, Walker had a sudden flash of inspiration. Excited, he ran to Dixon and explained his idea.

"You're crazy, but it just might work," Dixon said skeptically. "Let me run it by Colonel Daggett."

The two of them approached the colonel. His reaction was similar to Dixon's. Looking at Walker with a raised eyebrow, he said, "If you're crazy enough to try it, go ahead." And then to Dixon: "Have your men provide covering fire. It's a suicide mission, but we don't have any better options right now."

The regiment opened fire on the Chinese forces atop the wall to allow the Tenth to advance to the foot of the wall. Once there, the black soldiers aimed their rifles upward and continued raking the parapet with a blizzard of bullets. Walker, leaning his rifle against the wall, found hand and toe-holds in the battered exterior of the brick fortress and began to climb.

The wall was so rugged that it was not difficult to find crevices and holes. As he scaled the wall, he realized that it was a lot further to the top than it had looked from the bottom. Glancing down, he also realized that descending was not an option—there was no turning back. Finally reaching the crenelated parapet, he grasped the top with his left hand and pulled his revolver. Peering over the edge, he was surprised to find that the Chinese soldiers had already retreated and there was no one in sight. It looked like an abandoned military camp on top of the wall, with mats, equipment, and cooking utensils lying about in disarray. He hoisted himself over the top and gave the "all clear" sign. Immediately other soldiers began scrambling up, and in minutes the "Stars and Stripes" was waving on top of the wall. A huge cheer went up from the American regiments, who surged forward and pushed past the disorganized and confused Russians, forcing the inner gate with help from soldiers on the inside.

They headed west, parallel to the Tartar Wall, looking for an opening to let them into the old city where the foreign legations were still under attack. Chinese resistance was dogged, consisting mainly of snipers and sharpshooters on the roofs of buildings. This slowed the advance, forcing the men to take defensive measures, running from building to building, and climbing to the rooftops to drive the snipers away. Having taken control of the wall itself, soldiers were able to use its vantage point to suppress the resistance. Casualties were few, but the rate of progress seemed agonizingly slow.

Skulls picked clean by birds and dogs, broken and rusted swords and rifles, shards of glass and thousands of brass cartridges littered the streets, reminding Walker that fighting had been going on here for two months already. The streets were deserted, and he could occasionally see distant figures running away, but couldn't tell if they were civilian or military.

After inching their way for several blocks they found a sluice gate, through which flowed a sewage canal. It was euphemistically called the "Jade River," due to its stagnant green water. The stench was terrible and Walker had to fight the urge to vomit, but sloshed through the canal along with the rest of the men, some of whom gagged audibly. One man slipped on the slick, slimy stones and fell, going completely under the water. He instantly leaped up to his feet, making an awful choking noise, only to slip and fall under again. His thrashing was splattering the soldiers nearby with sewage, and their laughter turned to cursing, which provoked even more laughter from those far enough away to be unaffected.

After a two-hour running battle in the streets they finally reached the foreign legation compound. Upon entering the compound Walker was surprised at how pleasant everything appeared. It had been feared that the inhabitants had all been massacred and the place destroyed, but the international residents were clean and neatly dressed, and there was minimal structural damage. He actually began to feel self-conscious about being so dirty, gaunt, and splattered with mud and sewage among such decent and sophisticated people. But then he looked closer and noticed the thousands of bullet marks on the walls. He saw that almost no windows had glass remaining, and the people were mostly thin and pale. They had the appearance of a community of invalids.

One young woman approached Walker hesitantly, and with a somewhat vacant expression, gave him a nervous smile. "I am glad you are here," she said, with a cultured British accent. "We've been waiting for a long time."

"Sorry it took so long," Walker said kindly, doffing his hat. "You're safe now."

"I hope so," she replied, almost in a whisper. She seemed to totter a bit as she walked away, stopping to speak briefly to other soldiers as she went. He noticed a number of British and American officers standing in a group under the shade trees, talking with some well-dressed gentlemen who were smoking cigars. He assumed that these were the diplomats who had been the targets of the Boxers' siege. They appeared well-fed, he noted, and a little too ebullient, laughing and talking loudly as they gestured energetically with their cigars. In the background he saw several Chinese watching from a distance. They were gaunt, staring.

Walking quickly, he caught up with the young woman. "Excuse me, ma'am," he said, touching the brim of his hat respectfully. "Can you tell me who those well-dressed men are, over there in that group?" With his thumb he indicated over his shoulder the group of gentlemen and officers.

"Oh, they are the ministers of the foreign legations," she said cheerfully. "They are the diplomats representing all of the foreign governments here in Peking."

"Were they the leaders of the defense against the siege, then?"

"Oh no, the military officers were in charge of the defense."

"Well, I guess they organized and led the civilians in support of the soldiers? Perhaps caring for the wounded, making sure food was distributed, and things like that?"

"Oh, no, the ladies took charge of that. You can't expect diplomats to be concerned with such things as that."

"Hmmm," mused Walker, noisily scratching his lightly bristled chin. "What exactly *did* they do, then?"

"Oh—" she said again, and paused. After thinking for several seconds, she finally said, almost triumphantly, "They talked a lot. It was very interesting to hear them. Our British minister—MacDonald—he gave a lot of orders to everyone. He was in charge."

"I see," Walker nodded. "One more thing—who are those Chinese over yonder? Are they friendly?"

"Oh, yes!" she smiled, apparently happy for a question easy to answer. "They are the Chinese Christians who took refuge here from the Boxers. They would have been slaughtered on the outside. We protected them here in the legations."

"That's wonderful. Why are they so thin and hungry looking? They look half-starved."

"That's because they *are* half-starved. We've been living on rice and horse meat ourselves, and there wasn't enough to share with the Chinese too, especially since we didn't know how long the siege would last. I'm afraid they've suffered quite a bit. It's a shame, too. I wish we could have helped them. I know that several Chinese babies died of hunger. I felt really badly for them. Maybe now that you soldiers have arrived, we can all have enough to eat." She finished with a cherubic smile, pleased to have been able to share her knowledge.

"Thank you, ma'am," Walker said quietly, touching his hat brim again. "I hope that you do get enough to eat." As she walked away, Walker stared at the growing group of ragged, thin Chinese on the periphery of the commons. He could almost feel their hunger in the pit of his stomach.

Impulsively, he walked toward the group. As he approached closer, they noticed him and he felt their eyes focus on him. They were all watching him, clearly wondering why he was coming their way. Walker wasn't actually sure why he was going to them, either, but a purpose crystallized in his mind as he walked—and he realized that it was his intention all along, even though he hadn't known it. When he reached the group he took off his backpack and set it on the ground. Opening it, he took out his ration sack of hardtack, beef jerky, and canned peaches and tomatoes. Handing it to an older man with a white beard, he waved his hand broadly to indicate that it was for everyone and put his hand to his mouth as if eating. The old man's eyes widened, and the group began to cluster around him, expectantly.

Suddenly someone was standing beside Walker. It was Dixon. He had opened his backpack also, and was pulling out his ration sack. Walker glanced over his shoulder and saw that every man of the Tenth squadron was coming toward them, swinging their backpacks off. In a few minutes a significant amount of food had been distributed among the famished Chinese, who were excitedly opening the containers and beginning to eat.

The white-bearded old man turned toward them and spread his hands as if to embrace the soldiers. There were tears in his eyes as he said, in broken English, "Tank you, 'Mericans. Tank you."

A chorus of replies such as "You're welcome" and "No problem" arose from the soldiers as they backed slowly away and then turned to go back to their places. The act of charity meant that they would probably have to go without supper, but no one complained.

Walker noticed an old artillery fieldpiece between two buildings, braced with sandbags. He strolled over to take a look. There was a young American marine standing next to it, wearing the big slouch hat typical of the U.S. Marines.

"We was beginning to wonder if y'all was gonna get here or not," said the marine, with a distinct southern accent.

"We did the best we could," replied Walker. "That was the hardest eighty miles I ever marched. Where you from, soldier?"

"Georgia. You?"

"Alabama. Long way from home, ain't it?"

"Mighty long way."

"That's an unusual looking cannon you got there."

The marine laughed with genuine mirth. "We call this the

'International Gun,'" he said. "It's a British barrel tied to an Italian carriage with Chinese rope, worked by American marines, firing Russian shells packed with German gunpowder and using Japanese fuses."

"Well, I guess you got to do what you can, where you are, with what you've got."

They both laughed, and for the next half-hour they shared stories about home, bragging about their mama's cooking and what they were going to eat when they got back. Walker shared the story of his battle with the python, and the marine talked about enduring the siege. They felt almost like brothers in a short time.

"Looks like we're 'bout to move out," Walker said, reluctantly. "More work to do."

"Watch out for the jingals," advised the marine. "They're dangerous."

"What's a jingal?"

"The biggest rifle you ever seen. Seven foot long, at least .75 caliber, maybe more. Takes two or three men to work it, and they prop it on a support 'cause it's so heavy. Very accurate long-range. More like a cannon than a rifle."

"Thanks—I'll pass it on."

After their brief rest in the legation compound, the American soldiers moved back out into the city streets to drive out the last of the Chinese army forces and Boxers. They moved in two single-file lines, one on each side of the street. They advanced cautiously but quickly from street to street, house to house, carefully watching the rooftops and upper windows, as well as the alleys and side streets, peering ahead as well as to the rear. It was tense, exhausting work, but before sundown they had pushed all the way to the gates of the Forbidden City itself. Almost all of the resistance had already fled the city, and those who remained were mostly unarmed civilians, petrified with fear. They later learned that the Empress Dowager had also escaped, disguised as a peasant woman. The Imperial Palace was abandoned.

The American troops bivouacked that night in the courtyard of the palace. It seemed a different world than the desolate and shattered city beyond its red walls. Inside the wide moat and massive gates, all was quiet and serene. Outside, the pillaging of the city had already begun, abating only slightly with the coming of darkness. The sounds of gunshots could be heard all through the night.

At twilight the company cook suddenly appeared in a doorway with his arms full of bread loaves, found in a pantry storeroom inside the palace.

"There's more where this came from!" he shouted, as he staggered down a half-dozen steps. "And all kinds of fruit and vegetables, and cakes!"

The prospect of fresh food for supper instead of canned rations spurred the soldiers into action, and many stampeded through the doorway. The hungry men of the Tenth were at the front of the charge, emerging with arms laden with all sorts of tasty prizes, and knapsacks stuffed with supplies for the next few days.

"That's the first chow line I been in front of since this war started!" exclaimed Dixon, grinning. The other black soldiers hooted their glee as they tore into the bread, pastry, and fruit. Walker, sitting on the paving stones, laughed with them as watermelon juice ran off his chin. He spat out the seeds and took another huge bite.

"This is the best watermelon I ever ate!" he chortled, tossing the rind aside with red juice dripping from his nose.

"Wait 'til you try them oranges!"

"That brown cake's got nuts in it—watch out you don't break a tooth!"

"Them dark rolls got some kinda jelly in 'em! Gawd, I love China!"

"I sure am glad we gave our rations to those Chinese Christians. Made more room for this stuff!" This produced a chorus of "Amen's" and "You got that right!"

They continued with such banter until everyone was too stuffed with food to talk, and then they lay on their backs on the cobblestones, groaning and belching. Within minutes, snoring could be heard.

Walker, gazing up at the sky, wondered if its red glow was the sunset or fires burning in the city. As the glow faded slowly, he concluded that it was from the sunset. He admired the beautiful, yellow-tiled roof of the palace, silhouetted against the darkening sky, its tiles tinted faintly orange in the sun's dying rays. It occurred to him that the setting of the sun was symbolic of the demise of the Chinese nation. *Soon*, he thought, *it will be dark. But come morning, the sun will rise again. Maybe one day, China will also rise again.*

Suddenly thirsty, he stood up and scanned the courtyard for a source of water. He spied what appeared to be a well in the far corner, and grabbing his canteen, headed over to it. He was not disappointed. Cranking the handle on the pulley he brought up a bucket of cool, fresh water. After filling his canteen, he splashed his face and then poured water over his head.

"Hey! Don't waste all that water on a lousy corporal!"

"Help yourself, Lieutenant. Can't beat a drink of cool water on a hot day."

When Dixon was done with the water bucket they stood silently, watching the hundreds of soldiers milling about in the huge court-yard. As the daylight faded to darkness, they began settling down for the night. Eventually, Walker spoke.

"So, what's next? Is this going to be like Tientsin?

"Worse, probably. I 'spect we'll be patrolling the city to keep order, but it won't do any good. There won't be nothin' worth having left in this city by the end of the week."

"War is kind of a mess, I reckon."

"It ain't even civilized. Men from civilized, Christian countries turn into the worst rascals you ever saw, soon as they git the opportunity to loot and rape and kill with no fear of punishment. The Injuns we fought on the plains was more civilized than some of the whites. The red men only killed soldiers, but the soldiers killed men, women, and children. Down South, white men lynch colored men on Saturday night, and then go to church on Sunday and sing with the choir. Civilization ain't no more than skin deep, but hypocrisy goes all the way to the bone."

Walker said nothing, but let the import of Dixon's words sink in. It was very uncomfortable, but he knew that he spoke the truth.

"We need sentries tonight," said Dixon, abruptly changing the subject. "I'll take the first watch. You relieve me at midnight. I'll have someone relieve you at three."

"Yes sir."

"Garrett."

Walker had started to walk away, but turned back when Dixon said his name. There was something in his tone that caught Walker's ear.

"Yes sir?"

Dixon fixed his eyes intently on Walker's for a long minute. Walker felt as though Dixon was staring into his brain. Shifting uneasily on his feet, he repeated, "Yes sir?"

"I never heard a white man say 'sir' to a black man before. It don't seem to bother you none. Does it?"

"No sir, not a bit. I'm a corporal, and you're a lieutenant. That's all there is to it."

"When McFarley went down, I figured they'd make you the lieutenant, not me."

Walker laughed. "Liscum said I wasn't officer material. And then he said they'd have to transfer me to a different unit because putting a white man under a colored officer just wasn't done. I said it was alright. I said I wanted to stay in the Tenth—it's my unit. I belong here. He just shook his head and stomped off."

"Huh," Dixon grunted softly. Giving Walker another long, piercing look, he said, "Get some sleep, Garrett. I'll see you at midnight."

"Yes sir."

At midnight Walker rose stiffly from the hard ground, stretched, and yawned. Slinging his rifle over his shoulder, he stepped over the prone bodies of sleeping soldiers and made his way to the gate of the courtyard. Beyond the gate was a bridge over the fifty-foot-wide moat, and a long, broad street leading away through the city. Dixon stood in the archway of the gate, chatting with a couple of other soldiers.

As he approached the group the moon emerged from behind a cloud, illuminating the scene with its soft light. In the distance, far down the avenue, a movement caught his eye. Squinting as he studied it, he saw three figures of men scurrying into the middle of the street almost a half-mile away. Two of them appeared to be carrying a beam of wood, one end of which they propped on a stick held by the third man. The beam pointed at the gate where the men stood. Walker realized suddenly what was about to happen.

"Get down!" he shouted and ran to the side of the archway, unslinging his rifle and chambering a round.

Dixon hesitated, but only for a second, and then he ran to join Walker. The other two soldiers did not move, but only looked around curiously. The roar of the jingal was so loud that it reverberated down the street like a crash of thunder. One of the two soldiers was knocked completely off his feet, his jacket a bloody mess. Walker squeezed the trigger of his .30 caliber Krag, worked the bolt and fired again, five times. One of the jingal crew collapsed in the street and the other two lugged the heavy weapon away. One of them appeared to be wounded. Dixon added several shots of his own, but the Chinese were gone before the other American soldier could join in the shooting.

"What the hell was that?" gasped the stunned soldier.

"A jingal—a sort of Chinese rifle-cannon. Large caliber, long range."

"Good Lord! Look at the size of the hole in Ferguson's chest. You could stick three fingers in it. He never had a chance."

He and Dixon carried the body away while Walker took up a less exposed position against the wall of the archway. He was joined shortly by a couple of soldiers from other units, but no one felt like talking. They kept a close eye on their surroundings, and the rest of the three-hour watch passed quietly.

Walker returned to his blanket to get a couple hours more sleep. As he lay down he realized that the mission in Peking was nowhere near finished—it was just beginning.

26

____

NO REST FOR THE WEARY

August 8, 1900

Dear Ma,

I am in Peking, China now. We have been helping put down the Boxers, who were trying to kill all foreigners. Fortunately, we got here in time to stop them. Things are starting to settle down now, I think. China is very different from any place I've ever seen. Everything here is very old. If I never eat rice again, it will be soon enough for me. We finally have horses. Imagine that—a cavalry regiment with horses! It's about time.

Your last two letters caught up with me yesterday. You don't need to apologize for moving to Corinth to live with Aunt Lucy. I'm sure it's been very lonely for you at Pond Spring without Pa. Yes, I will certainly come there to see you as soon as I get back home. There is still much to be done here. I will try to write more often.

Love, your son,

Walker

A week had passed since the storming of the city walls. Since then the Chinese capital had undergone an orgy of looting by the foreign soldiers. Homes and shops had been ransacked in search of valuables, and armloads were simply taken by the greedy men. Innocent Chinese numbering at least in the hundreds had been brutally murdered, and many women raped by the unrestrained conquerors. Many women and girls committed suicide rather than fall into the hands of the marauders. Weak attempts by officers to control the violence and pillaging were to no avail.

"This is worse than Tientsin," remarked Walker, shifting in his saddle as he watched a gang of Russian soldiers breaking into a house. "Do they not have any officers?"

"Those *are* the officers," rejoined Dixon, eliciting laughter from some of the other men.

From their vantage point they could see several Chinese men run out of the back of the house as the Russian soldiers kicked in the front door.

"I don't see no women running out of the house," commented one man.

"That's probably 'cause the French got there yesterday," joked another. Everyone laughed at that, knowing the reputation of the French soldiers for abusing women. According to a French general, the "gallantry" of the French soldier could not be restrained, even though they had managed to avoid the fighting to capture the city.

"I guess that's why so many Chinks are moving into our district. Can't blame 'em—it's the safest place in China right now, I reckon."

"If Chaffee keeps having us set up all those food kitchens and shelters for the poor, and digging latrines—before long the whole city will be coming our way."

The casual banter continued for a while, but before long they fell quiet. It was hard to be jovial while watching the lawlessness that had taken over the city. The barbarity that was evident in every street had a sobering effect on the men of the Tenth.

"All right, men," announced Lieutenant Dixon, at length. "Time for another patrol. Corporal Williams—take Lewis and Baker and do a clockwise circuit around our sector. Corporal Garrett—take Anderson and Johnson and do a counter-clockwise circuit. Make sure none of those Russian or French bastards are messing around with our Chinks."

"Yes sir!"

Relieved at the opportunity for movement, the men prodded their mounts and trotted briskly in opposite directions down the brick-paved avenue that marked the boundary of the district assigned to the Americans. Walker's trio turned left after several blocks and soon entered a small plaza.

It was about fifty yards in diameter, with four streets leading into it. In the center was a public well, sheltered by an ornately carved and painted wooden roof with curved eaves, equipped with a bucket and a windlass. The plaza was ringed by homes of prosperous Chinese families, with shops on the ground floor and glass windows looking down from the three stories above. Walker was admiring the appearance of the place when it struck him that there was no one else in the plaza. It was completely deserted and quiet. The oppressive heat seemed even more intense in the silence.

He turned to look at Anderson and Johnson. Their eyes met, and they all knew they were thinking the same thing. They walked their horses slowly toward the well, carefully looking all about them. He scanned the buildings around the plaza and, as a feeble breeze fluttered a lace curtain to expose a person in the interior shadows, he realized that they were being watched from almost every window. Walker felt very uneasy and drew his revolver, resting his hand on the pommel of the saddle.

"Something's not right," he muttered, and the other two nodded agreement. "We need to spread out." They took positions along the periphery of the plaza, distancing themselves from each other.

Suddenly a shrill, blood-curdling scream split the heavy air. Startled, they looked up to a balcony on the third floor of a house as a green-silk-robed young woman with long black hair flying wildly came hurtling down to a sickening thud on the stone pavement. She lay on her back, and a pool of blood quickly formed a crimson halo around her head.

"Mon Dieu!" They looked back up to the balcony to see a mustached French soldier, his jacket unbuttoned and the shirttail hanging out over his baggy red trousers. He spread his arms wide, a wine bottle in one hand, and cocked his head to one side, white teeth flashing in a grin.

"Such a waste!" he exclaimed in a thick French accent, and disappeared back into the interior.

Immediately, as if on cue, there was another piercing scream, this time from the ground floor of the same building. A similarly clad woman came bursting through the open door, hobbling as fast as she could on her tiny, bound feet. A French soldier, laughing drunkenly, ran after her and caught her by her hair before she had gone a dozen steps. The horrified woman shrieked as she extended her arms toward the lifeless body of the young woman lying in blood, right in front of her. He waved merrily to the three Americans, and began to drag the screaming woman back toward the house.

He found his path blocked by a Buffalo Soldier on a horse. Waving his hand as if to dismiss the American, he unleashed a stream of French in an angry tone of voice. "Shorty" Anderson leaned from the saddle to make direct eye contact with the man and said quietly, "Let her go, Frenchy."

Walker and Johnson joined Shorty, forming a forbidding wall. The three of them glared silently as Walker pointed to the woman and shook his head firmly. The woman stopped screaming, but knelt, bent over, sobbing hysterically. The Frenchman continued to grip her hair and shout angrily in French, waving his free hand energetically.

"What is problem?" came an accented voice from the doorway. The French soldier who had been on the balcony stepped to the threshold, still carrying the wine bottle.

"What is problem?" he repeated.

"Let the woman go," Walker said, "and get out of the American district. You don't belong here."

"She only Chinese!" he replied, smiling with another wide-armed gesture. "No problem, yes?"

"Yes, problem!" snapped Shorty. "Get the hell out of here before we run you out!"—and he pointed down the street.

"No, no problem!" insisted the Frenchman. "Come in! Have wine! Have woman! No problem!"

"You *are* the problem, Frenchy," spoke up Johnson, angrily. "Sortez d'ici maintenant!" *Get out of here, now.*

Surprised that a black American soldier could speak French, he hesitated, stammered, gestured, and then realizing that it was a hopeless situation, bowed dramatically with a flourish.

"Mon Dieu! We go!" He gave orders to the other soldier in French, and turned to walk away. The drunken man, still jerking the woman by her hair, responded with a stream of unintelligible French protests, and then, curling his lip in contempt, reached under his jacket and pulled out a pistol. Quickly pulling the hammer back with his thumb, he raised his arm to point the gun at Shorty.

"Look out!" Walker shouted, but it was too late. The gun roared and Shorty was knocked out of the saddle. Walker instantly fired two bullets into the Frenchman's chest and turned back to see the first soldier reaching under his coat also. Walker's gun and Johnson's both belched flame simultaneously and the man was slammed back against the door frame, sliding down to the ground, leaving a red smear behind. His jacket fell open to reveal a pistol tucked into the belt.

They leaped from their saddles to see how badly Shorty was hurt. He was conscious, but bleeding heavily from his left shoulder.

"We've got to get him to a doctor," said Johnson. "Let's get him back on the horse."

"Wait!" said Walker. Looking quickly about, he pulled his bayonet and stepped over to the dead, drunken soldier who had shot Shorty. He cut one of the red trouser legs from the man's pants and tied it tightly around Shorty's shoulder to stanch the bleeding. Together they lifted him into the saddle. Shorty sat hunched over, holding the horn of the saddle, moaning and swaying unsteadily.

"Take him back," Walker said to Johnson. "I've got to get rid of these bodies."

As they left the plaza, Walker turned to the Chinese woman. She had crept on her knees to the body of the dead young woman and was stroking her hair, crying softly. He tapped her on the shoulder and she shrank away from him with a frightened cry. Using signs he tried to communicate that he did not intend to harm her, and that he wanted rope. He pretended to wrap a rope around the ankles of the dead man and tie a knot, and then to pull the rope. She understood and nodded. She rose and, in mincing steps, went back into the house, stepping over the body of the dead officer. Returning, she handed Walker a coil of soft, pliable rope.

"Thank you," he said, bowing and doffing his hat. She returned the bow, and then knelt again to grieve at the side of the young woman.

Walker pulled the officer's body over beside the other soldier and tied one leg of each man together with the rope, and tied the other end to his saddle horn. With a final glance at the open windows around the plaza, now filled with faces watching intently, he mounted the horse and dragged the bodies away. Reaching the broad avenue that marked the boundary of the American district, he dragged them into the middle of the street, untied the rope, and left them there. At a bend in the avenue, about a half-mile away, he glanced back and saw several dogs circling the bodies, crouching and drawing closer. He prodded the horse into a canter and hurried on to the American barracks. *Serves them right*, he thought.

Dixon and Johnson came out to meet him.

"How's Shorty? Is he going to be all right?"

"Bullet didn't hit bone," replied Dixon. "Shoulder's pretty messed up, but he should recover. Doc's working on him now."

Dixon folded his arms, with a serious expression on his face. "Tell me what happened."

They described the incident together, alternating with details. Dixon blinked when they told of the young woman's fall to the street, and shook his head when they described the drunk soldier grabbing the older woman's hair, dragging her back toward the house. He put both hands to his head and groaned when they told how they had shot both of the French soldiers. Walker concluded with noting that dogs were investigating the bodies in the middle of the street.

"This is bad," he said painfully. "Really bad. We're going to have trouble from this."

"We didn't have no choice," said Johnson. "They shot Shorty first. Probably woulda shot us too, if we had let them."

"But you can't shoot European soldiers to save Chinks," said Dixon. "It just won't do. Even if they are French."

"There won't be any evidence left after the dogs get through with 'em," argued Walker. "Nobody will be able to tell if they got shot, or whatever."

"Hell, you won't even be able to tell they was *French*," chimed in Johnson, "Unless the dogs don't like red pants."

Dixon just shook his head.

"I don't know. I just don't know. I don't have a good feeling about this." He turned and walked away a few steps, and stood with his back to them, hands on his head.

"Say, Johnson," whispered Walker, "How come you can speak French?"

"My folks come from Haiti. We speak French at home all the time."

"Oh," said Walker, wondering where Haiti was and how that explained Johnson's knowing French. He nodded as if he understood, making a mental note to find Haiti on a map.

Then Dixon walked back to them, hands on hips. "Only thing we can do is, we got to go get those bodies and get rid of 'em. If the French find them first, this will blow up in our faces. Mount up!"

They galloped along the back streets to the avenue where the bodies lay. Reaching the bend from which Walker had seen the dogs, they each reflexively reined their horses to a halt. It looked like every starving dog in Peking had gathered in the street. It was a teeming mass of animals, writhing and swarming, climbing over each other in a feeding frenzy.

"My God," breathed Dixon.

"I don't think we need to go there," said Johnson. "It ain't safe."

Walker's voice stuck in his throat and he felt like he was about to gag, so he just kept quiet.

"Let's get out of here," said Dixon hoarsely. They wheeled their horses about and trotted back to the barracks. No one spoke until they were stabling the horses.

"You gonna report this, Lieutenant Dixon?" asked Johnson, looking worried.

"Report *what*?" asked Dixon, pointedly.

Johnson blinked. "Nothing, sir."

"We need to make sure Shorty knows nothing happened before he tells somebody over at the infirmary," said Walker. "They'll want to know how he got shot. We need a good story."

"Let's say his gun went off accidentally," suggested Johnson. They each nodded agreement.

They found Shorty lying on a cot in the far corner of the medical ward. His shoulder was wrapped with white bandages, and he was sleeping soundly.

"Morphine," commented the orderly. "Knocks 'em out every time."

"When do you think he'll be awake?"

"Probably next morning. How did he get shot, by the way?"

"His gun went off accidentally," said Johnson, and Walker and Dixon nodded, perhaps a bit too vigorously.

"Hmph," frowned the orderly. "Strange. How did those red French pants get wrapped around his shoulder?"

"We just grabbed the first thing we could find to bandage him," said Walker thinking fast. "A French soldier was in the bushes with a Chinese girl, so we just borrowed his pants."

The orderly burst out laughing. "That is hilarious!" he exclaimed. "Serves that Frenchy right!" And he continued laughing as he walked away through the rows of cots.

"That was quick thinking, Garrett," murmured Johnson.

"Don't know where it came from, but it just popped out of my mouth."

"Glad it did," said Dixon. "We need to be here in the morning when Shorty wakes up, and tell him the real story so he won't give them some cock and bull report about getting shot by a Frenchy."

"If he does," suggested Johnson, "we'll just say it's the morphine."

Somehow that seemed very funny to the three of them, and they began to giggle uncontrollably as they hurried out, bursting into gales of laughter as they staggered like drunk men toward the mess hall for supper.

A few days later, at morning roll call, the Tenth squadron had an unexpected visitor. General A. R. Chaffee suddenly appeared, followed by a small entourage of aides. The men snapped to attention, saluting crisply. Walker caught Dixon's eye, and both wondered if there was trouble brewing.

"At ease, men," said the General in an amicable voice. "I haven't had an opportunity until now to speak to your unit, but you've all done a splendid job here. Your attention to detail and your professional conduct is among the best of any unit here. You are to be commended, and I will be sure to say so in my report."

Walker and Dixon exchanged a look of relief.

"And that's why I've come to you this morning," the General continued. "I have an important job that has to be done quickly and effectively, and I need a cavalry unit to do it. This squadron of the Tenth is the ideal choice. You'll be making a trip of about a hundred miles north of Peking to rescue some American missionaries who are in danger of being massacred by the Boxers. The Boxers are still active in some of the more remote places in the north, and we've been tasked with the job of protecting these American citizens." Then, raising his voice he almost shouted, "Is the Tenth ready for action?"

"Yes sir!" they responded in unison.

"I knew I could count on you!" the General nodded, pleased. "My aides will fill you in on the details. You'll be heading out today, as soon as you can get supplies packed. You'll be traveling light. Speed is of the essence!"

The General spun on his heel and strode away as his aides stepped forward. The squadron commander, Captain Andrews, and his half-dozen lieutenants gathered around them as they began reading aloud from papers in hand. In only a few minutes all was hustle and bustle as they began the process of gathering supplies, weapons, ammunition, horses, and all the equipment needed for the mission.

Everything was ready to go by noon, and after eating a quick lunch they made two lines of mounted troops followed by two wagons loaded with supplies and extra ammunition, and moved out.

Their destination was the city of Kalgan, more than a hundred miles northwest of Peking. They kept a brisk pace, thanks to the supply wagons being drawn by teams of six horses each. Each day they started well before sunup and continued until after dark, taking a noon break to avoid the sweltering heat of the midday. A major trade route, it was broad and not as rough as most roads in China, and they made good time. The road was busy with camel caravans bringing goods from Russia and Mongolia to the Chinese capital. It was Walker's first close look at camels, and he was intrigued. They were so strange! *Sure am glad I'm riding a horse instead of a camel,* he thought.

They reached Kalgan in the late afternoon of the third day of the march, having had little sleep since leaving Peking. The Boxers were already present in Kalgan, but the rapid movement of the Tenth brought them to the city before the news of their approach and they caught the Boxers by surprise. They crossed a long, stone bridge into the city and were within its walls before anyone could react. Aided by a Chinese Christian who had accompanied them from Peking, they quickly found the small group of a dozen American and Swedish missionaries and their families sheltering in the administrative complex of the local mandarin, where they had been given temporary refuge. The Boxer response was swift—within less than an hour an armed and angry mob of more than a thousand had gathered, beating on the iron gate and howling at the top of their lungs. As the sun began to set, the mob steadily grew larger and louder. The situation looked grim.

Captain Andrews came out of the palatial residence of the mandarin, followed by some Chinese officials and missionaries. He summoned his men to gather around him.

"Come dark, the Boxers are going try to break in here," he said loudly, in order to be heard over the din. "We'll hold them off, and first thing tomorrow morning, we'll take the missionaries and head back to Peking. Hopefully, if we shoot enough of them tonight, they'll keep their distance in the morning."

The men absorbed this news in silence, casting uneasy glances toward the mob at the gate. They knew that traveling through the open countryside with thousands of inflamed Boxers in pursuit would be a recipe for disaster, especially if burdened with helpless civilians, including women and children.

"Grab some extra ammo off the wagons," he concluded. "It's going to be a long night."

The mandarin's yamen, or complex, included several sturdy buildings arranged around a central courtyard. The buildings served as a protective wall, with no outward windows below the second story. There were several horses and camels tethered in a group in one corner, with some wooden carts that belonged to the missionaries, and would serve as their transportation on the journey. He had actually seen only a couple of the men; the rest of the group remained safely indoors.

As the darkness of night descended, the mob suddenly withdrew from the gate and all was eerily quiet. The soldiers fidgeted but did not speak, waiting. Walker could feel the hairs on the back of his neck begin to stand up.

"The calm before the storm!" called out Captain Andrews. "Take positions!"

By prearranged plan half of the men knelt in a line in the middle of the courtyard, facing the gate. The other half stood behind them, so that all seventy of the soldiers had a clear line of fire. Any attempt to force the gate would be met with a hail of lead.

At least fifteen minutes of quiet passed, and then it began. A distant rumbling sound caught Walker's ear. He cocked his head and listened. It grew closer, and he recognized it as the howling and screaming of the mob. It had regrouped several blocks away, and was advancing down the broad avenue directly toward the yamen's gate. Through the bars of the gate, he could suddenly see the swinging of red lanterns and the whirling of swords and staves as the Boxers leaped and kicked in the air. They were working themselves into a frenzy, and would assault the gate with gale force when they arrived.

Walker glanced down the two lines of motionless soldiers, each with a rifle to his shoulder, aiming intently toward the gate. They would acquit themselves well, he knew, but would they be enough? *Why did Chaffee send so few men on this mission?* he wondered. *This is going to get ugly, fast.*

The Boxers crashed into the gate with such explosive force and noise that, even though Walker had watched them approach, he still flinched for a split second.

"Fire!" shouted Andrews, and seventy rifles spat tongues of flame from their barrels with a thunderous roar. Hundreds of bullets screeched into the mob, some deflecting off the bars of the gate. Bodies fell by the dozens, and the agonized shrieking rose to a higher pitch as they fell back briefly. With less than a minute's respite the attack was resumed, and the bullets continued to fly. The growing pile of bodies in front of the gate was preventing the attackers from breaking through, and they began to drag the dead and wounded away. The rifles did not stop, however, and before long, the bodies were simply left where they lay.

There was a long pause in the action and Walker suspected that something was about to happen. He was right. The Boxers had brought up ladders and were climbing into the second-story windows of the buildings that encircled the courtyard. Suddenly screaming Boxers poured out of the doorways into the courtyard from three sides of the yamen. The soldiers, with perfect discipline, turned and poured bullets into each stream of attackers. Captain Andrews and a pair of Chinese Christian men feverishly carried boxes of ammunition to the lines, ripped them open, and went back for more.

Walker felt a hand on his shoulder. It was Dixon.

"Come with me!" he shouted in Walker's ear.

Walker kept firing as he walked backward toward the front door of the main house. Inside, he saw that he was part of a group of six soldiers. Captain Andrews stood next to the mandarin, towering over him. The mandarin, wearing a golden robe of silk with a pig-tail hanging down to his waist, gave a short, quick bow, pointed toward a doorway in the back of the room and then hurried away.

"The missionaries are already leaving out the back gate," Andrews barked. "This is getting too dangerous, and they are going to escape through the Great Wall and head west. You men will see to it that they get there, and then come right back. The mandarin says that these Boxers are not local and they probably don't know about this route, so you should be able to make it. Your horses are waiting out back—get moving!"

Just at that second, there was a crashing sound from the court-yard. Walker looked back and saw that the Boxers had fashioned a battering ram and were breaking down the front gate. Things were about to get very ugly indeed. He looked at Andrews with a question in his eyes.

"I said get moving!" Andrews bellowed. "Those missionaries are our responsibility! Get them out of here!"

The six men dashed through the rear door and mounted their horses. The missionary families were almost entirely out of the back gate already, riding camels and horses, with the women and children in the carts. The gate slammed shut behind them and the caravan hurried through the dark streets as fast as their carts and camels would permit.

The city gate to which they were heading was at the end of a long, wide street that ran in front of the mandarin's yamen. The caravan kept to the side streets until it was necessary to enter the main street to approach the gate. When they did so, some of the Boxers saw them and sent up a loud howling as they set out in pursuit. The caravan had a head start of several hundred yards, but the Boxers were gaining rapidly. Walker estimated that there were at least five hundred of them, with stragglers bringing up the rear.

At the gate, they found the massive doors closed. A servant sent by the mandarin ordered the gatekeeper to open it. Walker did not understand the language, but he could see that the gatekeeper was not cooperating. Spurring his horse to the front of the caravan, he cocked his pistol and pointed it at the gatekeeper's head and with his other hand pointed to the gate. The gatekeeper blinked, hesitated, and then with a quick bow, motioned to some men in the shadows, who began laboriously cranking a large windlass. The gate slowly began to open, but they could see that it wasn't nearly fast enough.

"Slow 'em down!" shouted Dixon. The six soldiers began firing into the running crowd, which was now less than two hundred yards away. It took only about a dozen casualties to convince the other Boxers to change their approach. The mob split to either side of the street, scurrying from doorway to doorway, zigzagging and darting into alleys. Their advance was significantly slowed, but the gate still wasn't opening fast enough.

As soon as there was a gap in the massive doors, the horses and camels began squeezing through, single-file. The six carts, drawn by shaggy Bactrian camels, waited. The soldiers, still on their horses, slowly backed toward the gate as the caravan was getting through, keeping the Boxers at bay with accurate rifle fire. They were coming closer and closer, however, and the situation was getting desperate. Walker glanced over his shoulder at the carts and saw the terrified faces of the small children and their mothers, and he felt a surge of anger that these innocent ones were being placed in such danger.

Finally, the gates were open enough for the carts to pass through. Five carts hurried through the gap, but the camel pulling the final cart balked, apparently spooked by the noise of the mob, the gunfire, and the narrowness of the opening. The Boxers were within mere yards of the gate, and the soldiers each pulled their revolvers for close action.

"Go!" screamed Dixon at the cart driver. The soldiers, facing away toward the advancing Boxers, did not realize that he was addressing the driver and immediately spurred their horses and charged, firing right and left as they scattered the mob and escaped at a full gallop.

The driver cracked his whip over the camel's head, and then lashed the animal with all his might. The camel let out a braying, angry sound and bolted, leaping forward and jerking the cart violently. Two small children tumbled out of the back of the cart and sprawled in the dirt. Their mother screamed, straining backward with her outstretched hand, but the cart whisked through the gate, leaving the children behind.

The men cranking the windlass, seeing the last cart go past, let go of the beam. It spun furiously and the great doors began to rapidly close together. Instinctively Walker spurred his horse, and racing toward the gate, leaned low from the saddle and snatched one of the children up by its foot. Dixon, a bare length behind, grabbed the other child. Their horses made it through the closing gates just in the nick of time, before they slammed shut in a cloud of dust.

On the outside of the wall it was suddenly quiet, as the thick walls muffled the sounds from the other side. The howling mob inside the city could not pursue them through the gate, and the caravan hurried along the road, trying to put as much distance as possible between themselves and the city.

Walker and Dixon rode swiftly to the front of the caravan where they found Swedish missionary Franz Larson, who was the leader of the group.

"Who's in charge here?" demanded Dixon. "We got to get back into the city and rejoin our unit. Tell us how to get back in."

"I am afraid that is not possible, my friend," replied Larson calmly. "The gate will not open again tonight, and by morning your comrades will have already left Kalgan. To go back in by yourselves would be suicide. You have no choice but to go with us. We can certainly use your help."

"No, no, no!" exclaimed Dixon, frantically. "That's not right. We have to get back. Now! There has to be another way! We'll go around it!"

"I am telling you the truth," said Larson, sympathetically. "Turn around and look at this wall."

Walker and Dixon turned and looked. They beheld the massive wall, stretching out into the distance as far as the eye could see. It was breathtaking.

"This is the Great Wall of China," explained Larson. "It was built many hundreds of years ago, and it is thousands of miles long. You can't go around it. You can't go over it. And now that the gate is closed, you can't go through it."

"You don't understand," interjected Walker, nervously. "We are United States soldiers. We have to rejoin our unit. We can't stay out here."

"I'm afraid Mr. Larson is right, young man," said an older man on horseback. "I'm James Roberts, missionary from the United States." He shook hands with each of them.

"But we can't stay with your caravan, sir," begged Walker earnestly. "We have to go back."

"You were sent to Kalgan to protect us missionaries, yes?" asked Roberts.

"Yes, that's right."

"Well, that's what you are doing. We need your help. We are going to Urga, the capital of Mongolia. Seven hundred miles of hard road. You will be obeying your orders by helping us get there safely."

"But—but—"

"I'm afraid there are no 'buts,' my young friend. To go back now would be suicide, as Mr. Larson said. After you saved our children so bravely, we simply cannot let you walk back into a sure death trap. Stay with us. You'll get back to your people, eventually."

"Talk it over. Think about it," suggested Larson. "Give it until morning."

"Morning will be too late," said Dixon.

"It's already too late," replied Larson. "Believe me—I know. I've lived here for seven years. The Boxers are everywhere across northern China, and two Americans alone will not live long, especially in military uniforms. Accept it—when those huge gates closed behind you, you began your journey to Urga."

Walker stared at the two men, speechless. His eyes met Dixon's, and they each let out a long, slow breath. They looked back again at the incredible wall. Under the bright moonlight it seemed particularly ominous and forbidding as it disappeared into the distance in both directions.

"What are we going to do?" asked Walker, shaken.

"Looks like we're going to Urga," replied Dixon, and then added under his breath, "Wherever that is."

27

"THE WATERLESS PLACE"

Walker sat between the two humps of the tall, shaggy camel, swaying with every loping step, and feeling more than a little ridiculous. He looked over at Dixon, similarly mounted.

"I said I'd never ride one of these critters," he said ruefully. "I feel like a clown."

"We look like clowns," agreed Dixon.

Both, however, had come to realize the advantages the strange beasts had over horses in the sandy wastes of the desert. Their broad, padded feet did not sink into the sand like the hooves of a horse, and their easy, swinging gait conserved energy. They were also able to carry a surprising amount of weight, much more than a horse. Walker had to admit that these animals were invaluable in a desert setting.

The caravan stretched out for more than a quarter-mile. Having acquired some additional animals, it now consisted of twenty camels, nineteen horses, six carts, and two dozen refugees. Most of these were Swedish missionaries and their families, and several were Americans. In addition, there were seven Mongol men who were hired to perform various chores, including pitching tents, tending the camels, and driving carts. Their presence was mainly helpful in allaying the suspicions of the local populations they passed, who generally distrusted foreigners.

They traveled mostly at night and in the early morning to avoid the heat, camping at watering holes and wells wherever they could be found. It became Walker and Dixon's job to draw water at the wells, and this was no easy task. When they occasionally traveled for two days to get to the next source of water, the thirsty animals could easily drink five hundred gallons—two tons of water to be drawn in buckets from twenty or more feet below. Sometimes they watered only the horses since the camels could do without for a few days, if necessary. When there was no water to draw, they joined the group of men who gathered "buffalo chips" to burn as fuel for cooking.

The road to Urga was easy to follow due to the telegraph poles. Twenty-four poles per mile alongside the road made it a simple matter to stay on course, and also allowed the travelers to calculate how far they had come. There were telegraph offices scattered along the way, but since the Boxers had cut the wires, it was not possible to send messages to Peking.

The desert was a place of utter desolation—clumps of thorny weeds emerging from heaps of wind-blown sand, and rocks. Lots of rocks. The ground was covered with rocks, gravel, and bits of shiny flint of various colors which reflected the brilliant sunlight, causing Walker to have to squint and shield his eyes. There were very few actual sand dunes in this vast wasteland, and no human habitations at all. According to Larson, the word "Gobi" meant "waterless place." Walker could see why it was called that.

Traveling at night was preferable due to the cooler temperatures, but at the same time was exhausting. It was also quite cold at night. Larson explained that the desert plateau was more than five thousand feet above sea level, and was at a more northern latitude than New York City. The heat of the day dissipated quickly after sunset, and Walker found himself wishing for a blanket or coat.

"Here I am in the middle of the Gobi Desert, and this is the first time I've been cold since I left Alabama two years ago," he remarked to Dixon.

"Yeah," agreed Dixon, shivering. "This is crazy."

Fortunately Larson was able to buy shaggy camel's hair coats for them from a passing merchant caravan bound for Kalgan. They noted that the caravan's camels and oxen looked well-fed, which meant that better terrain with pasture lay ahead. However, it took another week to reach it, and in the meantime they and their animals had to make do with near-starvation rations.

Walker rode alongside Roberts and Larson as much as possible, plying them with questions about China and Mongolia. They seemed to enjoy his interest, and he was fascinated by their wealth of knowledge. They taught him Chinese and Mongolian words and phrases, which he would practice speaking to the hired men. In turn, Walker told them about his experiences in Cuba and the Philippines. They did not believe the story about the python attack until he removed his shirt and showed them the puncture scars from the snake's jaws.

Three weeks after leaving Kalgan they reached the Oude Telegraph Station, the halfway point. It was there that they saw a tree for the first time since they had left Kalgan, over three hundred and fifty miles back. They rested there for two days, enjoying a well of good, clean water.

Larson scouted the area on his bicycle, which he rode frequently along the way. Walker had watched with great interest, having seen only Lou Hoover's bicycle before. When Larson returned to camp, Walker approached him.

"Would you mind if I tried that? It looks like fun."

"Have you ever ridden a bicycle before?"

"No, I've only seen one before, but it looks easy."

"Come and see!" Larson grinned.

It wasn't easy, Walker quickly learned. He repeatedly fell over, skinning his knees and elbows. Larson began to run alongside, helping keep him upright, giving advice and encouragement.

Dixon came over to watch, and laughed uproariously at Walker's mishaps.

"Come try it, if you think it's so easy," he challenged Dixon indignantly.

"Not me!" Dixon snorted. "If the good Lord had-a wanted me to ride one of them things, he woulda put wheels on me instead of feet."

"Did you know that there are professional bicycle races all over America and Europe?" asked Larson. "No? It is a popular sport, and one of the best riders in the world is an American Negro. His name is Major Taylor, and he is about your age. Perhaps you should practice and become professional racers!"

"A black man is a world champion bicycle racer?" echoed Dixon, in wonderment.

"That's right," chimed in Roberts. "I saw him race once. An amazing athlete! And he makes a lot of money winning races."

"Well, maybe I'll give it a try after all," said Dixon. He and Walker spent the rest of the day taking turns on the bicycle until they were exhausted. They were starting to get the hang of it when the call to supper came.

The missionaries invited Walker and Dixon to join them in a worship service that evening. They awkwardly accepted, feeling out of place. At twilight, the group gathered around the lone tree, sitting on the ground. Mr. Roberts preached a sermon on the Israelites wandering in the desert for forty years before crossing the Jordan River into the Promised Land. Walker thought that this was not a good theme for the sermon, considering the circumstances, but everyone else seemed to enjoy it. They then sang a number of hymns in English, and some spirituals. Walker felt stirred by the sacred songs, which reminded him of church services back home. He began to hum along, and then to sing softly, almost in a whisper. Across the circle, he could see Dixon's lips moving, his eyes closed. The Swedish group sang a couple of songs in their own language, and then various ones prayed aloud. They gave thanks for their blessings, and asked God to continue to guide and protect them. Walker knit his brow, wondering how they could feel blessed in this situation. He tried to pray silently, but couldn't find the words. When the service concluded, the missionaries stayed together, talking and laughing. Walker, however, got up and walked away a short distance, sat on a large rock and stared out across the barren landscape. Stars were just beginning to twinkle in the heavens—soon there would be a vast multitude of them.

"May I join you, Corporal Garrett?"

Startled, he turned to see Miss Maria Engh, an unmarried Swedish missionary several years older than Walker. They had spoken to each other only very briefly so far, nothing more than a simple introduction. Her blond hair, usually covered by a bonnet, was braided and coiled at the back of her head. The plain blue dress matched the blue of her eyes, and her strong, pleasant face was illuminated by a warm smile.

"Well, yes, of course," he stammered, scooting over to make room. "If you're sure you want to. I'm not much of a talker. I mean, you might rather be with the others."

"Corporal Garrett—may I call you 'Volker'? Is someting wrong? You appear to be unhappy. What is bott'ring you?" Her frank, direct approach was disarming, and her sing-song Swedish accent made him return her smile.

"Oh, it's nothing, really. It's just been a long time since I was in a church service. It brought back some memories."

"Pleasant memories, I hope?"

"Oh, yes—definitely. My family went to church all the time when I was a child. I haven't had much of a chance over the past two years that I've been in the army. But it was nice—I enjoyed it."

She looked closely into his eyes, as if studying him. He suspected that she did not believe him and looked away, fidgeting with his hat.

"There is one thing that kind of confuses me," he went on, clearing his throat.

"And vot is 'at?"

"They prayed just now and thanked God for their blessings. Honestly, Maria, I don't see that we are very blessed. Here we are on the other side of the world in the middle of a huge desert, freezing at night and burning up in the day, almost out of food, running for our lives, depending on water holes and rain puddles for survival. What's to be thankful for?"

"Oh, Volker!" she exclaimed, putting her hand on his shoulder.

"Ve *are* blessed! Gott has provided for us everyting ve need! He saved us from being killed by Boxers, and ve are alive, and ze verst is behind us now. Ze desert is hard, but it protects us from ze Boxers, you know! Ze desert is a blessing in disguise. And you, Volker—yourself—you are a blessing, too! Gott sent you and Dixon to save our children in Kalgan. You help keep all of us safe. So, I am very tankful for you!"

"Well, I guess I hadn't thought about it like that. The desert is kind of protecting us, when it's not halfway killing us. And all those telegraph poles have been a blessing, keeping us from getting lost in the desert. Having these camels is a blessing—never thought I'd say *that*. I guess there are some things to be thankful for."

Maria smiled even more warmly. With one hand still on Walker's shoulder she made a sweeping arc with the other hand, gesturing toward the darkening sky.

"You see all ze stars, Volker? Can you count zem?"

"No, of course not."

"Every star is a blessing, Volker. You cannot count your blessings! You see zat really bright one?" She pointed toward a brilliant, sparkling light across the universe.

"That one? Yes, what about it?"

"Zat star is you, Volker. You are a special blessing. When I go to sleep tonight, I will tank Gott for you."

She stood and smoothed her skirt, and he stood, also. "Good night, Volker," she said, and turned to go, but stopped and looked intently at him again. "Open your heart to Gott, Volker, and He vill come in. You vill be happy." And then she walked back toward the group, whose talk and laughter could still be heard in the cool of the night.

Her final words pierced Walker's heart like a knife. *I don't know how to do that,* he thought sadly. Touching his hand to his chest, he felt the silver cross hanging around his neck and remembered Harriet and her confident sense of mission. *Why do some people know exactly what they're supposed to do in life, and I don't?* he wondered. *When am I going to figure it out?*

Taking another look at the myriad stars in the broad expanse of sky, he heaved a sigh. Picking out the bright one that Maria had singled out, he shook his head. *I don't feel like a star. Maybe a shooting star, like that one there. I'm waiting, God. Make me happy.*

He looked up into the millions of stars above for a long minute, listening. Then, shrugging, he went in search of his bedroll.

"Upstellning!" Larson's booming voice meant that, once again, morning had come too early. Walker and Dixon slept back-to-back for warmth on the cold nights in the desert, when they weren't trekking all night long. Dixon elbowed Walker in the ribs, producing a grunt and a groan.

"Time to get up, cracker," he growled over his shoulder.

"Upstellning yourself, brevet," yawned Walker, in return.

"That camel ain't gonna saddle hisself, so rise and shine."

"If that camel don't quit eatin' wild onions and stinkin' up the desert, I'm gonna choke him to death before we get to Urga," groaned Walker. "I never smelled anything so bad in all my life."

The caravan formed into a line after everyone had a bowl of boiled millet, and set out on another day of march.

"We'll stop at lunch, and rest in the afternoon," called out Larson, as he pedaled past on his bicycle. As midday approached, however, something surprising began to happen. The horses began tossing their heads and neighing excitedly, and even the camels accelerated their slow, swinging gait, holding their heads higher than usual. The caravan passed a half dozen trees, and sprigs of grass began to appear along the roadside.

And then, as they crested a low hill, a beautiful sight greeted their eyes—a field of green grass! The animals broke into a run, and the carts full of the women and children were in danger of jolting their occupants out onto the ground. The tin cups and cooking uten-sils hanging on the outside of the carts clanged and rattled noisily, and the children made high-pitched squeals. The half-starved beasts scattered over the pasture, grazing almost frantically. A couple of the horses actually lay down and rolled in the grass. No one needed to be told that the caravan would spend the rest of the day here.

Over the next few days of travel they saw clusters of Mongol yurts, looking comfortable and prosperous. The round, white huts, and the grazing flocks of sheep and herds of horses dotting the green valleys, bordered with low, purple mountains, made such a lovely sight, especially after three weeks in the desert. The distant barking of dogs and the visible activity of the people brought back a sense of civilization and humanity to the exhausted travelers. Even the afternoon heat didn't seem quite so harsh as before.

The road became increasingly steep and winding as they ascended into a mountain pass. They passed by massive red granite boulders, whose great size was accentuated by the tiny, colorful wildflowers which grew all around them.

At the crest of the pass they were greeted by the sight of the Buddhist temple of Chwerin, which was also the name of the mountain. There were three large, gilded, glittering temple buildings, surrounded by smaller houses painted white with red trim. Some three thousand lamas, or priests, lived there. A group of them rode out to meet the caravan and talked with Larson, who was fluent in Mongolian. Their heads were shaved, and they wore flowing yellow robes of silk. Their bridles and saddles were richly ornamented with silver. Afterward, Larson gathered the "gypsies," as they called themselves, and shared with them what he had learned.

"Trouble is brewing," he announced with a serious face. "There are many Boxers in Urga, gathered on the west side of the city. The Mongols are worried about what they intend to do, and so are the Russians. Russia is sending soldiers to protect their consulate and the property of Russian merchants. The Mongols are also calling for their men at arms to assemble at Urga, and thousands of them are coming. With so many armed men coming together, and none of them trusting the others, it does not look good."

"Is it safe for us to go into Urga?" asked one of the Swedish missionaries anxiously.

"We have no choice but to go there," replied Larson, spreading his hands. "But I know the Russian consul. There is a telegraph station just ahead, and I will send a telegram to let him know we are coming. Let us hope and pray that he will give us shelter. The Chinese and Mongol mandarins have said that they are not responsible for the lives of foreigners, which means that we are not safe from either Boxers or Mongols. We must make haste."

Sensing the changed mood of the group, one of the small children began to whimper and cry. Everyone returned to their place in the train in silence. Walker met Dixon's eyes with an unblinking gaze.

"I'm really startin' to not like these Boxer rascals," muttered Dixon.

"If they're smart, they'll leave us alone," scowled Walker.

As he walked back toward his camel, he passed the cart in which Maria rode. She reached out her hand and squeezed his arm.

"You see, Volker," she said with a tense smile, "Ve need you here. You are a blessing to us."

As the caravan approached closer to Urga the road became busier with local farmers' carts, flocks of sheep being driven to market, and merchant wagons. They passed several villages every day, each with ten to twenty families and a like number of yurts. The road ran through a valley with mountains visible all around. The scenery would have been quite pleasant if they hadn't been so concerned for their safety. Finally, they crossed the Tola River, the first river they had crossed since leaving Kalgan, seven hundred miles away. There were increasing numbers of Mongol riders to be seen, and the caravan attracted a lot of attention from them. They appeared to be very suspicious of the foreigners, and studied them from a distance. It made Walker and Dixon nervous about their intentions.

At the river they found the final telegraph station remaining before they were to reach the city. Larson pedaled his bicycle to the station, accompanied by Roberts on a horse, hoping to find a reply from the Russian consul in Urga. Walker and Dixon remained with the caravan, keeping their eyes on the Mongols watching them from the hilltop. They held their rifles across their saddles to show that they were armed. Both had begun wearing their camel hair coats even during the hot days to conceal their military uniforms. Fortunately, the men kept their distance.

Larson came back from the station, pedaling furiously and waving a small piece of paper over his head with one hand on the handlebars. From the big grin on the face of Roberts, it was obviously good news. Larson skidded to a halt at the front of the group, and stood with his feet straddling the bicycle.

"The consul has replied!" he beamed. "He writes, 'Please to make yours stop immediately in Consulate, where you will have some rooms first time. Schischareff.'"

A shout went up from the group, and they all hugged each other with cries of "Thank God!" and "Tak Gud!"

Dixon nudged his camel over close to Walker's. "Now all we got to do is get there in one piece," he murmured, casting a meaningful glance at the hilltop. As if on cue, the horsemen turned and disappeared beyond the crest of the hill. They were out of sight, but not out of mind.

There was a large group of Mongols standing in a field of grass near the telegraph station. They heard shouts and cheers coming from this group, and looking more closely, realized that they were having wrestling matches. Walker and Dixon watched as the wrestlers circled, closed, and strained at each other. The apparent objective was to throw the opponent to the ground by any means possible, including tripping and shoving. One wrestler lifted his opponent and threw him several feet to land on his back. Another darted in low to grab his opponent's knee and lift it high, toppling the other man to the ground.

"Looks like fun," commented Walker.

"I'd rather just knock his head off," growled Dixon. "A good uppercut would end that round pretty quick."

"Hitting is not allowed!" laughed Larson, who was unexpectedly standing behind them. "But almost everything else is permitted. Whoever touches the ground first with any part of his body is the loser. You should try it! Mongolian wrestling is very difficult."

"Have you ever tried it?" asked Dixon.

"I was once invited to join in at the Festival of the Seven States, which is held every three years, but since winning meant that one becomes the property of the Living Buddha, I declined," he laughed.

"Who is the Living Buddha?" asked Walker. "Is that a religious thing?"

"Quite right, Walker," he nodded. "The Living Buddha is the most revered religious figure in Mongolia. He exercises power like a medieval pope and is worshiped by all the people, who believe that he is a living God. They bring him offerings of the finest possessions they have."

"Sounds like a pretty good thing," commented Dixon. "How do you get to be a Living Buddha?"

Larson laughed again. "Well, first you have to be born a Buddhist in Tibet. Then, the lamas there have to decide that you are the one destined to be a Living Buddha, and they bring you to Urga while you are still a small child." He grinned, clapping Dixon on the back. "I think you have missed your chance, unfortunately!"

"When you said the winning wrestler becomes the property of the Living Buddha, does that mean that they practice slavery here?" Dixon asked, with a frown.

"Not like what you are thinking," smiled Larson, shaking his head. "If you are one of the Living Buddha's wrestlers, you are housed, fed, and clothed for the rest of your life in the finest way. You are a respected and honored citizen. Any Mongolian man would be proud to be one of the Living Buddha's wrestlers."

"I could handle that. So, when is this Festival of the Seven States going to be held again?"

"Not while we are here!" Larson laughed again. "You are out of luck again, Lieutenant Dixon!"

"Too bad. I think I could put 'em on the ground pretty quick." Dixon watched the wrestlers intently until Larson called for the caravan to continue moving.

After traveling several miles, they took a rest break in the afternoon heat. Walker and Dixon drew water from a well for the animals and for cooking. They had a supper of boiled rice and mutton, thanks to Larson purchasing a sheep from a nearby herder, along with some fresh cheese. After the pots and dishes were washed and put away and the sun had begun to set, they resumed the trek, intending to push on through the night. However, no sooner had they formed the caravan line and begun to move, when suddenly with a rush of hoof beats, they were confronted by the group of riders who had been shadowing them for the past day. A dozen men on horseback blocked the road, and a particularly swarthy, bearded rider with an eye patch came forward, gesturing vigorously and talking loudly in a demanding voice.

Larson and the rider engaged in a heated conversation for several minutes. Walker and Dixon dismounted and went forward to stand a few feet behind Larson, carrying their rifles. Walker noted that about half of the Mongol men also carried rifles, and he felt very uneasy.

Larson turned and walked back to the group, hands on hips and shaking his head.

"What do they want"? asked Roberts.

"They want our horses, our camels, and all of our money," he replied. "They will let us keep the carts, but of course, without the animals we can't use the carts. And without animals and money, we won't make it to Urga."

"Can't we negotiate something?" asked one of the missionaries.

"I've tried," said Larson. "They won't give an inch. They've got us outnumbered and outgunned, and they know it. I don't know what to do."

The Americans and Swedes began talking all at once, using both languages. Walker saw the women gather into a circle and begin praying. He caught Maria's eye as she bowed her head, and remembered her words. "You are a blessing to us," she had said. "You help keep all of us safe."

Suddenly Walker heard words coming out of his own mouth.

"I have a suggestion," he said. The idea was only forming in his mind as the words were being spoken. The missionaries stopped talking and looked at him. Walker felt a bit foolish, but the words kept coming. "They love wrestling, right? Challenge them to a wrestling match. Their best man against ours. If they win, they take what they want. If we win, they leave us alone."

There was a moment of silence as they stared at Walker and each other.

"Are you sure?" asked Larson. "You've never wrestled Mongolian style before. You would be at a great disadvantage."

"We're already at a great disadvantage," replied Walker. "This way, we at least have a chance. They won't refuse—it's a matter of pride."

"I watched those wrestlers earlier today," spoke up Dixon. "I got a good idea of what to expect. I think I can do it."

Larson looked back at the menacing group of riders. "I don't think we have a choice," he said hesitantly. "I'll see if they agree to it."

While Larson was walking back toward the swarthy bandit, Dixon took off his camel hair coat and shirt and began flexing his muscles. He stepped forward to stand a few feet behind Larson.

The Mongol was obviously surprised at the offer, and at first appeared to reject it. The other riders scoffed and jeered, laughing to each other and shaking their heads. Larson then said something that caused them to become angry. He later explained that he had asked if they were afraid to wrestle a black man, suggesting that they were cowards. They shouted angrily now, and shook their fists. Walker thought that they might be about to attack them, but instead they withdrew a short distance to talk it over. When they approached again the one-eyed leader accepted the offer, and one of the riders dismounted and stripped to the waist. He was a short, stocky, muscular man, with a queue of black hair hanging down his back and a short strip of black beard dangling from his chin. He snarled ferociously, displaying a gap in his yellow teeth.

Larson quickly stepped in between the two, holding up his hands. Speaking alternately in English and Mongolian, he stated the established rules—no hitting, biting, or hair-pulling. The first to touch the ground with any part of the body loses the match. Dixon never took his eyes off those of his opponent. As soon as Larson and the bandit leader stepped away, the match was on. The other Mongols remained in their saddles and began to chant and strike the air with their fists.

They were obviously excited and full of confidence, expecting victory for their man.

"Take 'im, Dixon!" called Walker. "You can do it!"

"Don't be in a hurry!" cried Larson. The other missionaries raised their hands into the air and began praying aloud.

Both men went into a crouch and began circling. Every few seconds the Mongol made a feinting dart forward, reaching for Dixon's arms or shoulders. Each time Dixon knocked his arms away. Once, the Mongol managed to grasp Dixon by the shoulders and reached out with his left leg to trip him. Dixon put both hands on the man's chest and using all his strength, lunged forward, shoving him backward. The man stumbled back and almost lost his balance, but recovered. The riders gave an involuntary cry of alarm at this, and became louder and more insistent in their chanting. The wrestler was clearly shaken at his near fall and became more cautious. This continued for several minutes.

"Don't hurry!" cried Larson again. The missionaries continued praying.

"Watch out for your knees!" called Walker. "He'll come in low!"

Sure enough, the Mongol made a sudden move, bending low and reaching out with his right arm for Dixon's knee. Dixon instantly sprang forward and put his hands on the man's head and, kicking his heels up, vaulted over him, landing behind him. As the Mongol straightened and turned, Dixon drove into him, reaching across with his right hand to grasp his opponent's right wrist. Slamming his left hand behind the man's elbow, he straightened the arm and used it as a lever to turn the man and propel him backward. The Mongol succeeded in getting his feet out in front of him to brace himself, but Dixon immediately responded by reversing the momentum, suddenly pulling in the opposite direction and putting his weight on top of him. This was too much for the man to withstand and he sprawled face first in the dirt, with Dixon crouching over his back.

The missionaries, men and women, gave a great shout of joy, embracing and pounding on each other's backs. The riders, however, sat in dumbfounded silence. Walker got a bad feeling that they were not going to go quietly.

The defeated Mongol suddenly whirled on Dixon, brandishing a knife with a curved blade several inches long. The riders gave a spontaneous shout of approval.

"Catch!" shouted Walker.

Dixon glanced quickly and snatched the handle of the Cuban machete as it slowly rotated in the air toward him. He whipped it back and forth making it whistle in the air, and then pointed it at the throat of the Mongol.

"Want a knife fight?" he snarled. "Bring it on!"

The spectators on both sides were suddenly silent at this unexpected development. The Mongol blinked in surprise, and stepped back. Then, scowling, he put away his knife and walked back to his comrades.

The bandit leader walked his horse forward to face Larson and Dixon. He spoke a few words, and then turned and raised his arm and made a circling motion. The group galloped away into the darkening twilight, and the caravan did not see them again.

"What did he say?" asked Dixon.

"He said you won fair and square, and that we are free to go. You saved us, Dixon! Thank you!" And Larson embraced him emotionally for several seconds. Then he added, "That was the best wrestling feat I've ever seen. Simply amazing!"

The other missionaries crowded around, adding their praise and thanks for Dixon's victory. Dixon, glistening with sweat, said little as he buttoned his shirt.

"See?" smiled Roberts. "It's like I said in Kalgan—you are carrying out your orders to protect us! It was God's will that you come with us on this journey. We couldn't have made it without you!"

It was an emotionally drained but happy group of travelers that resumed the journey. Larson, carrying his rifle, took the lead as usual, while Walker and Dixon brought up the rear. The women's voices could be heard, softly singing hymns, and as darkness fell, lullabies to the children.

"Just think," commented Walker, "You could be housed, fed, and clothed for the rest of your life as the property of the Living Buddha."

"The Living Buddha can choke on it, for all I care," Dixon snorted. "I ain't nobody's property. The sooner I get out of this country, the better."

They rode in silence for a while, their camels swaying slowly and rhythmically. Walker gazed up at the dark sky with its multitude of stars, and remembered what Maria had said. He picked out the bright star that she had assigned to him. It didn't seem quite so far away, now.

"Maria says we are blessings from God. She says that we are stars."

"I got my doubts about that."

"So do I, but I kinda like it anyway. See that bright one right up there? She says that's me."

"I guess that makes you 'Corporal Twinkles.'"

"See that other bright one, off to the right of mine? I think that's you."

"Mine's brighter than yours."

"Well, you are a lieutenant, and I'm just a corporal. Goes with the rank, I guess."

They continued to banter for a while, and then fell silent. In a few moments Walker heard a soft snore. Dixon was asleep, nodding as the camel plodded along. Walker let him sleep, knowing he would soon be awake and he would probably be the next to doze off.

Looking up again, he saw the streak of a falling star briefly light up the sky. Immediately the sky was again as it was before, and the falling star was forgotten. *Was that me?* wondered Walker. *Am I just a bright streak, soon forgotten? Or is Maria right—that I'm a blessing, here for a reason?* He considered this for a moment, and then decided. *That falling star is already gone, but I'm still here. I may not be the brightest star in the sky, but I'm not a flash of light, gone in a second. Whatever the purpose, whatever the reason, I am here. Blessing or not, I'm here to stay.*

28

ONWARD, CHRISTIAN SOLDIERS

Walker did not feel as relieved at reaching Urga as he had thought he would. The small city was dirty and crowded, and he observed beggars, skinny dogs, and filth in the muddy streets as the caravan filed through. There were pretentious yamens surrounded by high walls, shabby tents, and ornate temples. Prayer wheels and red and yellow-gowned lamas on fine horses were everywhere. Knowing that a force of Boxers was already outside the city and that Mongol fighters were gathering rapidly filled him with a sense of dread. Russian troops were said to be approaching, also. He wasn't sure that Urga was a safe place for the group to stay.

They were welcomed warmly at the Russian consulate. A hearty meal was prepared for them which they devoured like wild animals, and then they were shown to the rooms in which they would sleep. Lying on a bed instead of the ground for the first time in six weeks was a delicious pleasure for everyone in the group. In fact, sleeping at night was itself a pleasure which they had almost forgotten how to enjoy.

Their pleasure was short-lived, however. At breakfast the next morning Larson gave them the bad news—the consul general wanted them to leave immediately for Siberia. It was not safe for them in Urga, he said. Making matters worse, a great festival was about to be staged along the road that they would have to travel to reach the Siberian town of Kiachta, more than two hundred miles away. Bogda, the Living Buddha, would be there, and most of Mongolia was expected to attend. It was to begin in less than a week, and immense crowds would be gathering before that. Due to the xenophobic mood in the country, they needed to leave now in order to get safely away. In addition, several hundred Russian soldiers were enroute to Urga and needed the rooms at the consulate. Simply put, the caravan had to go.

There was much to be done in order to prepare for the departure. Fresh food supplies were needed, horses needed shoeing, and carts needed repairing. Help came from an unexpected source. A Norwegian missionary, Olaf Nästegard, had been in Urga for some time, forced there by the Boxer uprising. Nästegard was multilingual, speaking Mongolian, Chinese, Russian, English, and even some other languages. His linguistic skills and experience in that part of the country helped them complete these tasks quickly and economically.

The group's money was almost exhausted, so the consul sent telegrams to the American and Swedish consulates in St. Petersburg asking for funds to be sent to a bank in Kiachta. He also provided each member of the group with a temporary Russian passport, which later proved extremely valuable. After three full days of frantic preparations, the weary caravan once again hit the road.

A new crisis confronted them just a few miles outside of Urga. They had apparently been observed by Boxer sentries while leaving the city, and a detachment of Boxers was in full pursuit. One of the Swedish children riding in a cart turned and looked back, and seeing the large crowd in the distance, pointed and warbled something in Swedish to his mother. Glancing back, her eyes widened, her face turned white as a sheet, and she screamed in sheer panic. Suddenly everything was pandemonium.

Larson, on horseback, rode up and down the caravan shouting at everyone to make all possible speed. There was a small stand of trees at the crest of a low hill ahead and he wanted them to reach it, for whatever security and protection it could afford. Walker and Dixon positioned themselves at the rear of the column, rifles at the ready.

Reaching the shelter of the trees, the caravan gathered in a tight circle, with the carts, women and children in the middle, surrounded by the pack camels and horses. The dozen men, with whatever weapons they possessed, stood between the group and the Boxers, who appeared to number five hundred or more.

The Boxers could have easily overwhelmed them by sheer force, but for some reason did not. They gathered in a semi-circle only a few dozen yards away and began their shouting and leaping, working themselves into a frenzy. One man stepped forward, apparently one of their leaders, and approached, sword in hand. He wore a red tunic and turban and had a red kerchief tied around his neck. He stopped about twenty yards from them, pointed at them with the sword, and began to shout and wave his arms. Remarkably, the Boxer army behind him quieted down.

"What is he saying?" Walker asked Roberts, standing at his side.

"He says that foreigners are destroying China. He accuses us of taking their livelihoods, disrespecting their ancestors, and angering their gods. He says that we are responsible for stopping the rain and killing their crops. It hasn't rained here for a year, and Christian missionaries are to blame. Therefore, we must die so that the rain can fall again."

"Then ve must give zem rain." They turned to see Maria Engh standing behind them.

"How do you propose to do that?" asked Roberts.

"Ve must pray," she replied simply. Walking to Larson, she spoke to him in Swedish. His face was blank for a second, but then he nodded. Motioning them all to gather around him, he turned to the Boxer leader and spoke to him in Chinese.

"What's he saying?" asked Walker again.

"He told him that we will prove that we are not responsible for the drought by praying and bringing rain for them."

Walker looked up at the cloudless blue sky and scorching sun. "I don't think this is a good plan," he said hesitantly.

"Trust God," said Roberts. "We have no other hope."

"Bow your heads," called out Larson. "Brother Roberts! Pray out loud—in Chinese. I want them to understand what we are saying. Everyone else, pray as hard as you can! We need rain, now!"

Walker and Dixon instinctively removed their hats and bowed their heads, but each kept a close watch on the Boxers out of the corner of his eye. Walker had expected them to attack immediately, but they stood still, listening as Roberts prayed loudly in Chinese. Walker observed that the other missionaries were fervently praying with closed eyes and bowed heads. Maria had both arms raised toward the heavens as she prayed, face uplifted, radiant with faith and joy.

Minutes passed. Walker shifted his weight, his fingers moving nervously over the hammer, bolt, and trigger of the rifle. Closing his eyes for just seconds, he almost involuntarily found himself praying, too. *God, I don't know if you're listening, but we could sure use some rain right now. These are good people, and if we don't get rain, they may all be killed. Please, God, send rain.*

Suddenly a cool breeze made the hairs on Walker's neck stand up. A shiver passed over him. A shadow passed over the group, and Walker had the distinct sense that something had joined them. A loud rumble of thunder caused him to jerk his head up, startled. Looking up, he saw the sky half-covered with black storm clouds, rolling and racing wildly from nowhere. The next thunder was not a rumble, but a terrifying, crashing explosion which made them all flinch involuntarily, accompanied by a blinding flash of lightning. The wind suddenly rushed violently through the trees, making a ghostly moaning sound. Walker inhaled sharply. *This can't really be happening, can it?*

And then—the rain began to fall. It wasn't an ordinary rain. It was harder than anything Walker had seen in the Philippines. It was the heaviest downpour he had ever experienced. It fell so furiously that he couldn't even see the Boxers. The trees swayed and the wind howled. The thunder crashed so constantly that he could hear nothing else, and the lightning was so bright that he had to use his hat to shield his eyes. Crouching to brace himself against the onslaught, he expected to be blasted into ashes by a bolt of lightning at any second.

Finally, after a full fifteen minutes of the insane deluge, it suddenly stopped. The silence was so quiet it was eerie. Walker, shaken, raised his head and looked outward. The Boxers were gone. It was as if they had never been there at all. Looking up he saw the black clouds dissipating like fog and blue sky beginning to reappear. He touched his rain-soaked clothes to assure himself it had all really happened.

"Thank you, God," called out Roberts, raising his hands. "Thank you!"

Larson began singing a hymn which Walker recognized from hearing them sing it while crossing the desert: "A Mighty Fortress is Our God." The Americans and Swedes each sang in their own languages. *A bulwark never failing indeed,* thought Walker. *Nobody will ever believe this.*

When the song was finished, they trudged through the mud back to the carts. Fortunately the animals had been tethered securely, else they would have panicked and stampeded during the storm. Checking the packs and carts to make sure everything was in place, they got ready to move out.

Before the caravan could resume its journey, however, a column of soldiers appeared, coming up over the crest of the hill. Their white caps and tunics and the fact that they were marching southward clearly identified them as Cossack troops. Olaf Nästegard greeted the commander in Russian and had a brief, friendly chat with him. The column then proceeded on toward Urga. As they passed, Walker stared at them, dumbfounded.

Nudging Dixon, he nodded toward the soldiers. "They're not wet."

Dixon intently studied the men passing in front of him. "How can they be dry?" Dixon whispered. "We just had the worst thunderstorm in Mongolian history, and they ain't got a single drop of water on 'em."

After the Russians were past, the caravan moved on. Descending the other side of the hill, Walker and Dixon both saw that the road was dry. There were no puddles of rainwater. They looked at each other with disbelief. They rode their camels in silence until they stopped for the afternoon rest break.

A tent was set up for the women to change into dry clothes, and the men spread their wet shirts in the sun to dry. After a lunch of cheese and dark bread, washed down with water from a nearby well, everyone sought the shade of a clump of small trees to rest until evening, when they would resume the journey until midnight.

Walker and Dixon approached Roberts and Williams, the two American missionary men.

"What happened back there?" asked Walker. "There wasn't a cloud in the sky, and y'all prayed up a thunderstorm in five minutes."

"And them Russians weren't even wet, but they couldn't have been a mile away while it was happening," added Dixon.

The two missionaries gazed at them serenely.

"Do you believe in miracles?" asked Roberts.

"I don't know. I ain't never seen one," replied Walker. "Not 'til now, anyway."

"I know they're in the Bible," said Dixon, "But this ain't the Bible."

"God is the same yesterday, today, and tomorrow," smiled Roberts benevolently. "What he did in Bible times, he can do today. He answers prayer. You just saw it happen."

"Then why don't he answer all prayers alike?" countered Dixon. "Lots of prayers don't get answered. Don't seem quite fair, to me."

"I can't tell you why some prayers don't get answered," shrugged Williams, "but I'm not going to object that it's not fair when my prayer does get answered. I have to trust God to do what's best. He knows better than I do."

"Why weren't the Russians wet?" asked Walker, puzzled.

"Maybe they weren't praying for rain!" chuckled Roberts, and all four of them laughed.

"You—all of us—have witnessed something extraordinary today," continued Roberts more seriously. "It can't be explained in natural terms. Just believe it, and know that God is with us. And that will make all the difference."

Walker and Dixon stood at the edge of the camp, with a view of the rolling hills and fields across the landscape. After a few minutes, Walker turned to Dixon.

"Well?"

"I got nuthin' to say, Garrett," he growled. "And neither do you."

So they stood in silence, each immersed in his own thoughts. Soon they were back in the saddle, swaying and plodding along into the night. Walker could not help but look up into the cold, starry sky and wonder about what had happened that day. *Why did the missionaries even think to pray for rain? It was obviously not going to rain. But it did. Apparently, they know something about God that I don't know. And I don't think I'll ever know it.*

The next day they passed the site of the impending festival. A large fairground had been cleared, and already dozens of tents had been erected, with pennons flying. Walker decided that it was a good thing that they were getting past this before the main crowds arrived.

Two days later they crossed the Hara Gol, or Black River, using a cable-drawn ferry. After so many weeks in the desert, it was refreshing to see so much clear, clean water. The animals drank their fill, and Walker and Dixon swam alongside the ferry.

"Remember the last time we swam a river?" grinned Walker as he pulled his boots back on.

"Yeah—I still got the bullet marks to show for it," grimaced Dixon, buttoning his shirt. "That was crazy. That Funston is a wild man."

There was tall grass along the river, so they spent the rest of the day there, letting the animals rest and graze. They would need their strength to pull the heavy carts up the high hills that lay ahead. The camels were almost worn out, with sores on their backs and feet, and it would require careful coaxing to get them to Kiachta before they gave out completely.

Dixon and Larson went hunting and bagged four ducks for supper, to go with the prairie dogs they had shot earlier. Walker spent the day with Olaf, learning Russian words and phrases. Having picked up some Chinese and Mongolian vocabulary from the missionaries while crossing the desert, he decided that he enjoyed learning new languages. Maria had taught him a small stock of Swedish words also, which he practiced daily to pass the time. Even though having to keep weapons close at hand and an eye out for suspicious activity around them, it was a relaxing, pleasant day, for a change.

After traversing an endless stretch of pine forest accompanied by the howling of wolves silhouetted in the moonlight, and ferrying across another river in the rain, they finally approached the Russian border. They had traveled almost two weeks since leaving Urga, with the constant worry of attack by Boxers or Mongols, afflicted by the blazing heat of the day and the chilling cold of the night. They and the animals were fatigued to the point of exhaustion. When, upon ascending a low hill their eyes beheld the spires of the churches of Kiachta in the distance, their relief was too much for words.

The great white and blue church they had seen from afar stood near the road as they entered the city. As they trudged tiredly through the streets, a crowd of people emerged from the church. It was one of Russia's many holy days, and the townspeople had gathered for a late afternoon service. Each group looked at the other with curiosity. There were rich gentlemen and ladies in expensive clothes, with carriages and fine horses. There were plainly dressed women with scarves over their heads, and bearded men with cloth caps and pants stuffed into the tops of their boots. Some of the women smiled and waved at the children in the carts as they passed. The governor's escort, who had met them at the border, showed them to a log hotel on the other side of town, where rooms and a meal were ready for them.

The four unmarried men shared a primitive room, with a rough-hewn bed frame, unpainted log walls, and unfinished boards for a floor. Olaf and another Swedish missionary took the bed, and Dixon simply stretched out on the floor with a groan. Walker went to the window and looked out. Opening the window, he climbed out onto a section of low, sloping roof, and lay back, gazing up at the sky. He could hear the sound of snoring from inside the room, but in seconds he was fast asleep.

29

NO LOOKING BACK

October 2, 1900

Dear Ma,

I'm sorry that it has been so long since my last letter, but things have been pretty wild here. I crossed the Gobi Desert to Mongolia, and am now in Russia. We have endured heat and cold, Boxers, camels, and miles of sand. I will explain how all that happened when I get back. It was pretty awful, but I am alright, so don't worry none about me. I don't know if you will get this letter or not, but I will put extra postage on it and hope for the best. I am with a group of missionaries, so it is like being in church all the time. I don't know when I will see you, but save some grits and bacon for me. Howdy to Aunt Lucy and Uncle Robert.

With much love, your son,

Walker

He pushed the thin envelope through the cutout in the glass pane to the Kiachta post office clerk, and watched his letter sail into a box on a table behind the counter. The short letter seemed so inadequate, but how could he describe the past weeks in any detail? *It would take a book*, he thought. Nästegard had helped him address the letter in both Russian and English—hopefully it would get to America before he did. As he turned to leave he almost bumped into Dixon, holding a similar envelope in his hand.

"Letter to Beulah?"

"Yeah, and Daisy. They prob'ly think we're dead."

"Well, we came pretty close to being dead more than once. It's a miracle that we made it this far."

"Good thing we're with missionaries."

"Yeah, they can sure pray up a storm." At that, both laughed.

"And we can't tell nobody about that, 'cause nobody would believe it," Dixon added, ruefully. "I still don't believe it, myself."

"Me either. It don't look like they're going to be able to pray the Söderboms' baby back to health, though," Walker said, shaking his head. "That child sounds like it's gonna die any day now." Several of the children had been ill on the journey, but all of them except for one had recovered.

"Ain't that the one you snatched up at the gate in Kalgan, that night?"

"Yeah—Anna Elizabeth. She's a sweet little thing. I sure hate to see her suffer like this. I hope the doctor can do something to bring her around."

They walked on down the street, thumbs hooked in pockets, skirting mud puddles as they observed the town and its people. The buildings were almost all of wood, mostly single-story, some with tiled roofs, and others with thatch. There were a couple of imposing administrative buildings, but most structures were small and unimpressive. The wealthier class lived in a neighborhood of fine houses, separate from the crowded middle of town. Merchant shops featured display windows with stacks of canned goods, shoes, scarves, wool caps, candles, and other miscellaneous items for sale. Wagons, carts, and carriages populated the wide street, drawn by oxen, horses, and even an occasional camel. Nondescript dogs roamed the streets, barking, fighting, defecating, and drinking from puddles.

Walker was intrigued by the variety of people that they passed on the street. There were quite a few Chinese, including prosperous merchants and ragged laborers. There were some who were plainly Mongolian, dressed perpetually in riding clothes and always on horseback. The native Siberians were easily distinguishable by their fair skin and wide, prominent cheekbones. The women wore scarves over their heads and tied under their chins, and the men wore leather caps and overcoats. Both men and women wore sturdy boots, with the men stuffing their pants into the tops of their boots. Occasionally a woman would pass, dressed in festive traditional garb, with brightly embroidered blouse and apron and an elaborate headpiece.

Dixon drew curious stares from the passersby, none of whom had ever seen an African before. A group of small boys followed them, watching his every move. Eventually, Dixon turned to face them. Bending forward and with his hands on his knees, he motioned for them to approach. Instead, they backed quickly away, wide-eyed, almost tripping over each other in their haste. Walker couldn't help laughing out loud.

Only one boy did not retreat. He stepped back with one foot, and stood sideways, watching Dixon, as if ready to turn and run. Dixon shrugged and extended one hand toward the boy, palm down, as if to show that he was also human. The boy stood unmoving, but it was clear in his eyes that his brain was spinning as he stared at Dixon's hand, unwilling to touch it. Dixon then closed his hand, leaving only his index finger extended. The boy looked at the finger, and then looked into Dixon's eyes, hesitating. Then he slowly inched forward, gradually raising his arm and extending one finger. It took several seconds, but at length, the two fingers touched. The boy quickly pulled his hand back, and then extended it again for a longer touch. The other boys exclaimed excitedly and elbowed each other from a distance of several yards away.

Dixon, still bent over, then removed his hat and ran his hand over his tightly curled hair. Resting both hands on his knees, he gave the boy a raised-eyebrow look that seemed to ask, "What do you think of that?" The boy's eyes widened, and he took a moment to summon his courage, but then slowly inched closer. Dixon did not move a muscle as the boy reached out, ever so tentatively and, almost shaking with fear, touched—and then lightly patted—Dixon's hair. There was another burst of exclamations and gasps from the other boys, but there were deeper notes this time, and Walker and Dixon realized that a small audience of adults had collected around them, also. Dixon turned to the crowd, bowing grandly. The group burst into laughter and applauded. He reached out and mussed the boy's hair, giving him a wink and a nod of approval. The boy grinned and ran back to receive the admiration of his fellows.

"Well, Lieutenant," remarked Walker, as they continued down the street, "You're quite the attraction, ain't you!"

"Huh! I feel like the carnival freak that everybody pays a nickel to look at—'cept I didn't get any nickels."

"Look at it from their side, though," remonstrated Walker. "What if you'd never seen a white person before? How would you react?"

"I'd be dancin' in the street, singin' 'Glory, Glory, Hallelujah.' That's what I'd be doing."

"No, seriously. Wouldn't you be just like that boy, or the others?"

"Nope. I wouldn't be rubbin' nobody's head. I'd say, 'Step'n fetchit, cracker.'"

"I give up, Dixon," sighed Walker. "I can't get nowhere with you."

"That makes us even, then, Garrett. Just leave it alone."

He was searching for a reply when Roberts and Nästegard emerged from a government telegraph office just ahead of them.

"We have bad news, I'm afraid," said Roberts, with a sympathetic smile. "You are not going to be able to go back to China and rejoin your units there."

"But we have to," objected Dixon, shocked. "We didn't have permission to come all this way, and we could be in serious trouble.

We may be considered deserters, and that could mean a firing squad."

"Well, you certainly can't go back the way we came," said Nästegard. "The only way to get back there is to go east to Vladivostok, the Russian port on the Pacific, and find a ship sailing to Tientsin. The problem is, first of all, you can't get to Vladivostok. You would have to take the Amur River, a section of which is controlled by the Chinese, and due to fighting between Russia and China, the Chinese would not look favorably on your presence, since you are carrying Russian passports. We've seen reports of Chinese soldiers massacring Russian civilians along the Amur. The Russian military has monopolized the railroad in that direction, and you can't get there, anyway."

"Furthermore," continued Roberts, "Tensions are building between Russia and Japan, and getting passage on a ship out of Vladivostok on the Sea of Japan will not be possible—even if you had money. The Russian government officials are insistent that it is not possible to travel east. We just received instructions from our Mission Board that we are to travel west to St. Petersburg and return to America. They have sent funds for all of us. If you go east, you will be traveling alone through hostile territory without money and without the ability to speak Russian, Chinese, or Japanese. I'm afraid there really is no choice. There is no going back."

Observing Walker and Dixon's stunned expressions, Roberts added, "I am truly sorry. You have been invaluable to us on this journey. We couldn't have made it without you both—we will all be eternally grateful. You are heroes, not deserters, and we will definitely advocate on your behalf."

"But, where is St. Petersburg, and how will we get there?" asked Walker, beginning to feel a sense of panic.

"It's a Russian port on the Baltic Sea, near Sweden," said Nästegard. "You will travel there on the new Great Siberian Railway, which has just been completed. Your expenses will be paid for you—it's the least we can do."

"I don't know," said Dixon slowly. "We need to think about this."

"Very well," nodded Roberts, understandingly. "We'll be here in

Kiachta for several days making the arrangements to go to Urkutsk, so you have plenty of time to think it over. I think you will see that there really is only one realistic path forward. Olaf and I will be happy to discuss it further with you, any time at all."

When the two missionaries had gone, Walker and Dixon continued standing on the street corner, staring at nothing. After a long moment, Walker released a heavy sigh and glanced over at Dixon.

"Don't ask me no questions," growled Dixon, before Walker could speak. "I ain't got nothin' to say. Got to think about this."

The two wandered aimlessly through the town, without talking. Past cottages, taverns, stables, stores, stately brick mansions, schools, and churches, they observed everything, occasionally pointing to something of interest, and moving on. Reaching the edge of town, they noticed a side street that appeared unusually active with carts, horses, and people. As they strolled curiously down this street, they realized that almost all of the people were Chinese. They had discovered the Chinese bazaar, a strip of shops and booths where you could buy practically anything you wanted. They each had a few Russian coins in their pockets, thanks to the missionaries sharing some funds with them, so they casually browsed the stalls and booths, inspecting the wares.

None of the Chinese spoke English, so they relied on hand signs to communicate. After some haggling they purchased four beautiful wool shawls with silver clasps, one for each of their mothers, one for Daisy, and Walker added one more simply because the shopkeeper offered it for a good price, and because it was easier to split the cost if they bought the same number of items.

"Say, Garrett," Dixon smiled as they left the bazaar, "who's that other shawl for? I bet you'll be giving it to 'Dancin' Dancy!'"

"Cut it out, Dixon," scowled Walker. "I'll keep it 'til the right person comes along, one of these days. It sure won't be Abigail Dancy."

"Maybe Maria?"

"Not a chance. She's almost thirty years old, and besides, she's going home to Sweden."

"Maybe you'd like Sweden."

"Maybe you'd like to shut up."

Dixon belly laughed. "That ain't no way to talk to a lieutenant, corporal!"

"I don't see no lieutenant straps on your shoulders," retorted Walker. "I don't think they make camel hair coats with shoulder straps."

They were in a jocular mood by the time they got back to the Limboski Hotel. As they walked in the front door, laughing, they realized that something was wrong. The other members of the missionary group were gathered in a circle, heads bowed, and they heard the sound of sobbing. One of the Swedish men was praying in a low voice while the women and children wept.

Walker and Dixon approached the group with soft, quiet steps. Maria raised her tear-streaked face and mouthed the words, "Anna Elizabeth," and shook her head sadly.

"Oh!" Walker and Dixon murmured simultaneously. Walker felt as if he had been hit in the stomach. He took a deep, shaky breath, as they both removed their hats. Walker instinctively bowed his head and closed his eyes. He couldn't understand the words of the prayer, but he felt that he had to offer some kind of petition on behalf of the Söderbom family. He didn't know what words to use, but he meditated intensely for several minutes. As he reflected back over the past weeks, beginning with that nightmarish escape through the gate at Kalgan, he remembered the delightful laughter of the little girl, her delicate voice, and the interminable coughing. Tears squeezed out of his clenched eyes, and ran down his cheeks. He wiped them away roughly, with the back of his hand. *Why do children have to die?* he wondered. *It just isn't right.*

Larson spoke, first in Swedish and then in English. He explained that the Russian Orthodox priest had agreed to allow the baby to be buried in the church graveyard, despite the missionaries being Protestant. It would take place the next day. The group sang a hymn softly, and then a Swedish lullaby, and then the Americans retired to their rooms, leaving the Swedish contingent to comfort the Söderboms. It was a somber evening meal that night, and everyone went to bed early.

Walker climbed out the window again, as had become his habit, and lay on the roof. Looking up at the myriad stars as he had so often on this journey, he struggled with his thoughts and emotions. He had seen a lot of death and carnage over the past two years, but the death of a small child seemed a special kind of loss. He remembered the bodies of dead children he had seen in the reconcentrado camp in Cuba, in rural villages in the Philippines, and floating in the rivers in China. The death of Anna Elizabeth was personal, though, and seemed especially tragic. He realized, with a sudden sense of insight, that the parents of those other children had probably felt as devastated over the loss of their children as he and the missionaries felt about the loss of this one. *We're not really different inside,* he thought. *We're all the same, no matter what color skin or what language we speak. We all look up at the same stars, see the same sun rise in the morning and set in the evening. There's enough sadness in the world to go around for everyone alike.* Images of José, Harriet, and his father floated through his mind, as he fingered the silver cross that hung around his neck. They all seemed to be from a different lifetime, so long ago.

That thought brought Walker back to the grieving family downstairs in the hotel. Somehow he understood that the Söderboms would be able to face their tragedy, and would not be crushed by it. Their faith and their friends would sustain them through it. Tomorrow would be a sad day, but there would be other days to come. The world would keep on turning—it couldn't be otherwise. There was no looking back.

The next morning, Walker went downstairs for breakfast. The Americans and some of the Swedes were already there, eating. Teacakes and hot tea were the usual fare, and he could never get enough to satisfy his hunger. As he slurped a cup of tea with a small cake in his other hand, Dixon appeared at his side.

"Never thought I'd wish for hardtack and beans, but this stuff don't get me through the mornin' at all," he muttered. Walker grunted agreement, his mouth full of tea-cake.

Larson and Nästegard stood together nearby, talking quietly in Swedish. Walker cleared his throat and stepped closer to them.

"Excuse me, but is there anything we can do for the Söderboms?" he asked. "Maybe get some flowers, or something?"

"No, thank you, Walker," replied Larson. "We have some flowers. Kind of you to ask."

"Anna and Carl are sad that they don't have anything nice to wrap Anna Elizabeth in," commented Nästegard, more to Larson than to Walker. "All they have is an old blanket they brought from Kalgan. Do you happen to know where we could get a nice blanket, or something to put inside the casket with her?"

"Ah, actually, I think I do," responded Walker, with sudden energy. "I'll just run upstairs and get it." He hurried out of the room, passing the Söderboms on their way in. Anna Söderbom embraced Walker impulsively with a sob. Carl extended his hand to Walker and said, with a thick Swedish accent, "Tak you."

It was clear from Walker's blank expression that he did not understand their gratitude.

Larson came over quickly and explained. "They are thanking you for saving their baby from the Boxers at Kalgan. If they had to lose her eventually, at least you gave them almost three more months to love her. They are grateful for that."

"Tell them that I am glad I could help," Walker said huskily, clearing his throat again and shaking their hands. He backed away and then hurried up the stairs, returning a moment later with a small, wrapped package in his hands.

"This is for Anna Elizabeth," he said to the Söderboms, pausing for Larson to translate. "I bought it yesterday at the Chinese bazaar. I want you to wrap her in it." He unwrapped the paper and held up a fine woolen shawl, beautiful in blue and yellow. The corners were held together by a nicely-tooled silver clasp.

Mrs. Söderbom gasped in disbelief, and exclaimed in Swedish as she reached out to take it.

"This is perfect, she says," said Larson, beaming. "These are her favorite colors."

This time both Anna and Carl embraced Walker, with tears in their eyes. He awkwardly accepted their thanks, and then returned to stand next to Dixon. He found that he had no more appetite for tea-cakes, so he just stood with his hands in his pockets, the room a blur.

"I told you you'd give that to your girl," whispered Dixon.

"Yeah," whispered Walker hoarsely. "And I did."

Walker and Dixon carried the small casket on their shoulders from the hotel to the graveyard at the front of the procession of about fifteen mourners. Men passing on the street removed their hats in a show of respect. The small grave had been dug for them on the slope beside the beautiful church, a gleaming white, towering cathedral with brilliant blue panels on its steep spires, topped with golden crosses. From the open doors came the heavenly sound of the choir, practicing its harmonies. The cemetery was full of large stone crosses and angelic statuary. From the gravesite, the distant hills of Mongolia could be seen. There was an autumn chill in the air, and there were splashes of yellow and red among the leaves of the trees. It was a lovely and peaceful setting, and it seemed to soften the grief of the parents that their baby would rest in such a place. Words were spoken, a hymn was sung, and then they walked slowly back to the hotel.

30

ON TO THE GREAT SIBERIAN
RAILWAY

Over the next few days, Larson and Roberts sold the caravan's horses, camels, and carts, and began stockpiling supplies for the trip to Lake Baikal. It would take five days by tarantass, a type of long-framed carriage. There would be seven tarantasses, each pulled by three horses, and they would need a sizable quantity of food for themselves and the drivers and feed for the horses. Walker and Dixon were part of the group, having accepted that it was their only realistic option.

They would now be traveling without Larson, however. He had been offered employment as a translator, and decided to stay in Kiachta. Having spent several years in this part of the world, he was loath to leave, explaining that when the Boxer uprising settled down, he hoped to be able to return to Manchuria or China and continue his work there. From here on they would depend on Nästegard to lead them.

The route chosen involved several stages. It required them to travel through the forests to Mysovaya, a small town on the eastern shore of the lake, cross the lake by steamship to little Listvyanka on the opposite shore, and then proceed a couple of hours by rail to Irkutsk, a more substantial city on the main rail line. From there it would be a three-thousand-mile ride to St. Petersburg by way of Moscow, on the Great Siberian Railway.

After two weeks in Kiachta they were finally ready to depart. As the caravan left the city behind, Walker felt a sense of relief. He appreciated the hospitality and friendliness of the Russians, but it wasn't "home," and he was ready to be on the move again.

The five-day trek to Mysovaya was, thankfully, uneventful. It was actually rather pleasant due to the beautiful scenery, the fragrant pine and spruce forests, snow-topped mountains, farms, and rivers. The horses wore bells that jingled continuously to keep wolves away, providing a cheerful accompaniment to the journey. The tarantasses did not have seats, but were well-padded with fresh hay and bedding which made the ride bearable—certainly more than the diabolical carts they were used to. There were established post stations along the way so that at night they slept indoors rather than on the ground, which was fortunate because the mountainous route reached elevations of eight thousand feet, and the temperatures at night were even colder than in the Gobi. Due to the constant threat of robbers along the way, Walker and Dixon kept their revolvers always close at hand.

Descending from an elevation of about three thousand feet down to the shore of Lake Baikal and the town of Mysovaya, an even more beautiful sight greeted their eyes. The lake was spectacular. It was more of a sea than a lake, stretching some four hundred miles long and as much as fifty miles wide, its deep waters transparently blue, mirroring the clear sky above. The small town on the shore looked picturesque and inviting. Unfortunately, the steamer that was to take them across to the western shore was leaving the dock as they reached the outskirts of town, so they would have to wait for its return the next day. The group found only two rooms in a small hotel, so, after a supper of cabbage soup, dark bread, and fish, Walker and Dixon slept on the floor in the corridor.

The next morning found them eating breakfast on the hotel veranda, enjoying a breathtaking view of the lake. As a special treat there were cucumber slices and butter to go with the sour bread and hot tea. After slurping several cups—and belching—Walker began to feel somewhat more alive and ready to face another day. The steamer arrived, disgorging more than a thousand men who piled into waiting train freight cars which then slowly disappeared into the east.

"Olaf," said Walker, pointing toward the departing train. "What's that all about?"

"They are conscripts for the Russian army," replied Nästegard. "The hotel manager says that groups like that come through here several times a day, all heading east. The expectation is that there will be a war with Japan before long."

Pausing, he sprinkled salt and pepper on his cucumbers and bread, and poured another cup of tea. Taking a bite, he continued, "This railroad is actually one of the reasons for the tension. The Japanese are expanding and have their eyes on eastern Asia for themselves. When the Russians built this railroad across Siberia all the way to the Pacific it became clear that they wanted it, too. Both sides are militarizing, and it looks like it won't be long before they clash."

"I guess Japan won't stand much of a chance against Russia, will they?" commented Roberts. "No Asian country has ever defeated a European power, and Russia is so much larger than Japan—it looks like an easy win for the czar."

The other missionaries were nodding agreement, but Dixon spoke up.

"Don't be so sure about that," he cautioned. "Russia being so big ain't necessarily an advantage. They got to send their troops and equipment thousands of miles across the country to get to the battlefield, and Japan is already there. Besides, we saw the Russian and Japanese soldiers in China. The Japanese soldier fights better than the Russians we saw—right, Walker?"

Walker nodded, munching on cucumbers and bread.

"Them Japs didn't back down from nuthin'," Dixon continued. "They took a lot of losses and kept right on fightin'. The Russian soldiers were brave enough, but their leaders were stupid. Both of 'em are happy to slaughter anyone who gets in their way, but I think the Japs are more dangerous. My money's on them."

"I'd have to agree," said Walker, swallowing his food and chasing it with another slurp of tea. "I'd a heap rather fight the Russians than the Japanese. And another thing—I don't see but one line of tracks heading east. If there's just one line going west to t'other side of Russia, they'll never be able to move enough men and material out here to win a war. I remember what it was like in Tampa—just one railroad line. It was a terrible logjam, and we like to never got out of there to go to Cuba. No, I have to side with Dixon—my money's on the Japs."

"Well!" exclaimed Roberts. "I must say that I am at a loss for words! With all due respect, I have to disagree! My money—figuratively speaking, of course—is on the Russians. Like I said, no Asian country has ever defeated a European power, and I don't think Japan will be the first. No, I think you have misjudged these two—if a war begins Russia will win, and rather easily, I'm afraid."

"Time will tell," returned Dixon with a one-sided smile. "But after that war, I think you'll be calling Japan a 'power' and Russia a 'country.'"

Roberts blinked, his teacup stopped halfway to his mouth, and his brows knit together as he thought about that.

"I think I'd like to take a look at that market in the square," said Dixon, rising from the table. "Never know what you might find."

"Me too," Walker mumbled, his mouth full. Taking a quick, last slurp of tea, he wiped his mouth with the back of his hand and put on his cavalry hat.

"Don't stay away too long," waved Nästegard. "We'll be boarding the ferry in a couple of hours."

The crossing of the lake took almost two hours. Upon disembarking at Listvyanka, tarantasses were hired to take them and their baggage to the railroad station. There was no hotel in the town and no train to Irkutsk until the next day, so the party spent the night camping on the train platform, surrounded by their trunks and bags. Walker and Dixon stood guard while the others slept.

The next day, an hour and a half on the first train out brought them to Irkutsk, where they stayed at a French hotel for two days while completing the required paperwork for permits to travel to St.

Petersburg. Nästegard and Roberts spent most of their time dealing with the railroad and government officials, leaving the rest of the group to wander the city on their own.

Walker and Dixon stood in front of the hotel deciding what to do when Walker observed a pretty, young woman wearing the uniform jacket of the hotel staff standing shyly nearby. Walker had noticed her at the front desk when they checked in. He thought she looked to be about his age.

"Pardon," she smiled, a bit nervously, "Parlez vous Français?"

"Ya geverit po-Amerikanski," replied Walker in the Russian phrase taught him by Nästegard. *I am American.*

"Ah!" she beamed. "I learn to speak English words," she said in a strong Russian accent. "May I walk with? I show you Irkutsk, and speak English with you."

"Yes, indeed! That would be wonderful!" said Walker, smiling and nodding. Dixon agreed, so the three set off together down the main street.

Her name was Anya, she said, and she had been working at the hotel for three years. She was learning Western European languages in the hope that she would be able to find work in hotels in the western part of Russia. Few European travelers came to Irkutsk, however, so she had limited opportunities to practice. Communicating all this with her broken English was difficult, and Walker tried to help with his few Russian words and phrases.

"Irkutsk is called 'Paris of Siberia,'" she said, "because wide streets. Pretty buildings." She gestured toward the broad avenue with a wave of her arm, and indeed there was a fancy hotel on the opposite corner, and next to it a theater.

"What is that colorful building over there?" asked Walker, pointing.

"Bogoyavlenskiy sobor," she replied. "Church. I don't know how to say in English. You like enter?"

The church featured multiple towers, each different than the others. One was topped with a conical spire, another was cylindrical, and a third was the bell tower. The brilliant whiteness of the exterior with its red, yellow, and gold paint and gilding did not prepare them for the explosion of color that greeted them upon entering the interior. Removing their hats and stepping into the coolness inside the church, they were speechless. Their jaws literally dropped and their mouths hung open as they stared, wide-eyed. Colorful paintings of religious scenes and figures covered the walls, massive gold chandeliers hung suspended in the middle space, and the high altar appeared to be made of solid gold. Sunlight poured in through its many windows, creating an otherworldly atmosphere. The sacred silence of the interior contrasted sharply with the noise of the street outside, adding to the spiritual impact. They stood in silence for several minutes, taking it all in.

"I never seen so much gold in my life," muttered Dixon.

"This can't be real," whispered Walker.

They were approached by a priest in a long black robe with a heavy silver chain around his neck bearing an elaborate silver crucifix. He had a thick black beard, and appeared to be about forty years old. He spoke to them quietly in Russian, and Anya replied rapidly. Walker picked up the word 'Amerikanski.' They talked together for a moment and then the priest spoke to them again, this time in English.

"Welcome to Irkutsk," he said cordially. "I am Father Kirilov. How long do you plan to visit?"

"Just for a day or two," replied Walker. "We're getting travel permits to go to St. Petersburg. We just came across the lake on the ferry yesterday."

The priest was curious as to why they were traveling in this part of the world, so they briefly explained that they were with a group of missionaries who were fleeing from the Boxer Rebellion in China, and due to the trouble in the east, had to travel west to get home.

"Yes," he nodded sympathetically. "The world is full of trouble these days."

"How is it that you know English?" asked Dixon.

"My brother emigrated to America five years ago, and I am hoping to join him. He sent me a book about the English language, and I have been studying it. It is hard, though, since there is not often anyone to speak with, so I am glad to meet Anya. I think we will practice together now."

"You're doing pretty good," observed Dixon. "You don't need much practice."

"Thank you," said Kirilov, with genuine humility. "That is very kind of you."

The priest invited them and Anya to come to his house for supper, to meet his wife and children and to have further conversation. They were glad to accept—the appeal of a home-cooked meal, even in a foreign land with strange foods was too much to resist.

Kirilov walked with them to the church entrance. As they stepped out into the sunlight, there was a crowd of people gathered around a nearby wagon on which a man with rimless glasses and a thick shock of dark hair, wearing an ill-fitting suit, stood giving a speech. The man spoke in a loud, strident voice, making forceful, almost angry gestures. The crowd of about fifty people seemed to be intensely interested in what he was saying.

"What's that all about?" asked Walker.

"That is Lev Davidovich Bronstein. He is one of the many political exiles here. Probably a third of the population of Irkutsk are exiles—politicals, criminals, who knows? He comes here often to make speeches about his radical political ideas."

"The government sends people here as punishment?" asked Dixon incredulously.

"Oh yes," nodded Kirilov. "They want more people to live in Siberia, and they don't want troublemakers in the west, so they send them to the east. They used convicts to build much of the railroad that you will be traveling on. Many people here like what Bronstein says against the government."

"What sort of things is he saying?" asked Walker.

"He says the workers are oppressed and robbed by the factory owners. The government supports the factory owners and forbids the workers to form labor unions, so they live in poverty and hardship. Soldiers break their strikes with force."

"Sounds like America," commented Dixon.

"He objects that the government controls the press, and does not allow criticism. He says that the workers must rise up and—how do you say?—overthrow the social order, I think."

"Sounds like he's a revolutionary!" exclaimed Walker.

"Oh, yes! Very much so. But it is useless. Someone like Bronstein will never overthrow the government. The Romanov family has ruled Russia for almost three hundred years. It is much too strong, and it has the army. He will spend his life here in Siberia preaching to exiles from the back of a wagon. He would help himself better by learning a trade and getting a job."

That evening Dixon decided to stay at the hotel and rest, so Walker met Anya in the lobby and they went to Father Kirilov's house. She was wearing a pretty, embroidered blouse and skirt, with blue ribbons in her light brown hair. Walker thought that she looked very lovely, and wished that he was wearing something other than his rough camel hair coat and scuffed boots.

Father Kirilov's wife had prepared a delicious meal. It was the first time in months that Walker had tasted potatoes, carrots, and onions. The platter of roast pork was indescribably wonderful. At the end of the meal the priest poured a small glass of clear liquid for each of the adults. The Russians quickly downed theirs in a single swallow, so Walker also tossed his head back and emptied the glass. His eyes bulged and his nostrils flared as he suddenly felt that he had drunk liquid fire. His face turned beet red, tears came to his eyes, and the room became unbearably hot. It took several minutes for him to regain his composure and stop coughing and wheezing. The others found great amusement in watching him and he was extremely embarrassed, and apologized profusely.

Conversation during the meal was somewhat labored, but with Kirilov translating it went well enough. When Walker began to sense that it was time for him to go, he rose and expressed his thanks for the hospitality of the family. The priest rose also, and stepping to a nearby trunk took from it a small package, wrapped in brown paper and tied with string.

"Could I ask a favor of you, Walker Garrett?"

"Of course, Father Kirilov. What can I do for you?"

"My brother—the one who emigrated to America—lives in New York City. I believe you will be there when your ship returns to America. Would it be possible for you to see that he gets this package? It is a warm neck scarf, socks, and mittens that my wife has made for him. His name is Mikhail, and his address is written on the paper."

"I'll be happy to do that, Father Kirilov. It's no trouble at all. I promise that he will get this as soon as I get back to America."

"You are a good man, Walker Garrett. May God bless you on your travels, and bring you safely home again."

Walker and Anya strolled slowly back toward the hotel along the nearly deserted streets. The sun had set, and although there was still ambient light, the temperature was quickly dropping, and Walker was now glad for the long-haired coat ruffling in the chill breeze. Conversing was more difficult without Kirilov to translate, but Walker enjoyed the challenge, and found Anya quite pleasant company. They taught each other some new words, and laughed at their attempts at pronunciation. She took his arm and bumped against him as they walked along, talking and laughing, oblivious to all around them. It was dark by the time they reached the hotel, and they stood across the street, continuing to talk.

Suddenly a burly man in dirty clothes with a straggly, dirty beard staggered out from an adjacent alley, brandishing a broken bottle. The smell of alcohol was strong, and he snarled at them with raspy, slurred speech. Walker did not need Anya to translate—it was obvious that this was an attempt at robbery. Anya spoke to the man but he only became angry and took a threatening step forward, raising his voice and thrusting the sharp edges of the bottle toward them.

Walker extended his arm in front of Anya and gently pushed her behind him. Handing her Kirilov's package, he positioned himself in front and crouched slightly, waiting for the drunken man to attack. The man stepped forward again, jabbing at Walker with the bottle. Walker did not move, but when the man, emboldened, advanced closer, Walker pounced. Grabbing the man by his wrist he smashed him in the face with his fist twice, bloodying his nose and mouth. The man twisted his arm free and slashed at Walker, leaving a red gash on the back of Walker's left hand. Furious, Walker sprang forward, striking the man in the chin with a left uppercut and then driving his right fist with all his strength into the middle of his face. The man sprawled full length on his back, writhed in pain for a couple of seconds, and then lay still.

"Walker!" cried Anya. "Blood!"

The back of Walker's left hand was covered in blood and it was dripping on the cobblestones. Anya grabbed his arm and propelled him across the street to the hotel, steering him through the empty lobby into a back room where she took a pillowcase from a shelf and began ripping it into strips. Through an open door Walker saw a sink with a water pump in the next room, and working the pump handle with his right hand, washed off the blood. Anya came into the room, which was apparently the laundry room of the hotel, and searched through the cabinets and drawers until she found a bottle.

"Ah!" she announced triumphantly, pulling the cork from the bottle. Walker thought it looked suspiciously like the bottle Father Kirilov had produced at the supper table, and when Anya poured it over the cut on his hand he knew he was right. He jerked his hand away with a stifled gasp at the intense burning sensation, but Anya, with surprising strength, forced his hand back over the sink. Locking his arm between her own arm and side, she doused his hand repeatedly with the vodka while he hyperventilated and danced from one foot to the other, gasping through clenched teeth. Finally the bottle was empty, and she wrapped his hand in the strips of linen and tied them securely.

Walker looked at his bandaged hand, then at the empty liquor bottle, and then at Anya, and cleared his throat. "Spasebo," he breathed, exhaling slowly. *Thank you.*

She hesitated, and then put one hand to her mouth and began to giggle. Walker started to feel offended, but then the humor of the situation struck him and he grinned sheepishly, and then joined her in laughing.

"Someone will be very unhappy," he smiled, pointing to the empty bottle.

"Shhh!" she whispered, putting a finger to her lips and making a face of pretended alarm. She put the cork back in the bottle and replaced it in the cabinet, and then pulled Walker after her back into the lobby.

They sat close together on a sofa in a shadowy area behind a row of decorative columns, and talked. Walker had never talked so much with a girl in his life, and he didn't know what to say, but he knew he wanted it to last as long as possible. Fortunately, Anya did most of the talking. He found the sound of her voice very pleasing, and he was enchanted by her accent. He watched her face as she talked, admiring her clear blue eyes and fair skin. He found himself hoping that it would take a few days to arrange the travel permits so that he could spend more time with her. A church bell began to chime somewhere in the distance, and Walker was shocked to count twelve strikes. Could it possibly be midnight? He'd had no idea that so much time had passed. Anya's head was resting on his shoulder, and her hand was on his bandaged hand. He then realized that she had dozed off, and he sat quietly, not moving a muscle so as not to disturb her. He thought that he might just close his eyes for a minute, and wait for her to wake up.

"Garrett! Wake up!"

It was Dixon, poking Walker in the shoulder. It was early morning, and gray daylight filtered into the lobby.

He awoke with a start, rubbing his eyes and stretching. Anya was gone and he was on the sofa by himself.

"You sleep down here all night?" asked Dixon. "What happened to your hand?"

"Yeah, I sat down here to relax for a few minutes, and I guess I just dozed off."

"What happened to your hand?" he repeated.

"Oh, that," said Walker, with feigned indifference. "Accidentally cut it on a broken glass at Father Kirilov's house last night. Looks worse than it is." Walker had instinctively lied, and he wasn't sure why.

"Wonder what's going on over there," Dixon pointed, standing at the front window of the lobby, looking across the street. There was a group of uniformed men standing around a body lying on the ground.

Walker joined him at the window. His pulse quickened as he realized that the body was that of the drunkard he had punched the night before.

"I don't know," he said. "Looks like maybe the police found some drunk sleeping off his liquor. Let's go get some breakfast."

At breakfast Nästegard informed them that the permits had all been approved the day before and that they would be going to the train station as soon as they had eaten. Walker was dismayed to realize that he would not see Anya again, but he hid his feelings and said nothing. Everyone was curious about his bandaged hand, but he told them all the same thing he had said to Dixon.

When they were leaving for the station in the tarantasses, a body wrapped in a sheet was being loaded into the back of a wagon across the street. Walker asked Nästegard if he had heard anything about it.

"The desk clerk says that a drunk man died last night. Apparently beaten to death. The police are asking questions to see if anyone witnessed it. I told them that we were all in the hotel last night."

"Yes, I fell asleep on the sofa in the lobby and didn't wake up 'til morning. Dixon woke me up and we saw them across the street and were wondering what it was about."

As he turned to climb into the tarantass, he saw Dixon looking at him. Something in his eyes told Walker that Dixon knew, somehow. Dixon quickly climbed in after Walker and elbowed him over to make room.

"Accidental cut on a broken glass at the priest's house?" he hissed in Walker's ear.

"Later," Walker whispered back, and hid his bandaged hand inside the shaggy coat.

At the station they found that a separate car had been reserved for their group. Their baggage loaded on board and everyone settled in the four-seat compartments, they were finally about to depart. Walker studied the platform, hoping vainly to catch a glimpse of Anya.

The train, without sounding a whistle, began to move, and in minutes they were amidst rolling countryside. Walker felt both relief and sadness, looking back at Irkutsk as the train rounded a bend. It was a gloomy, rainy day, matching Walker's mood. He had no interest in watching the scenery gliding past the window, but pulled his hat down over his eyes and slumped down in his seat.

31

ACROSS THE OCEAN OF LAND

"I'm not going to be able to relax until we're out of this country," Walker moaned, as he leaned against the side of the compartment and stared out the window at the dense pine forest sliding past. "They're gonna arrest me and send me to Siberia to work on the railroad."

"Just stay on the train and keep your head down," advised Dixon. "Nobody saw anything, did they?"

"Nobody but Anya, as far as I know. I don't think she'll say anything to anyone."

Dixon studied him for a moment before speaking. "Then you should be alright. Keep an eye out for the police whenever we stop, and don't call attention to yourself. The farther away we get from Irkutsk, the safer you'll be."

The train moved slowly. Excruciatingly slowly, it seemed to Walker. It frequently stopped on sidings to allow military trains to rush past, going eastward. Every two or three hours it let the passengers off to buy meals and refreshments at the rail stations. Food was plentiful and cheap—bread, butter, cheese, milk, roast chickens— and always boiling water for tea. A delightful surprise for the Americans in the party was that coffee was also available—the first they had tasted since their long trek had begun.

For the first two days Walker stayed on the train during the station stops, peering furtively out at the platform, watching for uniformed men. He was alarmed on day two at seeing a large number of colorfully uniformed men on the platform in Krasnoyarsk, but then realized that they were army officers, and not police. When the conductor came through the car checking tickets he would pull his hat over his face, turn to the wall, and feign sleep. The others in the group thought he must be sick, and he admitted, honestly, that he did not feel well. He spent most of his time reading a dense book by a Frenchman named Toqueville, borrowed from Roberts.

By the morning of the third day, despite the fact that Dixon had brought him food at each stop, he was hungry enough—and bored enough—to risk venturing out. The train pulled into the depot at Novosibirsk and the passengers exited the cars, walking stiffly and stretching as they converged on the food vendors. After downing a plate of sausage, eggs, and buttered bread, Walker felt better than he had in days. He was draining the last of his second cup of black coffee when, from behind him, a man spoke to him brusquely in Russian. He turned to see a policeman glaring at him.

It was such a shock to Walker that he caught his breath. He began a coughing fit, doubling over with coffee coming out of his nose and his face turning beet red as he coughed uncontrollably. He staggered away still coughing, hoping the policeman would not follow. Some of the passengers were laughing and pointing at him, but he pretended not to notice. Wiping tears from his eyes he bumped into Nästegard, who gave him an amused look.

"All he said was that you were blocking the way to the samovar."

"He surprised me and I snorted the coffee up my nose," said Walker in a choked voice. "Made a fool of myself."

Nästegard called out something cheery to the officer and waved. The man responded with a bored shrug as he filled his cup with tea. "Let's get back on the train. I think you need to lie back down."

Walker locked himself in the lavatory until the train had left the station, and didn't get off the train again until the next afternoon when they reached Omsk. After that he disembarked regularly with the other passengers, but always ate quickly and returned to the compartment.

Having left the pine forests behind, the train rolled across flat prairies for two days. Pastures, fields, orchards, and thatch-roofed huts dominated the landscape, and Walker could not help but admire the endless fields of grain. Shocks of harvested wheat dotted the landscape, while wagons piled high crept toward barns.

"I feel like I'm crossing the ocean again, 'cept this time on land," groaned Dixon. "I'm losing my mind."

"At least it's better'n riding a camel," replied Walker. "We're already halfway to Moscow, and we'll be out of this God-forsaken country in another week."

"I wouldn't call it a 'God-forsaken country,'" objected Roberts, sliding into the seat opposite them. "It's actually a very Christian country with much to recommend it."

"What's to recommend it?" scoffed Walker. "It's poor and dirty, and there's always gangs of prisoners on the train platforms with irons on their legs. China had more culture in one city block than I've seen in all of Russia."

"Perhaps so," conceded Roberts, "but China has had thousands of years to develop its culture, while Russia is really just getting started. They expanded eastward to the Pacific while we were expanding west. We built a transcontinental railroad with laborers imported from Ireland and China, while they built one three times as long with Russian labor. They're grabbing land from Manchuria, and we grabbed it from Mexico. They inhabit a harsh land of extreme heat and cold, but they have warm hearts. Remember how they cared for us in Kiachta when the Söderboms' baby died? They saved us from the Boxers, and have given us special permits to travel all the way across their country. They are a religious people. Their churches are the most impressive buildings in every city and village. This train even has a shrine car for worshipers. They worship the same God and read the same Bible as we do. If God has a 'manifest destiny' for America, then He may also have a 'manifest destiny' for Russia. They have a formidable task in civilizing this part of the world, but they have made a good start, and I believe they will succeed."

"Well," grumbled Walker reluctantly, "Since you put it like *that . . .* ," and his voice trailed off.

Dixon threw his head back and laughed out loud. "Admit it, Garrett," he hooted. "You're just grumpy 'cause you had to leave Anya behind!"

Walker reddened and glared at Dixon.

"Don't argue now, fellows," remonstrated Roberts. "I admit I'm partial to the Russians, but they have been good to us and I would be ungrateful if I didn't speak up on their behalf. I only hope that our two countries will be friends and not enemies."

"That fella Toqueville doesn't think so," averred Walker. "He says we'll be enemies because we're so different."

"Yes, he did," agreed Roberts. "But he had not visited Russia and didn't know the people. Also, he wrote that book more than sixty years ago. A lot has changed since then, and I'm hoping and praying that he will be proved wrong."

"That's something worth praying for," Walker conceded. "The world's got enough wars already."

It was suddenly darker in the compartment. Raindrops began streaking the windows, and thunder could be heard above the clacking of the rails.

"You been praying for rain again, preacher?" demanded Dixon in mock anger.

Roberts protested his innocence as everyone laughed. "I think this is a good time to go to bed early," he said, rising to his feet. "We'll be in Yekaterinburg by morning. Sleep well, brothers!"

Within minutes everyone else in the compartment had dozed off, lulled to sleep by the rhythm of the rails and the patter of the rain-drops. Walker, however, was not sleepy. He propped his elbow on the window frame, and rested his chin in his hand as he watched the dim countryside illuminated by occasional flashes of lightning. *All of them are going home,* he thought, *but I don't have a home to go back to. There's nothing for me at Pond Spring anymore. Maybe I'll just have to stay in the army—unless they shoot me for desertion. Or maybe I can get hired as a cowboy out West on a cattle ranch. Or maybe I could teach school—after all, I graduated from the Decatur Academy. Or maybe—*

Walker was too despondent to speculate further about his future. It didn't seem that he had any good options. He wished that General Wheeler was there to advise him—he was always so wise and practical, making clear what was confusing and making simple what was complicated. Thinking of the old General made him feel better, but also nostalgic at the same time. He sat deep into the night, looking out at the rain, thinking of days gone by, and wondering what lay ahead.

The terrain changed again as the train made its way slowly westward. They now entered a region of rich farmland with broad rivers, numerous large villages, and more frequent rail station stops. The stations became larger, better equipped, and more luxurious. There were more passengers milling about, and unfortunately for Walker's nerves, more policemen and soldiers. None of them seemed to be interested in him though, so while he remained watchful and cautious, he regularly exited the coach with the others for food and simply for the sake of moving about.

He ceased to care about the names of the cities they passed through: Perm, Kirov, Yaroslavl, and many others. He took some interest in the remarkably long and high steel bridge across the wide Volga River, but eventually turned his back on the window and stopped looking out at all. He did not even react to the announcement that they would shortly be arriving in the city of Moscow.

As they approached the city there was finally more than one rail line so that they no longer had to sit on sidings while eastbound trains rushed past. It was late afternoon when their train pulled into the Yaroslavsky station, which was impressively large and grand.

Thankful to finally be able to leave the train behind, at least for a couple of days, Walker paid attention to the sights of Moscow as they navigated its busy streets en route to the Great Moscow Hotel, in the center of the city. This city was a qualitatively different experience than anything he had yet seen, and he began to feel his energy returning as he anticipated exploring it before they continued on to St. Petersburg.

Since they were the only unmarried men in the group, Walker shared a room with Dixon and Nästegard. Nästegard had a trunk and handbag, but Walker and Dixon had nothing but coarse cloth bags containing their military jackets and the spare wool shirts which they had purchased in Kiachta. Their disassembled rifles were also in the bags, along with their revolvers, and Walker's machete, wrapped in the clothing.

Walker's eyes took in the high ceilings, lavish furnishings, velvet drapes, and gilded chandelier with electric lights. A side room provided a porcelain toilet, sink, and bathtub—all with running water. Everything was spotlessly clean. He then looked down at his battered boots, threadbare pants, and camel hair coat.

"I don't think I'm good enough to stay in this hotel," he remarked ruefully.

"What about me?" retorted Dixon. "Back in the States, I wouldn't even be allowed in a hotel with white people, 'less it was to shine shoes and wash dishes. And here I am, sleepin' in a nice, big bed with clean sheets. These Russians must think I'm a real man, same as anybody else."

"You'll find that to be the case across most of Europe," commented Nästegard. "Jews are often discriminated against, but not blacks."

"They never had slavery here, did they?" asked Walker.

"Yes, actually, Europe did have its own version of slavery—it was called serfdom. Serfs were not free people, but were the property of the landowner. This ended several hundred years ago in Western Europe, but Russia only freed its serfs about the same time as America freed its slaves, almost forty years ago."

"Are you serious?" Dixon asked incredulously. "Russians had white slaves up to forty years ago?"

"I am quite serious!" laughed Nästegard. "There were more than twenty million serfs—a third of the population of the country. And Czar Alexander II freed them without a civil war, without killing hundreds of thousands of civilians and soldiers, and without wrecking half of the country. And—" he added with emphasis, "he made it possible for the freed serfs to own land."

"You mean they got forty acres and a mule?"

"Well, they received government loans to help them buy land. It wasn't free, but it was better than nothing. It's interesting that both he and Lincoln were assassinated."

Walker and Dixon absorbed this in silence for a moment. Nästegard spread his hands in a gesture of helplessness as he continued. "But then, Socrates, Joan of Arc, and even Jesus himself were all put to death, so apparently making a positive difference in the world can be very hazardous to your health. Very hazardous indeed!"

"You make it sound like not getting assassinated is a bad thing," said Walker, with a wry smile.

Nästegard laughed out loud, sincerely amused. "Of course, it depends entirely on why you are assassinated! It's certainly one way to become famous, but I don't recommend it!"

As Nästegard turned to go check on how the others were settling into their rooms, Walker asked one last question. "Olaf, what are these buildings that we can see out the windows? They look very unusual."

"The huge, red brick fortress on the right is the Kremlin, which was the traditional seat of the Russian government before Peter the Great moved it to St. Petersburg about two hundred years ago. Beyond it, the church with the colorful onion domes is St. Basil's Cathedral. We'll visit them tomorrow, if you like."

A hot bath, a shave, and a clean shirt put Walker in a much better mood. Dixon also seemed to feel rejuvenated, and they went down the grand staircase for supper. The large dining room was brilliantly lit with blazing chandeliers, and the blue carpet and white tablecloths presented a stunningly beautiful sight. Nästegard motioned them into a smaller dining room which had been reserved for their group of twenty persons. It was furnished in the same colorful style, with large paintings and mirrors on the walls. Walker took a seat next to Maria at a table.

"I hope you don't mind," said Nästegard, "but I took the liberty of ordering your meal for you, since the menu was in Russian."

"As long as it ain't prairie dog, it'll be just fine by me," said Dixon.

"Amen to that!" seconded Walker.

When the plates of steaming food were placed before them, they each deeply inhaled the intoxicating aroma.

"What's this called?" asked Walker.

"It is beef stroganoff," explained Maria. "A traditional peasant dish."

"If peasants eat like this," said Dixon, licking sauce from his lips, "I don't want to be king."

Neither of them spoke again until they had completely cleaned their plates. It was their first sit-down meal in almost two weeks, and in the most luxurious setting either had ever seen, surpassing even the Tampa Bay hotel. At length Walker put down his silver utensils with a satisfied sigh and looked around.

"I can't believe we can afford this," he marveled. "I think maybe I should be a missionary!"

The American missionaries burst into laughter, and after Nästegard translated for the Swedes, they joined in.

"Yes, Walker," laughed Roberts, "We all agree that you and Dixon should become missionaries. It is your calling!"

"Whoa there, now," interjected Dixon. "Don't try to rope me into being a missionary. I'm a soldier, plain and simple. No preachin' for me! I'm not much of a talker."

"I think you would be good at it, lieutenant," chimed in Williams. "But God can use you in any walk of life. He has certainly used you in a powerful way over these past weeks, and we are all thankful that He did."

Roberts added, "I believe that it was St. Francis of Assisi who said,

'Preach the gospel at all times. Use words if necessary.' Actions really do speak louder than words, so you don't have to preach sermons to be a missionary. In a way, all Christians are missionaries."

"I don't think some of 'em know it," commented Dixon skeptically. "But I'll keep it in mind."

When the group began to head back upstairs to bed, Walker and Dixon decided to take a stroll. Stepping out of the hotel into the night air they discovered that the temperature had dropped dramatically since the afternoon. With hands shoved into the pockets of their coats and their breath forming clouds of fog in front of their faces, they walked briskly across the street toward the Kremlin. There were very few pedestrians in sight, and their footsteps echoed off the high brick walls.

"These walls are even higher than the ones around Peking," said Walker, squinting up at the sixty-foot-high barrier.

"Yeah, and you can prob'ly see Peking from that tower yonder," added Dixon, nodding toward a lofty tower more than two hundred feet in height.

"Wonder how far it is around this thing."

"One way to find out."

Hiking the Kremlin's mile and a half circumference took them along the banks of the Moscow River for a half mile, and then through the huge square in front of St. Basil's Cathedral. As they stood gaping at the turrets and onion domes of the cathedral, a flurry of snowflakes swirled down upon them.

"Snow!" exclaimed Walker, holding out his hands. "I ain't seen snow since I was fourteen! It's beautiful!"

"Plenty of snow in the Dakotas," said Dixon, unimpressed. "This ain't nuthin' compared to that. But seeing as this is barely October, they'll prob'ly have a lot more, come winter."

Walker, undeterred, turned his face up, mouth wide open and tongue out, trying to catch snowflakes.

Dixon watched with a disgusted look on his face. "Garrett, you are such a peasant."

"Don't care if I am. Just keep the beef stroganoff coming."

They gawked at the fantastic architecture of the cathedral for several minutes, shivering in the snow shower. Heading back to the hotel they stopped several times in the middle of the huge square to look back in admiration.

As they were about to cross the avenue to the hotel they were accosted by two baton-wielding, uniformed policemen. The officers spoke to them aggressively, waving the batons in a threatening way. It was clear that they were asking questions, but of course Walker and Dixon were not able to respond.

"Ya geverit po-Amerikanski," ventured Walker, remembering the phrase taught them by Nästegard.

"Amerikanski?" demanded the policeman, who then held out his hand toward them as he spoke a stream of Russian, which ended in the identifiable word 'passport.'

"Passport!" exclaimed Walker and Dixon in unison. They fumbled through their pockets and triumphantly produced their temporary Russian passports, issued by the consul in Urga. The policemen snatched the passports from their hands, took one look at them and snarled in anger. Waving the passports at them and shouting in Russian, they used their batons to prod the two of them, pointing in the direction they were to go. It was clear that they were being taken into custody.

"But this is our hotel!" protested Walker, gesturing to the Great Moscow Hotel across the street.

"Ha!" shouted the policeman in derision. Pointing with his baton at the shabby clothes worn by the two and then at the grand hotel, both officers laughed harshly as they made sneering comments and prodded them more vigorously.

"I think we're in trouble," said Dixon under his breath.

"We need Olaf."

They were not moving quickly enough for the policemen's liking. A couple of sharp blows across their shoulders with the batons fixed that, and within a few minutes they found themselves in a small, dingy police station a half-mile from the hotel. They were ushered roughly through the front room and shoved into a large cell where a half-dozen poorly dressed men sat on a bench, slumped over. A couple of men lay on the brick floor. One sat on the floor, resting his head on the bench. It was a dismal scene, lit only by a flickering candle in a wall bracket in the corridor. The cell door, consisting of vertical iron bars, admitted just enough light to let them find places on the bench.

The cell door clanged shut. None of the other men even looked up. They sat in silence in the semi-darkness, Walker's heart sinking into his stomach.

"You think they'll send us to Siberia?" he whispered. "In chains?"

"You, maybe. I ain't done nuthin'," replied Dixon brusquely.

Walker leaned forward, head in his hands, and sighed heavily. Seeing his distress, Dixon spoke again, less harshly. "Olaf will get us out of here, come morning."

"He don't know we're here. I'm a goner. It doesn't matter—I ain't got a home to go back to, anyway."

There was no more talking. It was cold in the cell and Walker could see his breath fogging. *Might as well get used to it,* he thought. *It'll be colder than this in Siberia.*

The night crept slowly past. Unable to sleep, Walker could hear distant church bells chiming the hours throughout the night. At about eight o'clock in the morning, the cell door screeched open and an officer motioned for Walker and Dixon to follow him. They stiffly got to their feet and went into the front room to stand in front of the desk, hands clasped behind them, military-style. A small stove provided welcome heat.

Behind the desk sat a stout, bald, bearded man in an elaborate uniform. He continued making notes on a pad, ignoring them for a long minute. Finally he put down the pen, opened a drawer, and took out their two Russian passports. Standing up, he looked at them rather irritably, impatiently tapping one passport against the other.

"Amerikantsy." He said the word as if it was a verdict, and paused dramatically, looking at them authoritatively.

"Russkiy pasporta?" He continued, with a quizzical note in his voice, holding the two passports out as if they were exhibits to be examined. He paused again and then delivered a rapid, long sentence in which Walker recognized the names of Schischareff and Urga. He then closed his eyes, shook his head, and gestured as if to say, 'I've seen everything now.'

Handing them the passports, he motioned toward the door to the street as if brushing them away. "Do svidaniya." *Good-bye.*

"Do svidaniya," they both responded quickly and backed to the door, bowing repeatedly as they went. Once outside they walked for a few steps and then simultaneously broke into a run. There was still a light dusting of snow on the pavement from the previous night's flurries and the frosty air stung their cheeks, but they did not stop running until they reached the hotel.

Pausing in the opulent lobby to catch their breath, they saw that the rest of the group was assembling for breakfast. They strolled calmly into the dining room to join them.

"There you are!" Nästegard sounded surprised. "Where have you two been?"

"We went for a walk," said Dixon, perhaps a little too casually.

"Again? Your bed didn't look like it had been slept in."

"That's the army for you," Walker yawned. "If you can't bounce a quarter off it, you didn't make it up right."

"Well, come on and get some breakfast! We've got a big day ahead of us."

Walker and Dixon shared a quick look and headed to the table.

"That coffee sure smells good," Walker smiled, tiredly. His feeling of relief was so intense that even his bone-deep exhaustion could not keep a smile off his face. *A big day indeed,* he thought. *You have no idea!*

Nästegard kept them moving throughout the day. They attended Sunday services in the cathedral inside the Kremlin, and also visited two other churches there. They walked all over the vast complex looking at Napoleonic cannons, historic monuments, paintings, and other treasures, and climbed to the top of one of the tall towers to enjoy panoramic views of the city. They arrived back at the hotel in time to wash up for supper.

Walker was too tired to admire the sumptuous dining room, but not too tired to appreciate another dish of beef stroganoff. After the meal he and Dixon were the first to head to their room. Trudging heavily up the stairs, Walker groaned, "I may just go to bed in my clothes—if I get that far."

After climbing several more steps Dixon wearily responded, "Don't care, long as you take off your boots. Don't want you kickin' me in your sleep."

Walker collapsed into the bed and looked up at the gilded chandelier. "Feels weird to be in a bed that's not moving," he murmured. "I could get used to this."

Dixon's only response was a soft snore. Walker turned over on his side and in seconds sank into oblivion.

Another night on a train brought them to St. Petersburg, on the shore of the Baltic Sea. They were met at the train station by the U.S. embassy's chargé d'affaires, Mr. Herbert Pearce. An equivalent representative from the Swedish embassy was there to take his countrymen to their lodgings, and it became apparent that the group was now going separate ways.

It was an emotional scene on the train platform as they bid one another farewell. It was particularly difficult for Walker to say goodbye to the Söderbom family, Maria, and Nästegard. He found himself choking on the words as he tried to speak, and furiously blinked back his tears as they walked away. He hadn't realized how attached he had become to all of them, and parting left a deep ache in his heart.

That left only the six Americans—Roberts and Williams and their wives, and Walker and Dixon, standing among the remaining trunks and bags. Pearce, hat in hand, stepped forward with a sympathetic smile.

"Well, my friends, you've reached the western end of the Great Siberian Railway! You have come a long, difficult journey, but you will be home soon, I promise! Come with me now, and I'll get you squared away."

Exiting the train station to the street, Walker shivered as he looked up at the cold, blue morning sky. Taking a deep breath to fill the emptiness he felt inside, he got into the carriage. It was going to be another long day.

32

CHASING THE SETTING SUN

The impressive sights Walker had seen in Moscow paled in comparison to the spectacular beauty of St. Petersburg. There were palaces and ornate churches without end, picturesque canals, and lovely parks and plazas with statues and fountains. After a day of traveling in the city and touring the Hermitage museum's fabulous collection of art, Walker's mind was numbed by the incomprehensible display of wealth and power. He had not imagined that such things existed. Boarding the train for Berlin, he settled into his seat thinking how little he really knew about the world, feeling that he must be as ignorant and uncultured as any peasant in Siberia.

"So, what did you think of all those paintings, statues, vases, and jewels?" he asked Dixon. "Wasn't that the most amazing bunch of art you ever saw?"

"Yup," said Dixon. "It was alright, I reckon." Reaching into his shirt pocket he pulled out a small, white crocheted square with a red star and blue ribbon. "But this means a heck of a lot more to me than all that fine, showy art in the museum. They can keep all that, and I'll keep this."

Walker blinked. Dixon had a way of seeing through the clutter and getting to what really mattered. He self-consciously touched the silver cross hanging around his neck and thought of Harriet. He wished that the crocheted pieces sent by Abigail Dancy had actually been her work, so that they could mean something to him, too.

Roberts and Williams with their wives joined them in the compartment, filling the remaining seats. The train began to move, and as the daylight faded they left the city behind, heading south by southwest at a rapid clip.

"So," smiled Mrs. Roberts, making conversation, "What did you two like the most about the Hermitage museum? Did you have a favorite artwork?"

"I really liked that giant green vase," said Walker, leaning forward with elbows on the arm rests. "That was really something!"

"Giant green vase?" She seemed confused. "Ah, yes!" she nodded. "The Kolyvan vase. The label said it is the largest piece of jasper in the world, made by Russian stoneworkers about fifty years ago. I agree, that's a very remarkable piece! There's nothing else like it in the world." She gave Walker a tight, compressed smile, and he leaned back in his seat, pleased with himself.

"And you, lieutenant?" She directed her gaze to Dixon.

Dixon cleared his throat. "Well," he said, perhaps a bit hesitantly, "All the paintings, statues and things was real nice. But I have to admit, the thing that impressed me the most was that staircase—the one they called the Jordan Staircase. That was a mighty nice staircase, for sure!"

"The staircase?" she echoed blankly. "Well, ah, yes—yes, indeed! That was certainly a very nice staircase, I agree with you. Very nice indeed!" and she nodded and smiled her approval to him also.

"Personally, I liked the Rembrandts," chimed in Roberts.

"The Raphael collection was exquisite," exclaimed Williams.

"I loved the Diamond Room, with all the beautiful jewelry," gushed Mrs. Williams.

"I've always been fascinated by the ancient Greek pottery," said Mrs. Roberts. "They have some marvelous pieces on display!"

"On the other hand," said Roberts with an impish smile, "was there anything that you did *not* like?"

It was Walker's turn to clear his throat. He felt his cheeks redden and was glad for the dim light in the compartment. "Well," he said awkwardly, "I don't think they ought to be painting pictures of all those naked people. They even had statues of naked people that looked like they were alive. They ought to have had some clothes on, I think. It was embarrassing."

"I didn't mind," drawled Dixon laconically.

"Artists have been depicting nudity for the last five hundred years," objected Williams, "not counting the ancient Greeks and Romans, who started it two thousand years ago. Nudity in art isn't a bad thing—it's a way of enjoying the beauty of God's creation."

"Maybe so," said Walker, "but even God gave Adam and Eve clothes to wear. I don't think he likes artists taking those clothes off of people just to look at them."

"But—but—" sputtered Williams indignantly.

"I think the boy's got a point there, Mark," grinned Roberts. "He knows his Bible stories. You can't argue with that!"

Williams held up his hands in surrender. "I concede your point, Walker!" he laughed. "More fig leaves and less nudity in art! Let's go get some supper!"

Just before noon the next day they reached the small Polish town of Illowo on the German border. There the passengers had to exit the train to have their passports checked, while crews of workers changed the wheel carriages of the cars. Walker presented his newly-printed American passport to the agent, and was gratified to see it stamped and returned to him without any fuss.

"What are they doing to the train?" he asked Roberts.

"Changing the bogies. Russian rails are wider apart than those in Western Europe, and they have to put different wheel carriages on the cars so they can continue on the track. They have to do the reverse process on trains going east."

"Wouldn't it be smarter to just use the same gauge?" asked Dixon. "Sure would save a lot of time and trouble."

"I've heard two explanations of that," said Williams. "One is that the Russians use a wider rail gauge because it's safer and more stable.

The other is that the different rail gauge makes it difficult for an enemy to invade Russia, since they can't use the Russian railroads to move their armies."

"Napoleon didn't need no railroads," commented Walker. "And he went all the way to Moscow. They might ought to look for a better defensive plan."

"Besides that," said Dixon, pointing toward the work crews, "it don't take but two or three hours to change the wheels, and then they can use the Russian railroads. Don't seem like much protection to me, either."

"You fellows are hard to argue with," laughed Williams, with Roberts joining in.

"Just common sense," scoffed Dixon. "I said the Russians won't be able to handle the Japanese, and this just proves it to me. They ain't got the brains for it."

This provoked a debate with the two missionaries, who energetically defended the Russians against Walker and Dixon's criticisms. The good-natured argument lasted through the lunch of bread, cheese, and hot tea, and by early afternoon the train was ready to go again.

The locomotive raced along without further interruption. The landscape continued to be flat and unremarkable, with no large towns. By early evening it steamed into Berlin's Schlesischer Bahnhof, the rail station on the eastern side of the city. It was necessary to have their baggage carted to the Lehrter Bahnhof on the western side of the city to continue onward to France. Due to the lateness of the hour the missionaries decided to spend the night and resume the journey the next day. Carrying only their handbags, they hired a carriage to take them to the Hotel Kaiserhof. Arriving in front of the imposing 260-room structure, they entered the luxurious lobby.

"I thought we stayed in some fancy places in Moscow and St. Petersburg," marveled Walker, "but this is the fanciest one yet."

"Wouldn't it be cheaper to stay in a smaller hotel, without all the trimmings?" suggested Dixon.

"Yes," said Roberts, "but none of us speaks German, and the

better hotels are more likely to have staff that speak English. Don't worry—the Mission Board sent us enough money to pay our expenses, and besides, we'll only be here for one night."

Walker and Dixon took the lift up to their room on the fourth floor. Dixon held on tightly to the handrail in the elevator as it rose, looking very nervous. Walker grinned at Dixon's reaction. "That's the same thing I did the first time I rode in one of these," he chuckled. Like the rooms at the Tampa Hotel, their room had electric lights, a private bathroom, and a telephone.

"I'm spoiled rotten," Dixon groaned. "I'll never be able to go back to living in the army barracks and using the latrine."

"And eatin' hardtack and beans," added Walker. "Not after that beef stroganoff!"

After a supper of würstel, sauerkraut, and roasted potatoes, they decided that Germany had even better food than Russia. Dabbing his lips with a cloth napkin, Dixon commented to the two missionaries, "I don't think Russia can handle the Germans, either. Any country that eats like this will be hard to beat on the battlefield."

"Don't get me started on that again," sighed Roberts, shaking his head. "Someday you fellows will see the light and understand that the Russian people have a resilience and solidity that will see them through the severest of trials. They may take a pounding, but they will persevere and they will prevail in the end!"

"Well, preacher, if the Russians are going to prevail over the Japanese and Germans in a war, they better put off that war until they have time to catch up, 'cause they are behind right now, and honestly, it don't look good for 'em."

"Russia's greatest weapon is its land," argued Williams. "There's just so much of it. The vastness of the Russian countryside is what ultimately defeated Napoleon and the Swedes, and will defeat all others who dare to invade them."

"You're forgetting one thing, though," countered Walker. "Bogies. All the Germans have to do is switch the wheels on the trains and they can steam all the way to St. Petersburg. They'll be there before the Russians can tear up their own railroads. The steam locomotive makes Russia an open door for invaders, and the Germans are the ones who can do it. We saw the German soldiers in China, too, and the Russians aren't in their league."

"You make good arguments," admitted Roberts. "Only time will tell which of us is right, and let's hope and pray that we never find out."

At that moment, across the opulent dining room a door opened and from a smaller, private dining room, out came a tall, husky man with close-cropped hair and dramatically swooping mustaches. He wore a military uniform decorated with rows of medals, and with him were a half-dozen men similarly attired, and several others in business suits.

When they had passed by, Walker motioned to the English-speaking waiter. "Who was that big man with the mustache?"

"That was General Paul von Hindenburg. He is one of Germany's best generals. Beside him was General Helmuth von Moltke. He is Germany's most important general." Then he added, "You also saw Herr Friedrich Krupp, who owns the steel company that makes Germany's weapons. They are three of the most important men in the Fatherland, next to the Kaiser himself."

"What do you reckon they was doing in there just now?" asked Dixon. "Planning a war?"

"They are always planning a war," replied the waiter solemnly. "It is what they do." He then picked up some used plates and carried them away.

They all shared a meaningful look as these words sank in.

Roberts cleared his throat and spoke quietly, "Like I said, you fellows may be right. Let's hope we don't find out."

Late the next morning their train departed Berlin, heading to Paris. Roberts had calculated that traveling to Paris and thence to Calais, on the Channel, would be the fastest route to reach London. Unfortunately, his inability to speak German resulted in failing to get tickets on the express train, and they discovered to their dismay that their train stopped in most of the towns along the way. Therefore, it took them until midday on the following day to reach the French capital city. Walker didn't mind, however, as the scenery from the train window was infinitely more interesting than they'd had while crossing Siberia. Neat houses with flower boxes, cobblestone-paved streets, and picturesque church spires filled every town and city, and the countryside was equally lovely, with well-tended farms and fields, sturdy horses pulling loaded wagons, and laborers harvesting the grain in the chill autumn air. He was excited to see an occasional castle in the distance. Altogether it seemed like a fairy tale land.

By the time they reached Paris it was too late to change trains and continue the journey on to Calais, so they once again made their way to a hotel. With only a couple dozen rooms the Hotel de Vendôme was much smaller than the Kaiserhof in Berlin, but it was still very nice.

Walker and Dixon decided to go for a walk before supper, and Walker asked the desk clerk if there were any interesting sights in the vicinity. The clerk, a balding, middle-aged man with a short, thin mustache, gave them a withering look of scorn as he surveyed their rumpled clothing, and turned and disappeared through a doorway.

"Not too friendly, is he?" Walker observed, as they headed for the street.

Dixon commented, "Maybe there ain't no interesting sights around here."

That could not have been further from the truth. After walking just a short distance from the hotel they reached the Place de la Concorde, a huge plaza featuring a tall Egyptian obelisk in the center. But what caused their jaws to drop was the towering entrance to the Paris International Exposition, just off the plaza. The graceful white arches formed a dome crowned by a soaring pedestal, supporting a statue of an elaborately clad female figure. A huge crowd of people was milling about, moving forward into what looked like a fairground of fantastic structures of all kinds. They could see a huge Ferris wheel with compartments the size of railroad cars, and in the distance a sky-scraping spire painted a bright golden yellow. They were irresistibly drawn to the entrance gate.

Beyond it they crossed a river on a bridge ornamented with

colossal statues of winged horses. Bumping and jostling in the crowd, they soon climbed to a platform above the street and found themselves on a moving sidewalk. Holding onto hand grips as they whisked along, both were wide-eyed and slack-jawed, heads swiveling as they drank in the sights along the way. They arrived shortly at the yellow spire and found that it was an iron tower, rising from a four-footed base to a point a thousand feet high. Taking an elevator up part of the way and then climbing several flights of stairs, they ascended to the observation platform at the top, over nine-hundred feet above the ground. Looking down, both recoiled in sudden panic, colliding with other visitors as they backed away from the railing.

"Good Lord!" gasped Dixon "I'm gonna die up here!" He began wheezing as if he couldn't breathe, and pressed both hands to his chest.

"Shouldn't have come up here," moaned Walker, sinking to his knees and swaying back and forth, hands over his eyes. "They're gonna have to carry me down."

After several minutes however, they managed to calm down and breathe normally, but still stayed away from the railing. Watching the other people—including children—enjoy the view, they gradually edged forward. Standing tensely with flared nostrils and clenched jaws, they inched closer to the railing, but stopped more than an arm's length away. The cool wind in their faces was both stimulating and frightening. Scanning the horizon and gazing down upon the vast expanse of the city of Paris from such a dizzying height, Walker felt unsteady on his feet. Crouching, he summoned all of his courage and crept to the railing, gripping it with both hands, and peering over it at the street far below, pulling back, and then peering again. He heard the sound of laughter behind him and turning, saw a group of people watching him, grinning and laughing. Blushing, he stood up, but immediately felt the sensation of falling in the pit of his stomach and quickly stepped back from the railing. Finding Dixon standing beside him, he grabbed his arm and said, "Let's get down from here."

"I'm way ahead of you," responded Dixon, and they quickly exited the platform. Back on the ground a few minutes later, they looked up at where they had just been.

"If God had a-wanted us to be up that high, he woulda give us wings," said Dixon.

"That's the scariest thing I've ever done," observed Walker, "except maybe for that python in the Philippines, and that wasn't by choice."

They strolled back along the left bank of the Seine, taking in all the astonishing pavilions of countries from around the world. They rode the giant Ferris wheel, which took them to more than two hundred feet above the street, but after the Eiffel Tower experience it was not alarming—or at least not as much as it would otherwise have been. Dixon elbowed Walker and pointed to a pavilion structure that looked surprisingly familiar.

"Hey—that looks just like the U.S. Capitol in D.C."

As a matter of fact, it was the United States' pavilion. Once back on the ground they joined the crowd entering it and looked curiously at the exhibits, taking some pride in knowing that this was from their country. A featured display was The Exhibit of American Negroes, with hundreds of photographs and books, and a statuette of Frederick Douglass. Browsing through these materials Walker found a set of four volumes describing inventions and patents by black Americans—almost four hundred of them. He flipped through the pages, grunting in surprise as he skimmed the lists.

"What are you gruntin' about, Garrett?"

"Say, did you know you could send a telegraph from a moving train?"

"Never heard of it."

"Says here that Granville T. Woods invented it in 1887. He was colored."

"These pictures over here are all taken in black colleges and universities. And all these books were written by Negroes."

"Black colleges and universities?" There was a note of surprise in Walker's voice.

Dixon came over to examine the books of patents, and Walker

stepped over to look at the hundreds of books and photographs. While they were engrossed in their investigations, a well-dressed black man with a goatee approached them.

"Puis-je vous aider, messieurs?" *Can I help you, gentlemen?*

"We're Americans," said Dixon. "We don't speak that language."

"I am also an American," he smiled, extending his hand to shake Dixon's. "'That language' is French, which is what the people speak here."

"That would make sense, I reckon, considering that we're in France." They both laughed.

"I am Dr. Du Bois. Welcome to my exhibit! Let me know if you have any questions."

"Doctor Du Bois? So, you're a doctor?" Dixon asked with raised eyebrows.

"Not a physician. I have a doctorate in sociology from Harvard, and I study and write about the lives of black Americans."

"That would make a pretty short and sad book, wouldn't it?" Dixon frowned. "I don't think I'd want to read it."

"Quite the contrary! Just take a look at the materials I've assembled for this exhibit, and you will see for yourself that black Americans have been very successful indeed. Considering the obstacles we've had to overcome, we have achieved remarkable things in science, business, education, literature, music—in all areas of life! You should be proud to be an American of African descent. You have a great heritage!"

The doctor abruptly turned away to greet another group of visitors. Walker heard him speaking German to this group.

"He must be a pretty smart fella," he whispered to Dixon.

"Smarter'n you and me put together," Dixon muttered.

Back on the street outside they were astonished to see that, with twilight setting in, the Exposition was illuminated by countless electric lights. Entranced by the beauty of the colored arcs, they wandered slowly along the crowded avenues, gaping and pointing like children in a toy store. They walked through the Palace of Electricity, marveling at the giant dynamos which generated the electricity powering the Exposition. They were amazed at the exotic sea life exhibited in the world's largest aquarium. Optical illusions, motion pictures, electric trains—there was simply too much to absorb.

It was very late when they finally got back to the hotel, having forgotten all about eating supper. When they stumbled into the lobby, dazed at their whirlwind experience, they were met by the same desk clerk they had seen when leaving earlier.

"Did messieurs find anything interesting in the vicinity?" he asked, in a voice dripping with sarcasm.

"Oh, I s'pose you could say that," drawled Dixon, affecting a bored tone. "There's a carnival over by that little river, with some jugglers and a trick pony. Nothin' we ain't seen before."

The desk clerk froze, his eyes narrowing as he glared furiously at them, his chin beginning to tremble and his upper lip to curl. Before he could explode, Walker asked nonchalantly, "What time is breakfast?"

Sucking in a deep breath between his clenched teeth, the clerk spun about and disappeared through the doorway again, this time slamming the door behind him.

"That was kind of mean," Walker said to Dixon.

"He asked for it," he growled in reply. Taking two red apples from a basket on the counter and tossing one to Walker, he added, "This looks like supper. My treat."

They slept so soundly that they almost missed breakfast, getting downstairs just in time to grab a bread roll and a cup of coffee before rushing to catch the train to Calais. They talked about all that they had seen the night before for almost the entire five-hour trip, and kept the missionaries entertained.

The steam-powered ferry took about two hours to cross the English Channel to Dover, and the train to London another two hours. By the time they arrived at a hotel, it was already dark. Since finding a hotel where English was spoken was not a concern, they went to a much less luxurious establishment than they had used in the continental cities for the past few nights. Only three stories in height, its exterior walls were a dark, red brick, with small windows and green awnings. The entrance was a large, dark, wooden door at the top of a half-dozen steps. The rooms were small and did not have electricity, and communal toilets were located down the hall from the guest rooms.

"Funny how fast you can get used to fancy, ain't it?" commented Walker, looking around critically at the well-worn facilities.

"I know what you mean," agreed Roberts. "But remember how thankful we were to have the Limboski Hotel in Kiachta? It was nothing like this nice."

The hotel also did not have a restaurant or dining room, so they went to a nearby pub for a supper of beef stew. The other diners appeared to be local and well-acquainted with each other, and conversation was loud and active.

"I thought they spoke English here," Walker said to Roberts, in confusion. "I can't understand anything they're saying."

"It's British English. They have their own local accent. They'd probably have trouble understanding you, too. Keep listening—you'll get the hang of it."

But he didn't. Walker was very frustrated. "I learned a lot of Spanish, and some Russian, Chinese, Mongolian, and Swedish, too. But I can't make heads or tails of anything they say—just a word now and then."

"Just remember," smiled Roberts sympathetically, "this is where English came from. Our ancestors took it to America and we speak it our way, but it's still England's language. We actually speak American."

"If you think *this* is hard to understand," interjected Williams, "just wait 'til we get to Scotland. Nobody murders the English language like the Scots."

"Scotland?" Walker was even more confused "Why would we go to Scotland?"

"Sorry—I guess I forgot to tell you," Roberts apologized. "Our ship for New York leaves from Glasgow, Scotland. Our trunks are already on their way there, and we'll be following tomorrow. I'm afraid we'll have no time to see London."

"Suits me," said Dixon. "This place smells like horse—" he hesitated, glancing quickly at the missionaries and their wives—"stuff," he finished lamely. "The streets are covered in it. And the air tastes bad."

"Maybe on our way to the train station we can at least pass by the Houses of Parliament, the Tower of London, London Bridge—I'd like to see those places while we're here." Mrs. Roberts gave her husband a beseeching look.

"And I'd like to ride the Underground!" exclaimed Williams. "This is the only city in the world with an underground railroad. It's too good a chance to pass up. When will we ever be here again?"

"Underground railroad?" Now it was Dixon's turn to be confused. "I thought that was what helped slaves escape to the North before the Civil War."

"No, I mean an actual railroad underground, running beneath the city. London first built it in the 1860s, and they have quite an extensive system of tunnels and tracks now."

"Well, that's for me!" Dixon grinned. "Can't wait to tell everybody that I was on the Underground Railroad!" Everyone laughed.

"That's settled then," announced Roberts. "We'll take the Underground part of the way to the railroad station, and try to see those famous places, too. We'll need to get an early start though, so don't stay out too late."

Exiting the pub they paused on the sidewalk to get their bearings. A dense fog had descended upon the city, giving the gas street lights an eerie glow. The effect was quite ghostly. It took several minutes for the group to find its way across the street and around the corner to the hotel again. They actually walked past it in the fog and had to double back when they realized they'd gone too far. Visibility was so poor that there was no point in going for an exploring walk, so they retired to their rooms.

Fortunately the fog was gone by morning, but it was overcast and the sun was a vague glow in a pale gray sky as they left the hotel early, before eight. The smell of horse manure was still strong, and the two women held handkerchiefs to their noses as they walked a short distance to the Clapham underground station. They were all astonished at how far they had to descend below street level to reach the train platform. They were also quite surprised to discover that the passenger carriages were pulled by an electric-powered engine. The only sound was that of the wheels rolling on the iron rails and the wind rushing past. They emerged a few minutes later at the King William Street station and found themselves in front of the London Bridge. Walking out onto the bridge they enjoyed a dramatic view of the Tower Bridge and the Tower of London, not far away to the east. They then boarded a horse-drawn tram and rode a couple of miles westward along the Thames River to the Westminster Bridge and saw the Palace of Westminster, where Parliament assembles, the clock tower called "Big Ben," and Westminster Abbey. Mrs. Roberts announced that she was satisfied now, and they hired a cab to take them on to the Kings Cross railway station to catch their train.

As he stood on the platform waiting to board the train, Walker looked up at the arched iron-frame roof, with its translucent panels admitting dull sunlight. Industrial, definitely not fancy, he thought. He compared the station with those he had seen in Russia, Germany, and France, and found it rather plain.

Turning to Roberts and Williams, he asked, "Why are the train stations in the other countries, like Russia, so much fancier and expensive-looking than this one? I mean, the big arches out front are nice, and this roof is alright, but it's nothing special. England is supposed to be the wealthiest country in the world, but this is really pretty ordinary."

"That's an interesting observation, Walker," replied Roberts. "Think of it like this—who owned those railroad stations in Russia and the other countries?"

"I don't know. I never thought about it."

"The railroads and the stations belong to the government, and the government pays for it all with tax revenues. It doesn't have to be profitable. The fancier the stations, the better the government looks.

In England the railroads are built by private businesses, and they are not as likely to spend money on expensive decorations because they have to earn profits for their shareholders. It's capitalism—less waste, more efficient. Did you notice what is written above those arches out front, just below the big clock?"

Walker shook his head.

"It says 'Great Northern Railway Station.' That's the name of the company that owns it—it's a private corporation, not the government. And you don't make money by spending it on decorations!"

"'Parently you don't make money by cleanin' up your city, either," noted Dixon. "This is the filthiest place I've seen yet. I'd rather live in Siberia than here."

"I'm sure we'll find that England, outside of London, is much cleaner and more appealing," suggested Williams. "We should get a good look from the train."

The "Flying Scotsman" blasted its steam whistle and pulled out of the station at ten o'clock. The four driving wheels—almost seven feet tall—turned faster and faster, until the train was racing along the rails at more than eighty miles per hour. Walker held the arm rest tightly, hoping they didn't go flying off the rails in a curve.

The scenery was pleasant at first, but not remarkable. However, as they moved further north it began to change, becoming hillier and more picturesque. Walker saw a particularly impressive gothic cathedral towering over the rooftops of York, both a cathedral and a castle in Durham, and then a castle in Newcastle.

"This is like being in a novel by Sir Walter Scott!" he exclaimed to no one in particular.

"Yes, it is," agreed Williams. "I think that England is indeed very lovely, outside of London."

They arrived in Edinburgh, Scotland shortly after six o'clock, and the Glasgow-bound cars were quickly decoupled from the train, attached to another engine, and soon on their way again. It was already dark so it was impossible to see much, but in the moonlight Walker could see beautiful mountain landscapes as they crossed the rugged countryside. He was mesmerized by the enchanting peaks and valleys, never taking his eyes from the window.

By eight they were in the Glasgow Central Station. To their surprise, a fine hotel was literally attached to the train station, and being tired from traveling they decided to take rooms there, even though it looked more expensive than they had planned. The Central Station Hotel was a large Victorian-style stone structure, dark and heavy, almost castle-like, with its entrance angled on a street corner.

"Howfur mony ur in yer pairtie?" greeted the desk clerk.

"We're Americans," said Walker. "We only speak English."

The desk clerk blinked, raised an eyebrow, and gave Walker a withering look.

"There are six of us," said Roberts, "and we'll need three rooms."

"Howfur lang wull ye be styin'?"

"Just one night."

The clerk pushed three room keys across the counter. "Th' stairs wull be thro' thare. Let me ken if yi'll be needin' anythin'."

As they walked toward the grand staircase, Walker looked at Roberts in consternation. "That wasn't really English, was it?"

Roberts grinned. "Actually, Walker, it was."

"Like I said," Williams chuckled, "Nobody murders the Queen's English like the Scots!"

Walker shook his head. "You're right about that! I was about to say that maybe we should've gone to a nicer hotel, where they speak English."

"Enjoy the night's rest, fellows," advised Roberts. "For the next few nights, you'll be sleeping on the ocean. I hope you don't get seasick—the North Atlantic is pretty rough this time of year."

"We crossed the Pacific, and a whole lot more," said Dixon, "so I think we'll be alright. The ocean liner will have to be better than sleeping in hammocks stacked three high, with no ventilation and one latrine for five hundred men."

"Oh, horrors!" exclaimed Mrs. Williams in disbelief. "That would be awful!"

"That's one way to put it," said Walker grimly. "After three or four days, you'd give your right arm to be back on dry land. Yes, I think we'll be just fine on the ship."

"You'll have much better conditions than that!" promised Roberts. "You won't be in steerage. We have tickets for second class cabins, so we will be quite comfortable."

"What is 'steerage?'"

"That's the area below decks where the poorest passengers stay—usually emigrants going to America. Conditions there are pretty bad, I've heard. It's unfortunate, but it's all they can afford."

"Of course, it's only for a few days," added Williams, "and they have the opportunity to make a better life in America, so I suppose it's worth it."

As they reached their room and closed the door behind them, Dixon snorted, "He supposes it's worth it? Who is he to say that it's worth it? He's not leaving his family and home, going to a new country where they speak a different language and having to suffer through a miserable voyage to get there."

"Well, actually, he did that," responded Walker cautiously. "He left everything to go to China. Maybe he didn't go in steerage, but he did go."

"That's completely different," argued Dixon. "He's a missionary. It was his job to go there. He wasn't poor, and he wasn't going to find a better life."

"No, he wasn't going to have a *better* life—he was going to have a *harder* life. And then had to escape across a desert to avoid being killed. I agree that it's very different than the emigrants' situation, but I think he understands something about it."

Dixon was quiet for a moment. "Alright," he said, finally. "I'll grant you that the missionaries left their homes and went to a foreign country where they speak a different language and had a harder life there. But they always knew that someday they'd go home again. For the emigrant, it's a one-way trip. That makes a big difference."

"That's true," admitted Walker. "That makes a big difference."

"I guess I might be a little hard on him," relented Dixon, softening a bit. "It just seemed to me that he was being—I don't know, insensitive. Making a judgment that wasn't his to make."

"Maybe so. I just hope, for the sake of those poor people, that it *will* be worth it. I hope they can look back later and say they're glad they did it."

"Amen to that."

The next morning at the dock, Walker was taken aback at the number of people there to board the ship. The first-class and second-class passengers numbered about three hundred, but there were at least six hundred roughly-clad men, women, and children slowly filing up the gangplank and disappearing down the steep steps and ladders into the open hold of the ship. Many carried packs, bags, and small trunks. Walker saw none of them smiling or laughing. From somewhere in the darkness below, he heard a baby crying.

It was a gray, windy day as the SS *City of Rome* left its berth and, towed by a tug, began its slow trip down the Clyde River toward open water. Walker and Dixon stood together on the deck, braving the chilling breeze, watching the city of Glasgow slide past. It looked crowded and dirty, with a foggy haze hanging over the dingy factories and warehouses. In the distance, a small boy in patched pants stood atop a dilapidated brick wall and waved at them. Walker waved back. Somewhere unseen, a dog barked. A light mist of rain began to fall, and a lone crow flew overhead, cawing pitifully.

"I take it all back," said Dixon, with a shiver. "It's got to be worth it."

33

THE PROMISED LAND

The *City of Rome* was a beautiful ship. Well over five hundred feet long, she boasted three smokestacks, or funnels, as well as four masts. When under sail she was a vision of grace and elegance unmatched by any other ocean steamer. Equipped with electric lights throughout and luxury accommodations in the cabins, she had been a popular liner in her day. She was, however, past her prime, as her iron hull made her too heavy to keep pace with newer, steel-hulled vessels, and was therefore relegated to secondary routes such as the one from Glasgow to New York.

Upon exiting the mouth of the Clyde River, the ship made a brief stop at Moville, on the northern coast of Ireland. There, several hundred more grim-faced emigrants trekked up the gangplank, only to descend into the gloomy steerage below deck. Having filled its capacity for passengers the ship began her voyage in earnest, and by the time the sun was setting on the western horizon, Ireland had disappeared from view and they were plowing steadily through the ocean.

The second-hand clothes Walker and Dixon had purchased in St. Petersburg were an improvement over their faded military togs, but were hardly of the quality to fit in with the passengers in the dining room of the ocean liner. They drew some curious stares as they joined the missionary couples at a table. A white-jacketed waiter handed them each a menu.

Walker took one look at the list of offerings and grunted in surprise. Roberts gave him a questioning look.

"They serve horse meat over grass?" Walker asked incredulously, pointing to the first items on the menu. Roberts blinked, and Mrs. Roberts literally snorted through her nose and looked away in embarrassment.

"That says 'hors d'oeuvres,' which means 'appetizers,' not 'horse'" Roberts explained. "And below that is 'pâté de foie gras,' not 'grass.' It's a delicacy, very popular in France. It's made from fattened goose liver."

"And what's this here?" asked Dixon, pointing to another item on the menu.

"Russian caviar," said Williams, sitting next to him. "Fish eggs, from sturgeon in the Volga River. Also a great delicacy."

"I saw a sturgeon in the aquarium at the Paris Exposition," said Dixon. "That was the ugliest monster I ever saw. Why would anybody want to eat those eggs?" He shuddered at the thought.

Turning to Walker he asked wistfully, "What do you s'pose they're having in steerage?"

Roberts laughed out loud. "You can skip the appetizers and just order the entrée, if you like."

The well-dressed passengers carried on lively conversations to the accompaniment of clinking crystal glasses and silver utensils, as a string ensemble played delicate music in the background. Furtively surveying the room, Walker saw that many wore expensive jewelry and stylish clothing. The way they handled their forks and knives was definitely not like how he did it, and he began to try to copy them. He and Dixon waited quietly while the others finished eating, and then excused themselves.

Back out on the main deck, Dixon muttered, "I don't feel so sorry for those folks down below any more. At least they're with their kind of people. Not like us."

"We can put up with it for a few days," Walker deadpanned. "When we get there, it will have been worth it."

Dixon glared at him, and then burst out laughing. "Garrett, you are such a country boy."

"Can't help it. I'm from the country."

For the next couple of days their main pastimes were eating meals and walking about on the deck. There wasn't much else to do, other than listening to piano and violin music in the sitting rooms. Many of the upper-class passengers would gather around the railing above the steerage deck and look down at the crowded scene below. Walker heard them talking about the people beneath them as if they were zoo animals, commenting on their clothes, their shoes, hats, hair, and even how they smelled and sounded. Many of those in steerage were draped in coarse, gray wool blankets with "Anchor Line" emblazoned across the back, and some of the expensively dressed ladies held kerchiefs to their noses as they laughed and pointed. The emigrants could not help but hear all of this and some were clearly irritated by it, but said nothing.

After the evening meal on day three it was announced that there was to be a dance in the ballroom, beginning at eight o'clock. The cabin passengers seemed quite excited about it, but Walker and Dixon exchanged a look of distaste.

"Goin' to the big dance, corporal?"

"I'll be right behind *you*, lieutenant."

"We should put on our army jackets. You know how pretty girls love a man in uniform."

"Actually, I was thinking of putting on my camel-hair coat and taking another walk around the deck. I just love being stylish."

"You're such a dandy. I think I'll join you."

It was a clear, moonlit night, cold and windy on the deck. The shaggy camel-hair coats once again proved their worth as they turned the collars up around their necks and pushed their hands deep into the pockets. Pausing outside the ballroom they looked through the glass French doors at the colorful scene inside. Dozens of dancing couples rotated around the brightly-lit room, delicately turning and stepping as the orchestra played a lilting melody. Others chatted amiably at the refreshment table, sipping champagne from tall, slender glasses and nibbling crackers with caviar or foie gras.

"That don't look like hardtack to me," commented Dixon.

"Let's go get some," suggested Walker. "You never know—it might be good."

However, before they could even open the door they were accosted by two uniformed ship stewards.

"Where do you two think you're going?" demanded one.

"Get back down where you belong!" added the other.

"Where we belong?" echoed Walker in surprise.

"You don't belong up here with the cabin passengers. Back to steerage with you!"

They grabbed Walker and Dixon roughly by the arms and began to jerk and shove them. Both of them planted their feet and resisted, but then two more uniformed stewards appeared, one of them carrying a stout stick.

Dixon raised his hands and said, "We're going. No need to get rough. We're on our way back to where we belong."

With crude, verbal abuse and a few pokes with the stick, Walker and Dixon were escorted to the steep steps down to the steerage hold. As the crowd of emigrants watched, they descended to the lower deck and joined them.

"And don't come back up here, if you know what's good for you!" jeered one of the stewards, shaking his stick at them.

"We could've mopped the deck with those bums," Walker muttered to Dixon.

"Yeah, but then we wouldn't of got to come down to steerage," replied Dixon, with a one-sided grin.

"Welcome home!" called out a bearded man wearing a cloth cap. "Yer just in time!"

And then a fiddle began to play a lively jig, and was joined by an accordion. The clear space open to the moon above was suddenly a kaleidoscopic whirl of jigging, bouncing, twirling dancers, and those standing on the side were clapping and stamping their feet in rhythm. One of the girls, laughing, grabbed Walker's hand and pulled him into the action. He had no idea how to dance, but he quickly realized that it did not matter. Imitating the hops and leaps of the others he threw himself into the celebration with gusto, colliding with Dixon and others a few times, whooping and waving his hat overhead as he danced. It was a feeling of exhilaration and liberation like he had never known. It was like being drunk, but without the alcohol. The music changed tempo occasionally, and winded dancers sometimes moved to the periphery to make room for others to join, but the motion never stopped.

Out of breath, he collapsed onto a bench to rest. Looking up, he saw several of the cabin passengers standing around the railing, watching. Some of them clapped their hands and tossed coins down, laughing. A couple of burly, working-class men picked up the coins and fired them back, eliciting cries of surprise and pain from the onlookers above, and raucous laughter from the celebrants below. The railing was soon empty of spectators.

The moon high above appeared to be enjoying the spectacle. However, there was a curfew for the steerage passengers, and at midnight the announcement was made that it was time to retire for the night. Sleeping compartments for single women were in the bow of the ship, while those for single men were in the stern, and space for families was in the midsection. As the crowd dissipated, Walker and Dixon realized that they had nowhere to sleep below deck and would have to get back to their cabin. Stealthily ascending the steps, they slipped into the shadows and successfully made their way back to their room without encountering any of the ship's crew, so the evening ended without further incident.

At breakfast the next morning, Roberts greeted them and asked, "How did you fellows enjoy the dance last night?"

"It was outstanding!" exclaimed Walker. "The most fun I've ever had!"

"Same here," agreed Dixon. "We had a great time."

"That's odd," commented Williams. "I don't recall seeing either of you there."

"That's 'cause you was at the wrong dance," grinned Dixon.

"The ship's crew didn't think we belonged up here with the good folks," explained Walker, "so they tossed us down in steerage. That's where the real dance was."

"This is an outrage!" fumed Roberts. "I will speak to the head steward. I can assure you that it will not happen again!"

"Don't do that!" importuned Dixon. "We like it in steerage. They're our kind of people. I plan on goin' back."

"Me too," chimed in Walker. "Really, it's alright. No need to say anything about it."

The missionaries reluctantly agreed not to complain, but it was obvious that they were very displeased at the way the two had been treated. The situation took care of itself, however, because before they had finished eating, two stern-faced stewards appeared at their table and tapped the two of them on the shoulder.

"We told you two not to come back up here," one of them growled.

"Stop right there!" snapped Roberts, rising from his chair as other diners became quiet and turned to look. "They are part of our group and have every right to be here. This is Lieutenant Dixon of the United States Army, and this is Corporal Garrett. I am Reverend James Roberts and this is Reverend Mark Williams, and these are our wives. We have traveled from China, escaping the Boxer Rebellion. These men have saved our lives more than once—we would not have made it without them, and I will not have you treating them with disrespect!"

"That is absolutely correct," said Williams, as he and both women also rose to their feet.

The steward's face reddened, and he stepped back. "Please accept my apology, but why didn't you say something last night?" he asked Walker and Dixon.

"You wouldn't have believed us," said Dixon, "and besides—we wanted to go to steerage! They had a much better dance!"

The steward coughed involuntarily and a titter swept through the surrounding tables. The steward gave a quick, stiff bow, and quickly retreated.

"You could've left off that last part," commented Walker, frowning.

"Nope, I couldn't, either," replied Dixon with an impish smile.

A mustached and bespectacled gentleman from a nearby table turned and addressed them. "Did I hear you say that your party has come from China? You were involved in the Boxer Rebellion?"

Suddenly they were in the middle of a lively discussion with the surrounding tables. Everyone seemed fascinated with their story and wanted to hear the details of what it was like in China during the upheaval. Learning of the flight across the Gobi Desert, through Mongolia, and across Russia left them amazed. The conversations went on until the tables had all been cleared of dishes, and they moved to the adjacent salon to continue. They were still talking when it was time to eat lunch. The gentleman who had asked the initial question was especially interested in hearing all about Walker and Dixon's heroics. They tried to modestly downplay their roles, but Roberts and Williams insisted on praising them effusively. After eating lunch the two were exhausted, not being used to so much conversation, and excused themselves and rose to go back to their cabin. As they were leaving the dining room, the gentleman handed them each an embossed calling card with his name and address.

"My name is John Wilkie. When you get everything straightened out with the army, contact me. I can use young men like you."

Walker looked at the card and noted that the address was in Washington D.C. "Yes sir. Thank you, sir." Walker shook his hand, and Dixon did likewise.

That afternoon, the seas began to become rougher. They encountered a stiff headwind, and all of the sails were furled. The ship began to labor, slowing down and rolling more noticeably. The captain announced that they were experiencing engine problems which caused the ship to slow to half-speed, but promised that it would be fixed soon. Meanwhile the pitching and rolling of the vessel made virtually everyone on board thoroughly seasick. To make matters worse, the headwind brought up a storm. Rain fell in sheets, accompanied by lightning and thunder, forcing everyone to remain inside. Walker noticed that there were fewer people in the dining room for meals, and even some of the staff looked rather pale and wan.

"I hope our friends down below aren't getting it too bad," he said, peering out the rain-streaked porthole window at the tossing ocean waves. "It looks pretty scary out there."

"I don't think there'll be any dancing tonight," agreed Dixon.

There wasn't any dancing the next night either, as the storm continued with only brief lulls for another day. The ship's steam engine had to be completely shut off at one point so that a repair could be done, after which it was able to resume its normal speed. This helped stabilize the pitching of the ship, much to the relief of the passengers, though the rough waters continued to make some quite miserable. The two hours while the engine was dead were the worst, leaving the ship at the mercy of the waves, and the passengers at the mercy of the ship. Walker then realized the purpose of the barrels of sand strategically placed around the ship, as he and the other passengers made frequent use of them.

Finally the storm was past; the clouds parted, the sea calmed, and the sun shone. Passengers gratefully thronged the decks, upper and lower, taking advantage of the fading light while it lasted. No one had yet recovered enough to feel like dancing, so a concert by the ship's orchestra was staged that evening in the ballroom. All of the chairs were filled, so Walker and Dixon stood in the rear, by the French doors. While the audience was politely applauding at the conclusion of the first piece performed, they quietly slipped out. They stopped by their cabin to put on their camel-hair coats and hats, and headed for the steps to the lower deck. As they approached they could hear the sounds of music and singing.

It was an impromptu concert of diverse cultures. The singers were not professional, or even particularly good, but all sang songs from home, either with or without musical accompaniment. Walker recognized Russian, Scottish, Irish, German, and English songs being sung, and there were other languages that he did not recognize. It was very democratic—singers joined in without having to be invited, and everyone applauded and cheered for each performance as if it were the best they had ever heard. Walker and Dixon stood in the shadows, listening intently and joining the applause. When it appeared that everyone else had contributed a song or two, one of the girls pointed to Walker and Dixon and beckoned for them to come forward, laughing and calling out in a language that sounded vaguely like English.

"We 'aven't 'eard from yer two yet! Shake a leg an' give us a sahng frum yer 'omeland!"

It was impossible to refuse, as the crowd turned their way, clapping and cheering. Reluctantly they edged out into the circle of moonlight, hands in pockets, not sure what to do.

"I'll sing y'all a song I learned as a child," announced Dixon, removing his hat and holding it in both hands. The audience cheered and then became expectantly quiet. Dixon cleared his throat and began to sing expressively in a clear, strong voice.

> *Amazing grace, how sweet the sound*
> *That saved a wretch like me.*
> *I once was lost, but now I'm found,*
> *Was blind, but now I see.*

From somewhere, a bagpipe began to play. Dixon launched into the second verse, and voices from all around joined in. By the time he reached the third verse it seemed that the entire ship was singing, even those who did not speak English. Every instrument available was playing—bagpipes, fiddle, accordion—even a tin whistle, soaring above the rest. When he got through the verses, Dixon repeated the first verse again, and then bowed as the final notes sounded. The applause and cheering were prolonged, and Walker saw some men and women wiping their eyes.

"War ye frum, mate?"

Dixon hesitated, and then said boldly, "I'm an American."

"Then wot ye doin' down 'ere?"

"I'm going home. Both of us are. We're not really immigrants."

"We're just soldiers," added Walker. "We don't belong up there with the rest of them."

The crowd surged forward, and for an instant Walker feared that they had hostile intentions, but he needn't have been concerned. They gathered around the two of them, peppering them with questions. What's it like in America? What will happen to us when we get to America? Are the streets really paved with gold? Is everyone in America rich? Tell us about America! Tell us all about America!

Dixon raised both hands and the crowd began to quiet down. Someone pushed a stool into the circle and he stepped up on it, balancing with one hand on Walker's shoulder.

"What's it like in America?" he asked. "I can tell you something about that." There was absolute quiet. He paused, collecting his thoughts. Walker felt him grip his shoulder tightly, and was glad that it was Dixon making the speech, and not himself.

"The streets ain't paved with gold. Some of 'em ain't paved at all. There's plenty of rich people in America, but most of us are just gittin' by. There's honest people, and there's dishonest people. Kind people, and unkind people." Dixon paused here, realizing that his desperate listeners needed to hear something to encourage them. Taking a deep breath, he went on.

"I've been in Cuba, Panama, Hawaii, Guam, the Philippines, China, Mongolia, Russia, Europe, England, and Scotland. I've seen how people live in all them places. America ain't perfect, but I'd druther live in America than anywhere else. You can make a better life for yourselves there. It ain't easy, and it'll take hard work, but you can do it.

"Take me, for example. I'm a black man. My mama was once a slave. Black folks in America has it harder than white folks, for the most part. But I was just in Paris a week ago, and met a black man who graduated from the best university in America. He showed me a list of hunderds of inventions by blacks, hunderds of books written by blacks, and pictures of black colleges and universities. We got our freedom just a few years ago, but look at what black folks've already done! Some white folks ain't ready to let us be equals yet, but it's coming. We already had some black men in Congress, and someday we'll have a black president. You wait 'n see!

"There's 'bout to be an election for president in America, just a couple of weeks from now. In America you get to choose your leader ever' four years. If you don't like one, you can throw 'im out and get a new one.

"That's really what America is all about—making choices. If you make good choices, you can come out alright. You've already made one of the most important good choices—to get on this ship and go to America. That took a lot of courage, and I respect you for it. Keep making good choices and be patient, and good things will come your way.

"So, my advice for all of you is, roll up your sleeves and be ready to work. There's lots of people just like you in America. They're making it, and you can make it, too."

He stepped down from the stool to thunderous applause and cheering, which went on for several seconds. Suddenly from the back of the crowd, the bagpipe began playing "Amazing Grace" again, and the ship's hold reverberated with the impassioned singing from hundreds of hearts from many lands and languages.

Walker put his arm around Dixon's shoulders and felt him slump against him, leaning on him for support. He realized then how much of an effort it had taken for him to give that speech. Dixon summoned all his strength, however, and when the verse of the song finished he bellowed, "Let's dance!" and began rapidly stamping his foot and waving his hat. The fiddler instantly began a lively jig, and with a collective shout the steerage erupted into a wildly joyous celebration.

Dancing and singing continued until the midnight curfew. Once again the multitude melted away, retiring to their own berths. Walker and Dixon returned to their cabin, which seemed weirdly quiet after the noisy hour they had just left.

"That was a really good speech," Walker said. "I couldn't have done anything like that good."

"I told 'em what they needed to hear," Dixon said quietly, and then added, "and what I needed to hear."

Another day passed, and the *City of Rome* was now only a couple of days from New York, and making good speed. She was a beautiful sight, with white sails billowing from four tall masts, and dark smoke streaming from her three black-painted funnels. Her long, sleek, graceful lines glided so smoothly through the water that it was possible for the passengers to forget that they were on a ship in the ocean.

As they passed the coast of Newfoundland late that evening a dense fog enveloped the ship, cutting visibility to almost nothing. Walker, standing on the main deck, could not even see the ocean. He could faintly hear singing from the steerage, but the fog dampened sounds so that it seemed to be from very far away. He turned to walk toward the singing, barely able to see the layout of the deck, walking with hands outstretched to feel his way along.

Suddenly there was a horrifying crashing noise from the bow, and a shudder passed through the ship. The bow bucked upward and then fell back, sending Walker sprawling. He heard terrified screams from steerage, from the cabins, and from the salons. All was confusion and chaos. A siren began to wail, and the first mate, using a megaphone, began calling for all hands to report to emergency stations, and for all passengers to clear the decks and return to their cabins. The passengers in steerage, however, were in panic. Fearing that the ship was sinking, they were not about to remain below, and were stampeding up onto the main deck, adding to the chaos. Thanks to the dense fog it was impossible to restore order, as they milled about in confusion. The ship's officer continued to shout through the megaphone, but to no avail.

The ship's engines were quickly throttled down, and as the ship slowed she began to roll again. A particularly pronounced roll to starboard caused many of the passengers to fall down, and others to stagger sideways, out of control. One careened into Walker, knocking him off balance and sending him stumbling into the side railing. Driven by his momentum and the ship's tilt, he doubled over the railing, his feet flailing the air and his hands desperately clutching at the wet railing to keep from falling overboard. In the light from porthole windows, he caught a glimpse of the writhing sea below, and was seized by a sudden horror that he was going to fall into the night ocean and drown. He opened his mouth to scream for help, but nothing came out.

Just as he felt his fingers losing their grip on the slick railing and his body beginning to fall, his ankles were grasped by a pair of strong hands which stopped his descent. In a matter of seconds the hands dragged him back and up, and he was able to frantically hoist himself back onto the deck, landing on his knees with a sense of profound relief. The ship had rolled back in the other direction, which also helped, but the two strong hands had saved Walker's life.

He scrambled to his feet and turned to face his rescuer, words of gratitude on his lips. Standing before him was a strange looking man, dressed in a long black coat. He wore a flat-brimmed black hat, and had a lengthy dark beard with two braided pigtails dangling on each side of his face, to his shoulders. In the thick fog the effect was almost spectral, and Walker found himself staring, speechless. The man gripped Walker's arm with a powerful squeeze, said "Shalom!" and then disappeared into the crowd.

The siren was finally silenced, which helped calm the feelings of panic. After a few moments the mate was able to announce that the hull had been examined and there was no leakage found. The ship had struck a small iceberg—known as a 'growler'—and had only damaged the bowsprit and the figurehead, a bronze representation of Julius Caesar. The *City of Rome's* iron bow was dented, but not so seriously that it threatened the integrity of the ship's hull. It was a close call. The ship had struck the iceberg only a glancing blow—a more direct hit might have been disastrous. As the ship regained her normal cruising speed, the rolling motion abated. Slowly, the passengers returned to their places and calm was restored.

Dixon and Walker both agreed that his mysterious rescuer had to be a steerage passenger. Over the next two days Walker visited the steerage deck looking for the man, and asked the English-speakers there about him. He learned that the man was a Jewish rabbi from somewhere in Eastern Europe, probably from Russia, who kept to himself and was seldom seen. Despite his repeated efforts, Walker was unable to find him among the thousand souls below deck.

"Perhaps he doesn't feel safe mingling with the other immigrants," suggested Roberts. "Staying out of sight might be his way of staying out of trouble."

Walker scratched his head. "Why wouldn't he feel safe?"

"Jews in Europe have been persecuted for a long time, going all the way back to the Middle Ages. In Eastern Europe, and especially in Russia, they have been the victims of pogroms—massacres—and many have emigrated to escape the violence. Like the other immigrants, they hope America will be a land of freedom and opportunity."

"But why have they been persecuted? Why would people want to attack them?"

"First of all, because they're not Christians. All of Europe became Christianized long ago, and that made Jews into outsiders. Being different was not tolerated, and since they are only a small part of the population, they aren't able to defend themselves. Secondly, some Jews have been very successful in business, and that has made some people jealous. Some people just can't stand for anyone to have more than they do, especially if it's a Jew."

"Sounds like the Jews are Europe's black man," commented Dixon, frowning. "You get kicked for being on the bottom, and lynched for being on top. I hope the Jews have better luck than us colored folks have had."

"That's a very interesting observation, Dixon," Roberts nodded. "I have to believe that things are moving in the right direction, though. Surely we will learn from our past mistakes!"

"That rabbi is obviously a good man," said Walker, shaking his head. "He saved my life! He deserves a medal, not persecution. People should be judged by their actions, not by their religion, or the color of their skin. America should be a place of freedom and opportunity for everyone. It doesn't make sense to persecute people like that."

"I couldn't agree more," Roberts nodded emphatically. "You are absolutely correct. And don't take offense at this, Walker, but could you say that in your hometown in Alabama? What would your neighbors think if they heard you say that?"

"What do you mean?" asked Walker, his cheeks coloring.

"Just that there aren't many white people in Alabama who think that way, that's all."

Walker's nostrils flared as he inhaled sharply, and his eyes narrowed. "Well, you may be right, reverend, but it's high time they changed." Walker got up abruptly and went outside to pace on the deck. Roberts followed him and put his arm across Walker's shoulders.

"I didn't mean to upset you, Walker," he said in a fatherly tone. "I think you are an exceptionally fine young man, and I suspect that you have changed greatly since you left home a couple of years ago. You may not realize how much you have changed until you get back home and find that things there are just the same as when you left."

"That's what I'm afraid of, reverend," Walker said, almost in a whisper. "I don't really have a home to go back to, in more ways than one."

"God will show you the way," Roberts assured him. "He's brought you all the way around the world, through perils and dangers too many to count. There's a reason for all that has happened, and He will show it to you, all in good time. Have patience, and trust!"

"Thank you, reverend. I appreciate that."

Walker paced the deck alone until late in the night. Finding a dark, isolated place, he lay down on his back and looked upward, fingers laced behind his head. Many times in the past two years he had found comfort in contemplating the myriad stars above. The vastness of this heavenly scene always made him feel very small and humble, and inspired him to find new perspectives on his troubles. Tonight was no exception.

With Roberts' words echoing in his mind, he retraced his steps since leaving Courtland over two years ago. He thought about General Wheeler, Captain Joe, and Captain Pershing—men he looked up to. He smiled as he once again beheld José and heard his laugh. He listened again to the haunting song of the old crone on the beach in Hawaii, as the Queen came ashore. He touched the silver cross and thought of Harriet. He chuckled out loud as he remembered Miguel's terror as he pried the python's jaws off Walker's arm. The sadness of Aguinaldo, the prisoner. The selfless bravery of Lou Hoover, riding her bicycle as bullets flew around her. Larson, Nästegard, Roberts, Maria, the Söderboms, Anya, and so many others. Of course, through it all, there was Dixon.

As he savored these memories he felt a tinge of sadness, but mostly he felt gratitude. *I'm a rich man,* he thought. *I wouldn't trade my experiences for all the money in the world. I don't know what lies ahead, but it will be alright. I'm ready for it.*

He scanned the sky for the star that Maria had assigned to him. Finding it, he pointed at it and murmured, "You just watch. I'm going to shine, too." And then, shivering in the cold, he got up and hurried back to his cabin. The room was dark—Dixon was already asleep. Tip-toeing carefully across the room, he quietly undressed and slipped into bed.

"Night, corporal," came a low, muffled voice.

"Night, lieutenant."

As they were eating breakfast the next morning, there was a loud commotion outside on the deck. Alarmed, they all left the table and went to see what was afoot. The passengers from steerage were crowding the main deck, straining to look forward into the distance as the crew members shouted at them to go back below. Some of them were crying and embracing each other.

"What is going on?" asked Mrs. Roberts anxiously. "Is there going to be trouble?"

"Not at all," replied the reverend, with a big smile. Pointing ahead, he said, "Look yonder!"

On the horizon could plainly be seen a towering statue of a woman, holding a torch aloft.

Walker felt an electric shock of excitement. "There it is!" he shouted. "The promised land! We're there!"

34

FULL CIRCLE

Walker and Dixon were met at the dock by an army captain who bluntly informed them that he was to escort them directly to Washington, D.C., where they would be tried for desertion. Walker's heart sank. The captain put handcuffs on them, impervious to the protests from the missionaries. They said quick good-byes to the Roberts's and Williamses, gave them Father Kirilov's parcel and, with a soldier on each side, followed the officer to the Grand Central Depot, as passersby stared. The officer pushed them into a reserved compartment on a train with the two privates, and locked the door. Putting their cheap carpetbags on the overhead racks, they sat down and looked at each other nervously.

The train headed south at a rapid clip, racing through Newark without stopping. Thickets grew so close to the tracks that it was impossible to view the scenery, so they sat in silence and stared straight ahead.

"I saw a deserter get shot by a firing squad last year," grinned one of the privates. "Splattered him good."

"Should've hung him," said the other. "Shootin's too quick and easy."

"They say cowards die many deaths," sneered the first, "but only the last one counts."

"Y'all ever been in combat?" asked Dixon casually. "I don't remember seeing you at San Juan Hill."

"Or Calamba," added Walker. "Or Tientsin."

"Or Peking," continued Dixon.

"Shut up!" snapped one of the privates, raising a clenched fist threateningly. "You weren't in all them places. Nobody was in all them places."

Dixon laughed softly. "That was just the short list, private. You wouldn't believe the rest of it."

Turning red in the face, the soldier unleashed a stream of profanity and racial abuse at Dixon. "You shouldn't even be allowed to sit in this car! You oughta be back there with the other—"

Walker stood up and kicked the compartment door, making a loud banging noise.

The captain quickly opened it from the corridor. "What the hell is going on in here?" he demanded.

"Sir! We want this private removed from the compartment. He has no business cussing Lieutenant Dixon, and we won't put up with it."

"What the—?" he gaped. "You won't put up with it? Who do you think you are, corporal? You're under arrest for desertion, in case you hadn't noticed. You don't get to say what will or won't be done. Sit back down and shut up!"

"No sir! Either you get him out of here now, or I will do it myself, sir."

"Corporal, that's insubordination!"

"No sir, it's not. If you allow this private to continue disrespecting a lieutenant, *you* are the one responsible for insubordination, sir, and I will report you for it as soon as we get to Washington."

The captain's face froze as his eyes met Walker's glare for a long second. "Private—get the hell out of this compartment! Go stand down by the lavatory." And then to Walker, "You sit down, corporal! I don't want to hear anything else from you!"

The door slammed shut behind the private. The remaining soldier stared at Walker wide-eyed and did not speak for the rest of the trip.

Dixon's eyes met Walker's, and he just grinned and shook his head. "You're a long way from home, Corporal Garrett."

Walker understood perfectly what he meant. "Yes sir, lieutenant, sir. I am."

It was mid-afternoon when they arrived in Washington's gothic Baltimore & Potomac Railroad Station. Walker asked if this was where President Garfield had been shot almost twenty years earlier, but their escorts ignored him. Exiting the station to the street, they had a splendid view of the U.S. Capitol building on one side and the Washington Monument in the distance in the other direction.

They were taken to a military stockade at Fort McNair, a couple of miles away at the confluence of the Potomac and Anacostia Rivers, and placed in a cell until their hearing, which was scheduled for the following day. They had the cell to themselves, so it was a quiet afternoon and evening.

When a black orderly brought their supper to the cell, Dixon, by way of making conversation, asked, "Anybody famous ever locked up in here?"

"Yes sir," whispered the orderly, with a furtive glance over his shoulder. "The folks what assassinated President Lincoln was put here. They was hanged in the yard out yonder." He then hastily withdrew, obviously under orders not to fraternize with the prisoners.

"Well, this situation just gets better and better," remarked Walker sarcastically. "I'll sleep better tonight, knowing that."

"You should!" replied Dixon, with mock seriousness. "It is an honor to be incarcerated in the same place as such famous criminals. We may go down in history, ourselves."

"It's going down in the yard out there that worries me," grumbled Walker. "I'm not ready to go down in history—not yet, anyway."

The next morning they were handcuffed again and marched across the yard to an imposing brick building. Escorted by the same captain and two privates as the day before, they ascended a narrow staircase to an upstairs room. In the sparsely furnished room, there were two tables, several feet apart. There were three comfortable-looking chairs at one of the tables, which was flanked by a flagstaff bearing the United States flag. There were two rickety chairs at the other table, and the two prisoners were seated in these. The captain and guards stood behind them.

They soon heard the sound of footsteps in the hallway, and the door opened. The captain barked "Ten hut!" and he and the two soldiers snapped to attention, clicking their heels. Walker and Dixon rose awkwardly to their feet, hands still chained in front of them. Three immaculately uniformed officers marched into the room and seated themselves at the front table. The one in the middle carried a manila folder and a gavel, which he placed on the table in front of him.

"At ease, men," he said without looking up. "Sit down."

Walker felt his blood run cold when he saw the officer seated on the right.

"Well, if it isn't Garrett and Dixon. I knew you two would come to no good."

"Sir, good morning, Major Payne. It's nice to see you, too, sir."

"It's *Lieutenant Colonel* Payne, Corporal Garrett. Obsequious fawning will not help you now. You are about to learn that actions have consequences, boy. *Serious* consequences!" He smiled an evil smile as his lip curled in a sneer. He was clearly enjoying this.

"Congratulations on the promotion, sir. You're clearly on your way up the ladder, sir."

Payne's face turned pale and his eyes narrowed to slits as he leaned forward in his chair, clenched fists on the table. He had opened his mouth to speak, when the senior officer looked up from the papers and spoke first.

"So, you know these two, Payne?"

"Yes sir, Colonel Anderson. From Tampa to Cuba to the Philippines, I've watched these two, and I have to say I'm not surprised in the least to see them here now."

"Hmmm. Interesting," mused the colonel thoughtfully. "How do you men plead to the charge of desertion under fire?"

"Not guilty, sir," they responded in unison.

Payne snorted derisively, folded his arms and leaned back in the chair.

"Sir," said Dixon, "we have letters of recommendation from Reverend James Roberts and Reverend Mark Williams, who—"

"Don't need them, Lieutenant Dixon," murmured Anderson with a wave of his hand, absorbed again in the contents of the folder. Walker and Dixon exchanged an anxious look—this was not going well at all. He flipped through several pages, scanning each carefully. The room was quiet for a long minute.

Payne's contemptuous smile turned into an evil grin.

"Very interesting," Anderson said, finally. "I have to say, this is unprecedented in my experience." He looked up at Walker and Dixon. "You two seem to have some very powerful friends."

Payne blinked, and his grin vanished.

"This is a glowing letter of recommendation from General Joseph Wheeler," he said, holding up a sheet. "He says you are two of the finest soldiers he has ever known, and recommends you both for the Medal of Honor.

"This letter is from General Frederick Funston. He says that the two of you swam a river under enemy fire while towing ropes, and helped capture Aguinaldo. He also recommends you for the Medal of Honor.

"General Arthur MacArthur says you are two of the bravest soldiers he has seen.

"This one is from Captain John Pershing. He writes that you both have displayed exceptional character and bravery, and that the army needs more soldiers like you. He is proud to have been your commander.

"And this one," he held up another page, "is from New York's Governor Theodore Roosevelt, former colonel of the Rough Riders, and probably soon-to-be vice-president of the United States. He says that your bravery and resourcefulness helped secure the victory at San Juan Hill. He recommends medals for both of you.

"And there are two more from a couple of Swedish missionaries named Larson and Söderbom. They seem to think that you two are angels sent from God himself."

He handed the papers to the officer to his right who spent a moment perusing them, and then put them in front of Payne, who did not touch them. He was visibly pale, and had a panicked look in his eyes.

"I'd like to hear about how you two became separated from your unit," Anderson said softly. "Tell your story."

"Yes sir," said Walker, "but may we add these letters from the missionaries to that folder? They probably tell it better than we can." As they fumbled for the letters, the chains of the handcuffs clinked and rattled.

"Captain, hand me the letters, and remove those chains."

While Walker and Dixon briefly narrated their story of what happened at the Great Wall in Kalgan, the colonel read the letters from Roberts and Williams, nodding. When they were finished he exchanged a look with the officer to his right, and then turned to his left.

"Payne, do you have anything to add to this?"

Payne coughed and cleared his throat. "No sir," he said hoarsely.

"The charges are dismissed," Anderson said, rapping the gavel. "You are free to go. The captain will escort you to the bursar's office, where you will receive back pay for the last three months. I will forward these recommendations for decorations."

As they stood, the colonel came around the table and approached them. He extended his hand to shake theirs. "It is unfortunate that you have had to undergo this unpleasantness and spend a night in the stockade. I am going to put in for promotions for both of you as compensation for what you've gone through. You've earned it. Have a good day, gentlemen!"

As they left the room they heard the colonel say, "Payne, we need to have a talk."

Neither of them spoke a word until they stood alone on the street outside the front gate of the installation, money in their pockets and bags at their feet.

"Am I dreamin', or what?" asked Walker.

"Can't be real," breathed Dixon. "Pinch me."

They donned their ragged camel's hair coats, shouldered their bags, and walked slowly up the street. The trees were alive with autumn colors, the sky was a perfect blue, and a single white cloud floated motionlessly. The sun's warmth compensated for the chill in the air.

"Something ain't right," Dixon said. "This just don't happen to a colored man."

"This don't happen to nobody," rejoined Walker. "Roberts has to be behind this. He must've wrote letters to somebody. Maybe to General Wheeler. And then the General wrote to some more people. This didn't just happen." Walker's thoughts raced wildly as he imagined a chain of letters spanning the globe. It was dizzying to contemplate.

"So," said Dixon, after a long pause, "Where to now?"

Walker pulled an embossed card from his pants pocket. "Remember him? He said that when we got straightened out with the army, to come see him. There's his address—right here in Washington."

"Alright, let's go."

It was a handsome stone house, two stories tall, with a wrought-iron fence. They walked up the path, climbed the steps to the broad porch and knocked on the door, which featured an oval of beveled glass. The door opened and a plump black woman in a white apron and red kerchief looked at them sternly.

Before they could speak, she said, "Y'all want somethin' to eat, go 'round to the back door." She was closing the door when Dixon spoke up quickly.

"No ma'am, we ain't asking for food. We're here to see Mr. Wilkie. He asked us to come."

"We've got his card," added Walker, holding it up. "He gave it to us on the ship coming from Europe."

She looked at them skeptically and reached out her hand for the card. Examining it carefully, she made a face. "Alright then, come in—but wipe your shoes off on the rug. And don't sit on nothin'."

A few minutes later, Wilkie emerged from his study. "Gentlemen!" he exclaimed. "Come in! Thank you for coming—I didn't expect you so soon. Do come in!"

In Wilkie's study he offered them cigars and brandy, which they politely declined. They sat gingerly on the edge of expensive leather chairs and briefly described for him the morning's hearing.

"Let me get right to the point, gentlemen," he said, blowing a ring of smoke toward the ceiling. "I am the Director of the Secret Service. Are you aware of what the Secret Service does?"

Neither of them had ever heard of the Secret Service.

"In the past, our main responsibility has been to stop counterfeiters. However, since the assassination of Garfield and the threats against Cleveland, we have assumed the role of presidential protection. Our agents serve as bodyguards for the president, and the need for this is growing. I need quality men that I can depend on, and from everything I've seen and heard, you two fit the bill perfectly. Are you interested?"

"Yes sir!" responded Walker, astonished.

"Count me in!" said Dixon. "When do we start?"

"First of the year, in January. By then I'll have funding to expand the agency. We'll get you enrolled in a training program and put you straight to work. Glad to have you both on board!" Wilkie stood, and with the smoking cigar in his left hand, extended his right hand. They shook hands enthusiastically.

"There's just one problem, though," interjected Walker. "We're still enlisted in the army. I don't think we are free to work for the Secret Service just yet."

"Your unit is still in China, right?" asked Wilkie. They both nodded. "The army isn't going to ship two soldiers halfway around the world just to reunite you with them. There really isn't much that they can do with you. I'll talk to Secretary Root over at the War Department and take care of it. I don't think it will be a problem," and he waved his cigar dismissively.

Back on the street minutes later, Dixon exclaimed, "This day hasn't gone anything like what I was expecting."

"Didn't look too good at breakfast," agreed Walker, "but now I'm floating on the clouds."

"So, what do we do until January? We got two months to kill."

"Time to go visit our mamas, I'd say. Let's head back to the train station."

"Alabama ain't very high on my list of places to go," said Dixon grudgingly, "but you're right. Let's do it."

A white man and a black man traveling together through the South by train was not a simple matter. At first Walker attempted to sit in the colored car with Dixon. He remembered the scene that had erupted when a black man had attempted to sit in the white car, and neither of them were inclined to provoke such an unwinnable confrontation. However, he found that a white man was also not allowed in the colored car, and the black passengers did not seem to appreciate the gesture. So, they rode separately. They avoided the issue of overnight lodging by taking a night train across Georgia, arriving at the Decatur, Alabama, station at noon the following day.

They stepped out onto the familiar platform and looked down the street at the two landmark chimneys identifying the Dancy home.

"I reckon they're gonna be pretty surprised to see us," said Walker, feeling apprehensive.

"Yeah," replied Dixon, hoisting his bag onto his shoulder. "'Dancin' Dancy' is probably gonna be all over you."

Walker snorted a laugh and shook his head. "Not in a million years. Let's go to the back door."

They walked around to the back of the imposing house and knocked on the kitchen door frame.

"Could a couple o' tramps get somethin' to eat?" called Dixon through the open door, hat in hand.

"You'll have to come back in a while," said a pleasant, matronly voice, and Beulah appeared at the door, wiping her hands on a dish towel. "I'm fixin' dinner for the family and ain't got time right now to —" She stopped mid-sentence and stared for a second, and then literally screamed, throwing the towel into the air. Nimbly descending the two wooden steps, she enveloped Dixon in a bear hug, sobbing and moaning almost incoherently. Daisy appeared in the doorway, alarmed.

"Mama! What's wrong?" And then she saw her brother and she squealed in delight. Ignoring the steps, she leaped to the ground and joined the hug.

A moment later a third figure filled the doorway—a well-dressed man with a trimmed gray beard and gold-framed spectacles.

"What's all the commotion out here?" he demanded, with a note of irritation.

Walker lifted his hat. "Howdy, Mr. Dancy. Nice to see you again."

Dancy stared blankly.

"I'm Walker Garrett, sir."

"Oh—right. Garrett. I thought you were off with the army somewhere." He turned to Beulah. "And who is this one?"

"It's my boy, L.G.," said Beulah, through tears of joy. "He's home for the first time in more than six years."

"I see. Very well." Pulling a fancy gold watch from his vest pocket, he cleared his throat and said gruffly, "We'll be wanting to eat in about fifteen minutes—as soon as he gets here." And then he disappeared back into the house.

Beulah stood clutching Dixon with both hands, an agonized expression on her face.

"It's alright, Mama," said Dixon gently. "You go ahead and take care of fixin' dinner. We'll come back in about an hour."

"Don't you boys eat nothin' before you come back, you hear?" She shook her finger at the both of them. "I'll have y'all a plate of food fixed when you come back—fried chicken livers, collard greens, biscuits, and fried green tomatoes. And sweet potato pie for dessert."

"Good Lord!" exclaimed Walker, looking up at the sky. "Thank you, God!"

As he was looking up he noticed the lace curtain at a window moving. *Abigail must have been watching,* he thought. He was a little surprised that he did not feel an emotional response to this. In fact, he actually was rather amused. *Maybe she's not feeling well today, again,* he thought wryly.

They put their bags behind the kitchen door and walked around the house, heading back to the street. Past the carriage house, they strolled down the drive, gravel crunching under their feet. Suddenly a bright, feminine voice called out.

"Walker!"

Startled, he stopped and turned. Standing on the front porch steps was Abigail, wearing a soft yellow dress, her long dark hair coiled at the back of her head. She descended the steps and stood beside the rose trellis, which still boasted a few deep red roses. Walker caught his breath.

"I'll wait for you at the street," said Dixon.

Walker, feeling suddenly tense, walked over to greet her, unsure of what to say. He held his hat in both hands and gave her a quick nod.

"Abigail—it's good to see you." It seemed the polite thing to say.

"Walker, we thought you were dead! It's been so long since I heard from you. I'm so glad you are alright!"

"Well, ah, it wasn't possible—"

"You don't need to explain—I understand. Will you be staying for dinner? I want to hear all about your adventures."

"No, we won't be staying for dinner—"

"Then you must come for supper! I won't take 'no' for an answer. I insist! And I want to give you this—" She extended a yellow envelope which reminded Walker of the ones he'd received in the mail.

"There's something in it for you," she smiled shyly. "I know you must think my needlework is abominable, but it's only my own fault. Daisy does such beautiful work that I had her teach me. I've been copying her pieces and doing the best I can, and I think mine are almost as good as hers now. This one is my own design—I hope you like it."

He opened the envelope and held up a crocheted yellow diamond with a green circle in the middle, adorned with a blue ribbon. He stared at it, speechless.

"The green circle represents the planet Earth, because you've gone all the way around it. The yellow represents the sun, which shines the same everywhere on the Earth, and the blue ribbon is the ocean, which you have sailed. This is your special favor, Walker. Do you like it?"

Walker cleared his throat, feeling his face begin to redden.

"Yes, Abigail, I really do like it," he said, a bit hoarsely. "I like it a lot. It's amazing, really. You did this all by yourself—for me, I mean?"

"Walker! Of course I did it for you!" Her eyes shone. "I'm glad you like it." She put one foot on the first step and looked back at him with a smile. "Don't forget—supper tonight. Seven o'clock!" And she ran up the steps and disappeared into the house.

At the street, Dixon gave him a quizzical look. "What was that all about?"

"I'll tell you later. I'm having a hard time getting a handle on it, myself."

They were discussing where to go for the next hour when they heard a man's voice calling both their names. Coming toward them at a brisk pace was a diminutive man in a white suit, with a full white beard.

"General Wheeler!" Walker cried excitedly. "I didn't expect to see you here!" The three men shook hands vigorously, exchanging greetings.

"I'm running for reelection to Congress," Wheeler explained, "and am here in Decatur to make a speech tonight. Frank has invited me to dinner. Are you staying to eat?"

"No sir, we're not here for dinner. We came to see Beulah."

"Of course! Of course! We must make plans to talk soon. I can't wait to hear all about your experiences."

"I'll be heading over to Corinth to see Ma, so maybe we can meet when I get back."

The General looked at Walker in surprise.

"You haven't heard? No, of course you haven't. How could you?" The General removed his hat and looked at Walker with a sad expression. "I hate to be the one to have to tell you, Walker, but your mother passed away about six weeks ago. She was buried at Pond Spring last month, next to your father. I am so sorry!"

"Mother? Dead?" Walker was speechless. There was an awkward silence. The General continued.

"We had heard that the two of you were captured by the Boxers, and were presumed dead. After losing your father a few months earlier she just couldn't take the grief, and she died of a broken heart. I'm so sorry that you had to find out this way."

Walker heaved a deep sigh and rubbed his hands over his face, at a loss for words.

"At least you still have a family connection in Dixon," Wheeler said. "I know that will be a consolation to you in your loss."

"What do you mean, 'a family connection?'"

"You don't know?" Wheeler took a backward step in surprise. He looked at Dixon, who shook his head.

"I didn't tell him, sir."

"Didn't tell me what?"

There was another awkward silence, and it was Dixon's turn to heave a deep sigh. He looked to the General for help.

"You and Dixon are half-brothers, Walker. When Beulah was with child, I found her the position with the Dancys to get her away from Pond Spring. Your mother never knew of it."

Walker could only stare, wide-eyed. It seemed that his heart quit beating.

The General cleared his throat, seeming embarrassed. "It was a difficult situation for everyone," he said, uncomfortably. Turning to Dixon, he asked, "When did you learn this? Did Beulah tell you?"

"No sir. It wasn't hard to figure out, after you had us write those letters in Hawaii. My initials stand for 'Lemuel Garrett,' and my skin is brown, not black. I always wondered about that."

Walker looked at Dixon. "Why didn't you tell me?"

"I wasn't sure you'd want to know. Didn't want to cause problems."

Another awkward silence followed, broken by the General. "You men come to the big Baptist Church by the river tonight for my speech, and we'll talk afterward. I want to hear all about your travels." And then he shook hands again with them, and hurried off to dine with the Dancys.

They walked slowly down the street to the wharf, and stood looking out at the broad expanse of the Tennessee River. Several minutes passed without speaking. Finally, Walker glanced sideways at Dixon.

"How do you feel about it?"

"It is what it is. I made my peace with it a long time ago."

"I'm sorry for any hardship it caused you and your mama."

"It is what it is," Dixon repeated flatly, with a shrug. "No point in looking back."

Walker nodded agreement. They continued to watch the river for a long while, as a barge made its way slowly under the railroad bridge, steaming against the current.

"I thought yesterday was surprising," Walker reflected, "but it can't hold a candle to today. Today, I've lost my mother, and found my brother. It doesn't get much bigger than that."

"I guess not," agreed Dixon. After a short pause, he added, "How 'bout we head back up to the house? Them chicken livers is calling my name."

"Mine, too. You reckon Beulah might have some cold buttermilk to go with that?"

"I'd bet my Guam buttons on it."

With a short laugh, they turned and began strolling back up the street. About halfway to the Dancy house, they stopped at a street corner as Dixon gazed to the left, toward a cluster of trees on the courthouse square. Walker gave him a questioning look.

"That's the tree. That one there."

"What do you mean, 'the tree'?"

"The tree." Dixon repeated, unable to say more.

Then it hit Walker what he meant. The tree on which Daisy's father had been lynched.

"Oh!" was all he could say. They stood staring for a long minute, each lost in his own thoughts. Wheeler imagined that he saw the motionless figure of a man hanging from a rope around his neck, and he began to feel sick to his stomach. He suddenly remembered General Funston's bragging about having strung up dozens of Filipinos without trials, and his lip curled in disgust.

A slow southern drawl startled them both back to reality.

"You boys lost your way?" Three young men came slouching unsteadily out of a dark interior, two of them holding pool cues, and the other a glass of beer. The speaker was a freckled redhead with tousled hair, his white shirt, gold watch chain, and red suspenders suggesting money. The other two grinned drunkenly, their clothing also reflecting affluence.

"No," replied Dixon. "We know where we are."

"'Parently not, n----r," sneered the speaker. "'Round here, coloreds say 'sir' to their betters. You seem kinda uppity, to me, boy."

"I do say 'sir' to my betters. And I'm not a boy. I'm a lieutenant in the United States Army."

"Fellows, I think this n----r needs to be taught a lesson in respect," snarled the redhead, twirling his pool cue. The other two stepped forward to stand beside him, with expressions as threatening as they could muster in their intoxicated condition.

Walker glanced back down the street at the death tree and felt a cold anger rising in his heart. He forced a casual tone into his voice as he spoke, but it had a threatening edge to it, which Dixon recognized. "Robert Murphy? 'Red' Murphy? I knew you at the Academy."

The redhead stared intently at Walker and then a flash of recognition crossed his face. "Walker Garrett? I heard you'd gone off to the army. Gone to Cuba."

"Cuba. The Philippines. China. Russia. We've been all the way around the world, fighting all the way in jungles, deserts, cities. Got the scars and medals to prove it."

"Well, good for you, Garrett, but that doesn't mean anything here. You were just a farmer's boy, anyway—didn't belong at the Academy.

Step aside while we work this darky over and teach him a lesson he won't forget."

"You can't whip both of us, Red. Go back to your beer and pool, and save yourselves a lot of trouble."

"You're the ones who'll be having the trouble!" Red snapped, raising his pool cue as if to strike.

"Red!" hiccupped the one holding the glass of beer. "They're soldiers! Maybe we should just let them alone. I don't think—"

"Are you with me, or not?"

"Actually, I really need to pee," said the other, and retreated quickly back through the doorway.

"Coward!" yelled Red. He whirled to the other young man. "Are you going to yellow out on me, too, Baker?"

Baker hesitated, and then took a halting step backward. "I need to pee too," he said, and disappeared into the dark interior.

Red furiously broke the pool cue over his knee—except that it didn't break, and he staggered off balance for a couple of steps before regaining his equilibrium. He flung the cue stick into the street with a curse.

"Maybe you need to pee, too?" suggested Dixon, with cool politeness.

Red glared at Walker. "You're sticking up for a n----r?"

"He's worth ten of you, and then some," replied Walker icily. "Besides, I just saved your sorry butt from a serious beating. You should thank me."

Red roared something that sounded like "Bah!" and stormed off after his friends, slamming the door loudly behind him.

Walker and Dixon exchanged a look.

"I remember something about fried chicken livers," said Dixon.

"And buttermilk," added Walker.

They resumed walking up the street as Dixon added, "And collard greens."

"And fried green tomatoes."

"And some of Mama's biscuits."

"And sweet potato pie."

"Sure do wish we had some hardtack and rice and beans," Dixon murmured dreamily.

They both burst into laughter, as they hooted and belly-laughed their way up the street.

It was a perfectly clear, blue sky. The sun's warmth compensated for the autumn chill in the air. Orange, yellow, and red leaves fluttered down from the trees. A pair of crows flew overhead, cawing in unison.

HISTORICAL NOTES

1 THE ODYSSEY BEGINS

- Pond Spring is the name of General Wheeler's home. It can be visited today.
- The *Southern Belle* locomotive is fictional, however the *Dixie Queen* was a historical engine. It was in service in Alabama in 1910 with the Alabama & Mississippi Railroad.
- The Academy in Decatur is fictional.
- The Dancy house still exists, and was known as the Dancy-Polk house by 1898, but had by then ceased to be a private residence. It had two red brick chimneys and was located between the depot and the Tennessee River.

2 ON THE ROAD

- The Birmingham Terminal Station was a historic building for decades, razed in 1969. Its architectural style was controversial at first but it became known as one of the most distinctive terminals in the country.

- The *Age-Herald* was a real Birmingham newspaper, published on Tuesdays in the 1890s. The headline was from the May 24 issue, as was most of the other material mentioned.
- The incident with the black passenger echoes the Supreme Court's Plessy v. Ferguson case of 1896, in which the court ruled that having "separate but equal" facilities for whites and blacks was not unconstitutional.

3 TAMPA

- It is true that Tampa was served by only a single rail line.
- The army made its headquarters at the Tampa Bay Hotel. The description of the interior and exterior of the hotel is based loosely on first-hand historical accounts and photographs, available online.
- According to my research there were 4 bridges across Tampa's Hillsborough River in 1898, including the Lafayette Street Bridge, which was an iron-truss swing bridge.
- General Shafter did weigh 300+ pounds and suffered from gout.
- Henry Plant's Tampa Bay Hotel not only boasted tennis courts, a golf course, and a bowling alley, but a racetrack, a casino, a conservatory, a zoo, and more. It is currently the property of the University of Tampa, and includes a museum of the original hotel furnishings.

4 CUBA BOUND

- The chaos during the embarkation of the troops was widely reported in the press of the day. Descriptions here are based on contemporary and historical accounts.
- Descriptions of the rifles used by the regular troops and the volunteers are accurate. And though it may seem

strange, firearms that use black gunpowder produce white smoke.

- Descriptions of conditions on board ship for the troops are based on contemporary and historical accounts. The story about the tooth-grinding sleeper is borrowed from an account in a soldier's letter home from a Civil War prison camp in *The Blue and The Gray.*
- The "Buffalo Soldiers" are historical fact, and included the 10th Cavalry Regiment.

5 CUBA!

- Some men and animals died during the chaotic landing. A boat of black soldiers capsized, losing two men. Their rifles were retrieved by a Rough Rider.
- Crabs were a source of pain and lost sleep for many soldiers.
- Different accents would have been heard because, for the first time, the U.S. Army mingled soldiers from different parts of the country rather than forming companies from single towns. This was to prevent the devastating impact on a community if a company suffered heavy losses, and also to promote a sense of national identity among the troops.

6 FIRST BLOOD

- The Cuban rebels commonly carried machetes, and did not have regular uniforms.
- Numerous American soldiers were bitten by tarantulas. The bite is painful, but not lethal.
- The Spanish army used the Mauser C96 pistol, which featured a round handle (hence its nickname, the "broomhandle") and a box magazine.

7 FIRST BATTLE

- The first battle between American and Spanish forces was at the town of Las Guásimas, on June 24, 1898. The casualty numbers for the battle are accurate. I simplified the description of the action.
- The incident of the bullet going through the palm tree trunk and filling TR's ear with sawdust actually happened.
- Wheeler's exclamation about attacking the "Yankees" is well-known.
- The flanking maneuver by the Rough Riders is historically accurate, and they were assisted/rescued by the Tenth Cavalry's black troops. John "Black Jack" Pershing was a white officer commanding the Buffalo Soldiers. He is famous for his leadership of American troops in World War One.
- Confederate soldiers in the Civil War were known for the high-pitched "rebel yell," which was often disconcerting to the Union soldiers facing them. You can find audio/video recordings of Confederate veterans demonstrating it on Youtube.
- The comments about the Civil War battle of Sharpsburg are historically accurate. The battle is more famous by the name of Antietam, but Southerners called it Sharpsburg.

8 SAN JUAN HILL

- Spanish snipers hid in trees, communicated by simulating bird calls, and often shot wounded Americans and medics.
- More American soldiers died from tropical fevers and food poisoning from eating their canned meat rations— which they called "embalmed beef" – than from bullets.
- The story about Dixon rescuing Anderson from the San Juan River is historical, but the actual soldiers were named Baker and Marshall. Baker received the Medal of Honor

for his bravery. My source did not provide the first names
of the two historical soldiers.

- The roof-entry at the blockhouse actually happened.

9 SANTIAGO

- Joseph Wheeler Jr. and another soldier performed the
  changing of the flag at the Spanish fort in Santiago.
- Secretary of State John Hay did say that it was a "splendid
  little war."
- At that time in the U.S. Army, the rank of Private First
  Class was indicated by the wearing of insignia on the
  collar, reflecting the branch of service.
- Reconcentrado camps were real. The American press
  tended to exaggerate the numbers, but many Cubans did
  die—perhaps as many as two hundred thousand.

10 HALFWAY AROUND THE WORLD

- The Citation Star medal received by Walker was the
  forerunner of the Silver Star medal, given for gallantry in
  armed combat. The Silver Star was introduced in 1932.
- It is true that General Wheeler and some of the Tenth
  Cavalry were sent to the Philippines after the fighting in
  Cuba was done, but it wasn't quite as soon as this. I have
  accelerated the timetable to keep the story moving.
  Having the transfer occur while they were still in Cuba
  suggests the Panama route. Fictional, but plausible.
- The poem "The White Man's Burden," by Kipling, was
  published in America in early February, 1899. The poem's
  actual publication date fits well with the historical
  timetable for General Wheeler's transfer to the
  Philippines, so the dates for both have been accelerated
  here.

- I have no specific historical evidence that General Wheeler held the view expressed here, but he had been an outspoken advocate of going to war to liberate Cuba, and had fought for the Confederacy during the Civil War, so it is not much of a stretch to impute these opinions to him.
- The physical description of Colón, the railroad, and the Panamanian countryside are fairly accurate and are based on old photographs found online. The remarks by the fictional Frenchman are factually correct, though the number of deaths of railroad workers was probably much less. His estimate is what was widely believed at the time.

11 HAWAII

- The account of the return of Queen Liliuokalani to Hawaii is based on an article written by Alice Rix and published on the front page of *The San Francisco Call* on August 13, 1898. The description of the setting, the name of the ship, the queen's leaning on the arm of Governor Cleghorn, and the mournful song of the Hawaiian woman are all taken from her eyewitness account.

12 THE ANNEXATION

- The description of the Iolani Palace is accurate. The building still stands in Honolulu, but no longer serves a political function. Washington Place, the personal home of the ruling family, stands less than a block away, across the street. Queen Liliuokalani lived there for the rest of her life, until her death in 1917.
- The description of the ceremony is based on an eyewitness account by journalist Alice Rix, published on August 23, 1898 in *The San Francisco Call*.
- Contemporary accounts state that native Hawaiians stayed home that day in protest against the annexation.

- Cleghorn's tirade is mostly accurate, but he tweaks a few things. Slavery was not officially practiced in Hawaii, but forced labor was. Liliuokalani left Hawaii voluntarily after abdicating. Avoiding tariffs was indeed a major reason for the landowners' seeking annexation. He refers to *The Influence of Sea Power Upon History*, by Captain Alfred T. Mahan (1890), which did help move the U.S. and other countries to imperialism. The Iolani Palace truly did have electric lights and telephones before the White House.
- General Wheeler's visit to the Queen at Washington Place is fictional.

13 EXPANDING AN EMPIRE

- I have tinkered with the dates here again. These actual events involving the island of Guam occurred about six months earlier than depicted here, but they are presented accurately.
- The description of the flotilla of four ships bound for the Philippines is accurate. They were led by the USS *Charleston*, a cruiser commanded by Captain Henry Glass. The number of days required for the voyage is based on the actual speed of the transports. The change of course, the conference, the rumors, the naval cannon target practice are all factual.
- The account of the apology for not replying to the "salute," the request for gunpowder, and the ignorance of the state of war are all historically accurate, as are the beach meeting with Governor Marina and the role of Lieutenant Brauner (actually Braunersreuther), and the half-hour ultimatum. José Portusach served as a translator.
- The Americans raised the U.S. flag over the fort and then lowered it and took it with them. The reaction of the Chamorro troops to the departure of the Spanish is

accurate, and they did give their buttons to the U.S. troops as souvenirs.

- The facts presented by General Wheeler about black office holders during Reconstruction are all historically correct. His explanation of how black voters were kept from voting by state laws is also correct. General Wheeler praised the performance of black soldiers in Cuba, but the view on race relations attributed to him in the conversation with Walker is not based on any historical sources and may or may not represent Wheeler's actual views.

14 MANILA!

- The description of Walker's first sight of Manila is based on online photos and maps of the city from 1898-1900.
- Annie Wheeler accompanied her father to the Philippines, again serving as a nurse.
- Lieutenant/Captain John Pershing also served in the Philippines after his tour in Cuba. Major General Arthur MacArthur was second in command to General Otis, and later succeeded him as military commander in the Philippines.
- William Howard Taft was appointed by President McKinley to serve as Governor of the Philippine Commission, a civilian governing authority in the Philippines. Taft did not actually arrive for another year, so his appearance here is a bit early. Taft weighed well over 300 pounds. He accurately quotes McKinley's statement that the U.S. intended to 'civilize and Christianize' the Filipinos, and McKinley's stated policy for the Philippines was known as "Benevolent Assimilation."
- Some sources say it is unknown whether it was an American or Filipino who initiated hostilities by firing the first shot, but most say it was an American (or two) on

sentry duty. I assume that Otis would probably have blamed the Filipinos. The offer of a peaceful resolution by Aguinaldo was made a day later. Otis's response to Aguinaldo's offer is quoted here ("The fighting, having begun, must go on to the grim end.") Otis's whiskers are accurately described, as is Taft's mustache.

- The bridge was the Puente de España, built in 1630. The description of the fighting there is fiction.
- Emilio Jacinto was a real Filipino, but not exactly a journalist. He wrote revolutionary propaganda under a pen name for an underground publication called *Kalayaan*, which was the voice for the independence movement. *El Diario de Manila* was an actual newspaper published in Manila at that time, and *Kalayaan* was printed on its press, but in secret. His presence in the American-occupied fortress claiming to write for *El Diario* is fictitious, but believable. Had it actually occurred, it would have been an undercover intelligence-gathering mission.
- The things stated by Emilio Jacinto about the Philippines are all correct.

15 "NO MERCY!"

- The story about Wheeler dismounting and taking a soldier's pack is true. The part about the soldier being shot while on the General's horse is fiction.
- Ambushes and booby traps such as these were employed by the insurgents. The U.S. soldiers tended to retaliate with brutality.

16 CHASING AGUINALDO

- The expedition described here conflates two separate actions which, while in the same general area, occurred a few months apart. The description of the rainy weather was true of both historical actions.

- Colonel Funston was a historical person and an American hero of the war. The reconnaissance of the bridge was indeed his idea. It was carried out by Corporal A. M. Ferguson, who was given the choice of accepting or rejecting the dangerous assignment. This occurred during the "new moon" lunar phase in which the moon is not visible, so it would have been extremely dark. The roundtrip reconnaissance took Ferguson two hours.

- The swimming of the river with ropes was also Funston's idea. It was carried out by privates W. B. Trembly and Edward White. All three received the Medal of Honor for this exploit. The throwing of mud balls into the Filipino trench by Trembly and White actually happened.

- General Wheeler did, in fact, strip and swim down underwater to inspect the condition of the railroad track on the bridge over the Tarlac River.

- Wheeler and his family members returned to the States after he was relegated to a supporting role, away from the combat action.

- By the time the two American army columns converged at San Isidro, Aguinaldo had relocated further into the mountainous interior.

17 CALAMBA, Part 1

- The size of the force and its method of travel are historically accurate.

- Road-building and schools were a major focus of the American effort to undermine the insurgency. More than 500 teachers went to the Philippines, and were often called "Thomasites" due to having travelled on the USAT (U.S. Army Transport) *Thomas*. A few were murdered by rebels.

There was not an American school at Calamba at the time of this battle, and the teachers described are fictional.

18 CALAMBA, Part 2

- The historical battle at Calamba took place in 3 separate actions over 4 days, which have been condensed here for simplicity. There was a counterattack by the rebels the second day, but I have made it a night attack.
- Generals Lawton and Hall are historical figures, and were in charge of the Calamba expedition. Lawton's wife and young son accompanied him. The conversation and the debate over the use of racially insulting language is fiction. The "n-word" was widely used by white U.S. soldiers to refer to Filipinos.
- The "water cure" was a method of interrogation involving pouring water down a prisoner's throat until his stomach was distended painfully, and then forcing it back out by stomping on the stomach. It was sometimes fatal. I do not know if Hall or Lawton ever used it, but it was commonly employed by U.S. forces.
- The description of the Macabebe scouts is based on photographs available online. The nighttime mission is fiction.
- Miguel's hatred of the Tagalog rebels was typical of the feelings of the Macabebes, who readily joined the American war against the Filipino majority ethnic group.

19 PAYNE'S REVENGE

- Pershing was known to be humane and considerate in his dealings with the Filipinos, learning to speak the local dialects, preferring to use the "carrot" instead of the "stick" whenever possible. The story of his putting pig's blood on the bullets used against Muslim Filipinos has no historical validity.

- Forty miles is approximately the distance that they would have had to travel to get back to Manila. The current in the Rio Pasig changed direction with the tides, as noted in an earlier chapter.

20 EN ROUTE TO CASIGURAN

- Funston led the mission to capture Aguinaldo. The basic facts are accurately presented here, though the timeline has been modified for the story. Macabebe scouts were used, and the USS *Vicksburg* provided transport. The ship and its route are accurately described.
- Seaman Watkins is fictional.
- Funston's expedition did include a Lieutenant Hazzard, but the words attributed to him are from other sources. They reflect views typical of the U.S. Army during the Philippine War, but may not be those actually held by that officer.

21 AGUINALDO

- The route taken, the distance, and the exhaustion of their food supply are all historically correct, including the eating of snails.
- Many Americans, including Samuel Clemens ("Mark Twain"), criticized Funston for accepting aid from Aguinaldo and then capturing him.
- It was, in fact, the day after Aguinaldo's birthday celebration in the village, and decorations were still in evidence. This is according to the reports of the American officers in the expedition. One of the officers (Lt. Burton Mitchell) had taken along a camera and took numerous photos, which are available online.

- The information about David Fagen, the defector, is historically correct, though he was not actually in the vicinity of Palanan at the time of Aguinaldo's capture, as far as I know.
- On the return voyage Aguinaldo and his fellows were indeed allowed the free run of the ship, and were treated like guests. Walker could have easily encountered him. Aguinaldo did not speak English.

22 GOOD-BYE, PHILIPPINES

- The ceremony described is imaginary. However, Taft was made the civil governor (about a year later than presented here), and Funston did become a Brigadier General as a reward for capturing Aguinaldo. It is also true that Taft ate a large steak for breakfast every day.
- The discussion between Taft, MacArthur, and Funston is imaginary, but the statements attributed to Taft and Funston are almost entirely quotes of their actual words, spoken or written at other times.
- MacArthur sent the 9th Infantry Regiment to China, which left the Philippines on June 27, 1900. Squadrons were later sent from the Ninth and Tenth Cavalry Regiments. I have combined these two deployments to simplify and accelerate the narrative. Second Lieutenant McFarley is fictitious.
- Herbert and Lou Hoover were in the Chinese city of Tientsin, where the American troops saw their first combat. According to *The Boxer Rebellion*, by Diana Preston, Lou Hoover wrote to a college friend that "never have so many flags been in action together since our history began ... And such a motley array of troops ... Cossacks, Sikhs, Siamese, a couple of English Chinese regiments on our side—and a lot of our own darkies, who strike terror to the hearts of some."

23 HELLO, CHINA

- Mrs. Anna Drew was a historical person who was evacuated from Tientsin (known more commonly today as Tianjin) to the USS *Logan*, and her diary is a source of some detail about developments in Tientsin and onboard the *Logan*. Her explanation of the Boxer uprising is generally consistent with current historical interpretations.
- The conversations among the soldiers contain accurate facts, such as Seymour's abortive attempt to relieve Peking and the lack of horses. Myths about the Boxers are repeated by the soldiers as if true.

24 SAVING TIENTSIN

- The troops traveled by barge to Tientsin. The descriptions of the countryside and the floating dead bodies seen by Walker are taken from diary accounts by soldiers and others who were there.
- The details of the fortifications and condition of the Tientsin foreign settlement are taken from contemporary sources. The ineffectiveness of the Chinese artillery shells was true. Most of the shells did not explode on impact.
- Lou Henry Hoover rode a bicycle as she helped in the hospital and elsewhere, carrying a .38 revolver, and a tire was punctured by an enemy bullet on one occasion.
- The Tientsin Club in the British sector was converted into a hospital during the siege. I have no historical records to verify the segregating of patients by color in the makeshift hospital, but since it was commonly done at the time, I assume that it would have been done there. I have invented the name of the doctor.
- The bayonets used for the Krag-Jorgenson rifles in 1898 had an 11.6-inch blade, with an overall length of 16 inches.

When not affixed to the rifle it was carried in a scabbard at the hip.

- The night-time Boxer attack is not based on an actual event.
- "Shining Red Lanterns" were teenaged female virgins who wore all red and carried red shaded lanterns and red fans, possibly for incendiary purposes. They were reputed to have supernatural powers, such as flying and casting spells. I am aware of no recorded instances of their participating in direct combat. However, a song about them said "Learn to be a Boxer, Study Red Lantern. Kill all the foreign devils and Make churches burn." "The Boxers would fight down below," recalled a former Boxer, "while the Red Lanterns would watch from above, appearing, suspended in the sky. . . ." From their perch high above, the girls were supposedly able to strike down enemy soldiers, destroy artillery, and ignite buildings. Hopefully it isn't too much of a stretch to bring that activity down to earth.
- Colonel E. H. Liscum was the commanding officer of the Ninth Infantry Regiment. The exchange between Walker and Liscum is not based on any historical record, and is meant only to reflect conventional attitudes of the time.
- There were Sikh and Rajput troops from British India present in Tientsin.
- The wearing of a gold bar on the collar lapel to indicate the rank of a 2nd lieutenant was begun in 1917. Before that the rank was indicated by the wearing of shoulder straps.
- The description of the terrain between the Chinese city of Tientsin and the outlying foreign community is based on military and historical records of the event. The description of the day's fighting is based on historical records. Liscum was killed while the men were pinned down beside the canal.

- The descriptions of the aftermath of the capture of Tientsin are taken from contemporary accounts.

25 ON TO PEKING

- The description of conditions on the march to Peking are taken from contemporary accounts. The references to dead bodies floating in the river and the soldiers' drinking of unboiled river water are based on these sources, as are the descriptions of the tall corn and the brutality of the Russian and Japanese troops.
- The events of the battle at Peking are based on contemporary sources. The scaling of the wall by a soldier actually happened. The idea came from Colonel A. S. Daggett, and the wall-climber was a young bugler, Calvin P. Titus, who received a Medal of Honor and appointment to West Point for his brave exploit.
- The feeding of the Chinese converts by the American black soldiers is fictional, but the neglect of the Chinese refugees in the international compound is a well-documented fact.
- The "International Gun" is a well-known feature of the legation defense. Walker's comment is borrowed from a similar statement by Theodore Roosevelt. The Chinese "jingal" was used during the siege, and is accurately described.

26 NO REST FOR THE WEARY

- Peking was divided into occupation districts among the various foreign powers. General A. R. Chaffee set up food kitchens, shelters for the poor, health checkups for prostitutes, public latrines, and etc. in the American district. Many Chinese moved into the American sector.

- General Frey dismissed criticism of the behavior of his French soldiers toward Chinese women by saying that it was "impossible to restrain the gallantry of the French soldier."
- Captain Andrews is fictional.
- American and Swedish missionaries in the city of Kalgan (also known today as Zhangjiakou) were forced to flee into the Gobi Desert to escape the Boxers. This occurred several weeks earlier than indicated here, and no American troops were actually deployed to rescue them, so this episode is not entirely historical. However, American troops and those of other countries did provide protection for some missionaries elsewhere, so this departure from the historical record is not inconsistent with other actual events.
- The description of the escape route through the gate in the Great Wall and across the desert and eventually into Russia is based on book-length accounts by the American missionaries, James Hudson Roberts and Mark Williams, as well as some published letters by other participants in the trek, which are all available online. The Swedish missionary, Franz August Larson, led the caravan. The nighttime battle with the Boxers in Kalgan is fictional.

27 "THE WATERLESS PLACE"

- Franz Larson did indeed take a bicycle along on the trip. The information in the conversation about Major Taylor, the black professional racer, is historically accurate.
- Miss Engh was a real Swedish missionary in the caravan. I have found her identified only as "Miss M. Engh," and so have given her the name "Maria."
- I am sure that my representation of a Swedish accent is badly done, but I tried to give the impression of an accent without too much modification. I did not attempt to give

Larson an accent, since I presume that he was very fluent in English, having previously spent time in England, and was known as a gifted linguist.

- The propensity of the camels to eat wild onions and the horrible breath odor that resulted from it, is frequently noted in the contemporary accounts.
- In missionary James Hudson Roberts' book, *A Flight for Life and an Inside View of Mongolia*, he described the Buddhist temple of Chwerin, where they were met by lamas. I have invented the topic discussed with them.
- Roberts includes in his book the text of the telegram from the Russian consul.
- The description of Mongolian wrestling is accurate.

28 ONWARD, CHRISTIAN SOLDIERS

- Urga is today known as Ulaanbaatar. The description of the city is taken from Roberts' book, mentioned above.
- The multi-lingual Norwegian Lutheran missionary who joined the group in Urga is identified by James Hudson Roberts only as "Mr. O. S. Nästegard." I have assigned him the name "Olaf."
- The story of the missionaries' prayer bringing rain is taken from *A Thousand Miles of Miracle in China,* by Archibald Glover, 1904, ch.19. Glover tells how his family was fleeing the Boxers, and their prayer for rain—in loud Chinese— brought a torrential downpour from a clear sky and saved them from being massacred.
- "Williams" was the Rev. Mark Williams, mentioned in the notes on ch. 27. His account of the journey is found in his book, *Across the Desert of Gobi* (1901), which mostly parallels Roberts' account. They both tell of eating prairie dogs along the way.

- Roberts told of the Limboski Hotel, with its vermin and odors. He wrote that he would climb out the window and sleep on the roof in fair weather.
- The Limboski Hotel was actually in a town just beyond Kiachta, called Troits Kosavski (or Troitskosavsk). Kiachta was a trading town directly on the border, while Troits Kosavski was administrative. I have disregarded this distinction, as it is not important to the story.

29 NO LOOKING BACK

- The Söderboms were a Swedish missionary family in the caravan. Their baby girl, Anna Elizabeth, died in Kiachta (Troits Kosavski) and was buried there, as described here. The cause of death was not clear in Roberts' account, but Williams attributed it to whooping cough.
- The arguments made by Roberts and Nästegard as to why Walker and Dixon could not get back to their military units in China are, with minor modifications, those given in Roberts' book to explain why the missionaries could not return to their mission posts in China.

30 ON TO THE GREAT SIBERIAN RAILWAY

- The Trans-Siberian Railway was originally called the Great Siberian Railway.
- The town on the eastern shore of Lake Baikal is called "Myssowaiya" by Roberts in his book, *A Flight for Life*.... According to other sources, it was known as Mysovaya until 1902, when it became Mysovsk. Today it is known as Babushkin.
- Roberts records that the group of about two dozen people had only two rooms in the Mysovaya hotel, so that some slept in the corridor. Spending the night on the station

platform in Listvyanka is mentioned by both Roberts and
Williams.

- Roberts provided this phrase ("Ya geverit po-
Amerikanski"), explaining that the Russians were more
kindly disposed to Americans than to Englishmen. He
says it usually produced a friendly reaction.
- Irkutsk was, in fact, known as "the Paris of Siberia."
- Lev Davidovich Bronstein (a.k.a. Leon Trotsky) was a
political exile to Siberia; he lived in the Irkutsk district and
is known to have given public lectures there. Whether he
ever did so from a wagon bed, I don't know.
- The missionary accounts describe visiting the cathedral in
Irkutsk and staying at "the French hotel." The descriptions
of the interior and exterior of the Epiphany Cathedral are
based on online images.

31 ACROSS THE OCEAN OF LAND

- American novelist and travel writer Paul Theroux once
described the Trans-Siberian Railway as "like a cruise
across an oceanic landscape." That inspired the title of
this chapter.
- The description of the travel experience is based on
Roberts and Williams' accounts. Roberts made the dry
observation that it "was not like traveling by camel."
- Roberts made an extended, impassioned defense of
Russian character and government in ch. 32 of his book, *A
Flight for Life . . .*, from which this passage is condensed.
- Roberts says that the group stayed at the "Great Hotel of
Moscow" ("Belshaya Moskofskaiya Gostinitza").
- The name of the U.S embassy official is taken from both
Roberts and Williams' accounts.

32 CHASING THE SETTING SUN

- Neither Roberts nor Williams provided any details about their travel experiences after leaving St. Petersburg other than that their route went to Berlin, London, and Glasgow, and from there to New York. Williams identified the SS *City of Rome* as the ocean liner. All besides those details has been invented.
- The Russian-German border town of Iłowo-Osada, Poland, was the site of a facility where the bogies (wheel carriages) of trains were changed to accommodate the different rail gauges. Williams' explanations of the reason for the different rail gauges are traditional, and one or both of them may be correct.
- The details provided about the Hotel Kaiserhof are historically accurate. Hindenburg, Moltke, and Krupp are historical figures.
- The 1900 Paris International Exposition was still underway in the fall of 1900. Its Ferris wheel was later relocated to Vienna. The Eiffel Tower was painted yellow during the Exposition for the only time in its history. The bridge mentioned is the Pont Alexander III, crossing the Seine.
- The contents of The Exhibit of American Negroes are described accurately. W.E.B. Du Bois was one of the creators of the exhibit, but was not actually present at the Exposition, as far as I know.
- The "Flying Scotsman" later gained fame as the world's fastest steam locomotive. The engines in service in 1900 were capable of speeds up to about ninety mph.
- The Scottish pronunciation used in the conversation with the desk clerk is provided by a website translator. My apologies if it is not realistic.
- The SS *City of Rome* in 1900 could carry 75 first-class passengers, 250 second-class, and 1000 in steerage.

33 THE PROMISED LAND

- The description of the *City of Rome* and its route are accurate. The menu items are found on an actual *City of Rome* menu (online).
- Descriptions of steerage life are based on contemporary accounts, such as "The Fellowship of the Steerage" (1905), "The Steerage of Today—A Personal Experience" (*The Century Magazine*, 1898), and "On the Trail of the Immigrant" (1906), all available online. In the first of these sources, the author relates how the immigrants begged him for "a sermon about America."
- The *City of Rome* actually struck such an iceberg 'growler' in fog off the coast of Newfoundland in 1899, causing the damage described here.
- I use the term "emigrant" to refer to the steerage passengers as they depart from Europe, but switch to "immigrant" as they reach the other side of the Atlantic.

34 FULL CIRCLE

- The Baltimore & Potomac Railroad Station was located on the Mall, just a short distance from the Capitol. Within a decade of Walker's arrival it had been replaced by the Union Station.
- Fort McNair, formerly known as the Old Arsenal Penitentiary, was where the associates of John Wilkes Booth were tried and executed in 1865 for the assassination of President Lincoln.
- The hearing before the military review panel is entirely fictional and based on no historical sources.
- John Wilkie was the Director of the Secret Service at that time. Everything else presented here about him is fiction.
- General Wheeler was reelected to his seat in Congress in 1900.

ACKNOWLEDGMENTS

I would like to express my appreciation to all those who have assisted me in the writing and publishing of this book. Without their support and input, it would have been extremely difficult to complete the process. Many thanks to each and every one! In alphabetical order: David Anguish, Suzanne Connel, Linda Glenn, Tammy Hughes, Creston Mapes, Wayne Moltz, Scott White, and Tim Weekley. Special thanks to Wayne Joyner for the cover art, and to Natasha Fancher for editing the manuscript.

ABOUT THE AUTHOR

Michael Glenn is a native of Montgomery, Alabama. He earned his masters degree in history at the University of Mississippi, and taught history for more than forty years. Now retired, he currently lives in the Atlanta area with his family and a neurotic Sheltie.

He can be contacted at pageturnerbooks.llc@gmail.com.